SPARKS!

DOUBLE DOG DARE

WRITTEN BY **IAN BOOTHBY**

ART BY **NINA MATSUMOTO**
WITH COLOR BY DAVID DEDRICK

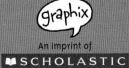

An imprint of
SCHOLASTIC

Photo by Vicky Van

Dedicated to Cohen aka Coco aka BubBub
— Ian Boothby and Nina Matsumoto

Text copyright © 2020 by Ian Boothby
Art copyright © 2020 by Nina Matsumoto

All rights reserved. Published by Graphix, an imprint of Scholastic Inc., *Publishers since 1920.*
SCHOLASTIC, GRAPHIX, and associated logos are trademarks and/or registered trademarks of Scholastic Inc.

The publisher does not have any control over and does not assume any responsibility for author or
third-party websites or their content.

No part of this publication may be reproduced, stored in a retrieval system, or transmitted in any
form or by any means, electronic, mechanical, photocopying, recording, or otherwise, without written
permission of the publisher. For information regarding permission, write to Scholastic Inc., Attention:
Permissions Department, 557 Broadway, New York, NY 10012.

This book is a work of fiction. Names, characters, places, and incidents are either the product of the
author's imagination or are used fictitiously, and any resemblance to actual persons, living or dead,
business establishments, events, or locales is entirely coincidental.

Library of Congress cataloguing-in-publication data is available

ISBN 978-1-338-33991-8 (hardcover)
ISBN 978-1-338-33990-1 (paperback)

10 9 8 7 6 5 4 3 2 1   20 21 22 23 24

Printed in China   62
First edition, August 2020

Edited by Adam Rau
Book design by Phil Falco & Steve Ponzo
Publisher: David Saylor

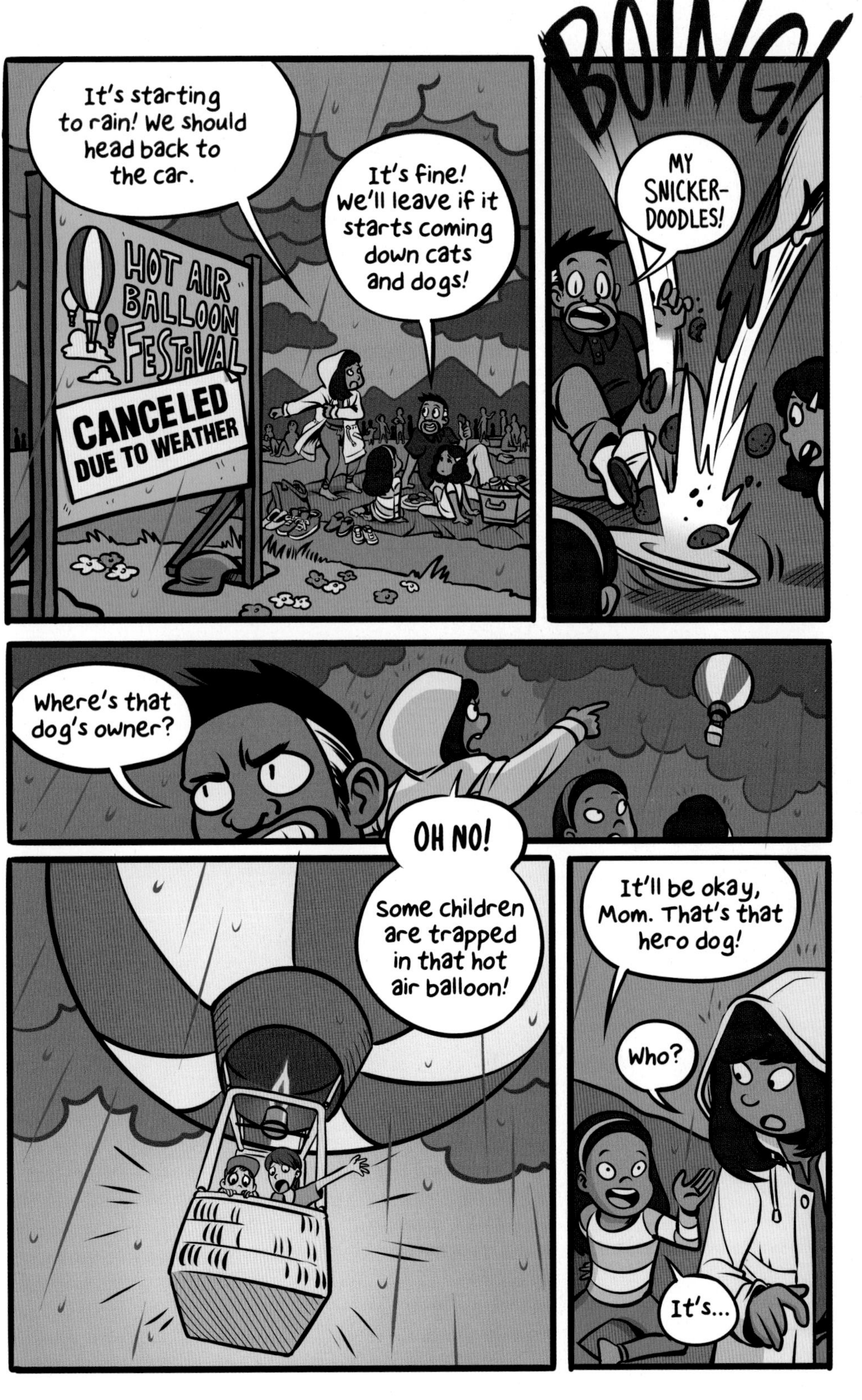
It's starting to rain! We should head back to the car.
HOT AIR BALLOON FESTIVAL
CANCELED DUE TO WEATHER
It's fine! We'll leave if it starts coming down cats and dogs!
BOING!
MY SNICKER-DOODLES!
Where's that dog's owner?
OH NO!
Some children are trapped in that hot air balloon!
It'll be okay, Mom. That's that hero dog!
Who?
It's...

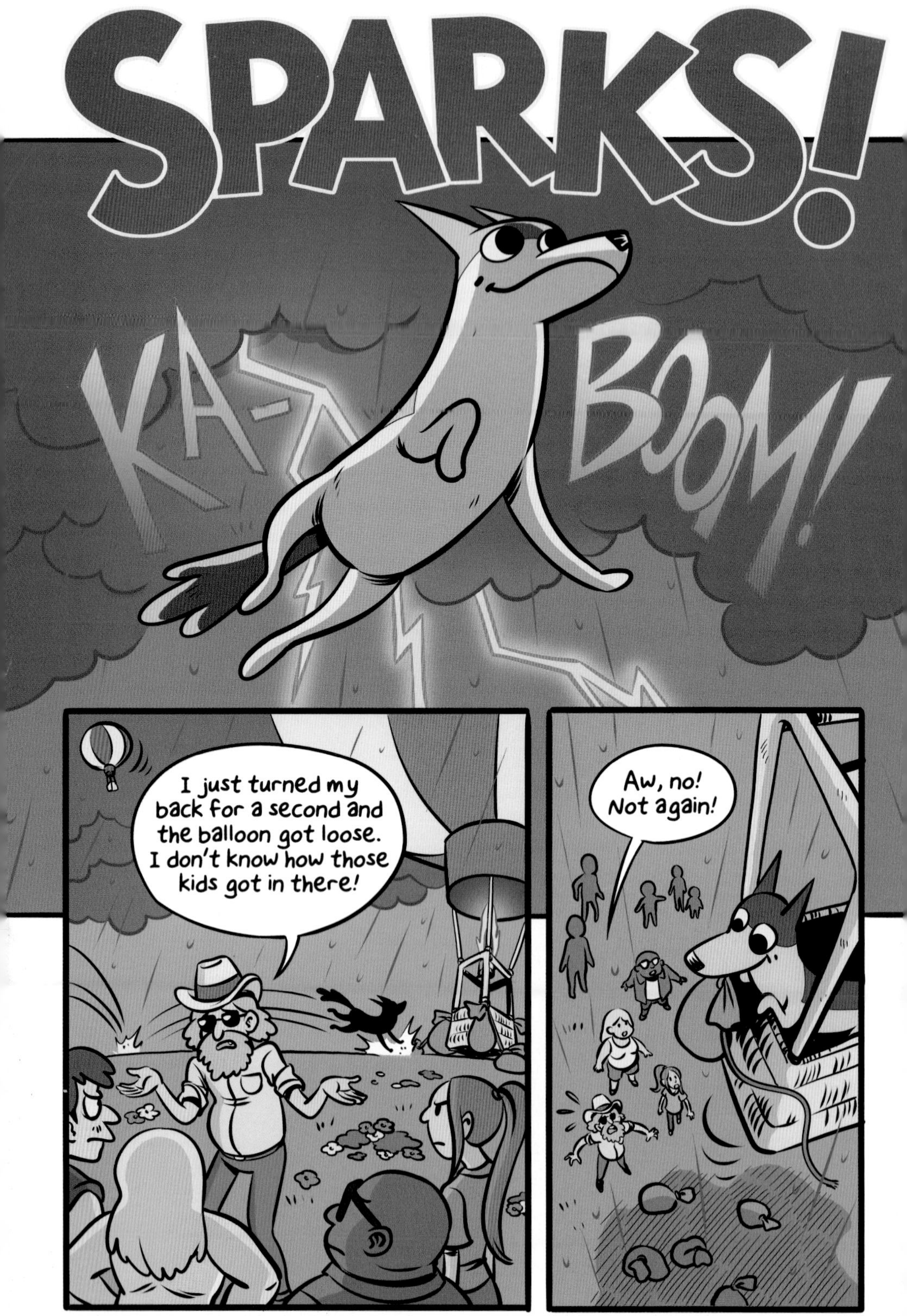
SPARKS!
KA-BOOM!
I just turned my back for a second and the balloon got loose. I don't know how those kids got in there!
Aw, no! Not again!

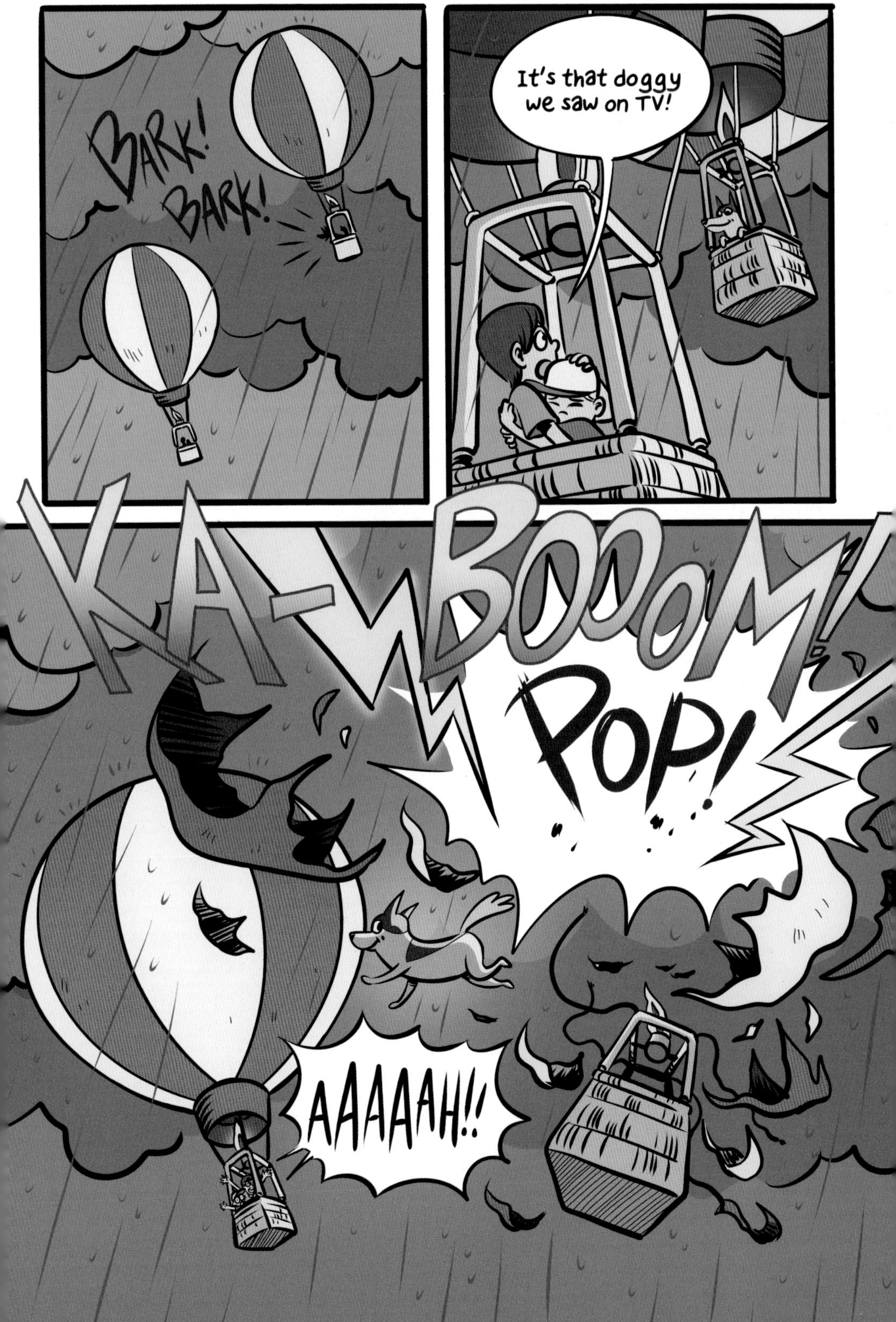
BARK!
BARK!
It's that doggy we saw on TV!
KA-BOOOOM!
POP!
AAAAAH!!

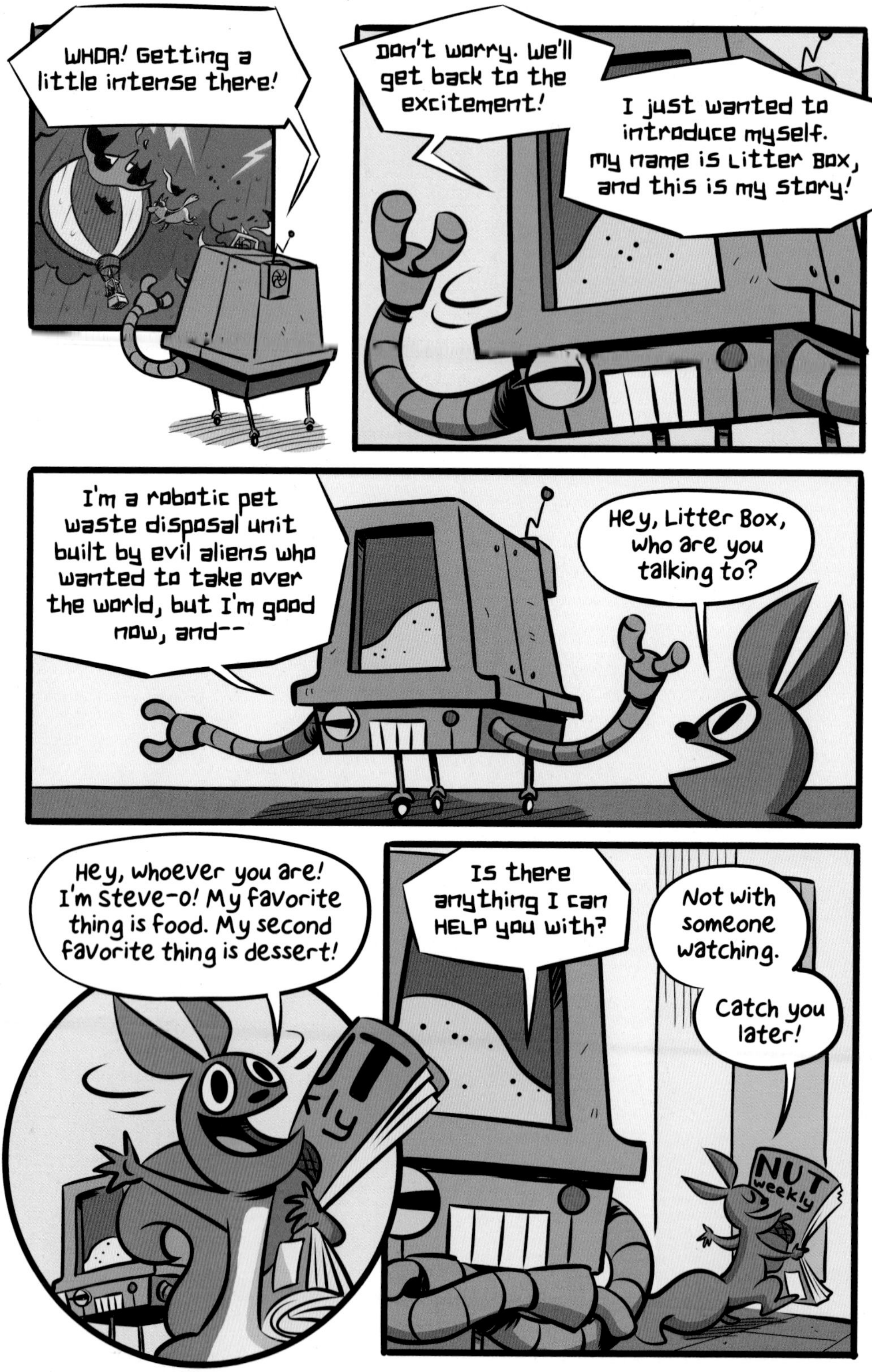
WHOA! Getting a little intense there!
Don't worry. We'll get back to the excitement!
I just wanted to introduce myself. My name is Litter Box, and this is my story!
I'm a robotic pet waste disposal unit built by evil aliens who wanted to take over the world, but I'm good now, and--
Hey, Litter Box, who are you talking to?
Hey, whoever you are! I'm Steve-O! My favorite thing is food. My second favorite thing is dessert!
Is there anything I can HELP you with?
Not with someone watching.
Catch you later!
NUT weekly

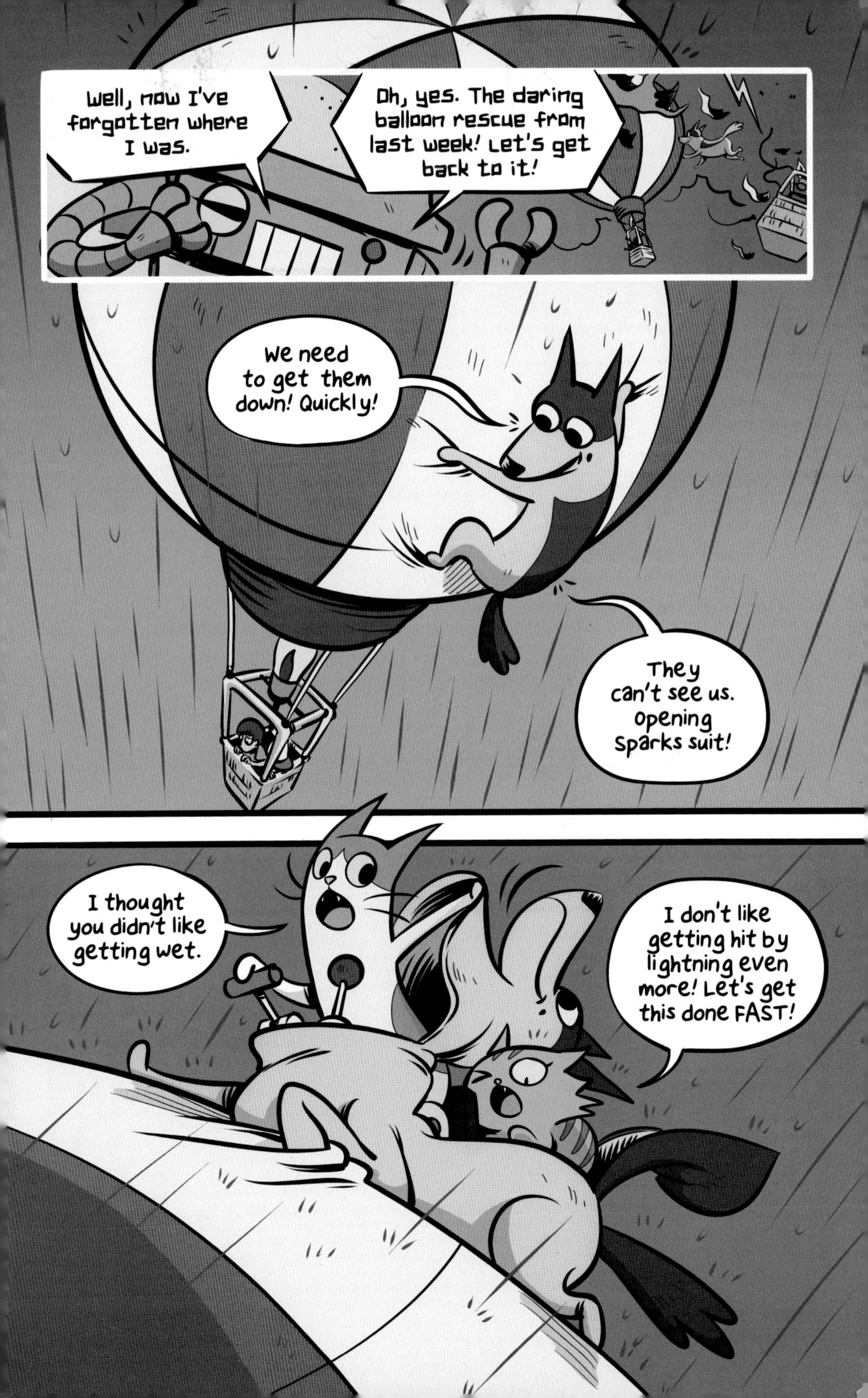
Well, now I've forgotten where I was.
Oh, yes. The daring balloon rescue from last week! Let's get back to it!
We need to get them down! Quickly!
They can't see us. Opening Sparks suit!
I thought you didn't like getting wet.
I don't like getting hit by lightning even more! Let's get this done FAST!

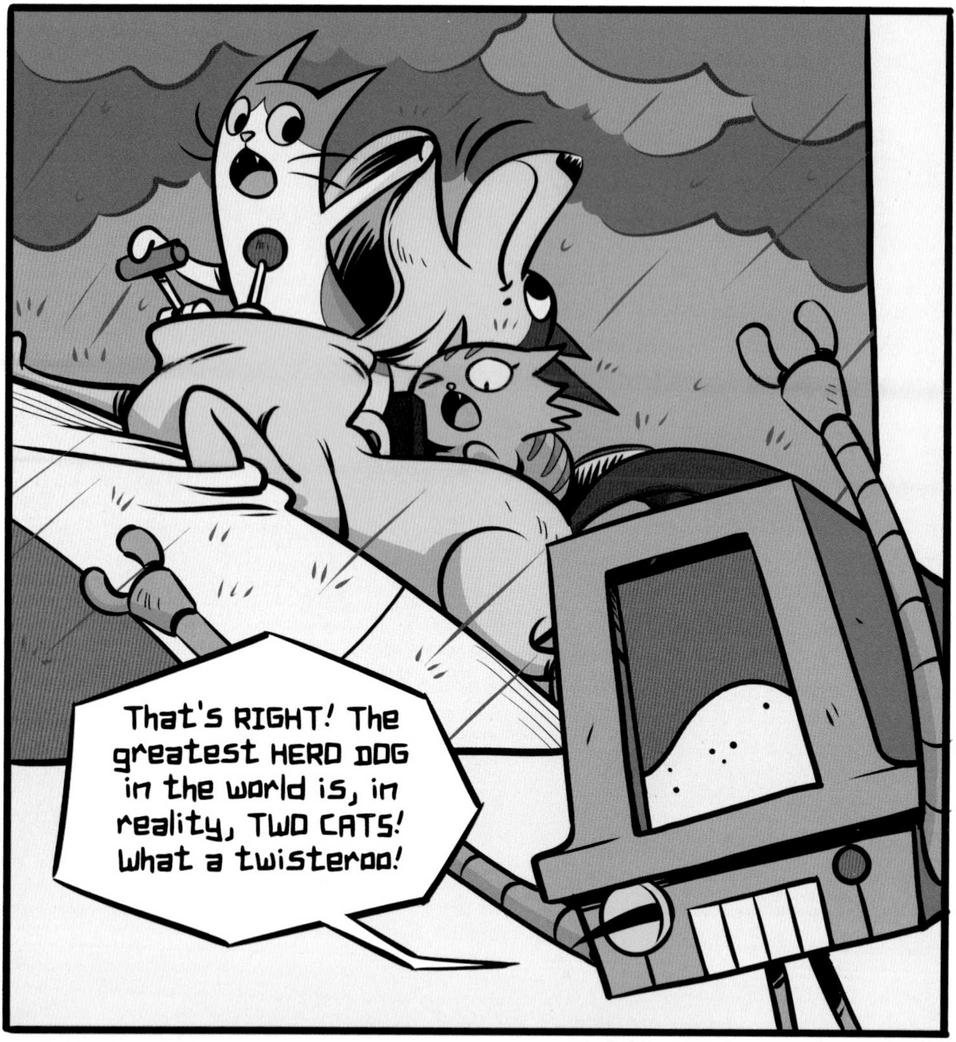
That's RIGHT! The greatest HERO DOG in the world is, in reality, TWO CATS! What a twisteroo!

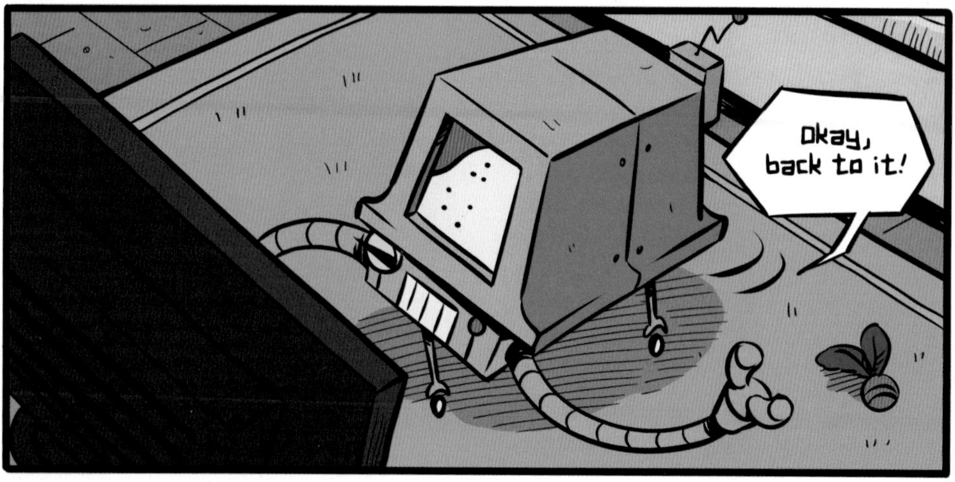
Okay, back to it!

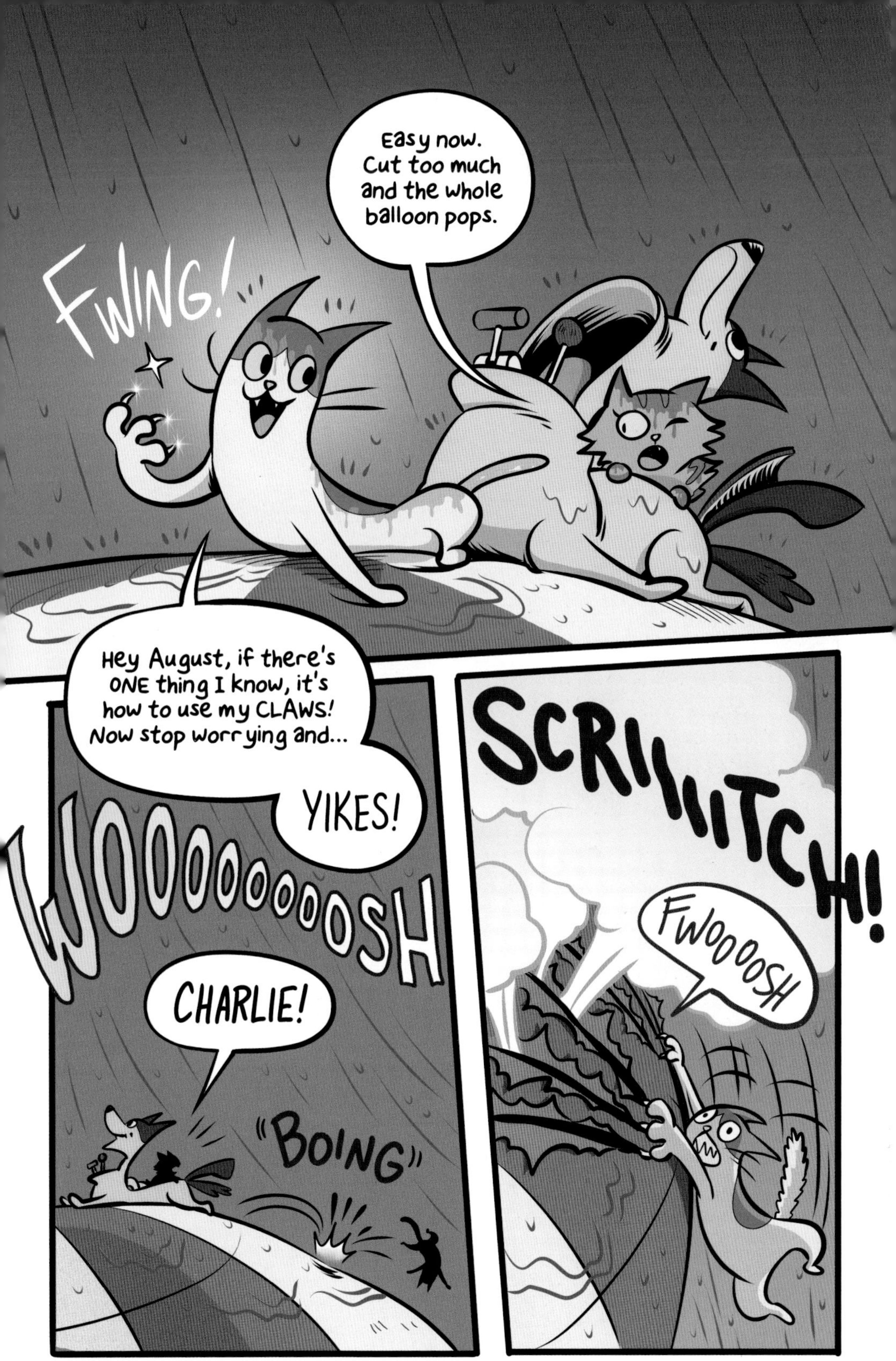
Easy now. Cut too much and the whole balloon pops.
FWING!
Hey August, if there's ONE thing I know, it's how to use my CLAWS! Now stop worrying and...
YIKES!
WOOOOOOOOSH
CHARLIE!
"BOING"
SCRIIIITCH!
FWOOOOSH

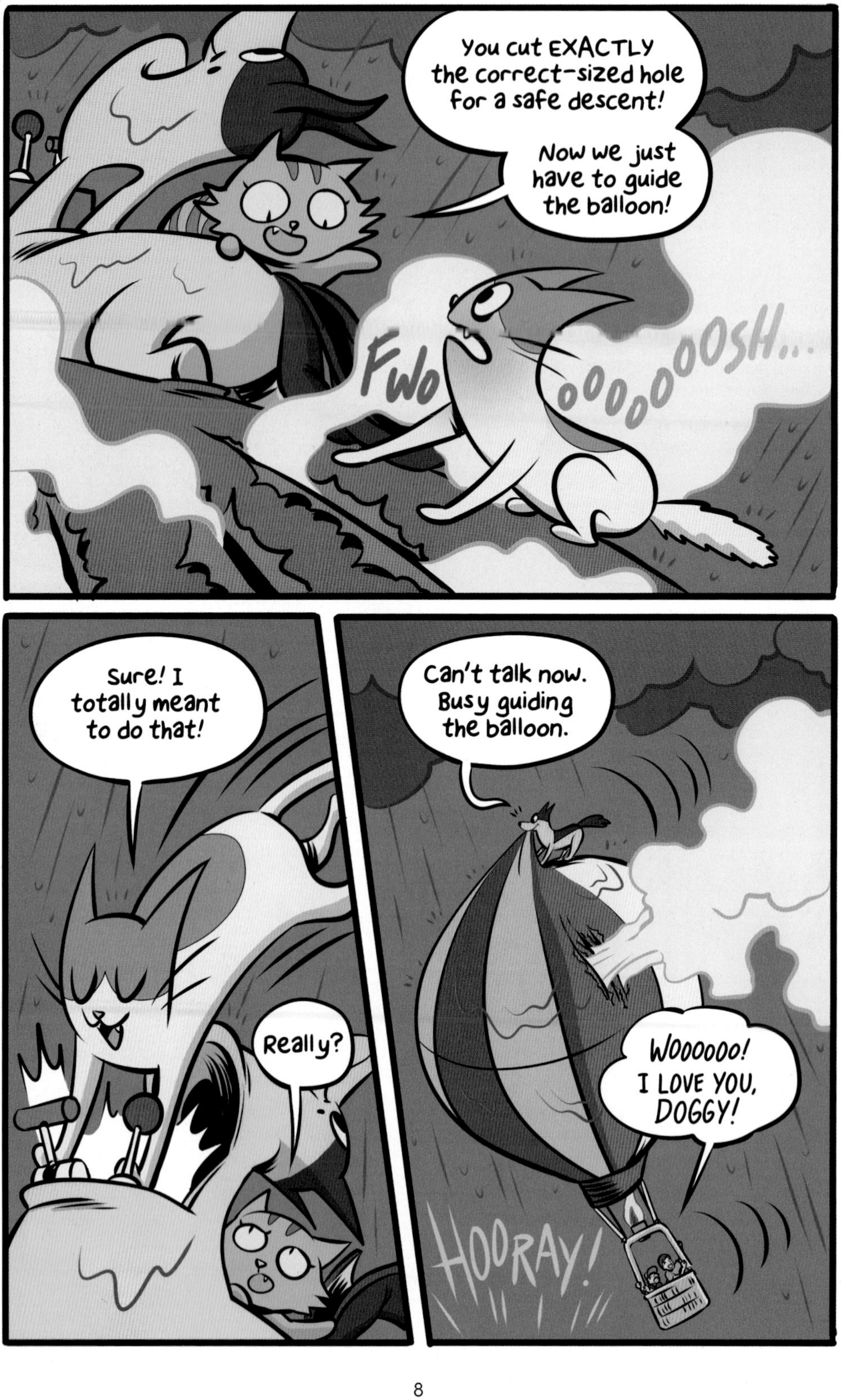
You cut EXACTLY the correct-sized hole for a safe descent!
Now we just have to guide the balloon!
FWOOOOOOOOOSH...
Sure! I totally meant to do that!
Really?
Can't talk now. Busy guiding the balloon.
WOOOOOO! I LOVE YOU, DOGGY!
HOORAY!

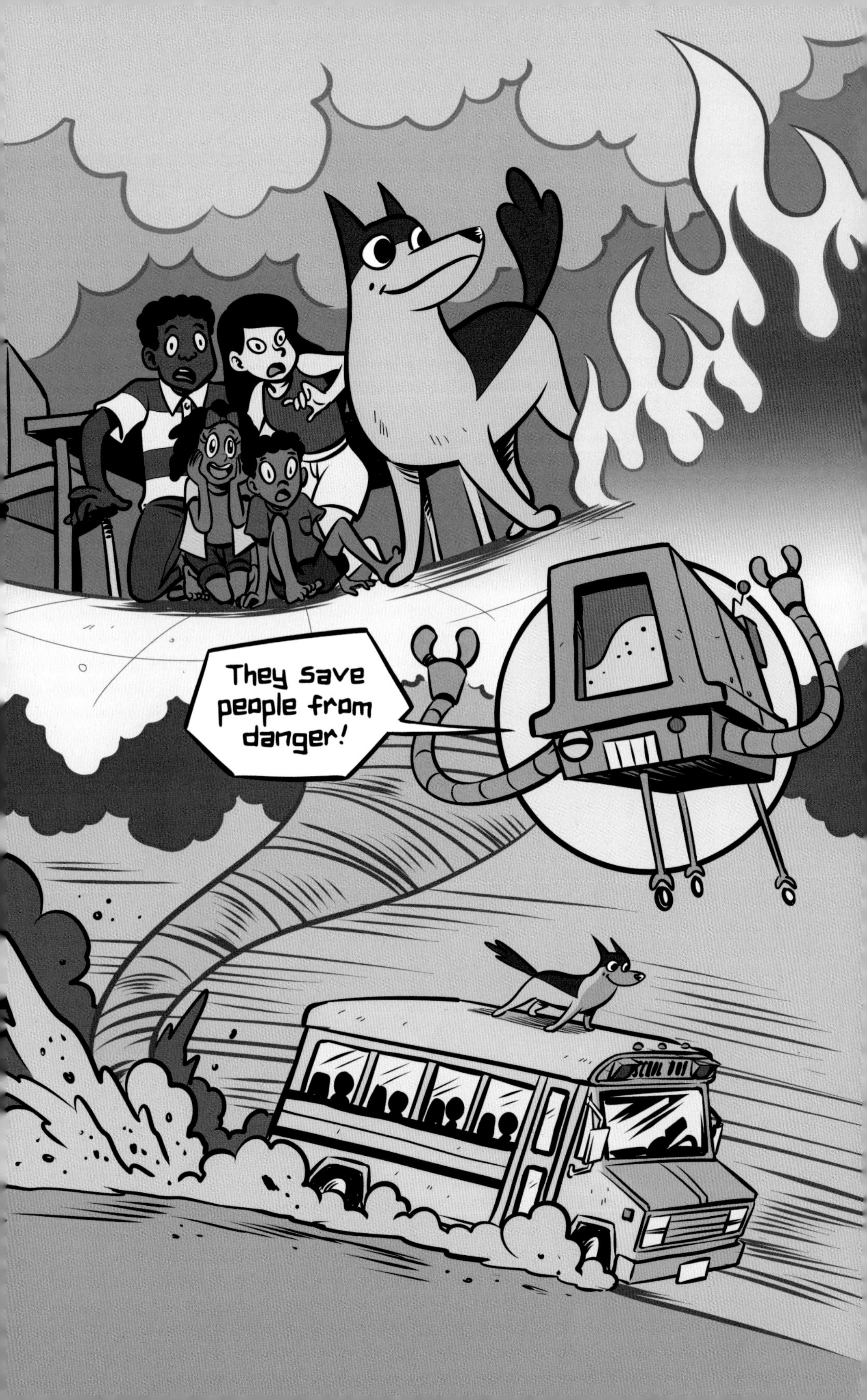
They save people from danger!

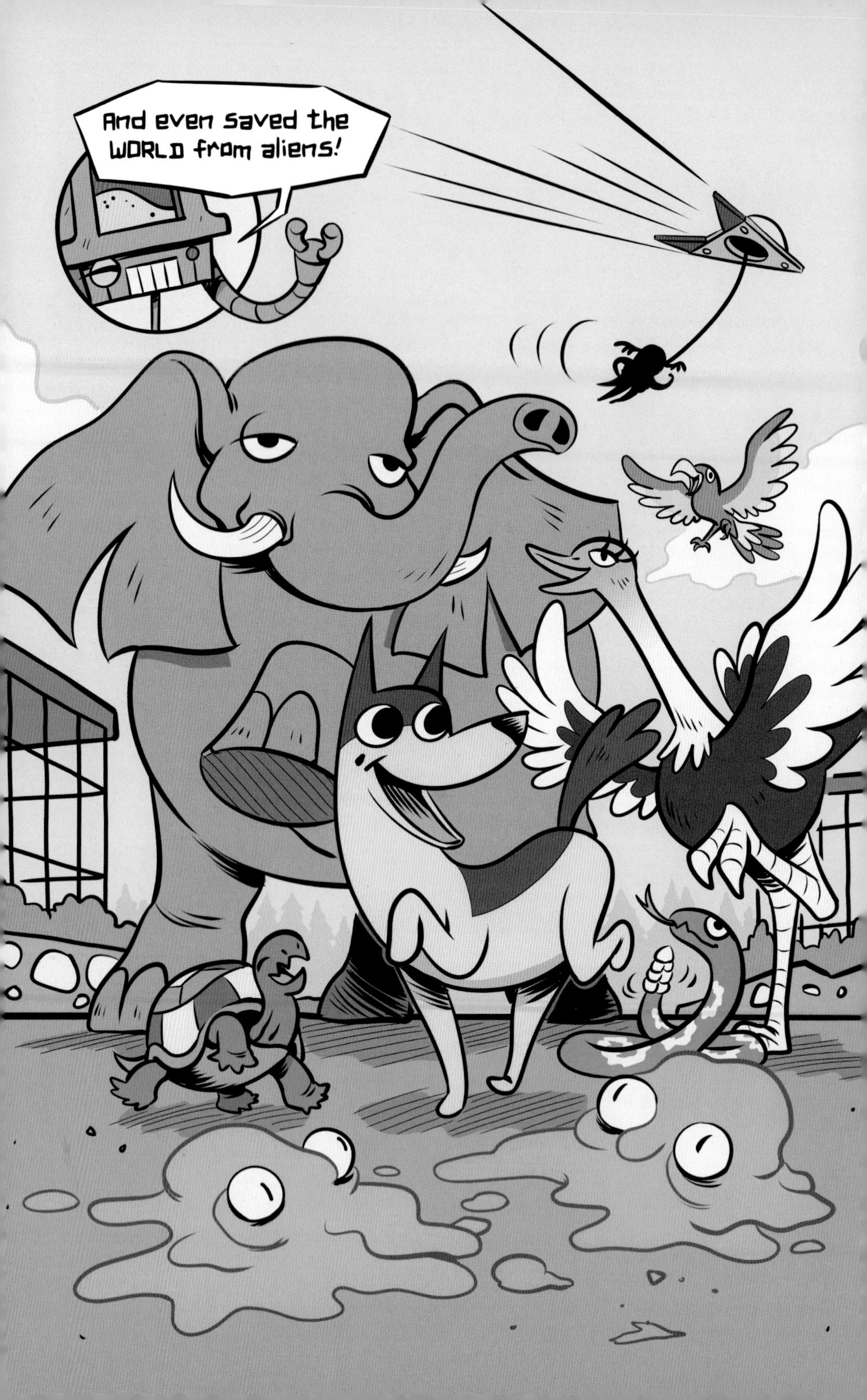
And even saved the WORLD from aliens!

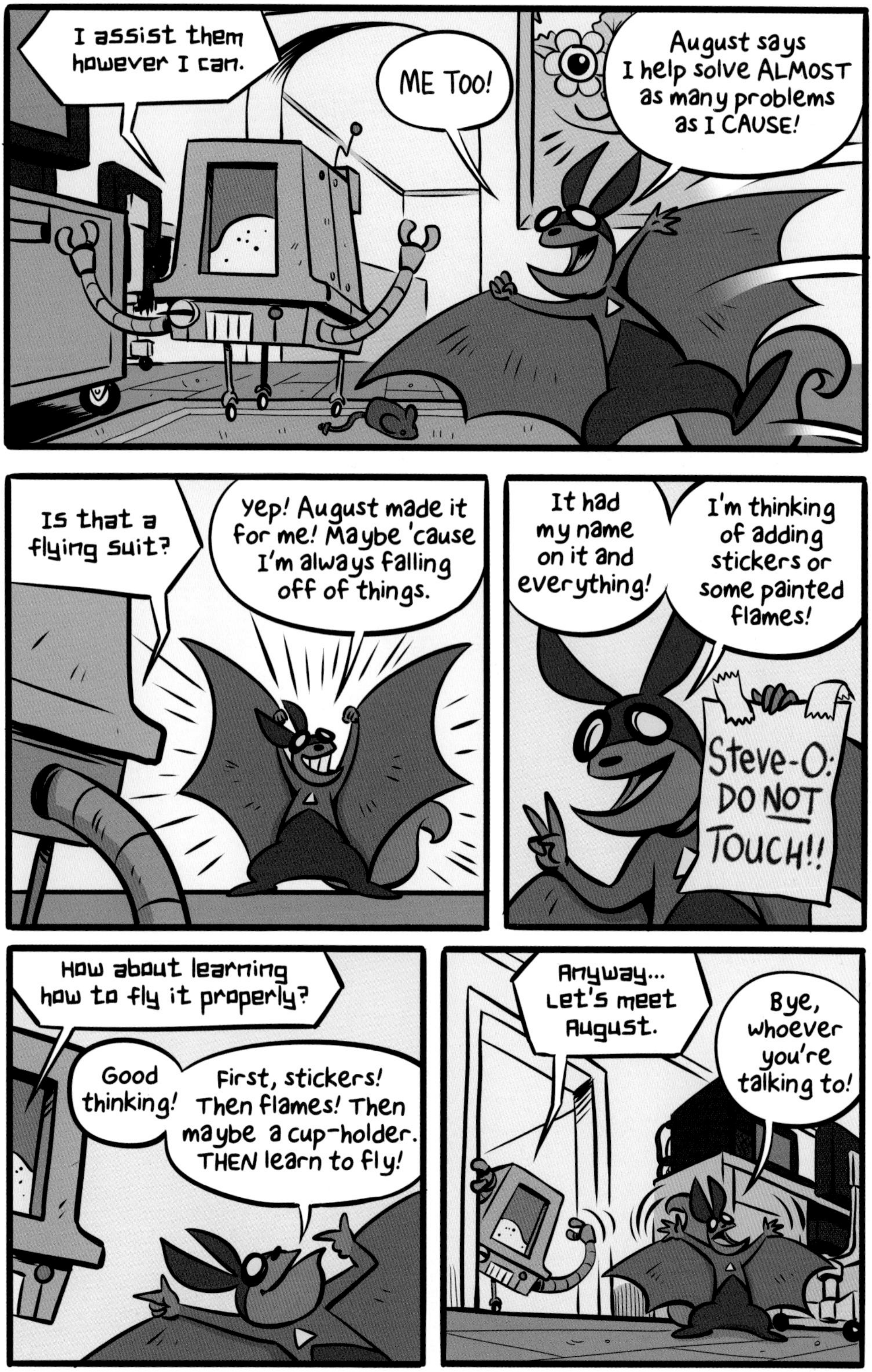
I assist them however I can.
ME TOO!
August says I help solve ALMOST as many problems as I CAUSE!
Is that a flying suit?
Yep! August made it for me! Maybe 'cause I'm always falling off of things.
It had my name on it and everything!
I'm thinking of adding stickers or some painted flames!
Steve-O: DO NOT TOUCH!!
How about learning how to fly it properly?
Good thinking!
First, stickers! Then flames! Then maybe a cup-holder. THEN learn to fly!
Anyway... Let's meet August.
Bye, whoever you're talking to!

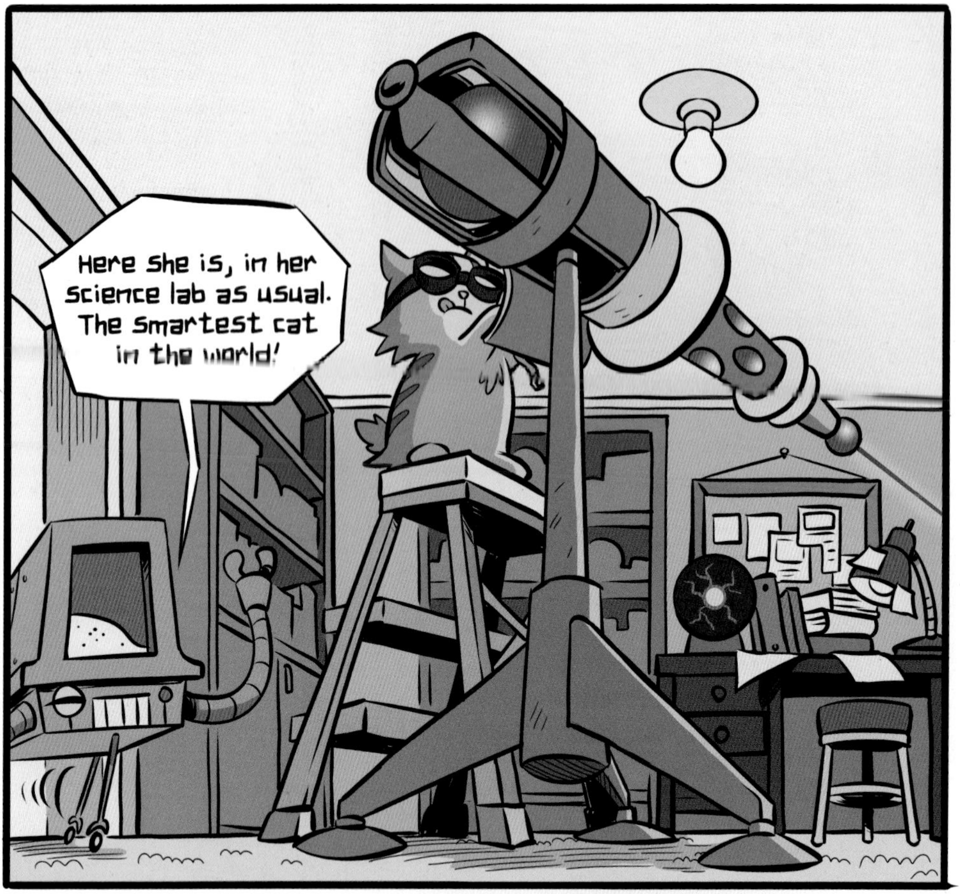
Here she is, in her science lab as usual. The smartest cat in the world!

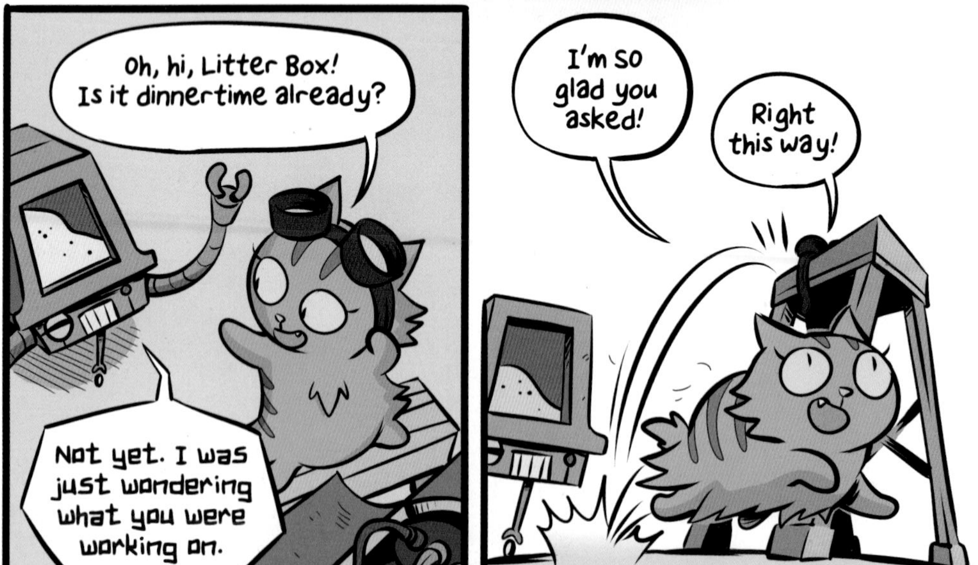
Oh, hi, Litter Box! Is it dinnertime already?
Not yet. I was just wondering what you were working on.
I'm so glad you asked!
Right this way!

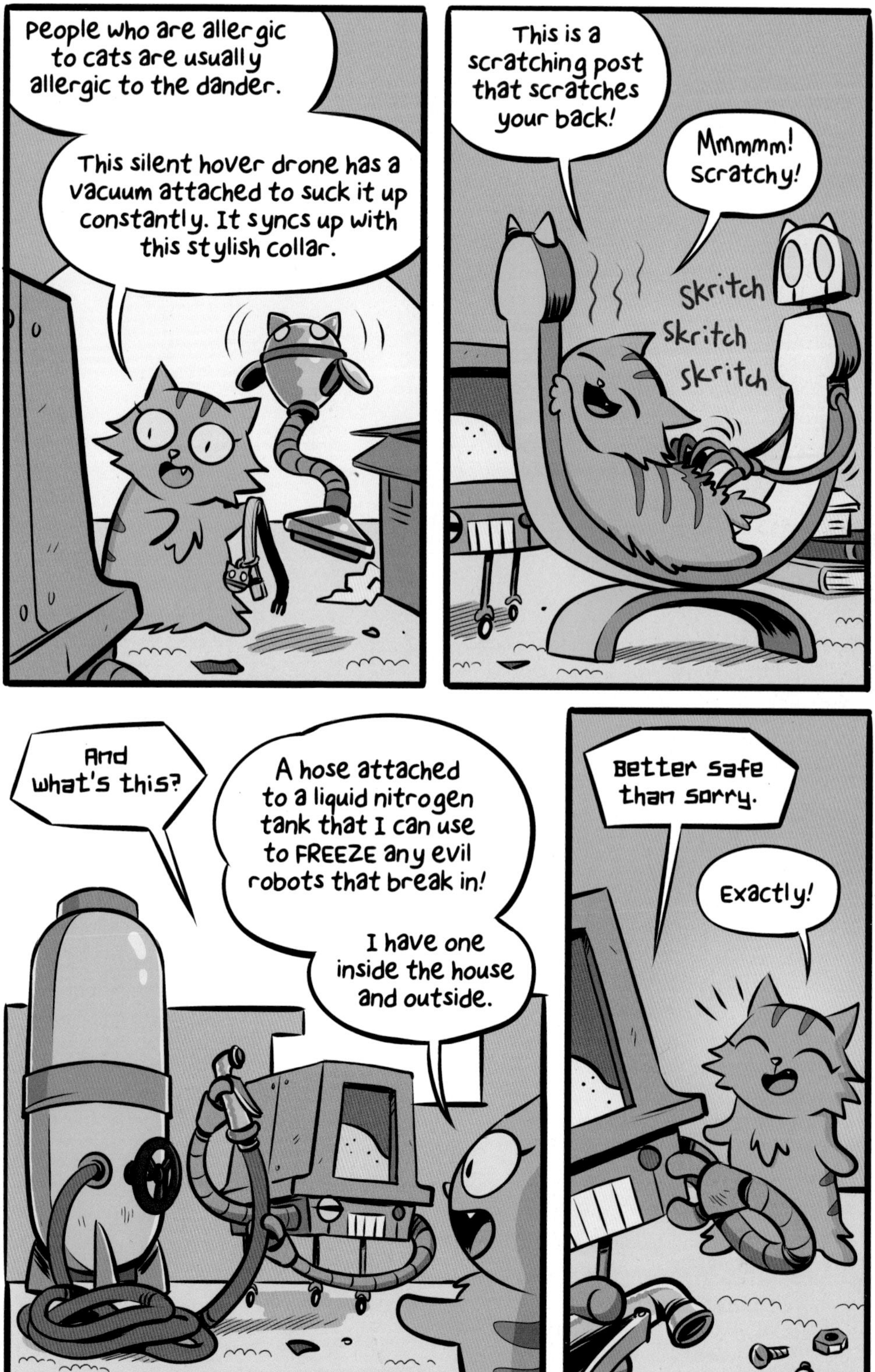
People who are allergic to cats are usually allergic to the dander.
This silent hover drone has a vacuum attached to suck it up constantly. It syncs up with this stylish collar.
This is a scratching post that scratches your back!
Mmmmm! Scratchy!
Skritch
Skritch
skritch
And what's this?
A hose attached to a liquid nitrogen tank that I can use to FREEZE any evil robots that break in!
I have one inside the house and outside.
Better safe than sorry.
Exactly!

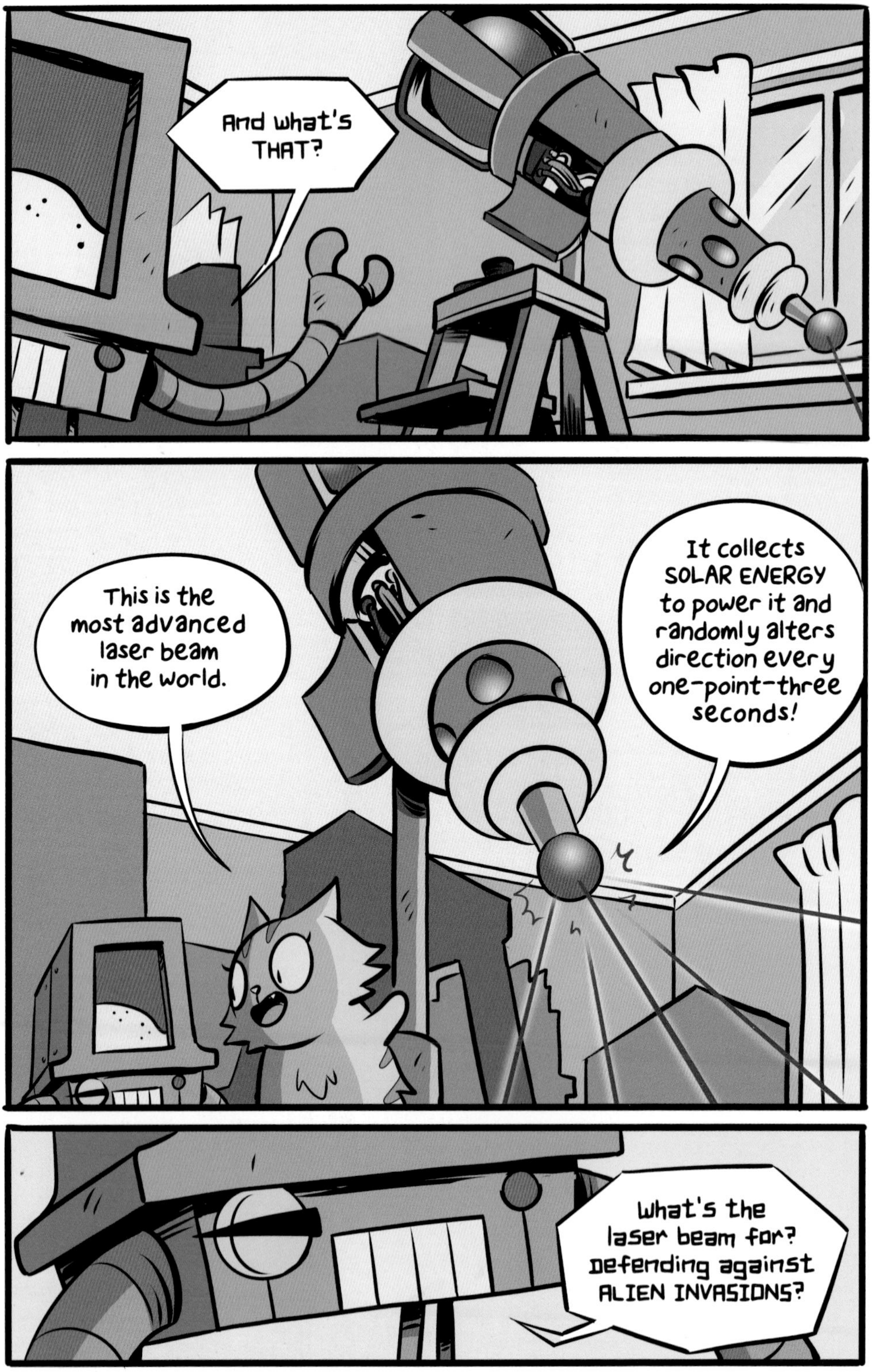
And what's THAT?
This is the most advanced laser beam in the world.
It collects SOLAR ENERGY to power it and randomly alters direction every one-point-three seconds!
What's the laser beam for? Defending against ALIEN INVASIONS?

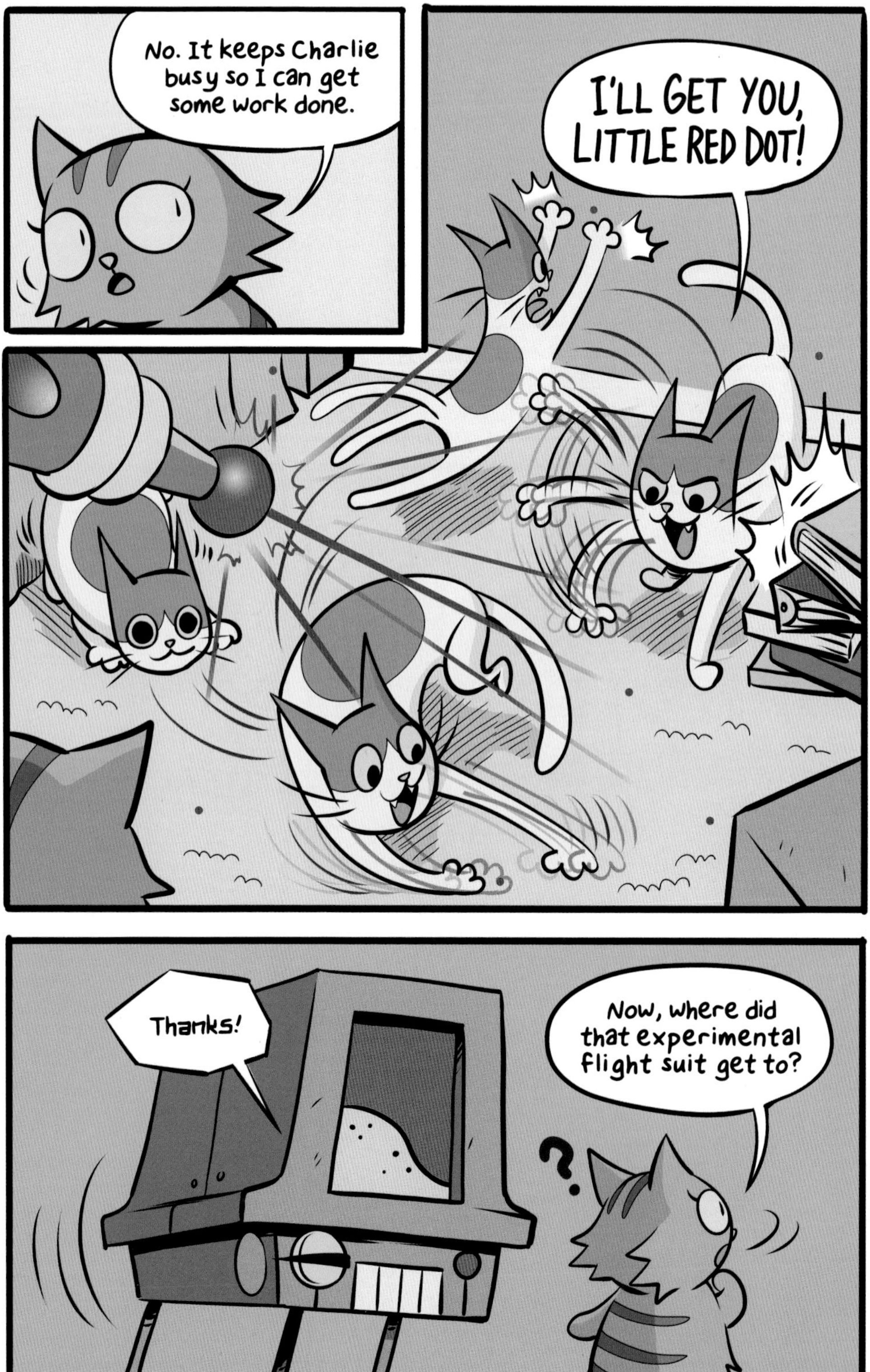
No. It keeps Charlie busy so I can get some work done.
I'LL GET YOU, LITTLE RED DOT!
Thanks!
Now, where did that experimental flight suit get to?

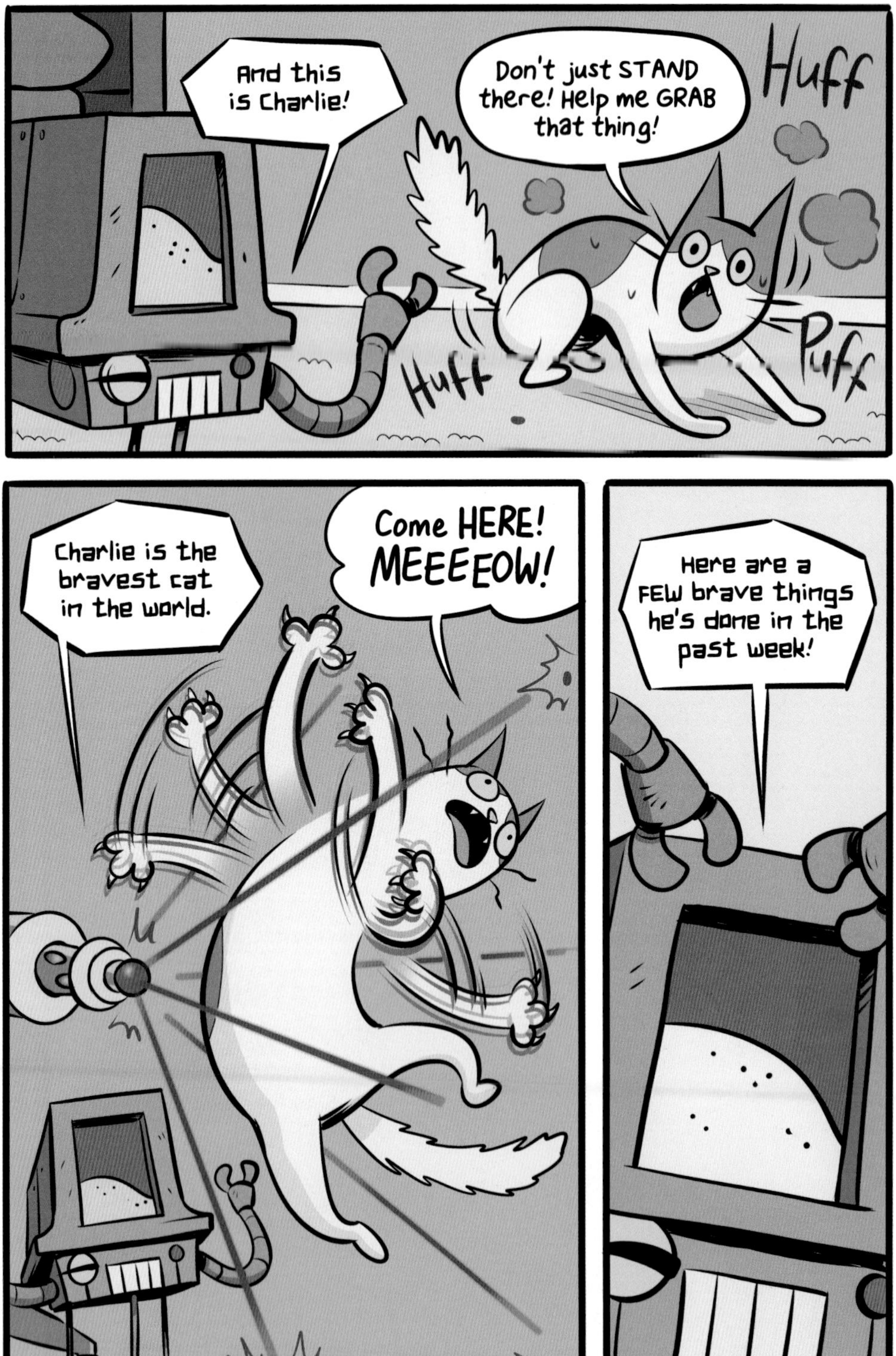
And this is Charlie!
Don't just STAND there! Help me GRAB that thing!
Huff
Huff
Puff
Charlie is the bravest cat in the world.
Come HERE! MEEEEOW!
Here are a FEW brave things he's done in the past week!

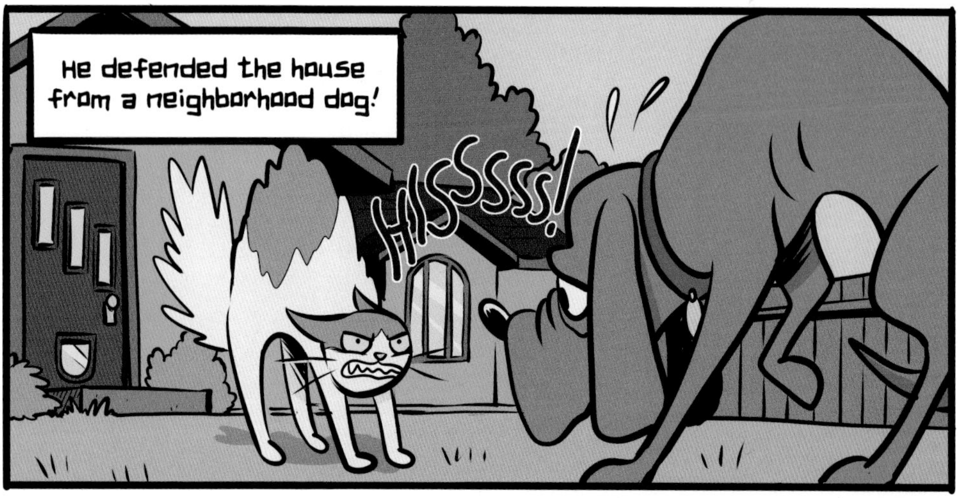
He defended the house from a neighborhood dog!
HISSSSS!

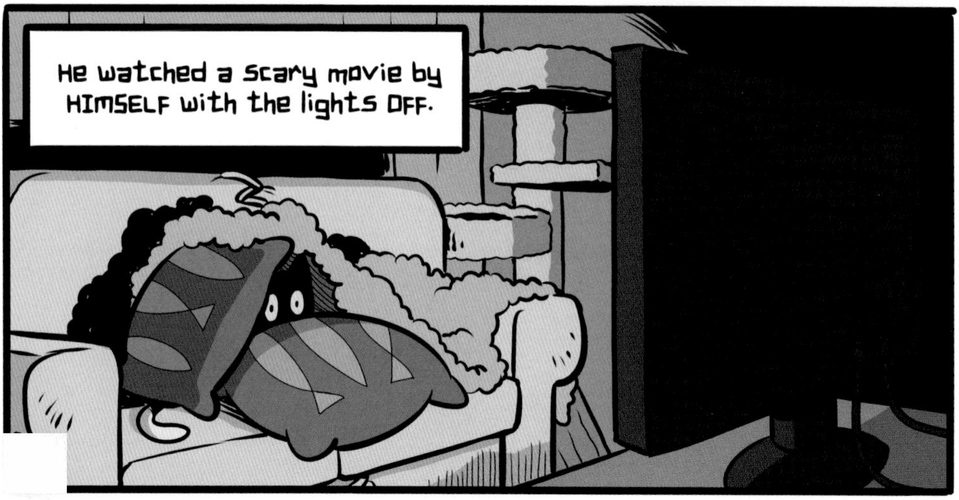
He watched a scary movie by HIMSELF with the lights OFF.

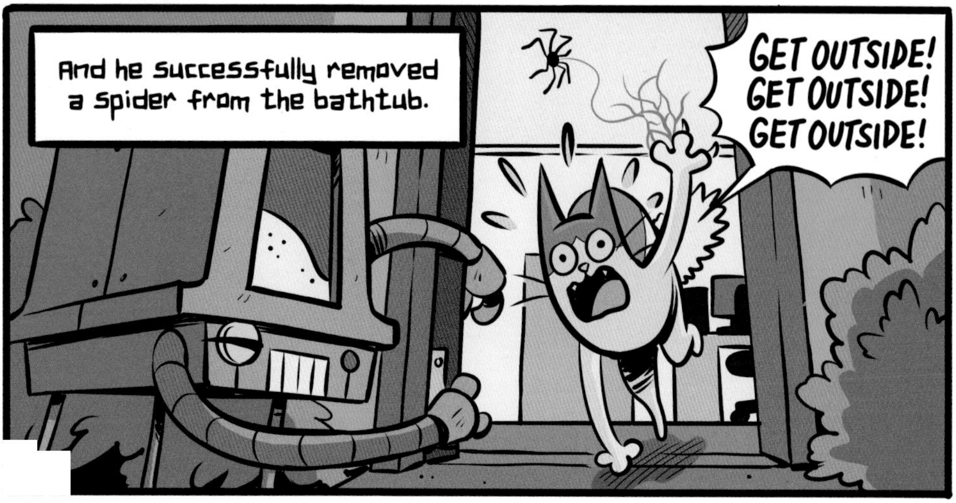
And he successfully removed a spider from the bathtub.
GET OUTSIDE! GET OUTSIDE! GET OUTSIDE!

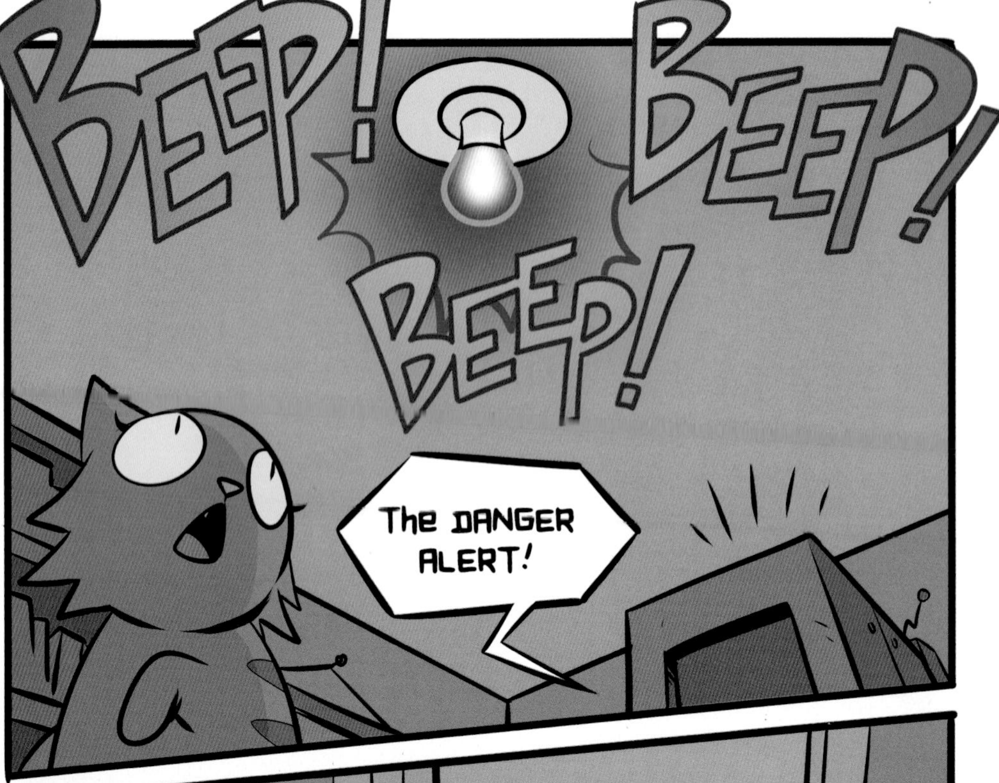
BEEP! BEEP! BEEP!
The DANGER ALERT!

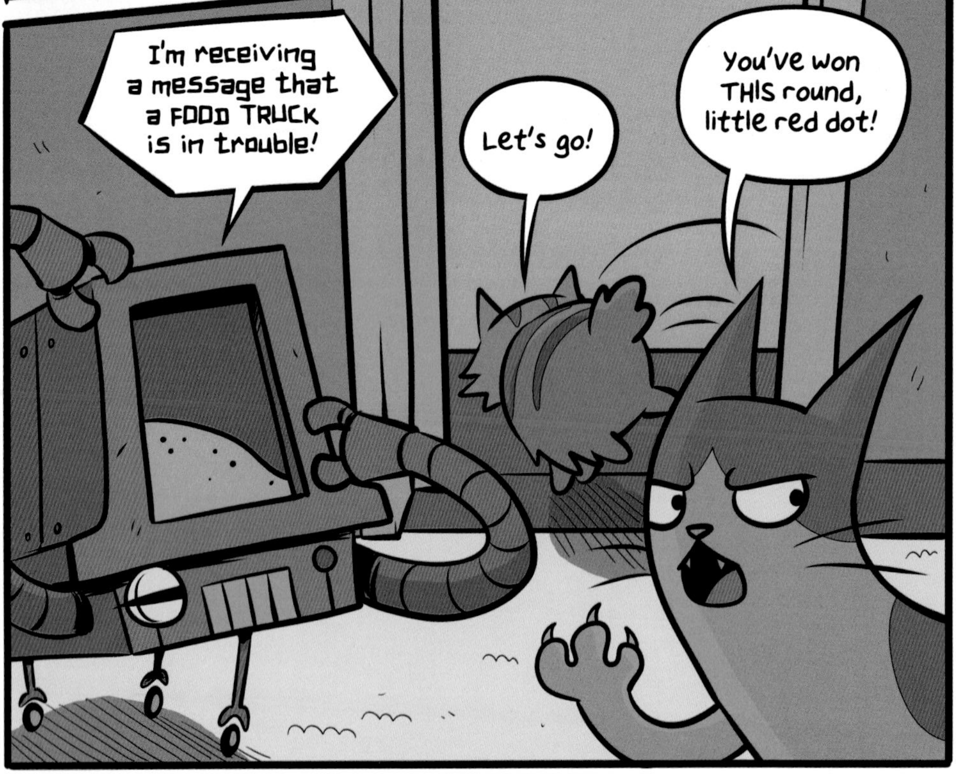
I'm receiving a message that a FOOD TRUCK is in trouble!
Let's go!
You've won THIS round, little red dot!

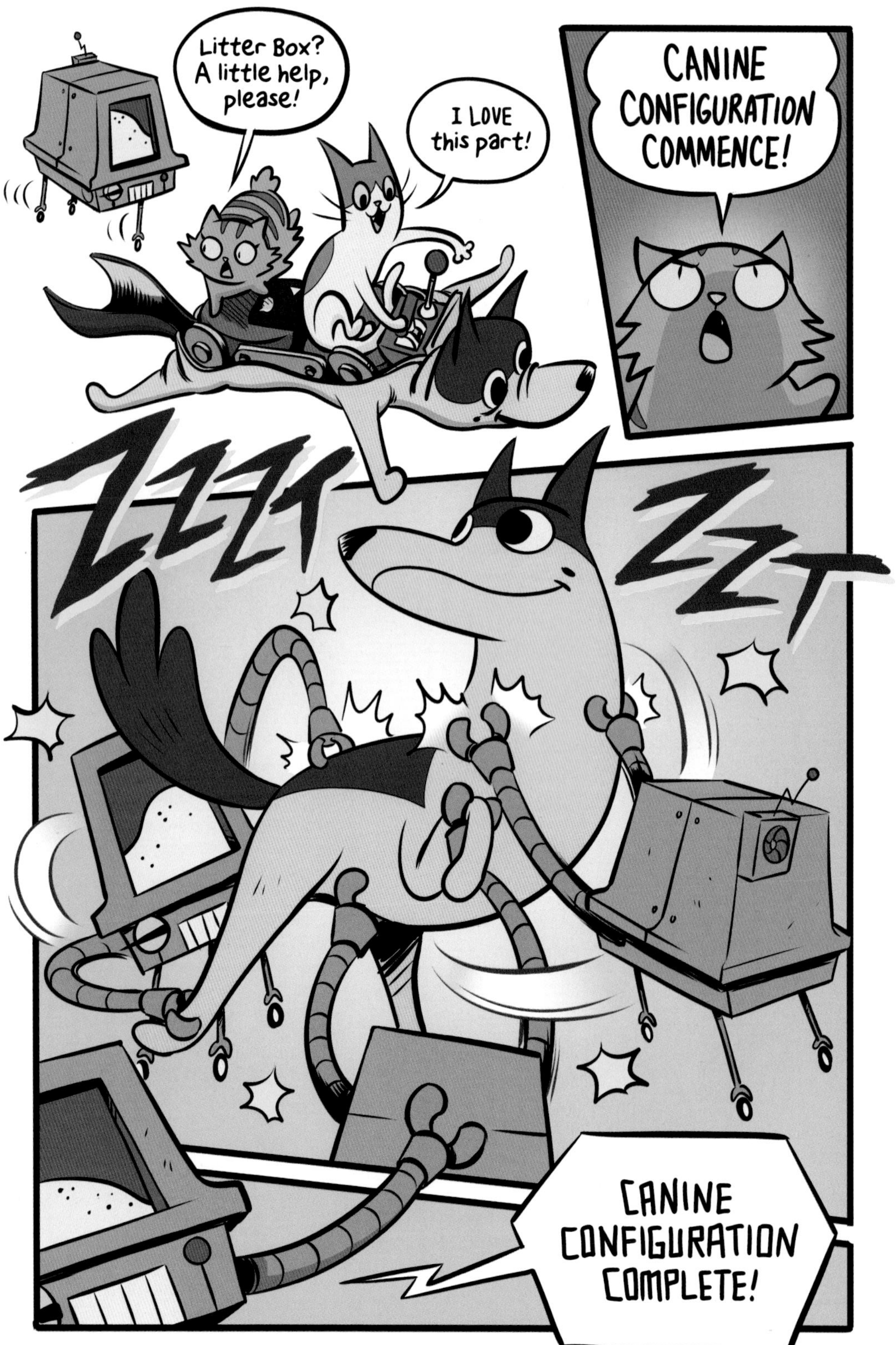

Litter Box? A little help, please!
I LOVE this part!
CANINE CONFIGURATION COMMENCE!
ZZZT
ZZZT
CANINE CONFIGURATION COMPLETE!

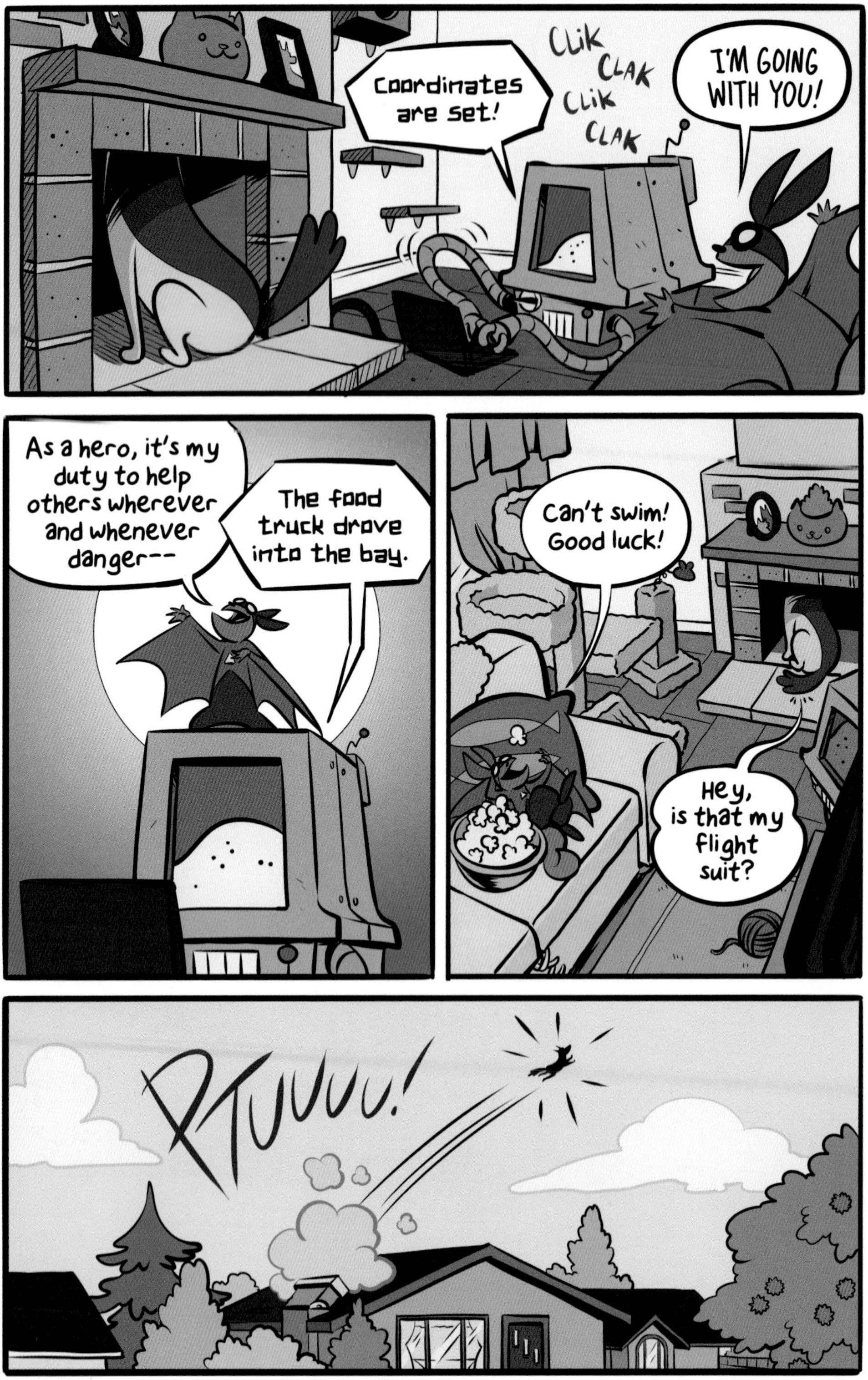
Coordinates are set!
CLIK CLAK CLIK CLAK
I'M GOING WITH YOU!
As a hero, it's my duty to help others wherever and whenever danger--
The food truck drove into the bay.
Can't swim! Good luck!
Hey, is that my flight suit?
PTUUUU!

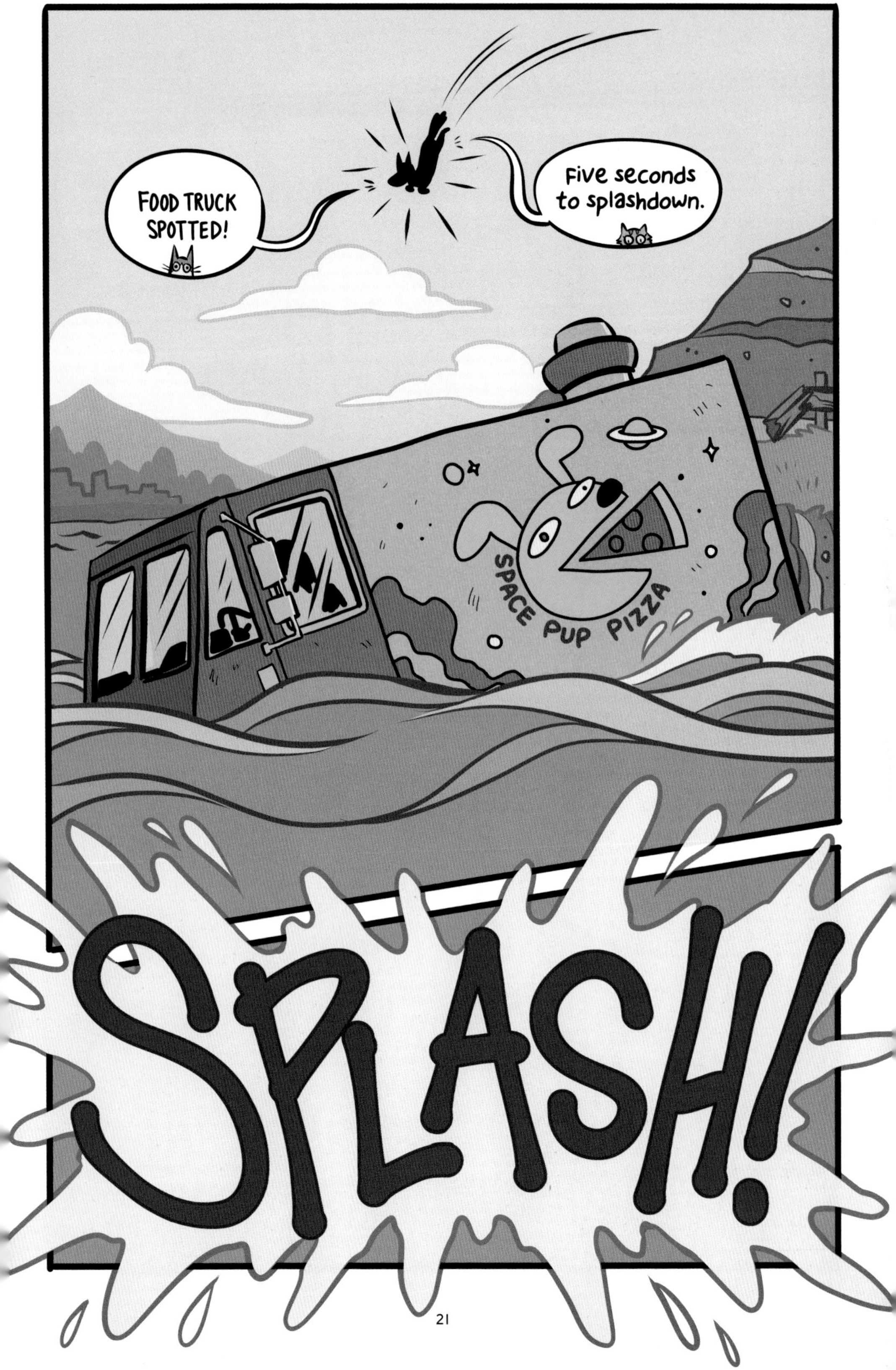
FOOD TRUCK SPOTTED!
Five seconds to splashdown.
SPACE PUP PIZZA
SPLASH!!

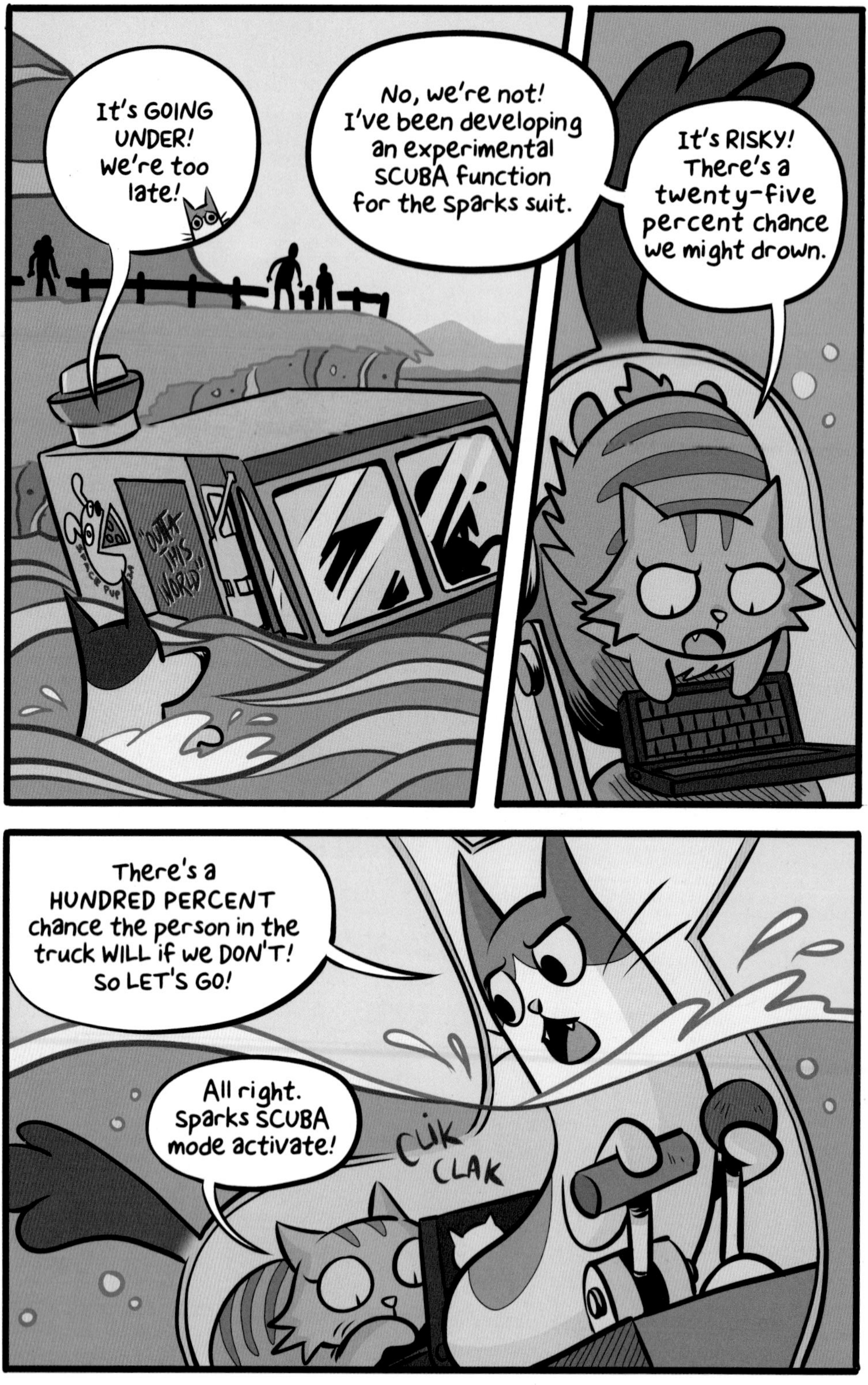
It's GOING UNDER! We're too late!
No, we're not! I've been developing an experimental SCUBA function for the Sparks suit.
It's RISKY! There's a twenty-five percent chance we might drown.
There's a HUNDRED PERCENT chance the person in the truck WILL if we DON'T! So LET'S GO!
All right. Sparks SCUBA mode activate!
CLIK CLAK

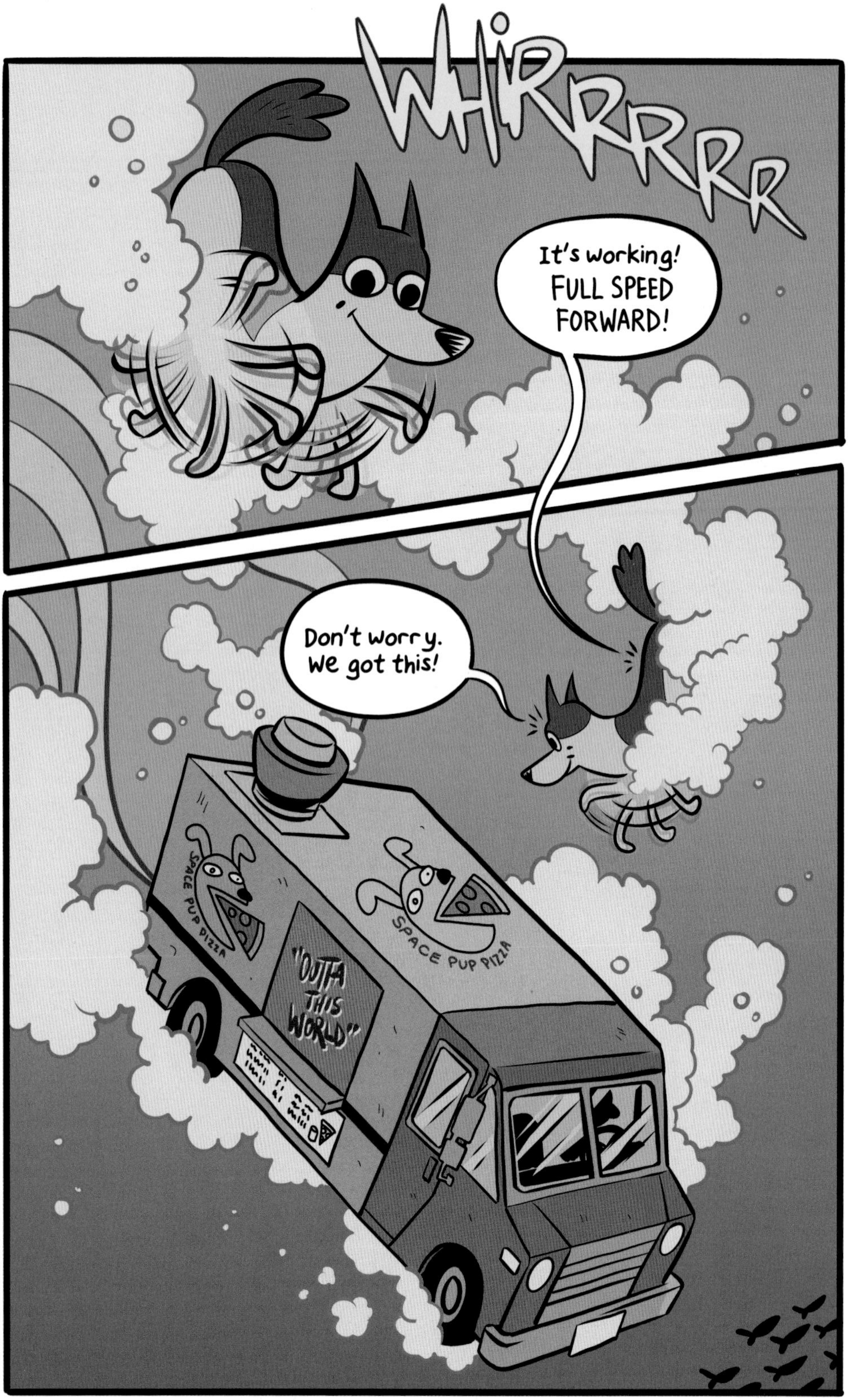
WHIRRRRR
It's working! FULL SPEED FORWARD!
Don't worry. We got this!
SPACE PUP PIZZA
"OUTTA THIS WORLD"
SPACE PUP PIZZA

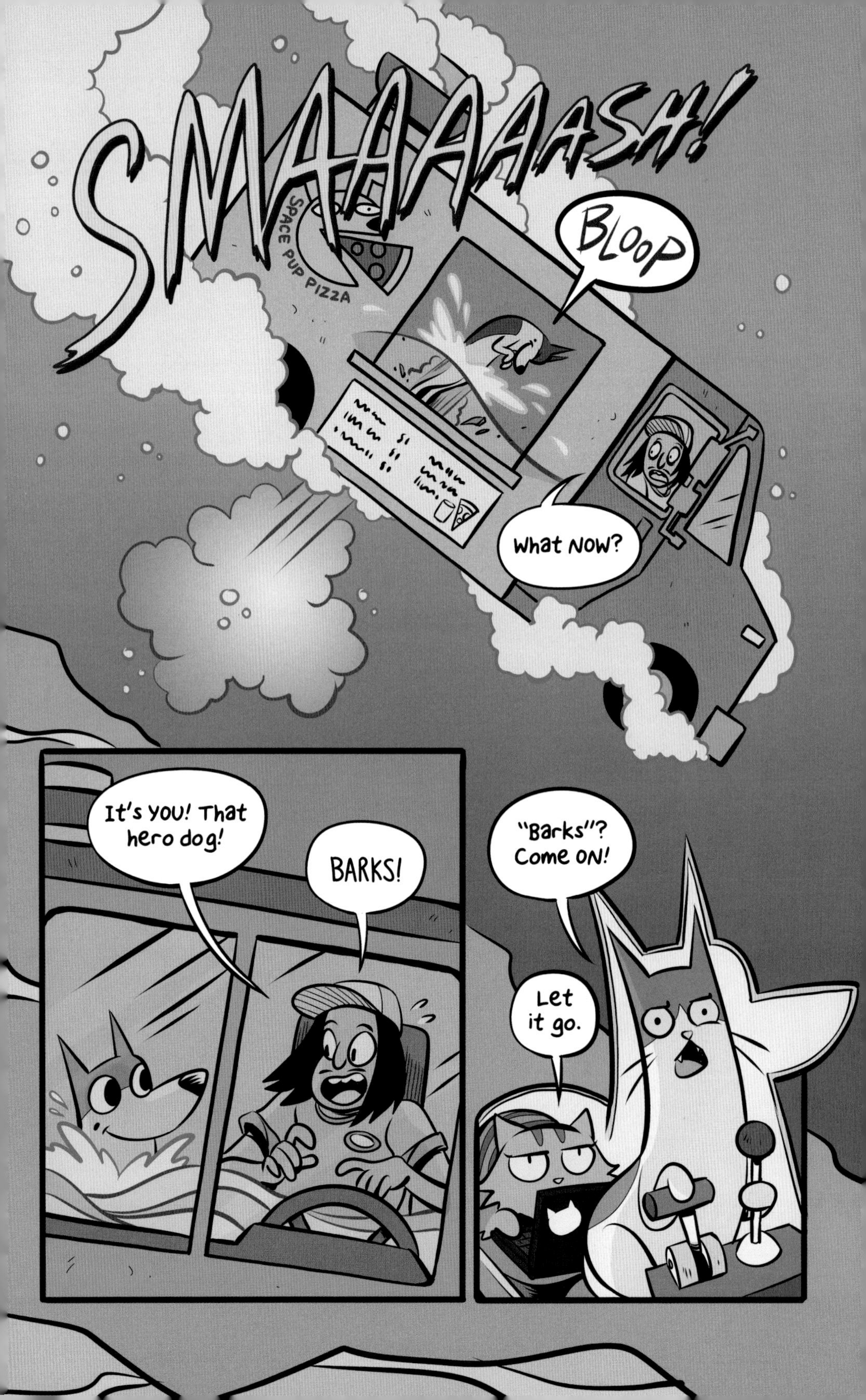
SMAAAAAASH!
SPACE PUP PIZZA
BLOOP
What NOW?
It's YOU! That hero dog!
BARKS!
"Barks"? Come ON!
Let it go.

26

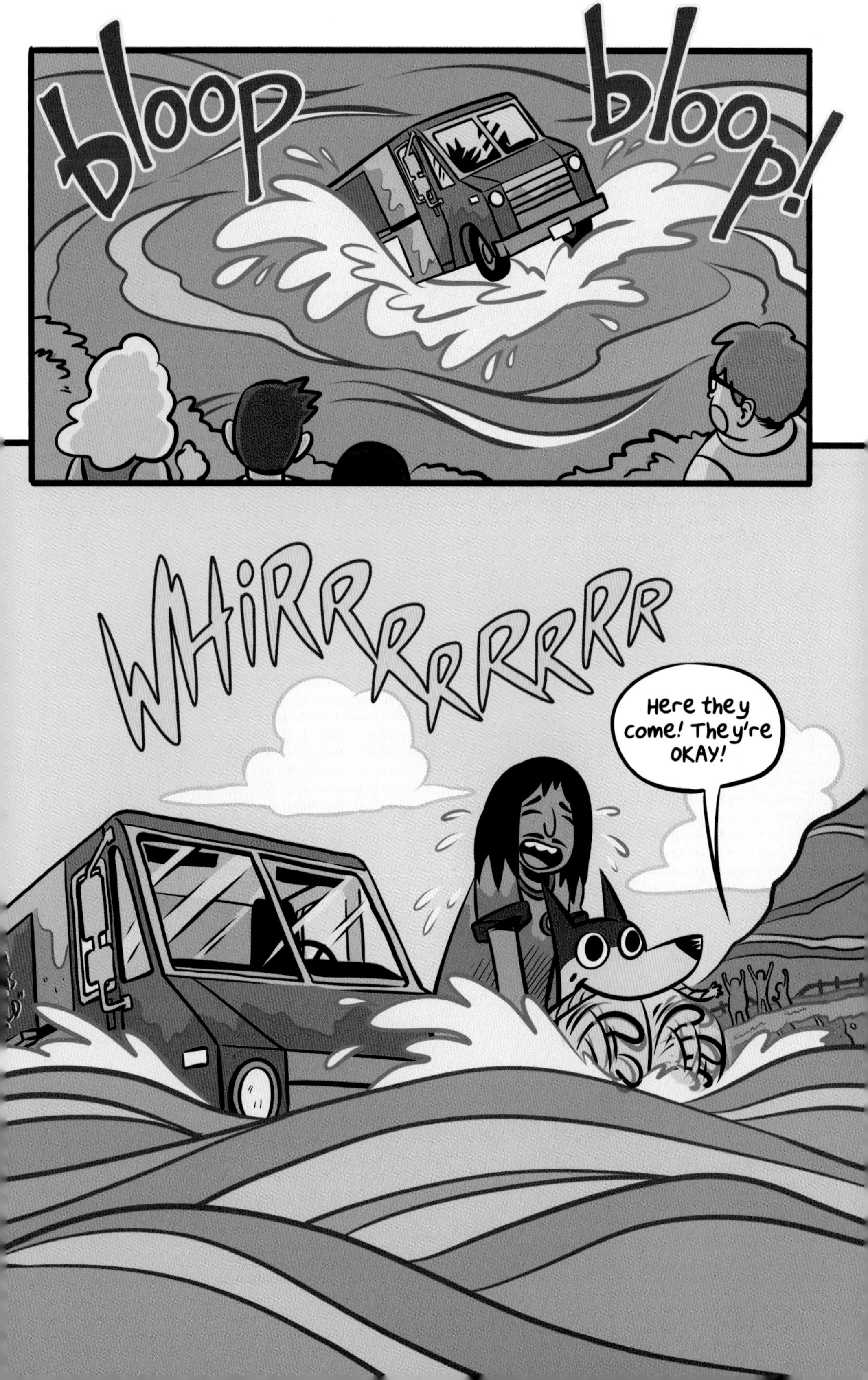
bloop
bloop!
WHIRRRRRRRR
Here they come! They're OKAY!

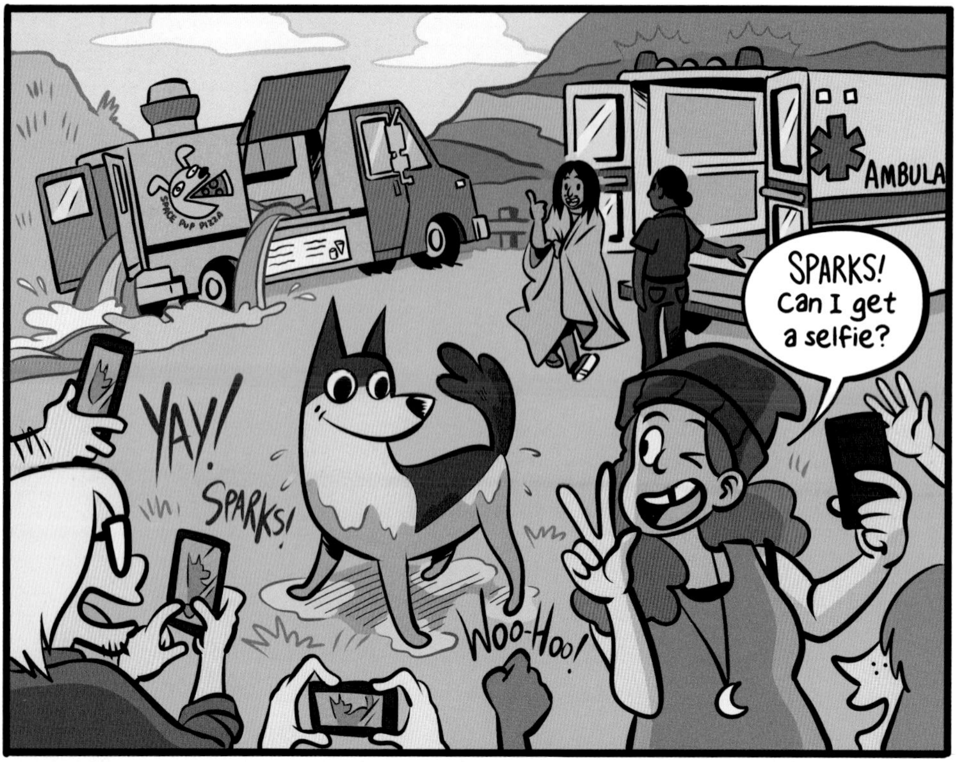
AMBULA
SPACE PUP PIZZA
SPARKS! Can I get a selfie?
YAY!
SPARKS!
WOO-HOO!

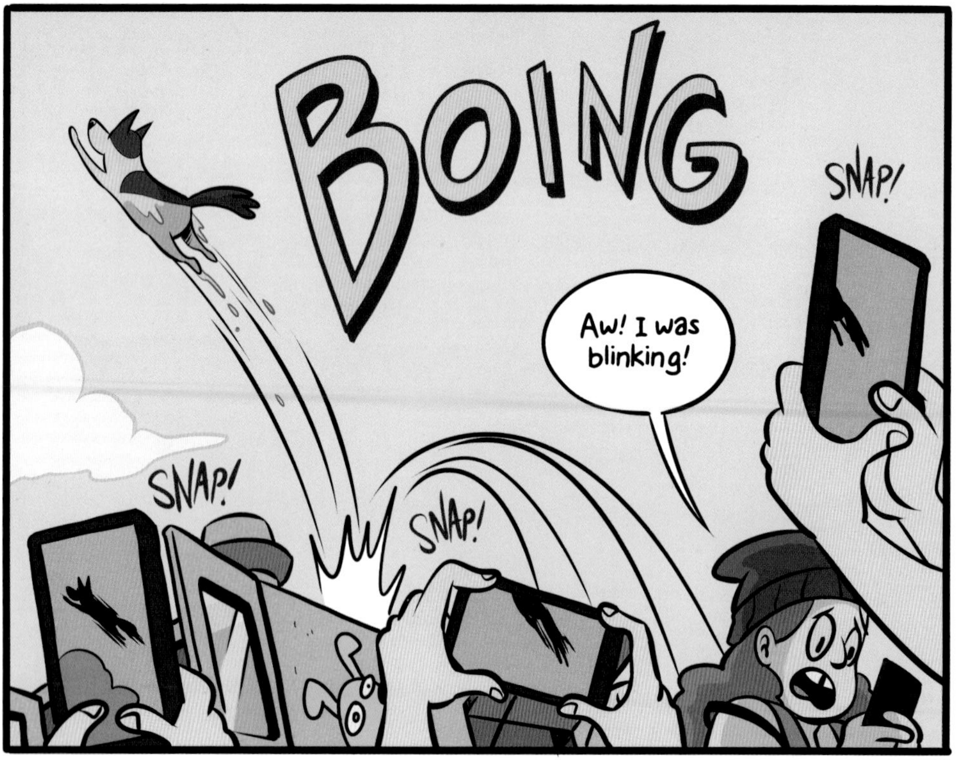
BOING
SNAP!
Aw! I was blinking!
SNAP!
SNAP!

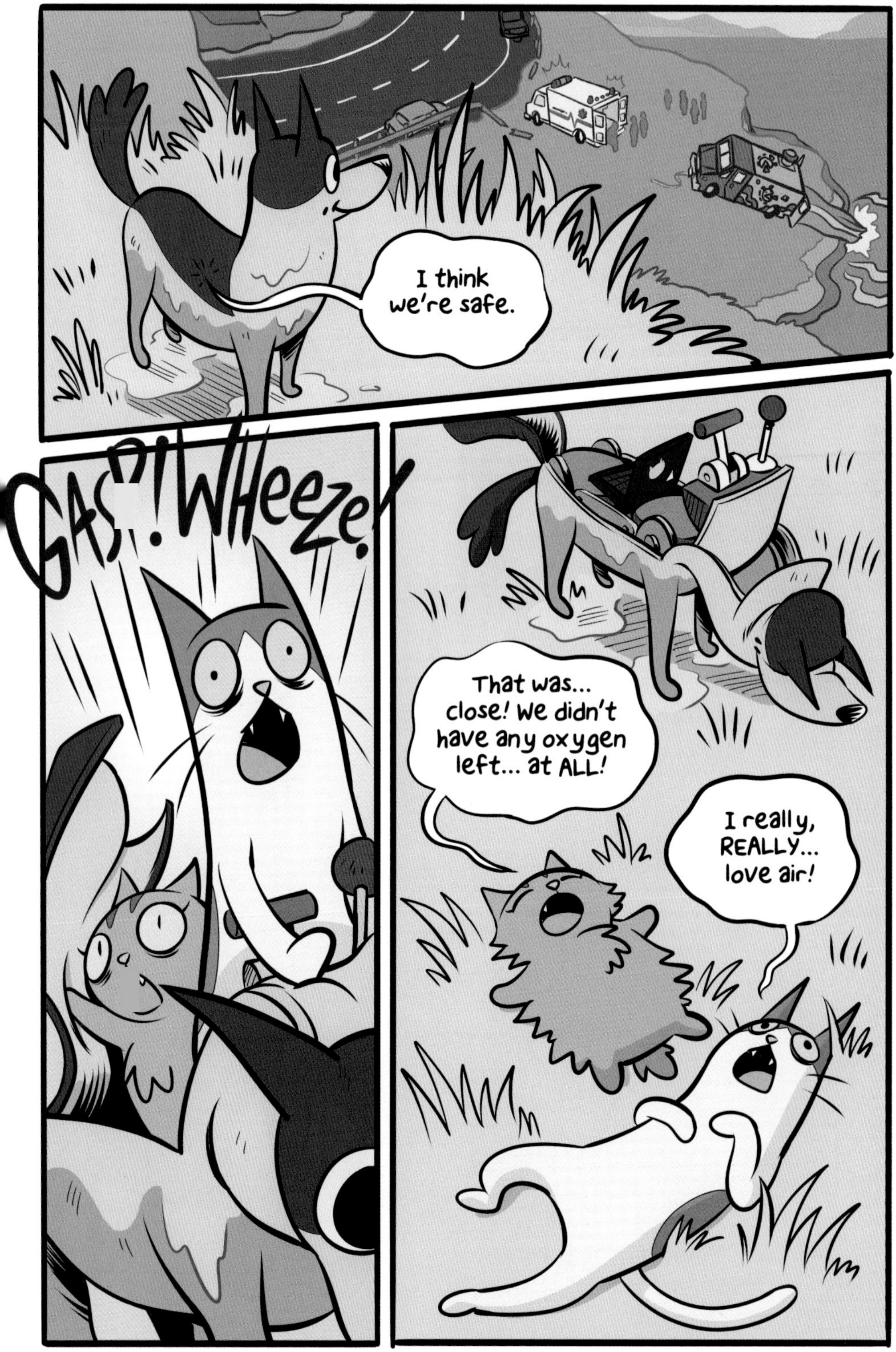
I think we're safe.
GASP! WHEEZE!
That was... close! We didn't have any oxygen left... at ALL!
I really, REALLY... love air!

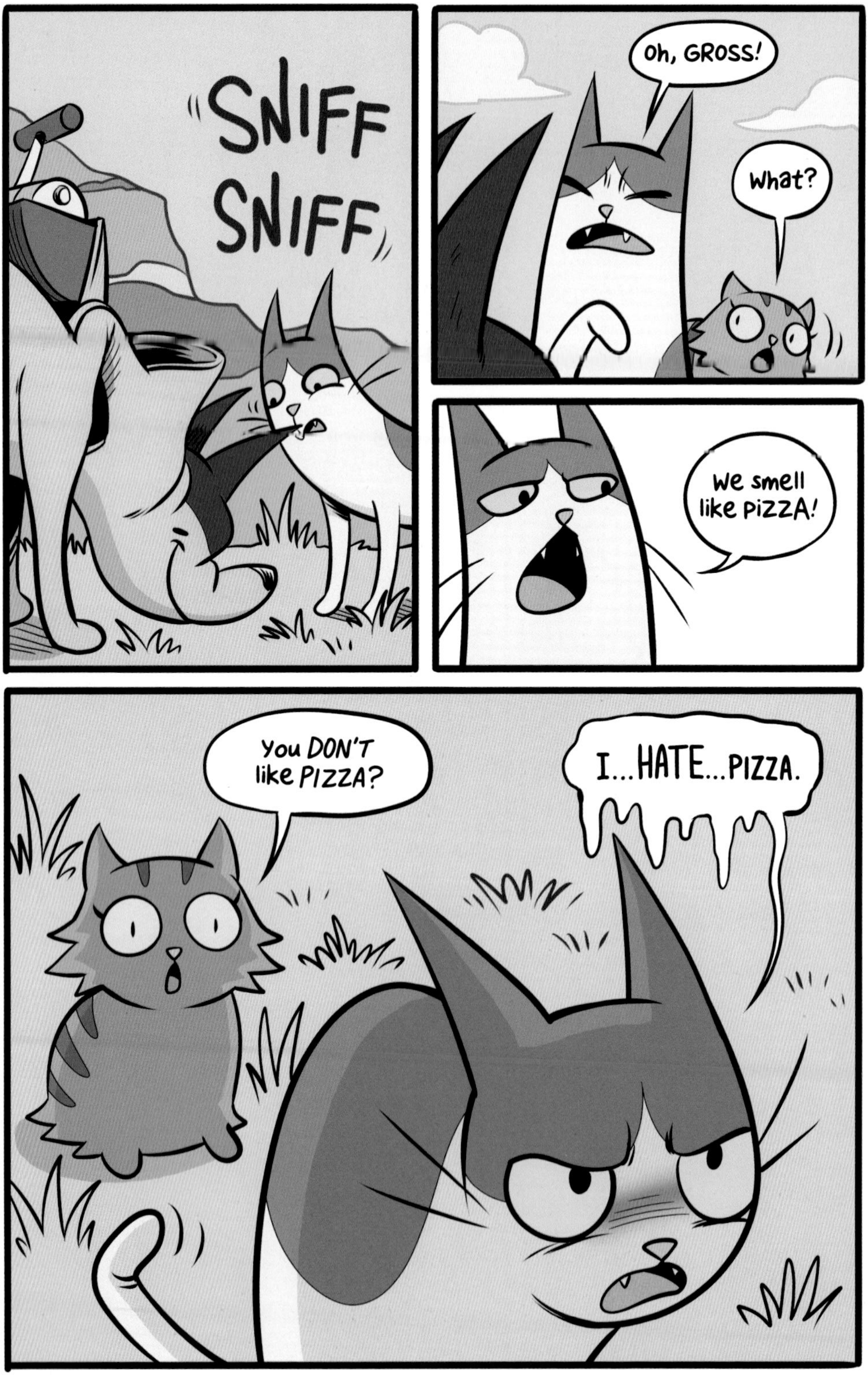
SNIFF SNIFF
Oh, GROSS!
What?
We smell like PIZZA!
You DON'T like PIZZA?
I...HATE...PIZZA.

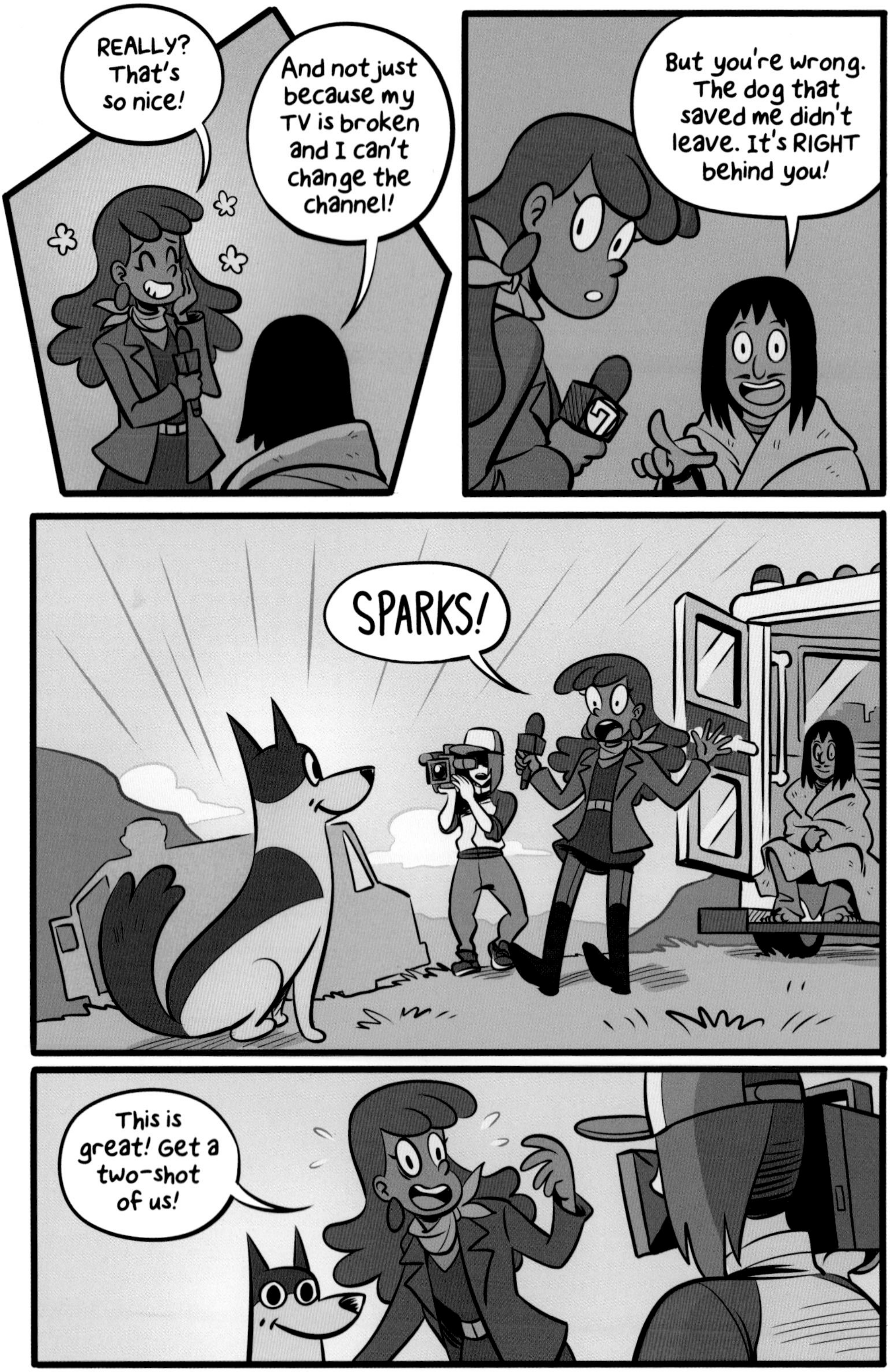
REALLY? That's so nice!
And not just because my TV is broken and I can't change the channel!
But you're wrong. The dog that saved me didn't leave. It's RIGHT behind you!
SPARKS!
This is great! Get a two-shot of us!

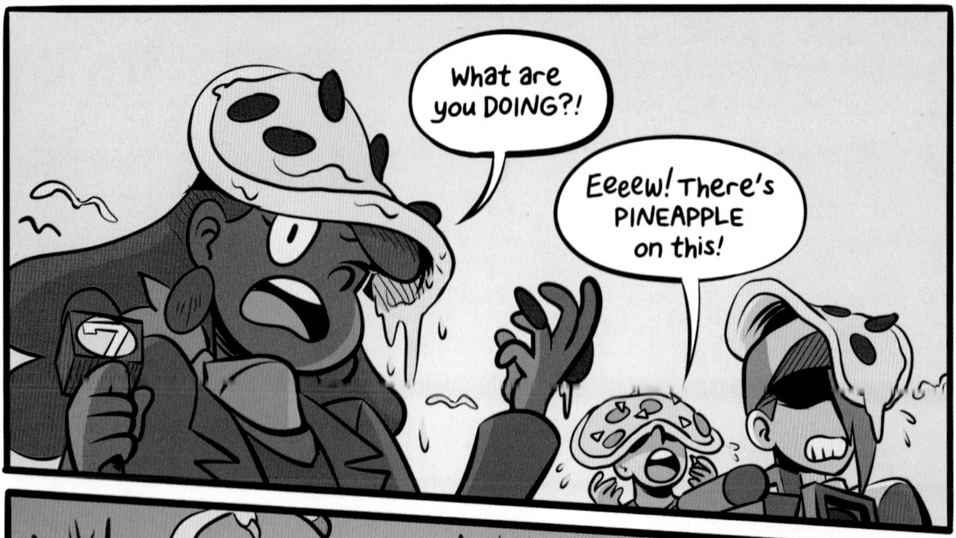
What are you DOING?!
Eeeew! There's PINEAPPLE on this!

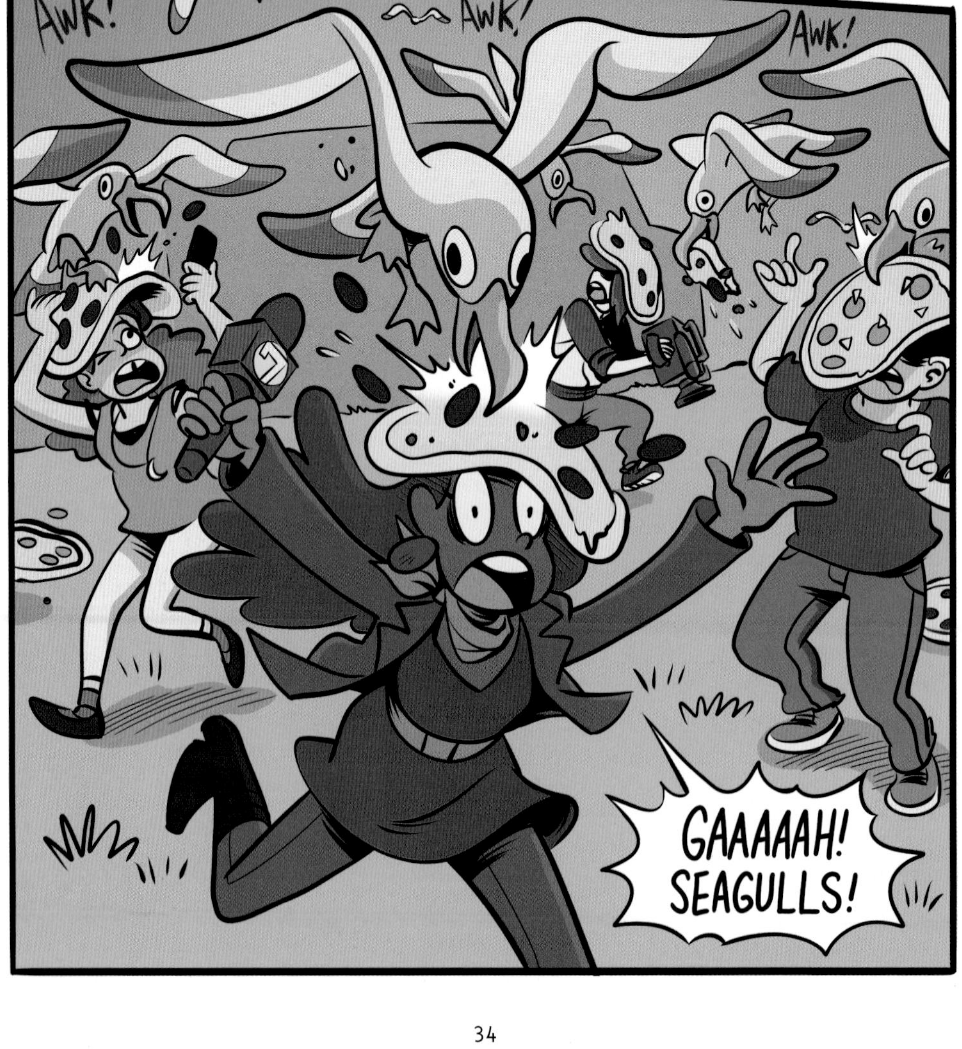
AWK!
AWK!
AWK!
GAAAAAH! SEAGULLS!

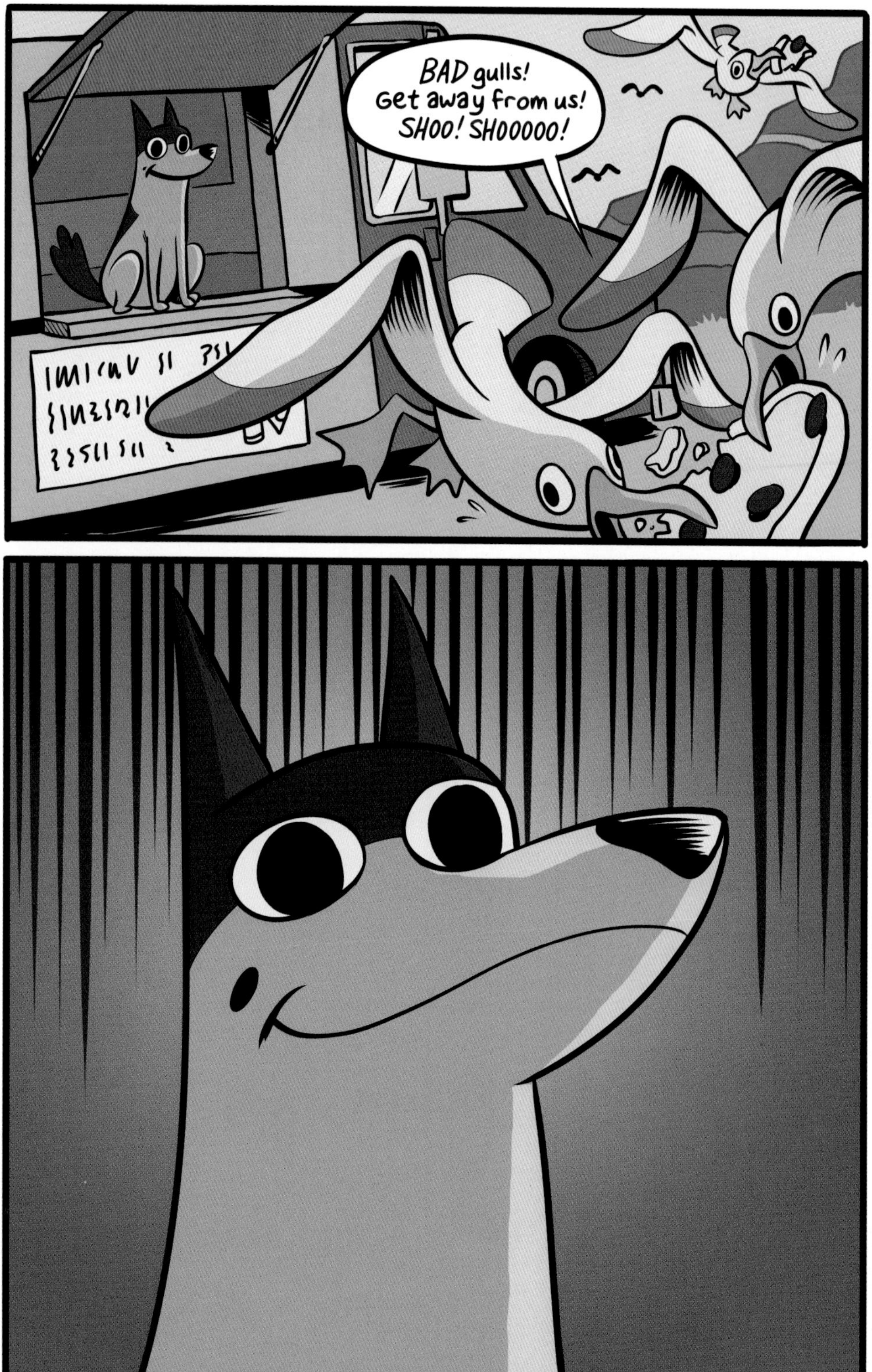
BAD gulls!
Get away from us!
SHOO! SHOOOOO!

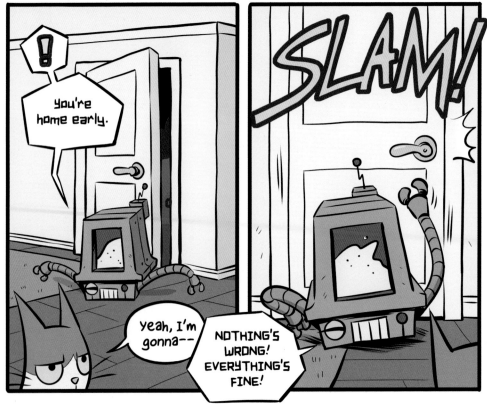

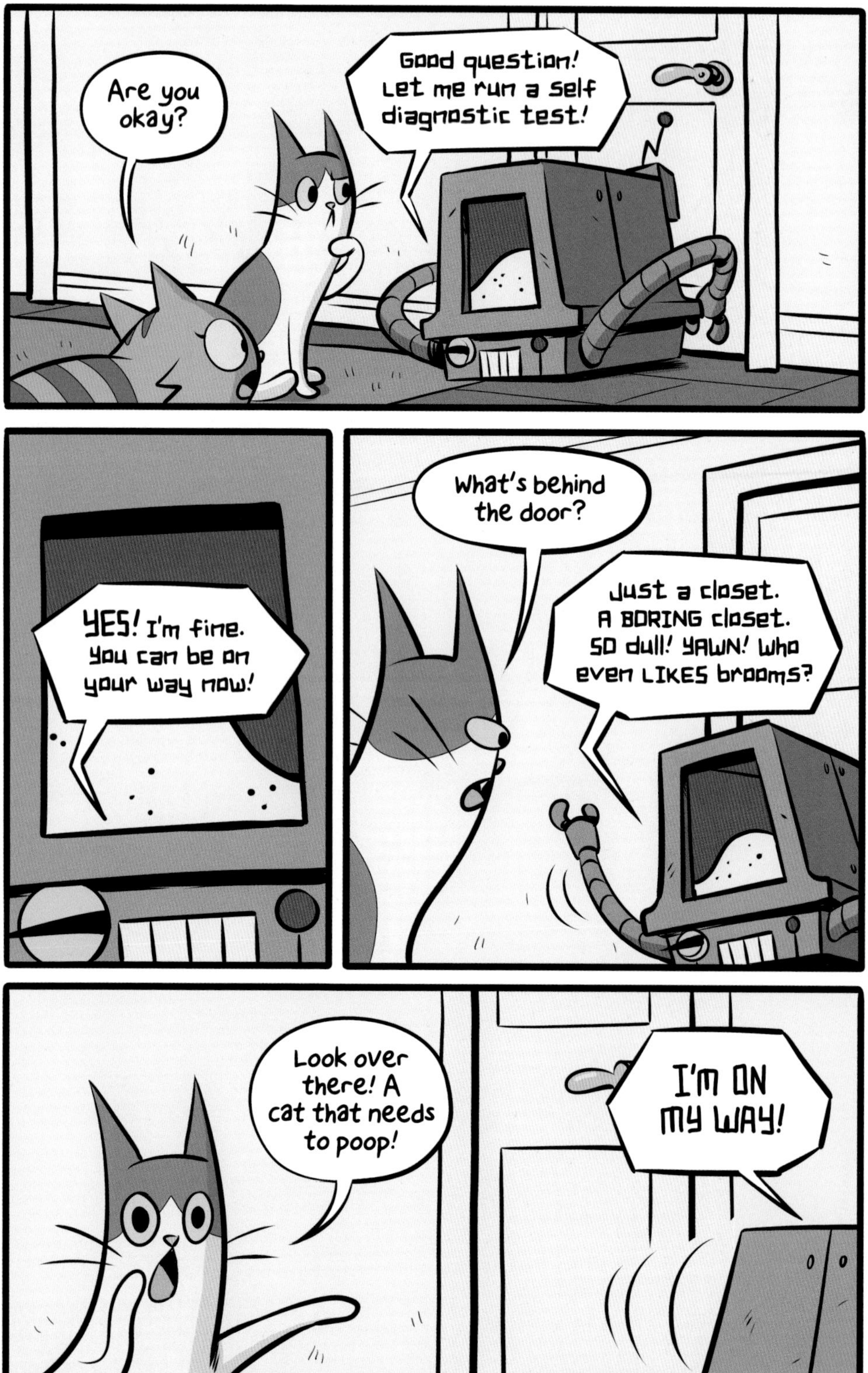
Are you okay?
Good question! Let me run a self diagnostic test!
YES! I'm fine. You can be on your way now!
What's behind the door?
Just a closet. A BORING closet. SO dull! YAWN! Who even LIKES brooms?
Look over there! A cat that needs to poop!
I'M ON MY WAY!

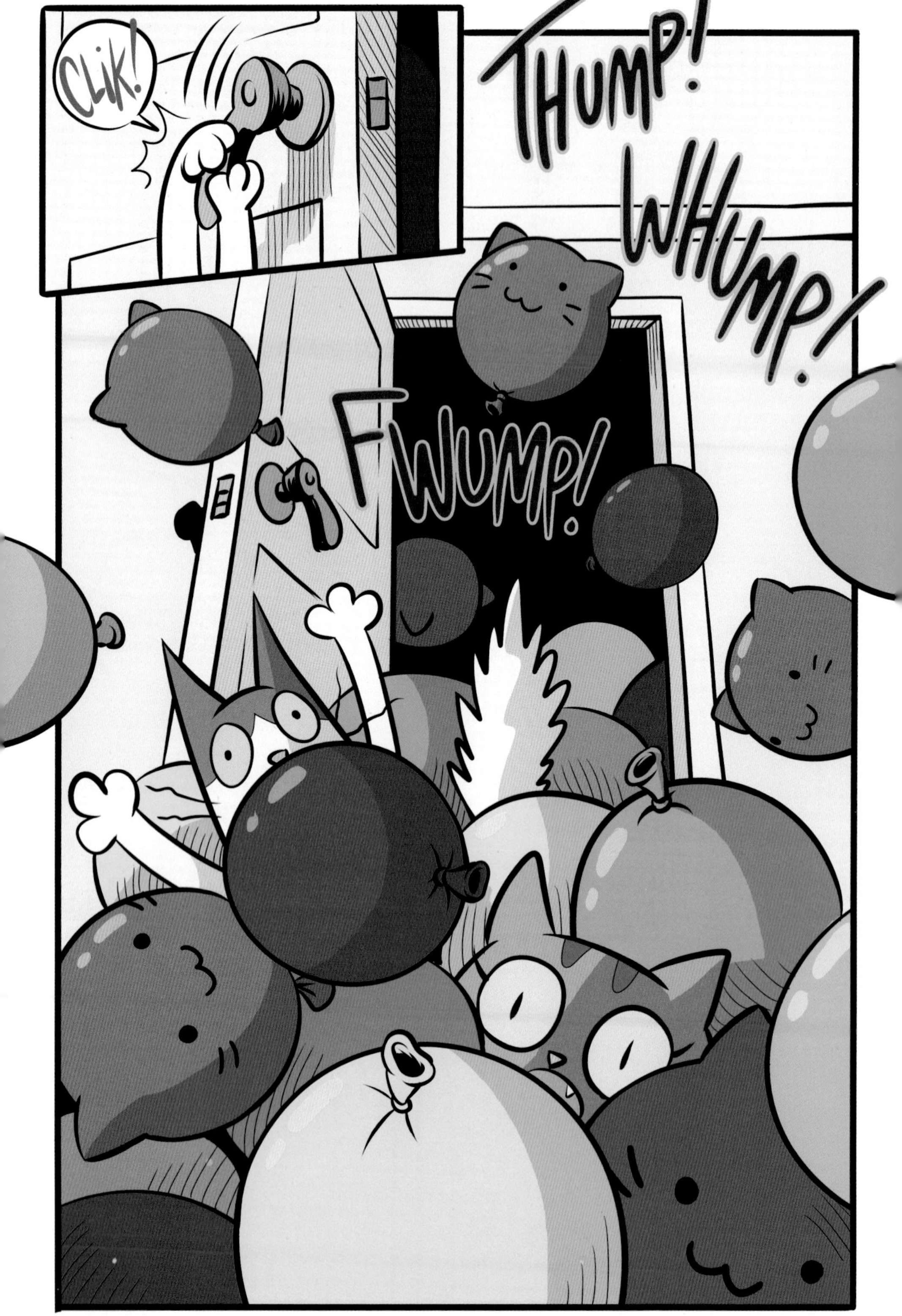
CLIK!
THUMP!
WHUMP!
FWUMP!

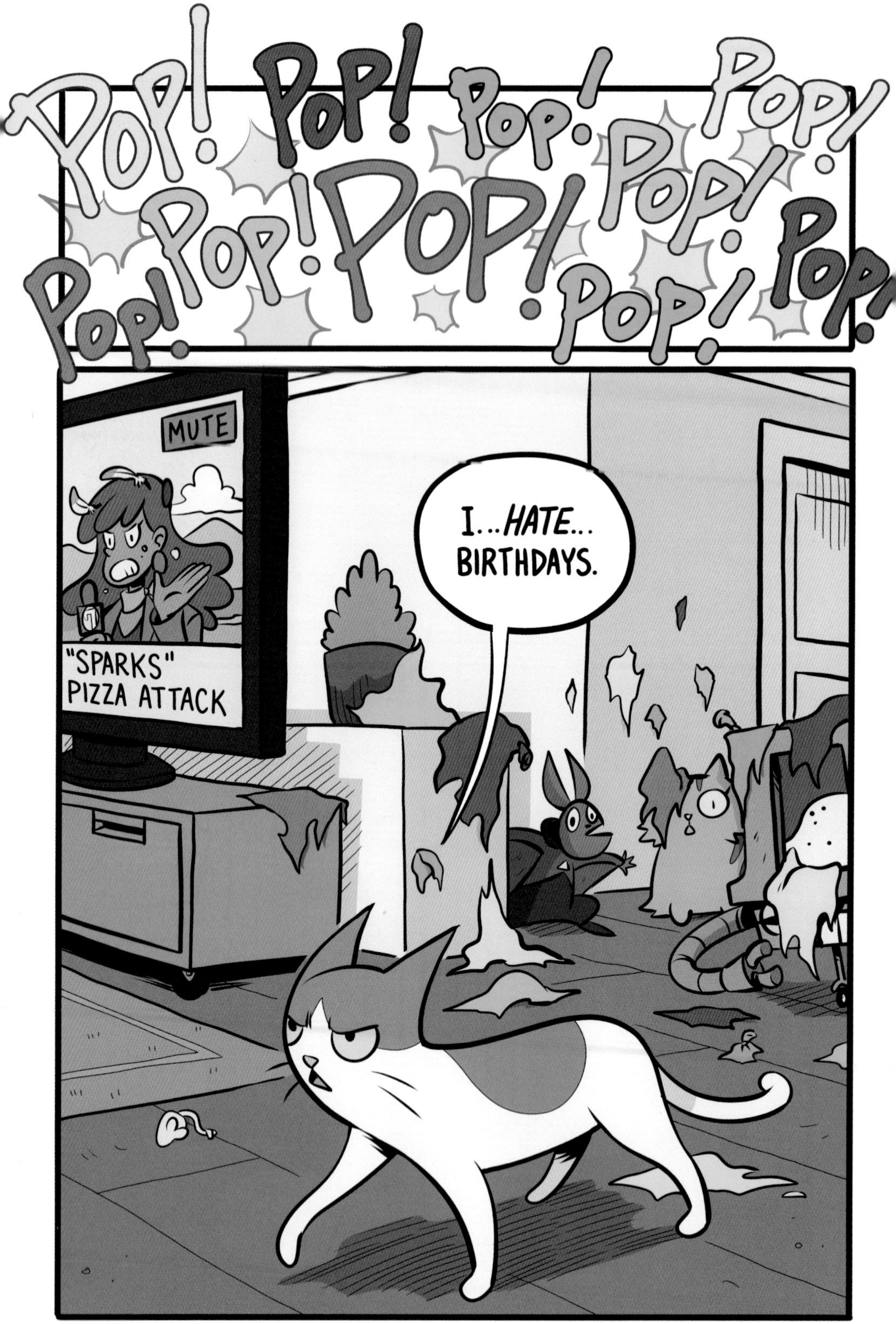
POP! POP! POP! POP! POP! POP! POP! POP! POP! POP! POP!
MUTE
"SPARKS" PIZZA ATTACK
I...HATE... BIRTHDAYS.

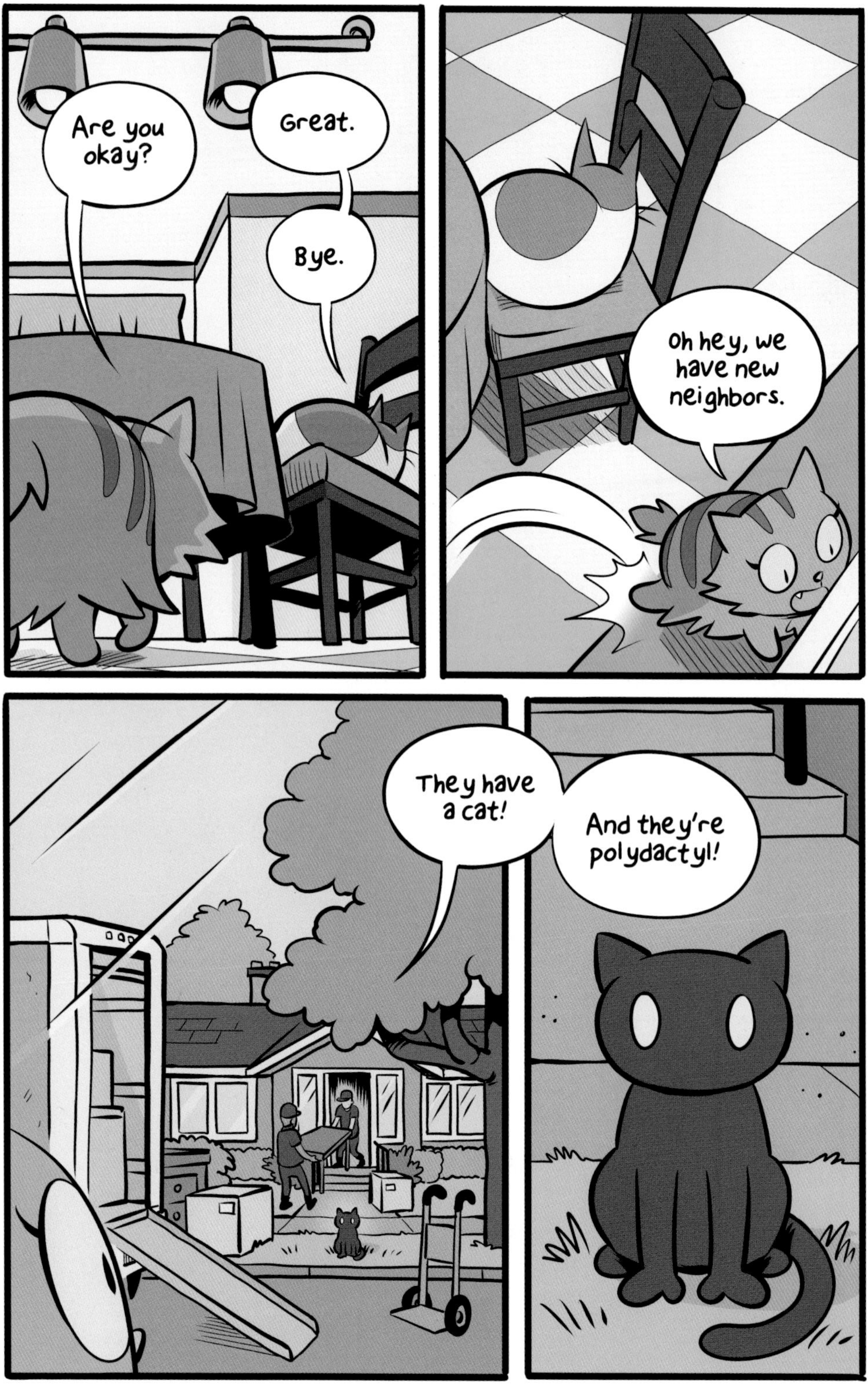
Are you okay?
Great.
Bye.
Oh hey, we have new neighbors.
They have a cat!
And they're polydactyl!

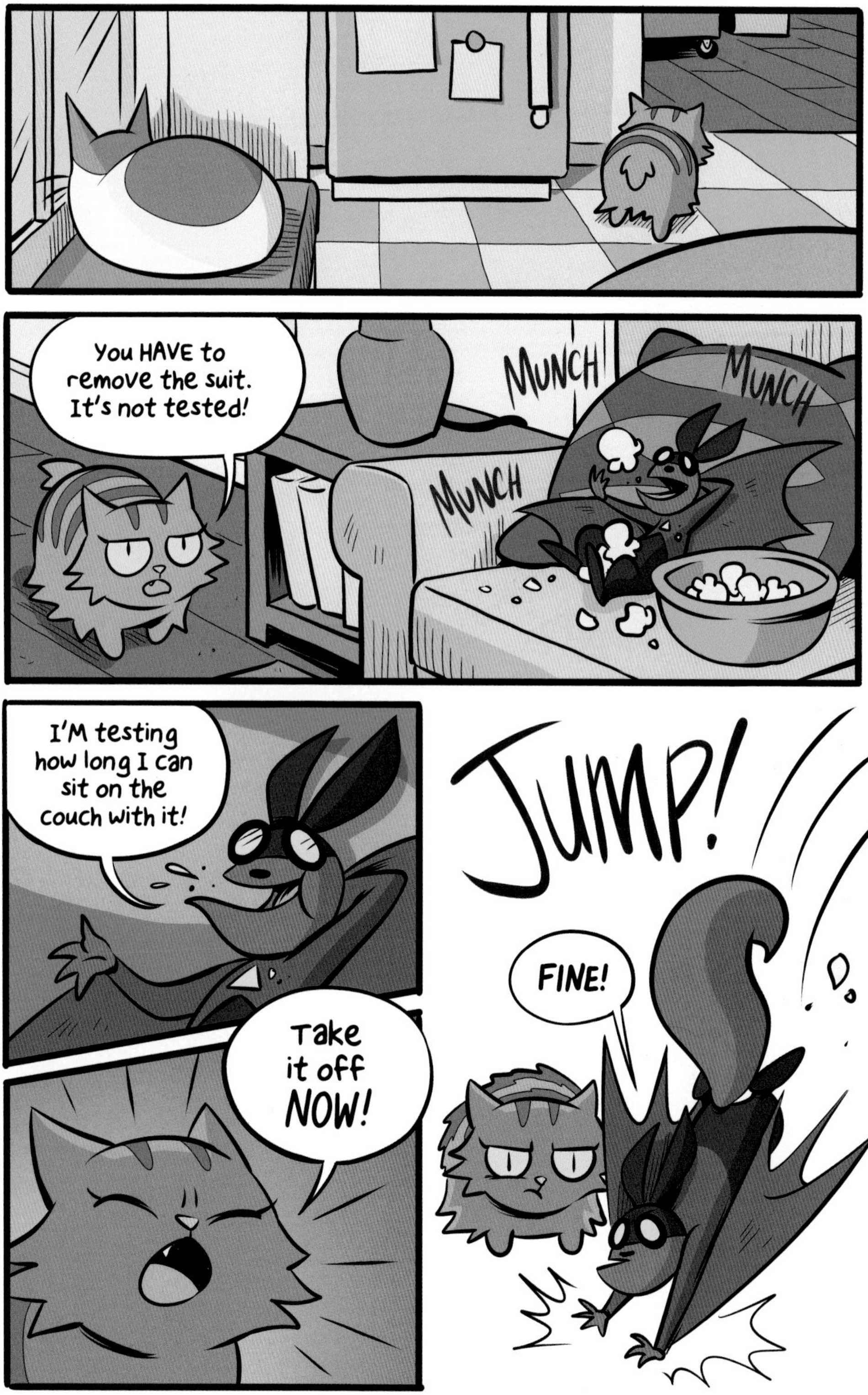
You HAVE to remove the suit. It's not tested!
MUNCH
MUNCH
MUNCH
I'M testing how long I can sit on the couch with it!
Take it off NOW!
JUMP!
FINE!

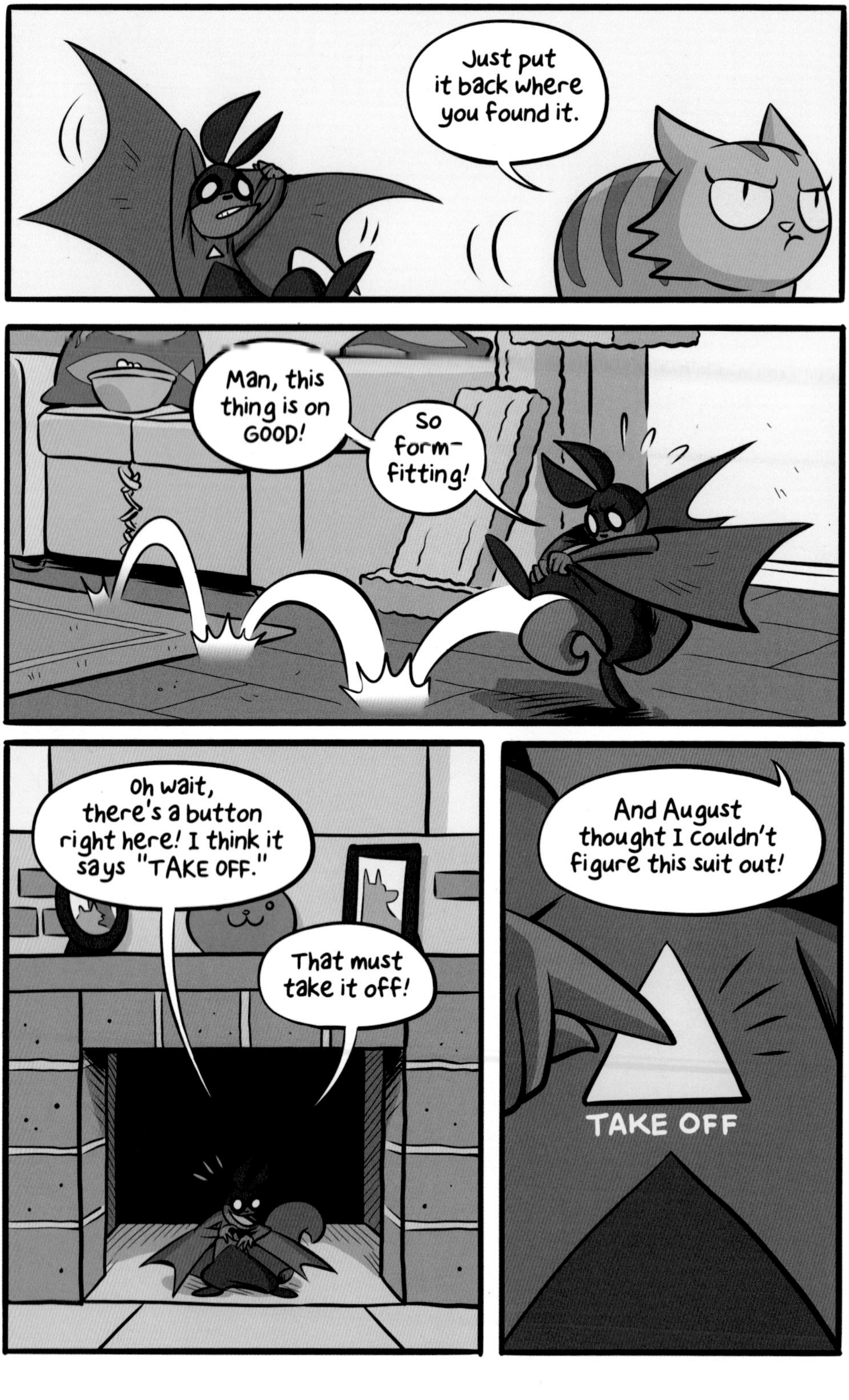
Just put it back where you found it.
Man, this thing is on GOOD!
So form-fitting!
Oh wait, there's a button right here! I think it says "TAKE OFF."
That must take it off!
And August thought I couldn't figure this suit out!
TAKE OFF

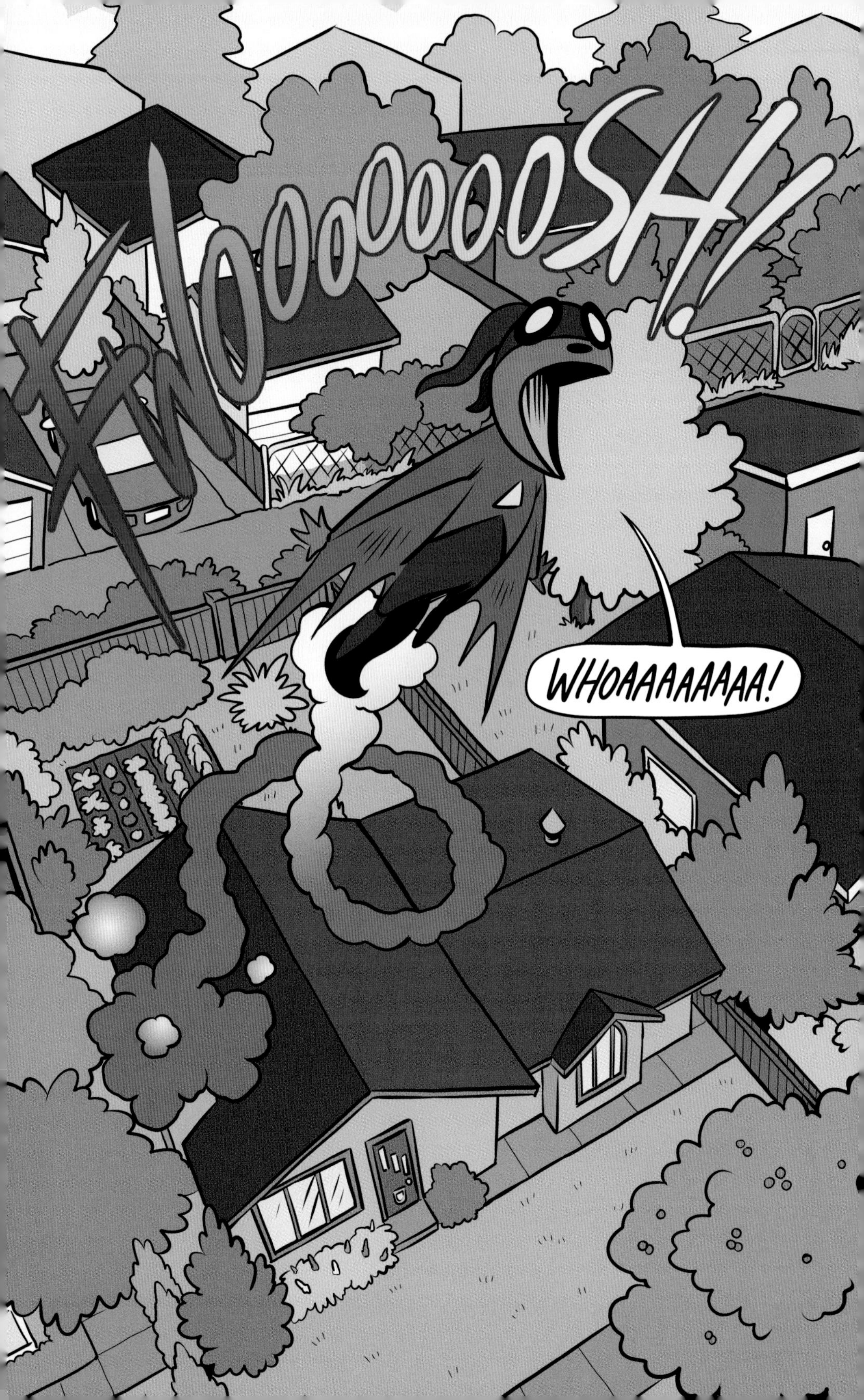
WOOOOOOOOSH!!
WHOAAAAAAAA!

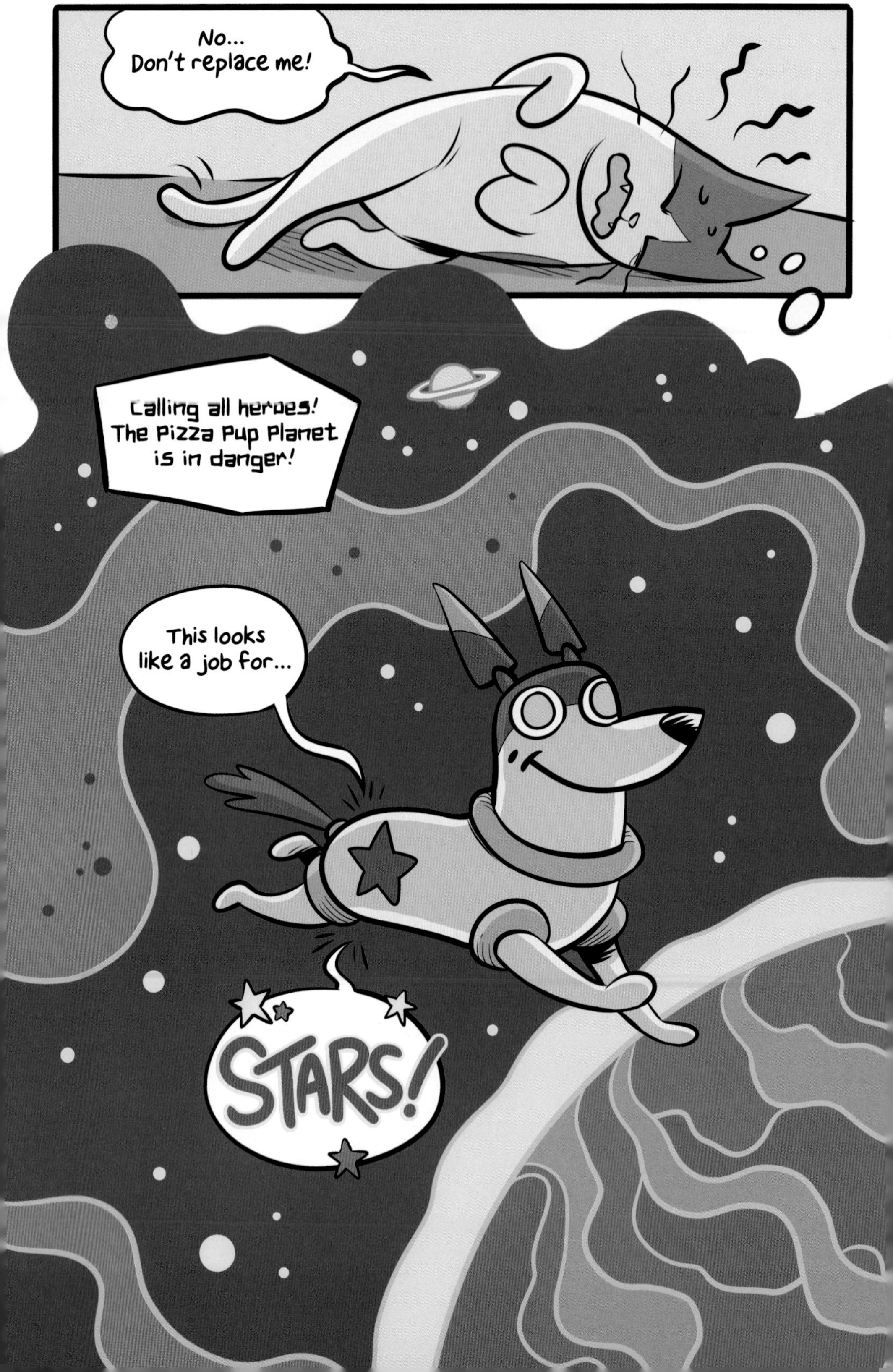
No...
Don't replace me!
Calling all heroes! The Pizza Pup Planet is in danger!
This looks like a job for...
STARS!

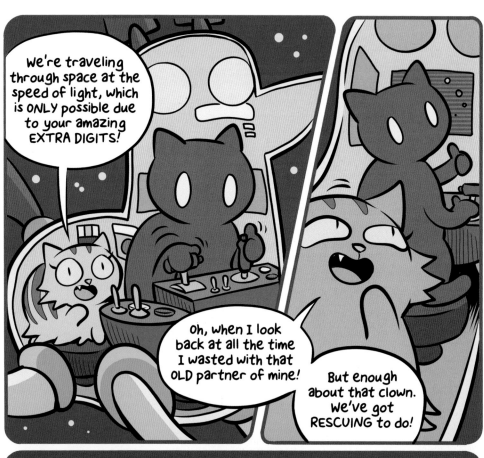

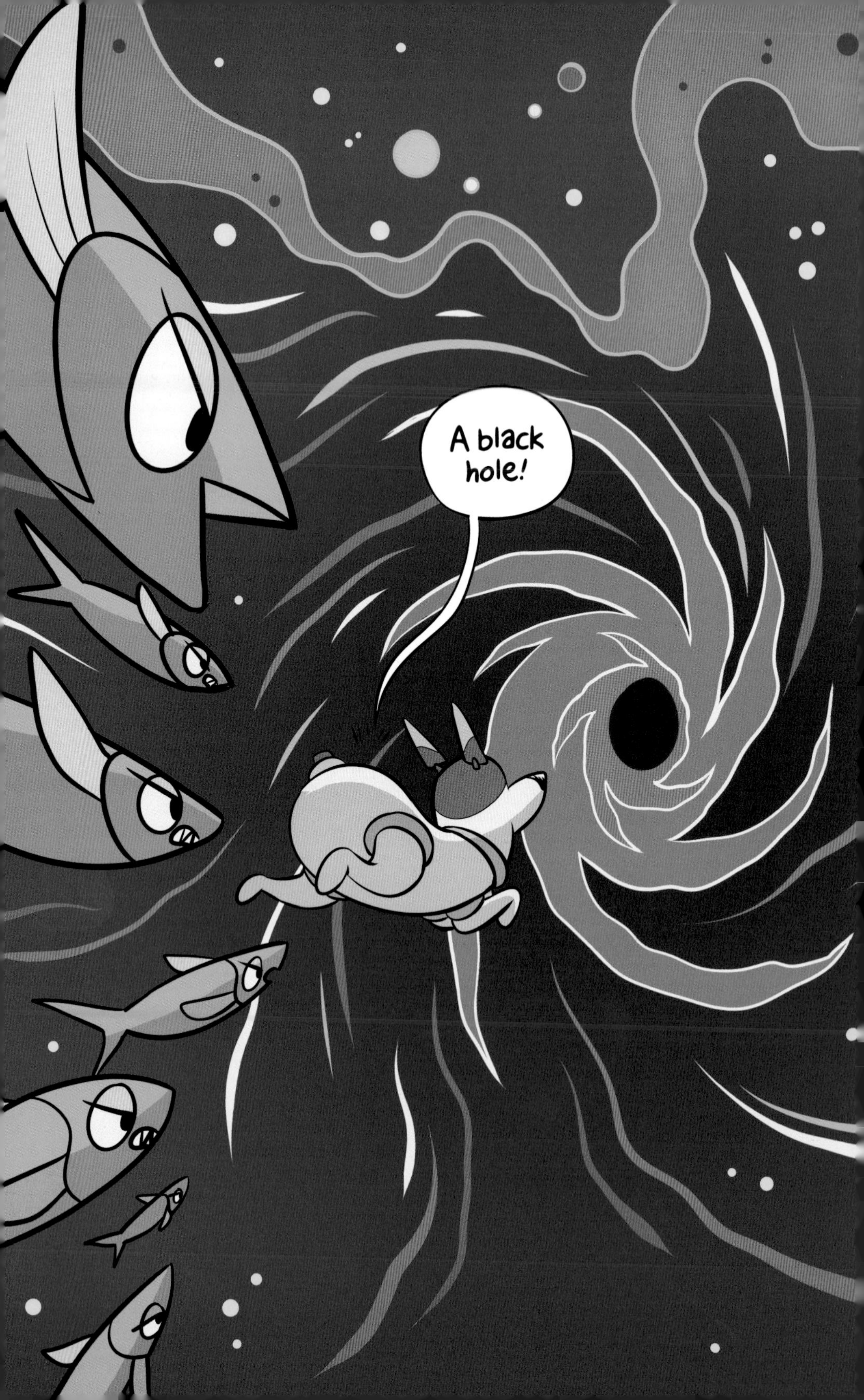
A black hole!

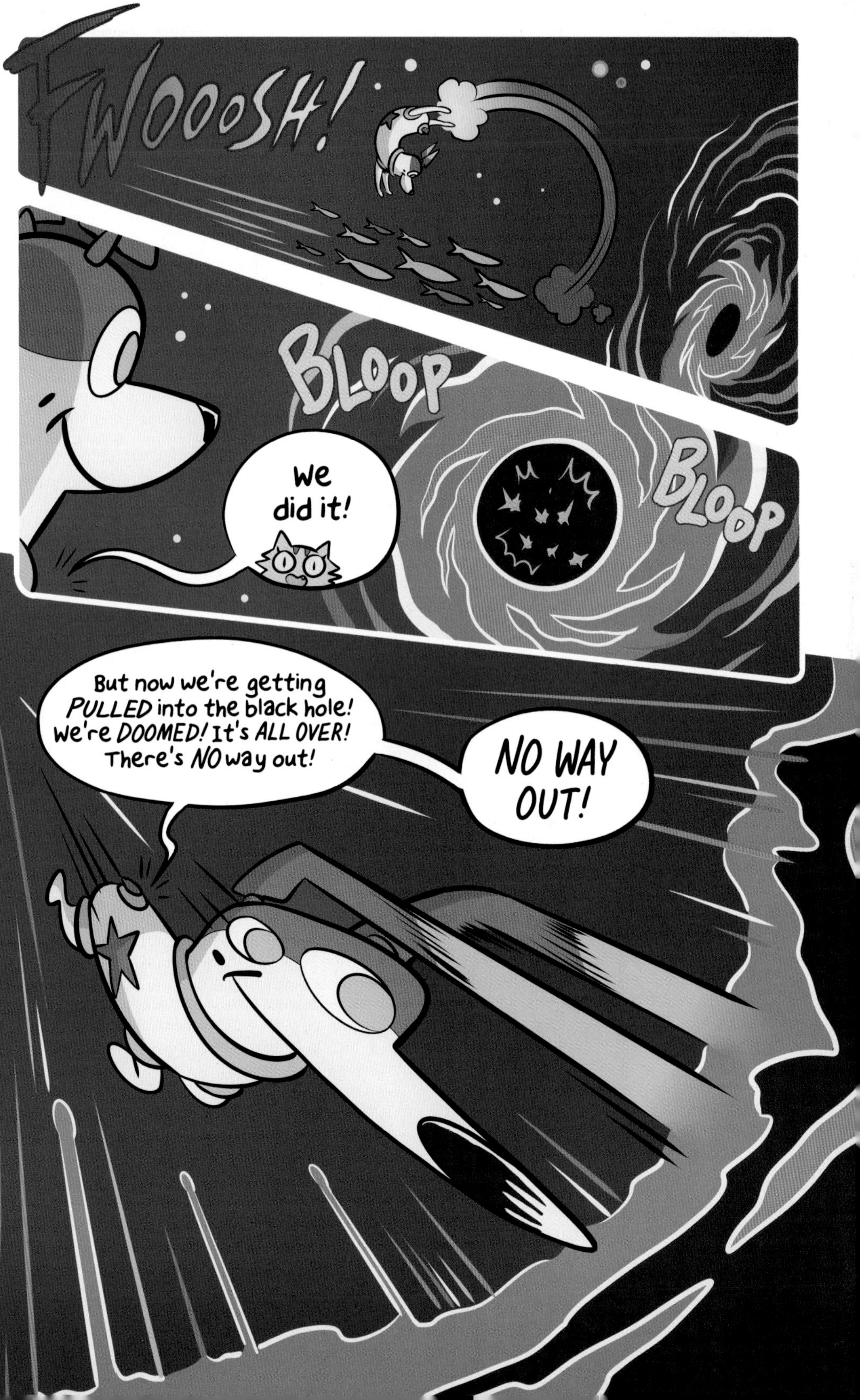
FWOOOSH!
BLOOP
BLOOP
We did it!
But now we're getting PULLED into the black hole! We're DOOMED! It's ALL OVER! There's NO way out!
NO WAY OUT!

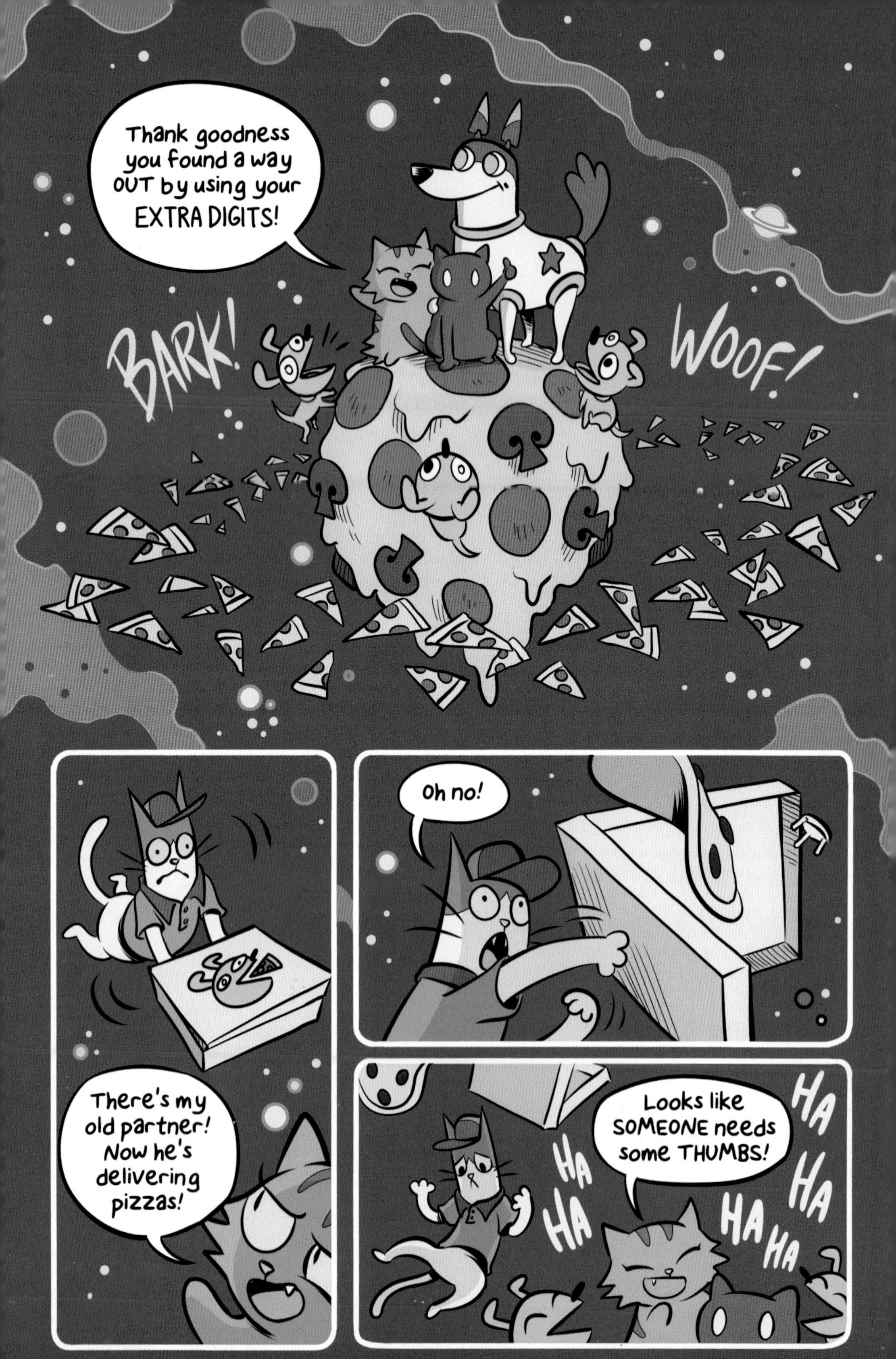
Thank goodness you found a way OUT by using your EXTRA DIGITS!
BARK!
WOOF!
Oh no!
There's my old partner! Now he's delivering pizzas!
Looks like SOMEONE needs some THUMBS!
HA HA HA HA HA HA HA

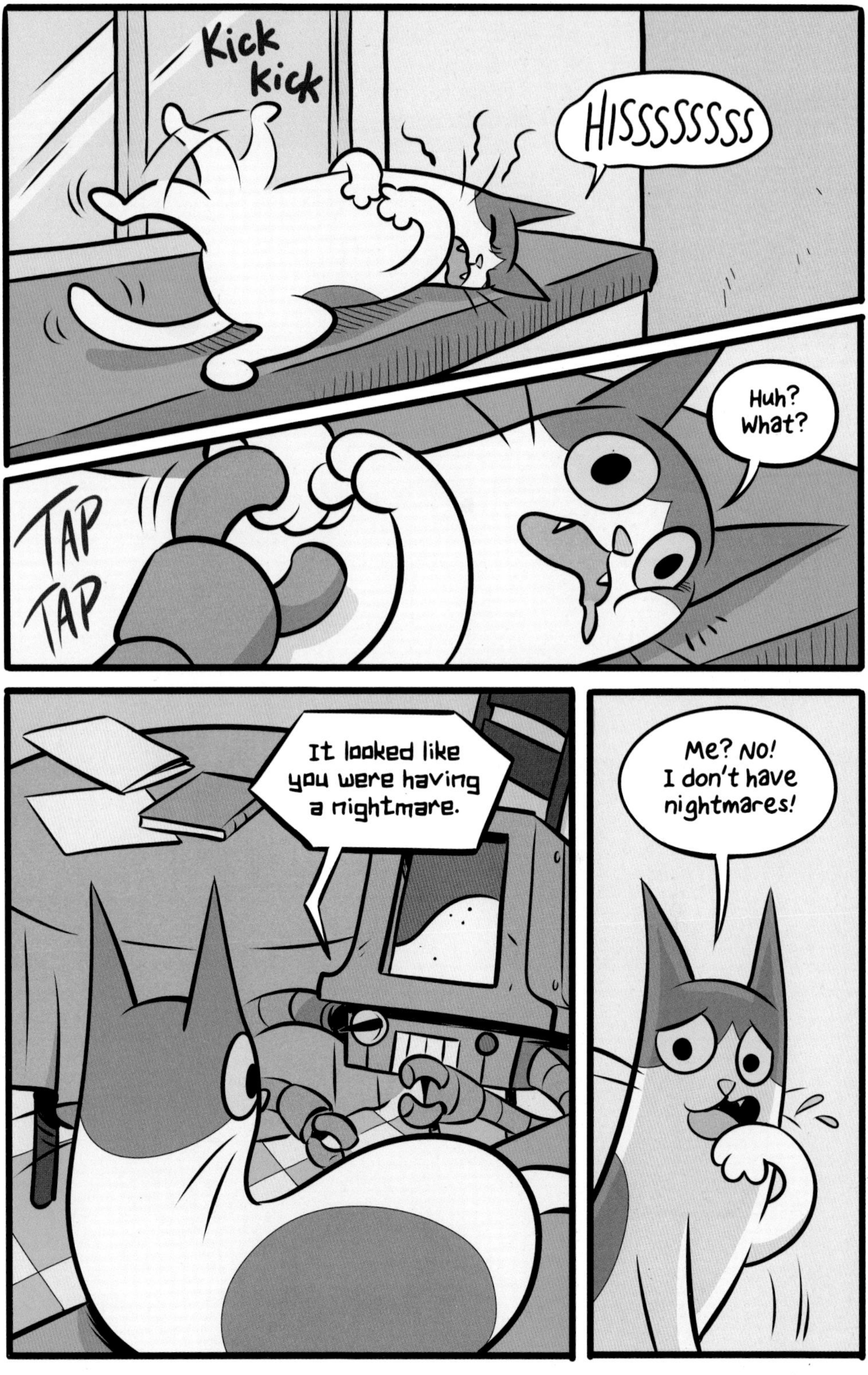
Kick kick
HISSSSSSSS
Huh? What?
TAP TAP
It looked like you were having a nightmare.
Me? NO! I don't have nightmares!

54

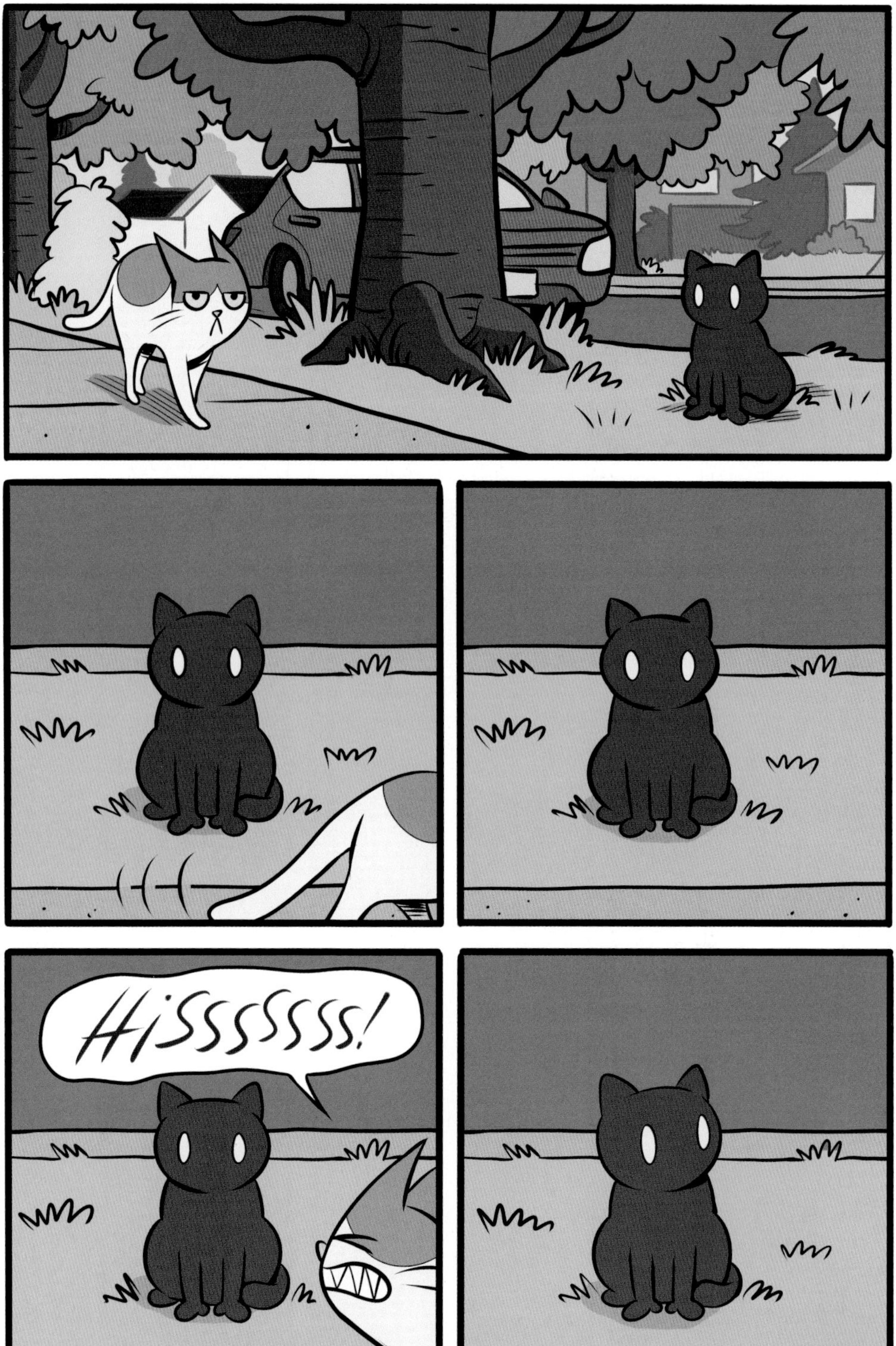
HiSSSSSS!

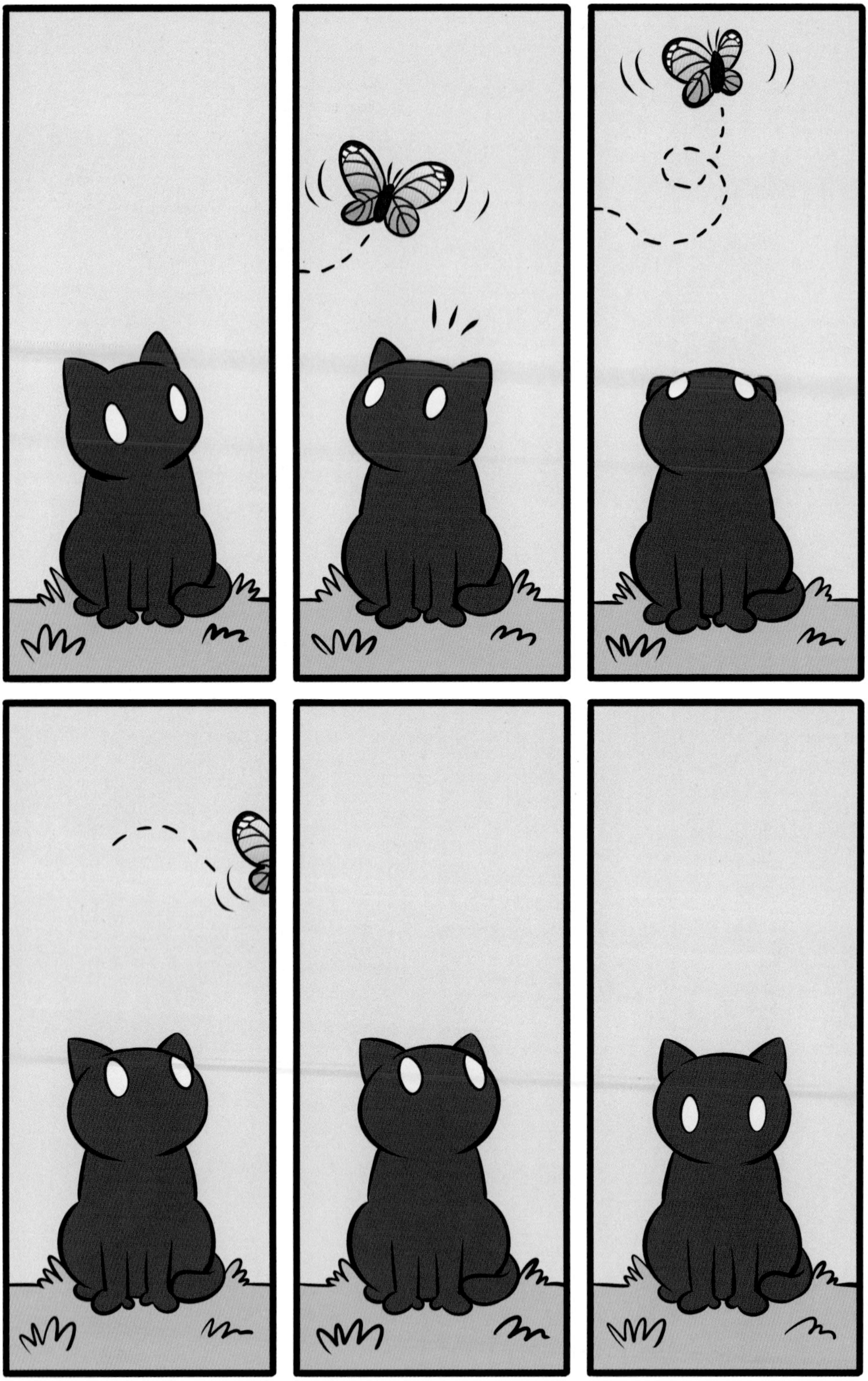

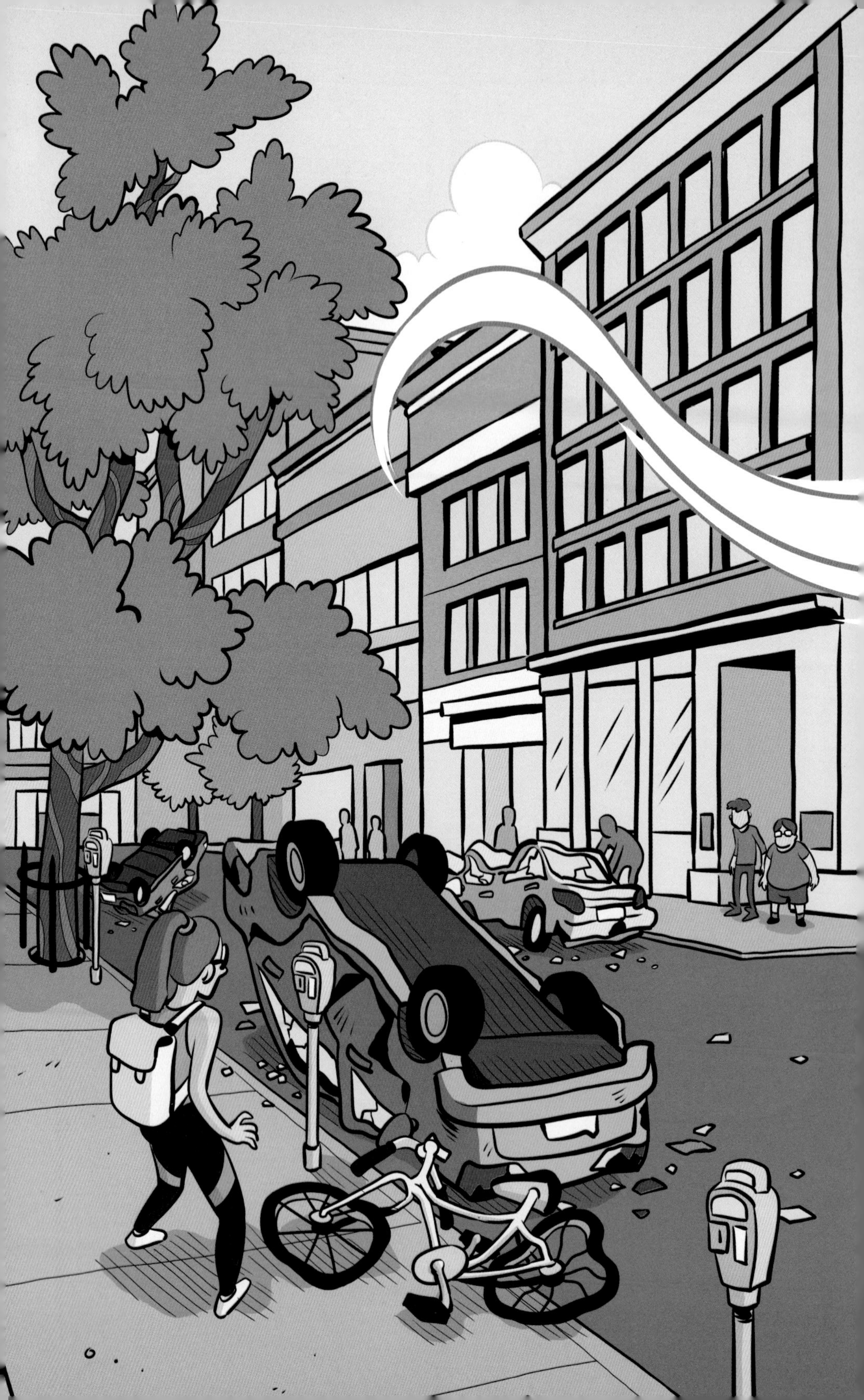

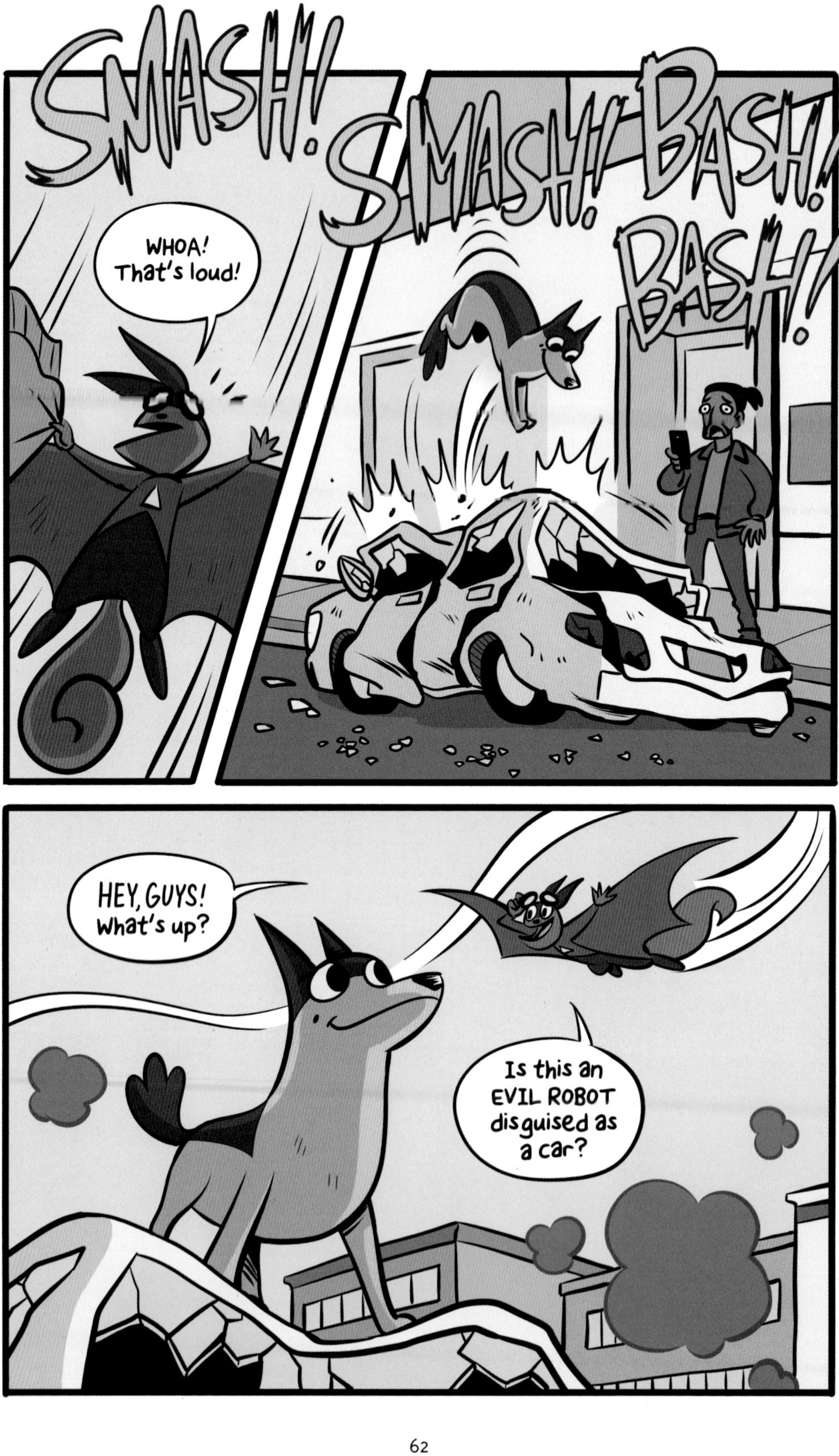
SMASH!
SMASH! BASH!
BASH!
WHOA! That's loud!
HEY, GUYS! What's up?
Is this an EVIL ROBOT disguised as a car?

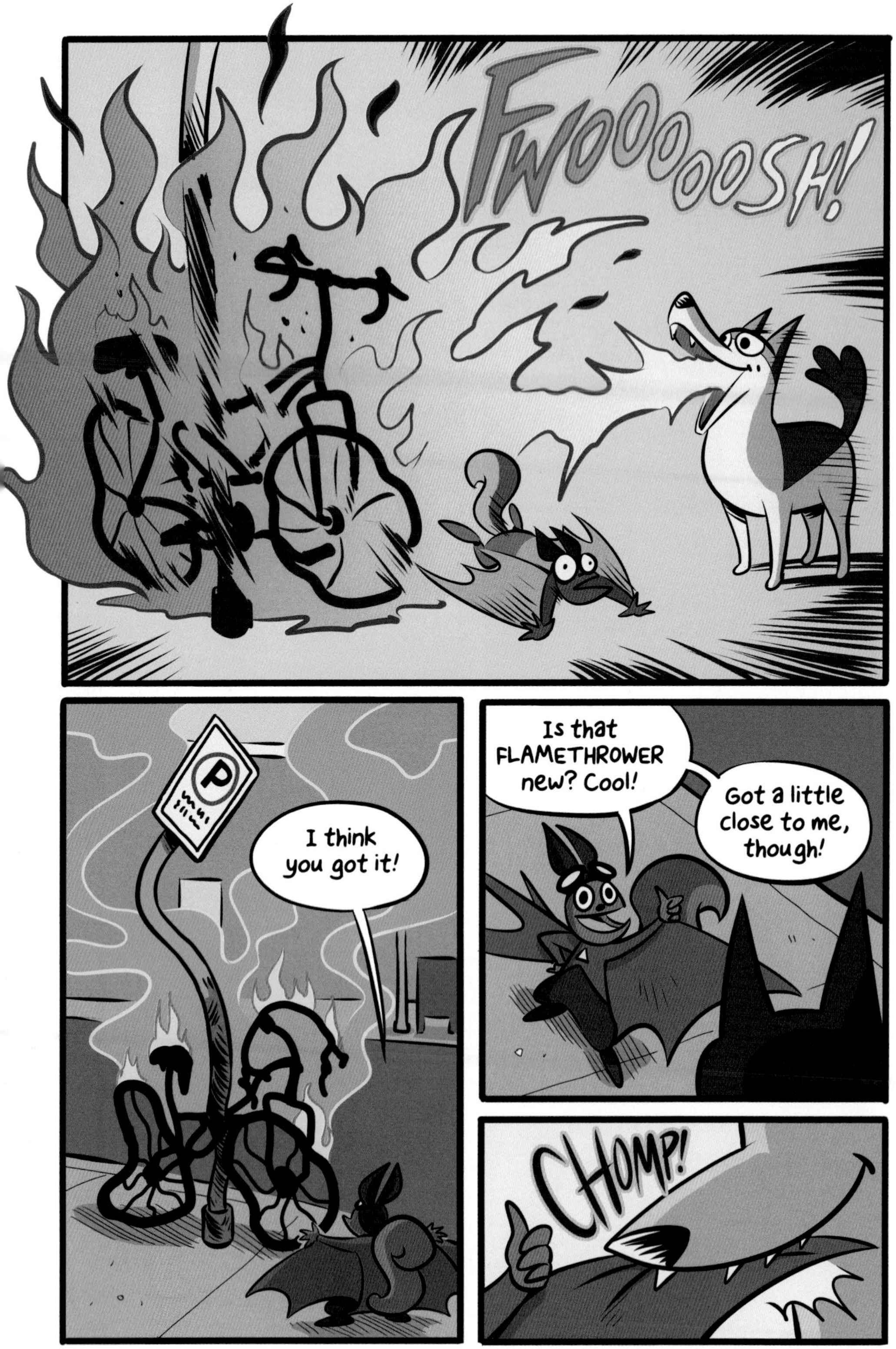
FWOOOOOOSH!
I think you got it!
Is that FLAMETHROWER new? Cool!
Got a little close to me, though!
CHOMP!

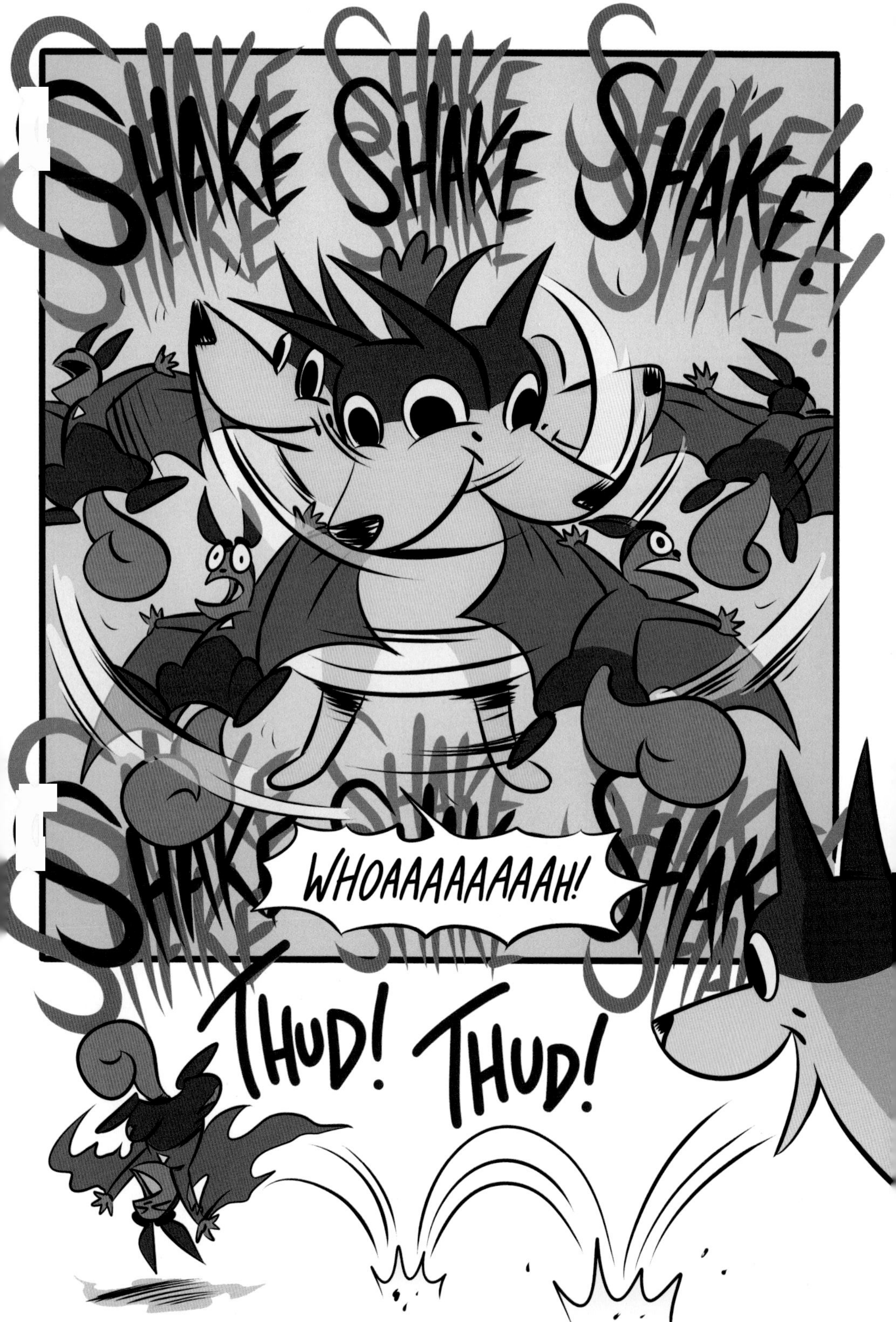
SHAKE SHAKE SHAKE!
SHAKE
WHOAAAAAAAAAH!
SHAK
THUD! THUD!

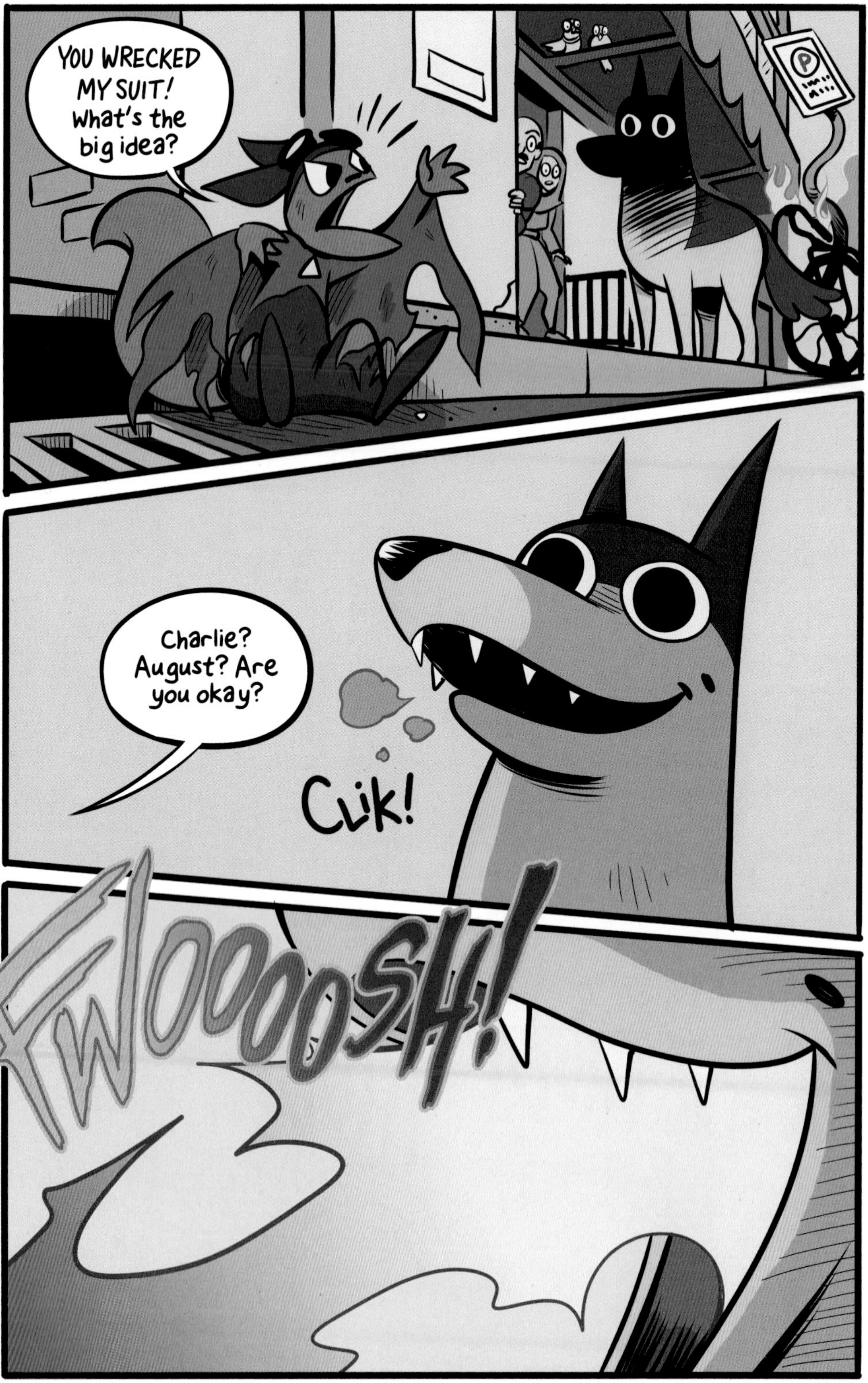
YOU WRECKED MY SUIT! What's the big idea?
Charlie? August? Are you okay?
CLIK!
FWOOOOSH!

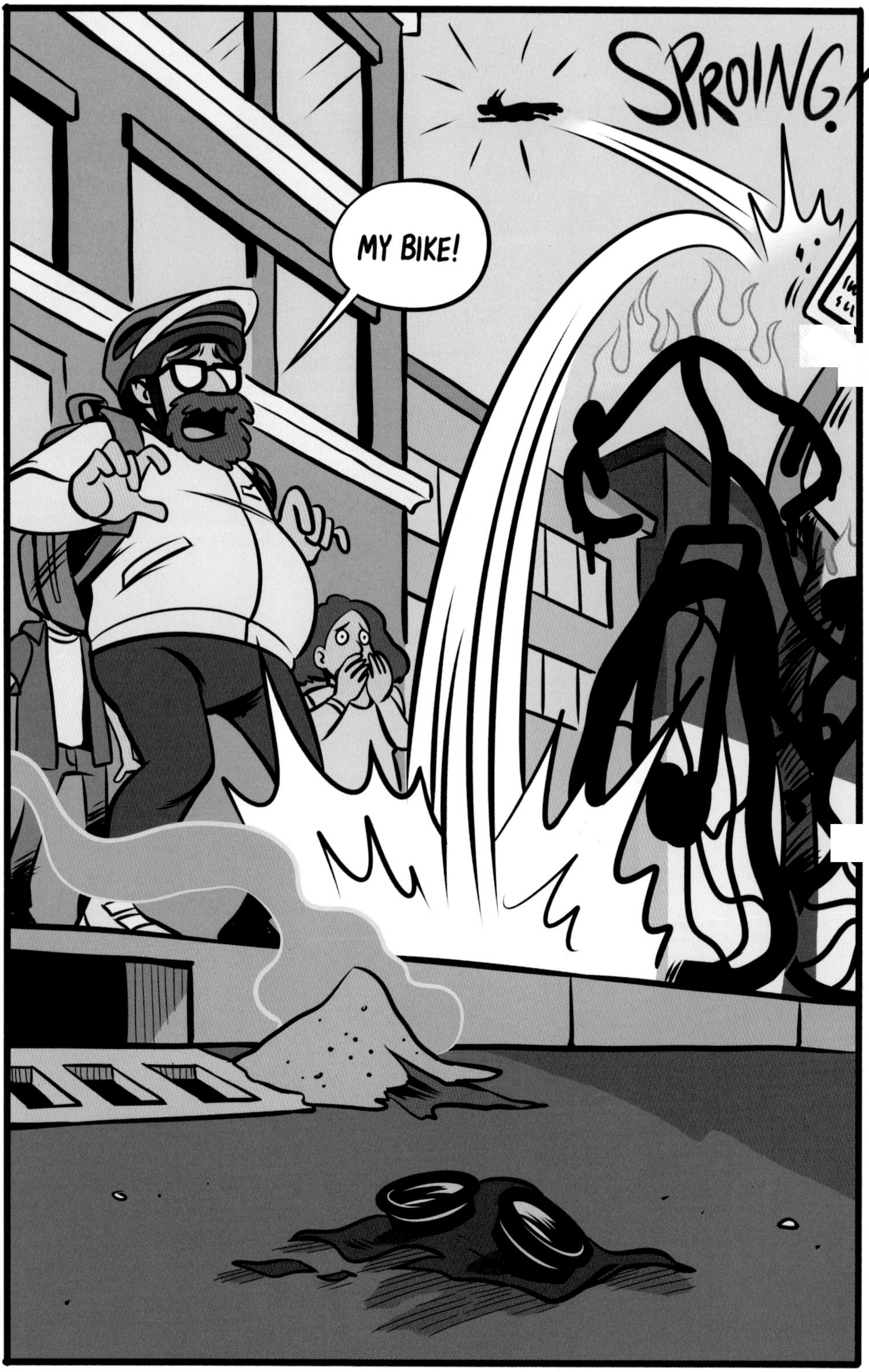
SPROING!
MY BIKE!

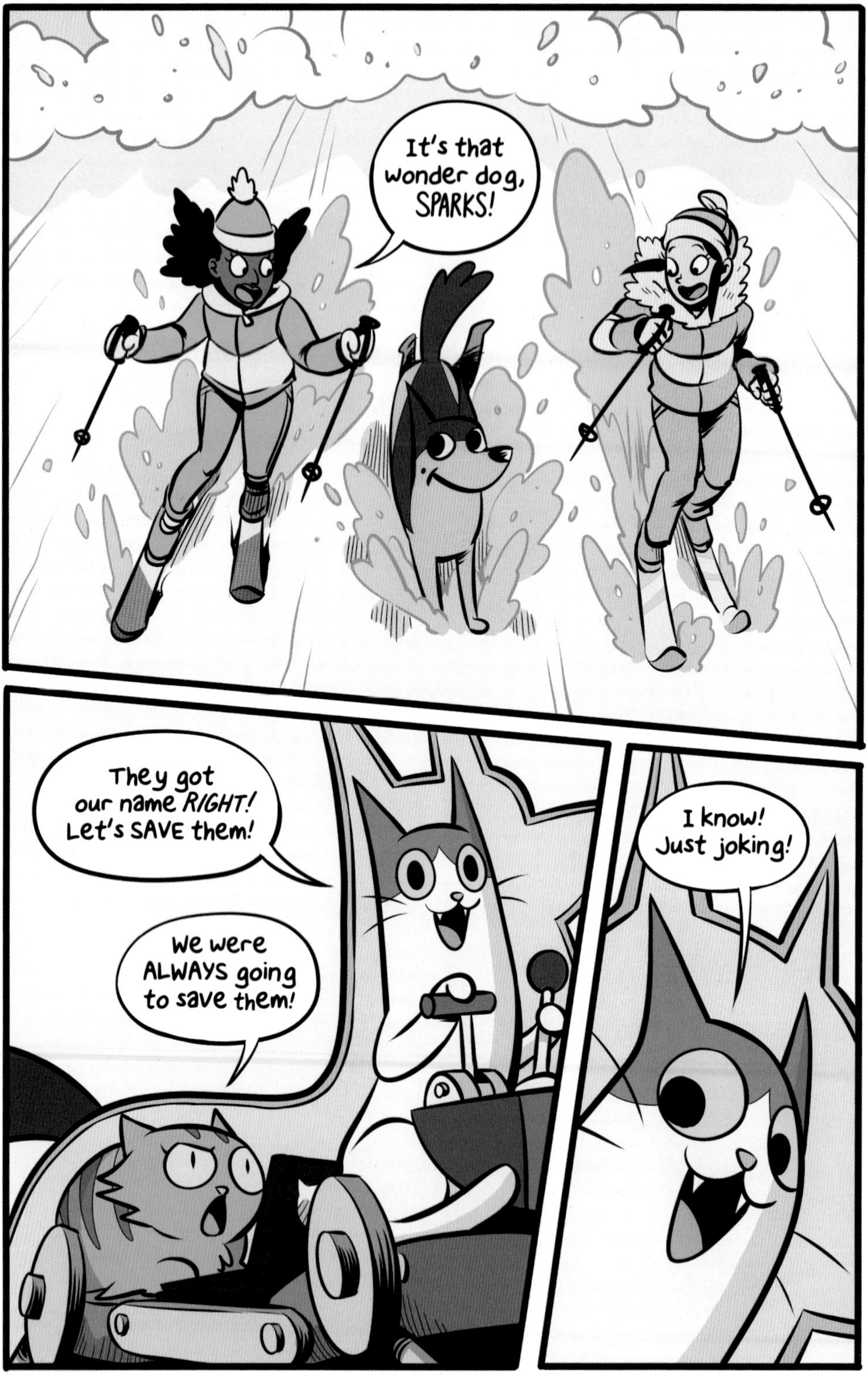
It's that wonder dog, SPARKS!
They got our name RIGHT! Let's SAVE them!
We were ALWAYS going to save them!
I know! Just joking!

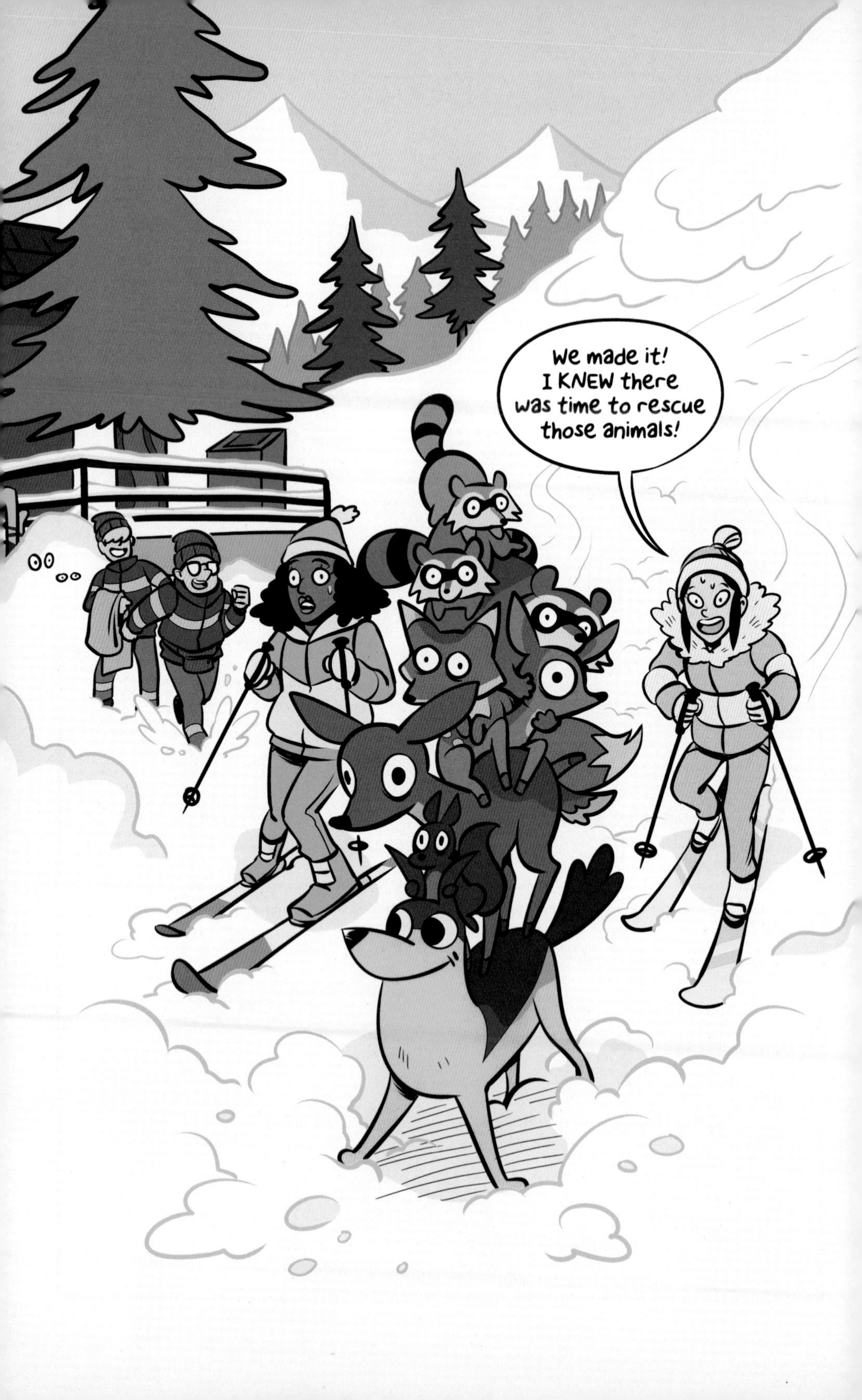
We made it! I KNEW there was time to rescue those animals!

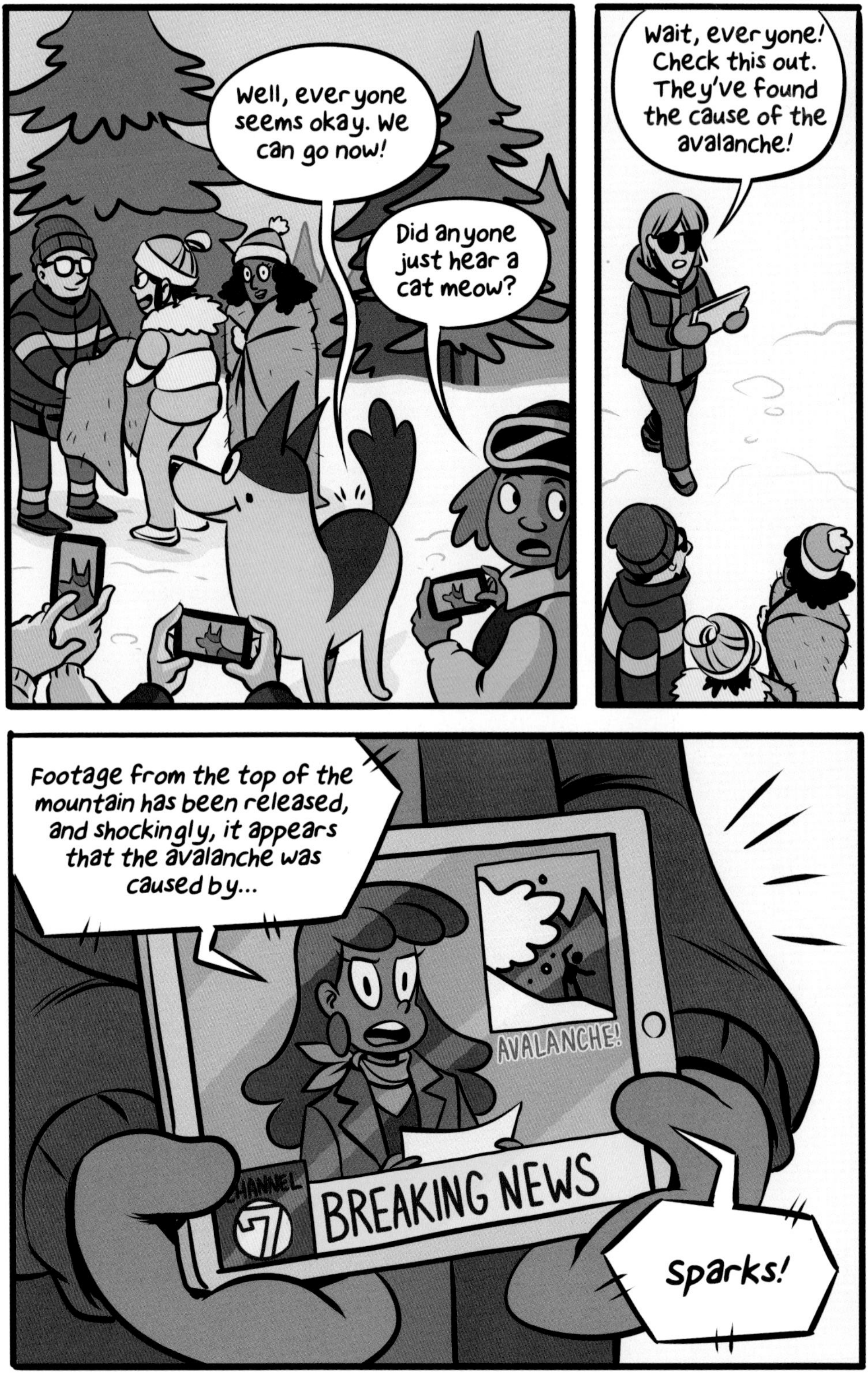
Well, everyone seems okay. We can go now!
Did anyone just hear a cat meow?
Wait, everyone! Check this out. They've found the cause of the avalanche!
Footage from the top of the mountain has been released, and shockingly, it appears that the avalanche was caused by...
AVALANCHE!
CHANNEL 7
BREAKING NEWS
Sparks!

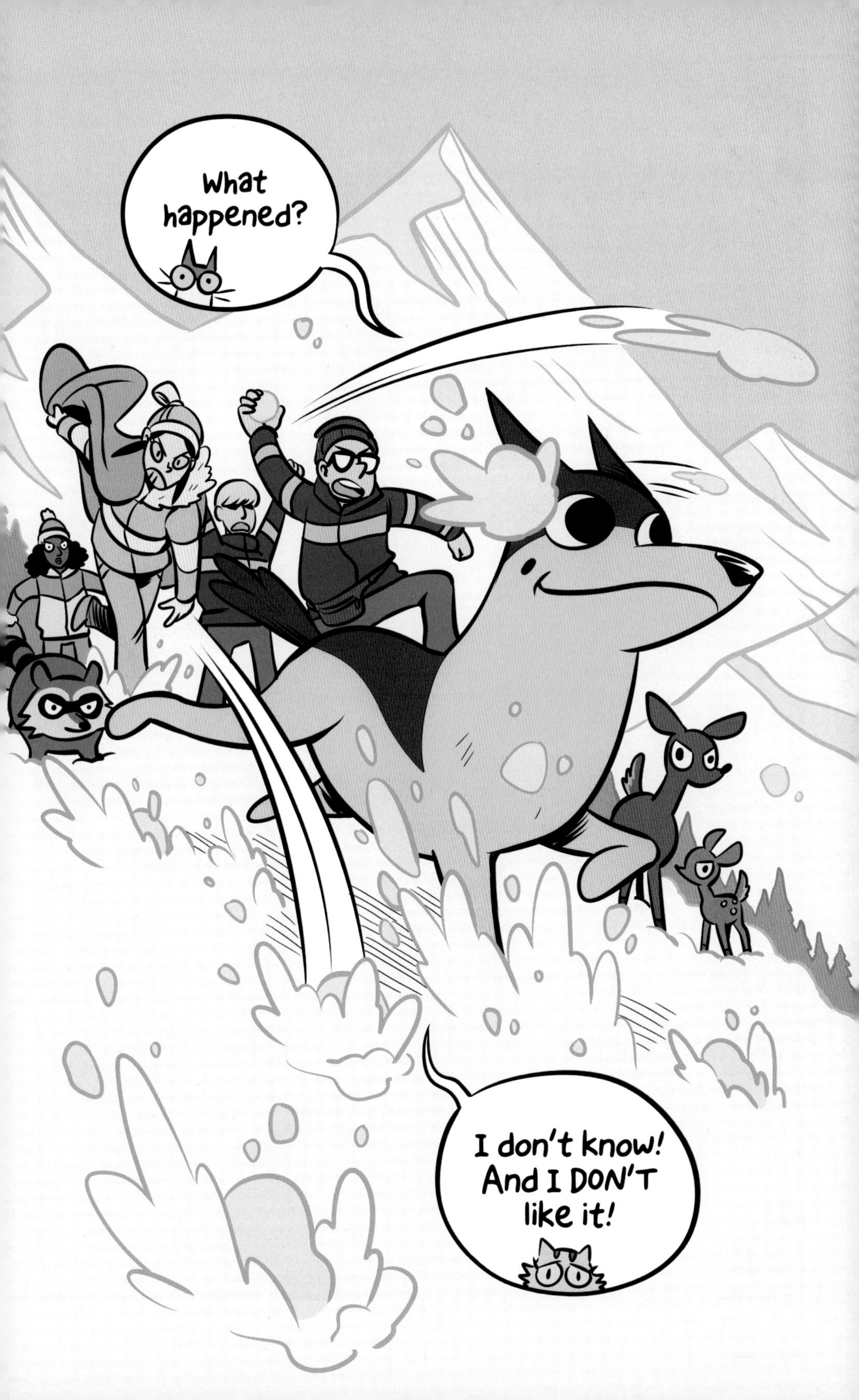
What happened?
I don't know! And I DON'T like it!

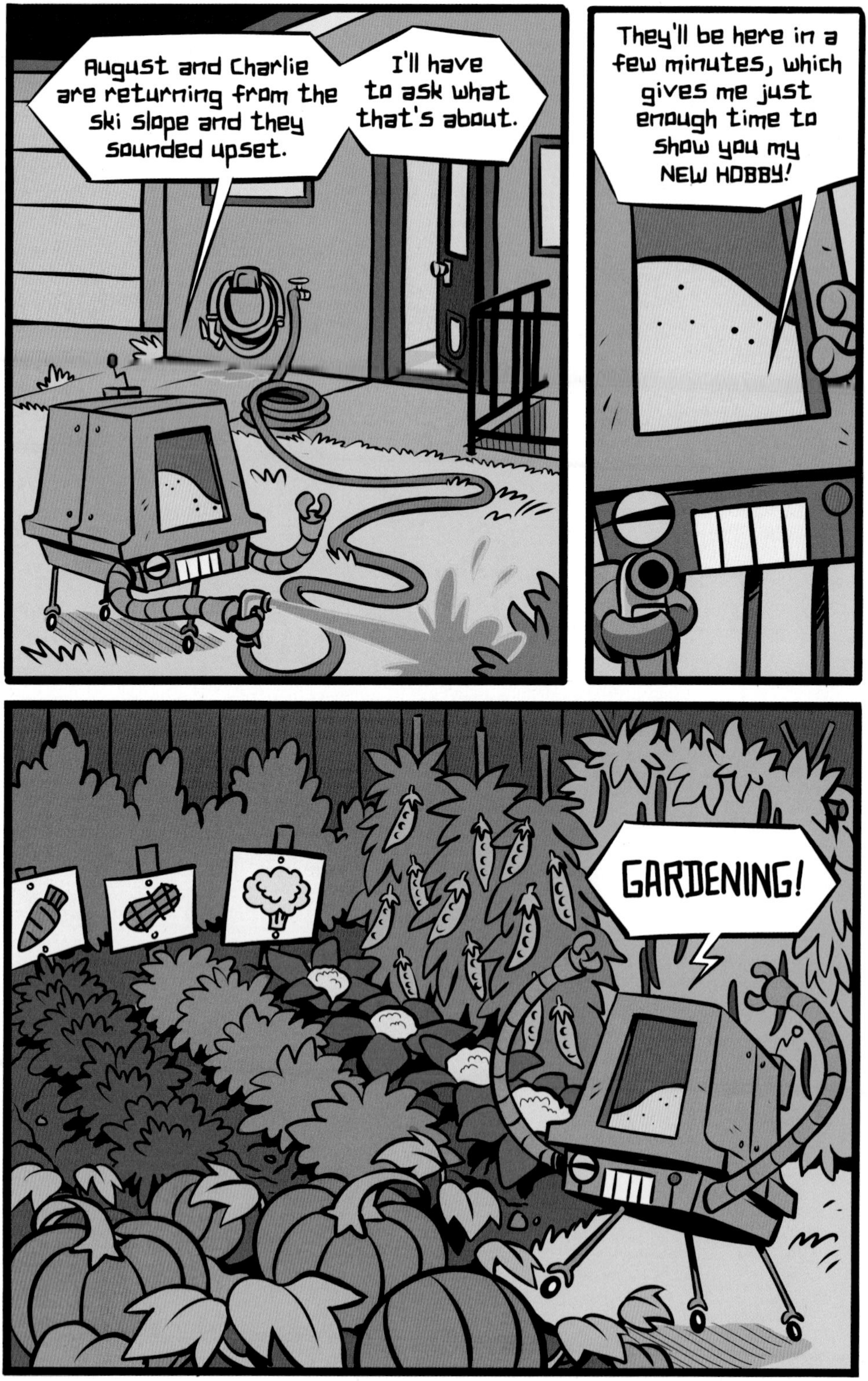
August and Charlie are returning from the ski slope and they sounded upset.
I'll have to ask what that's about.
They'll be here in a few minutes, which gives me just enough time to show you my NEW HOBBY!
GARDENING!

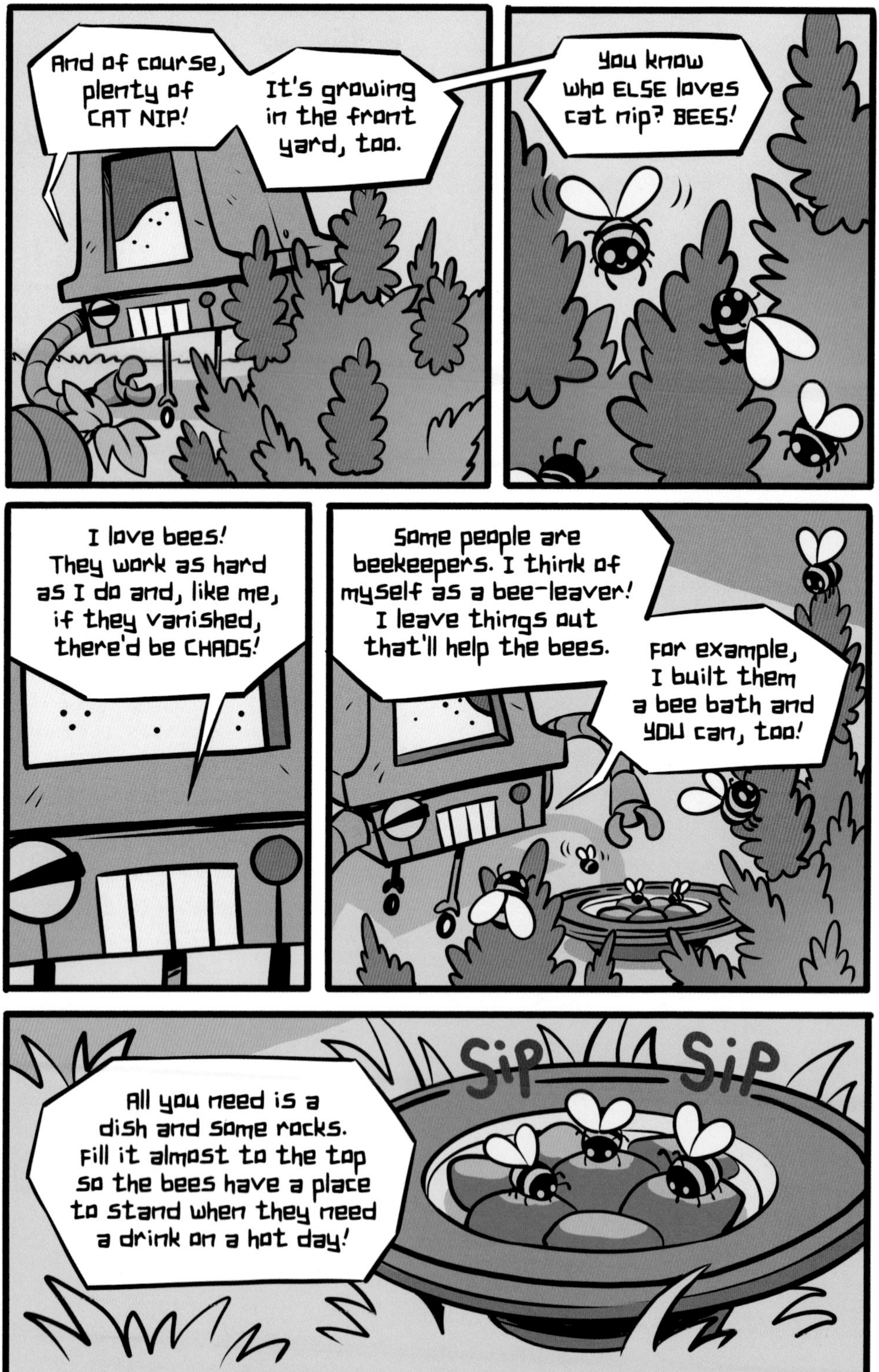
And of course, plenty of CAT NIP!
It's growing in the front yard, too.
You know who ELSE loves cat nip? BEES!
I love bees! They work as hard as I do and, like me, if they vanished, there'd be CHAOS!
Some people are beekeepers. I think of myself as a bee-leaver! I leave things out that'll help the bees.
For example, I built them a bee bath and YOU can, too!
All you need is a dish and some rocks. Fill it almost to the top so the bees have a place to stand when they need a drink on a hot day!
SIP SIP

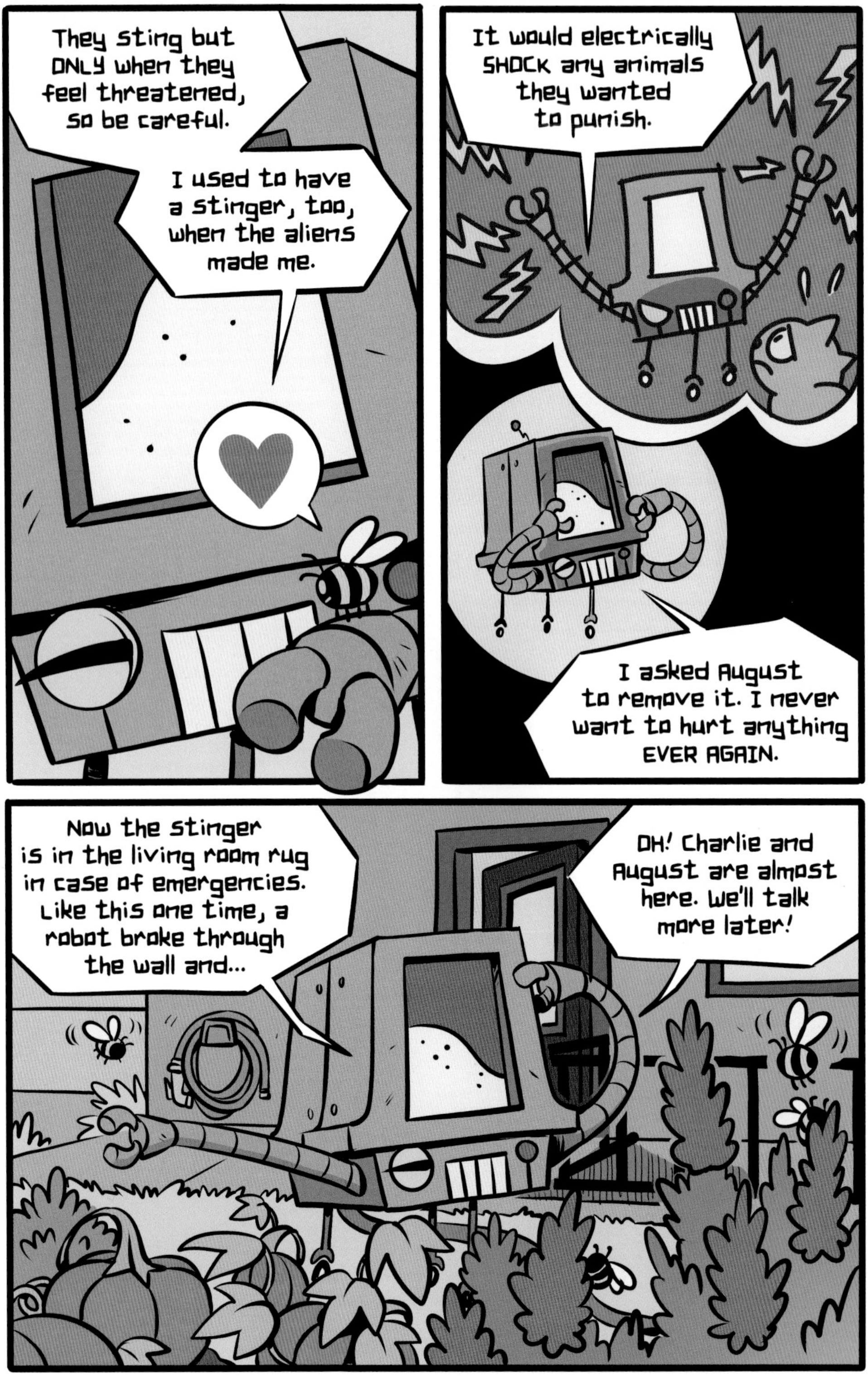
They sting but ONLY when they feel threatened, so be careful.
I used to have a stinger, too, when the aliens made me.
It would electrically SHOCK any animals they wanted to punish.
I asked August to remove it. I never want to hurt anything EVER AGAIN.
Now the stinger is in the living room rug in case of emergencies. Like this one time, a robot broke through the wall and...
OH! Charlie and August are almost here. We'll talk more later!

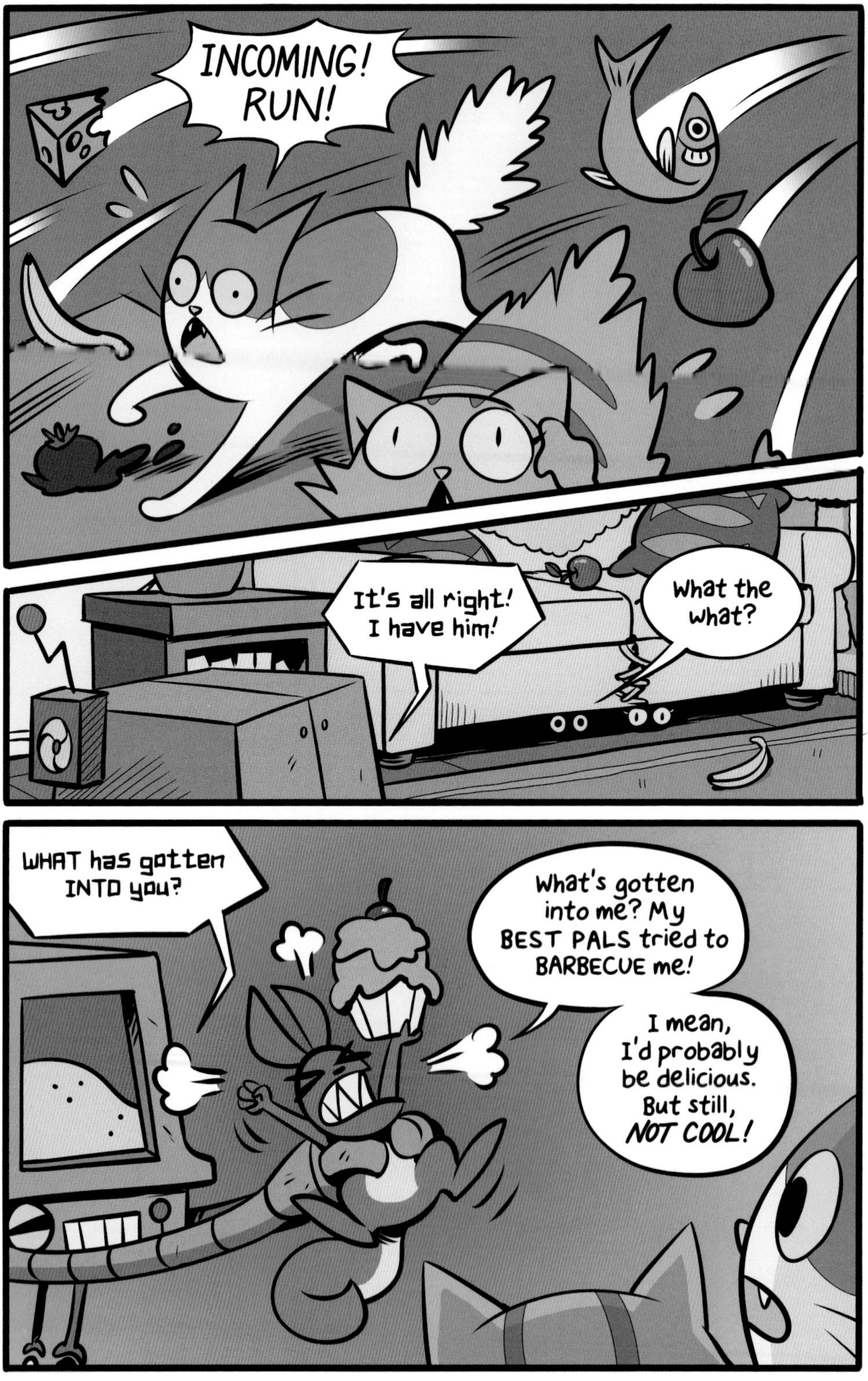
INCOMING! RUN!
It's all right! I have him!
What the what?
WHAT has gotten INTO you?
What's gotten into me? My BEST PALS tried to BARBECUE me!
I mean, I'd probably be delicious. But still, NOT COOL!

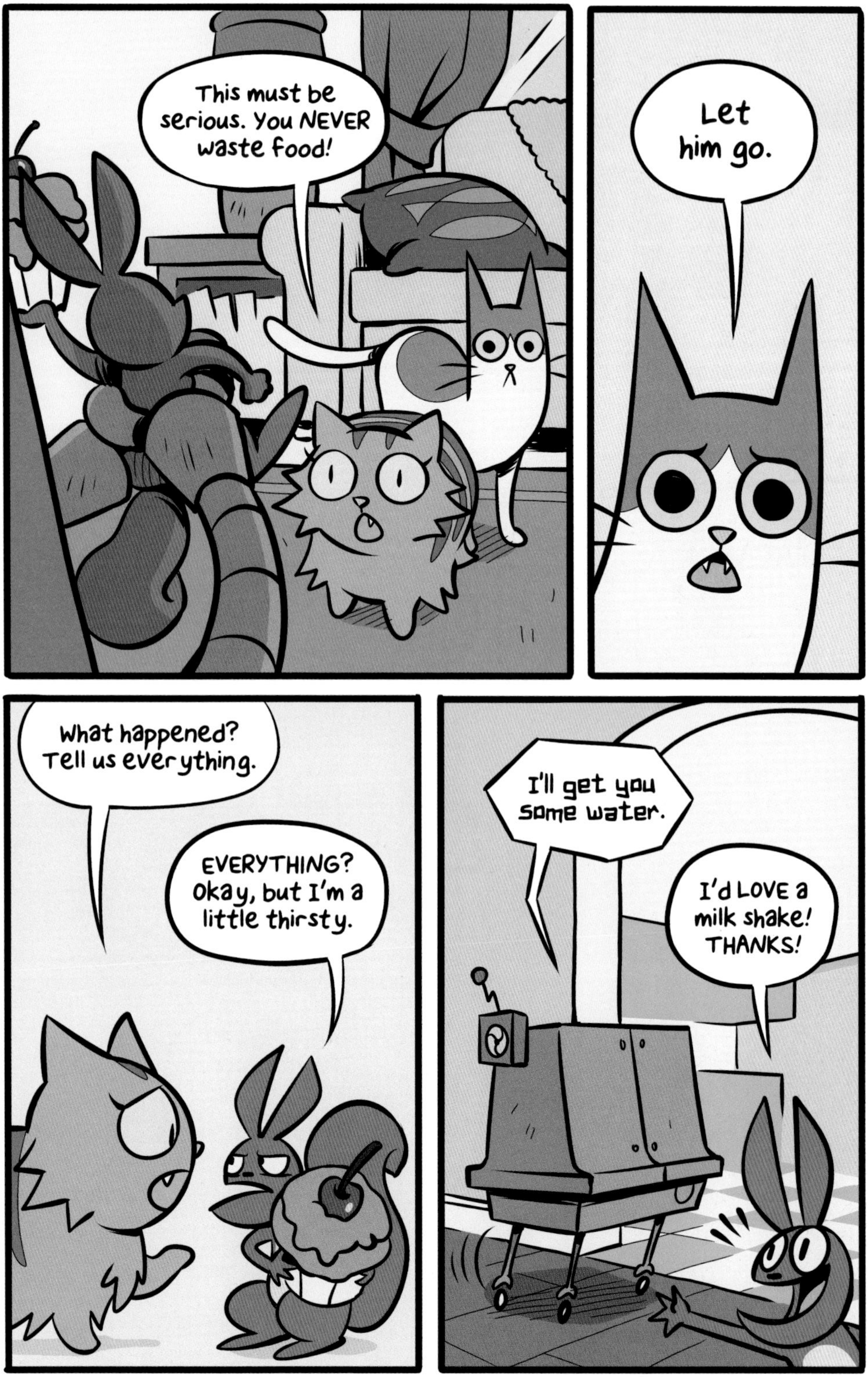
This must be serious. You NEVER waste food!
Let him go.
What happened? Tell us everything.
EVERYTHING? Okay, but I'm a little thirsty.
I'll get you some water.
I'd LOVE a milk shake! THANKS!

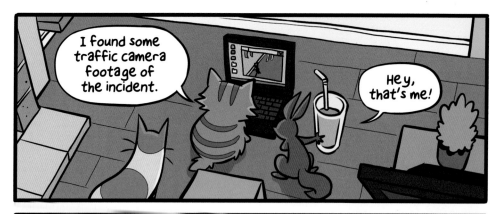

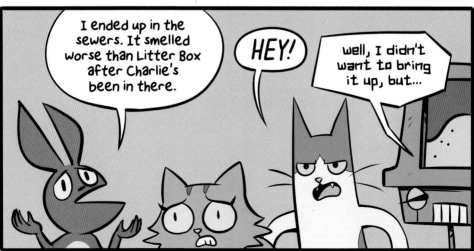

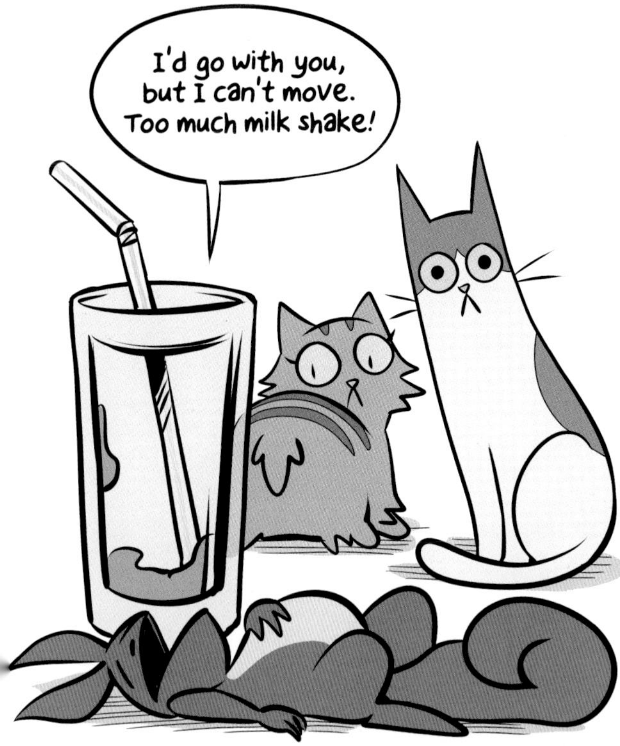
I'd go with you, but I can't move. Too much milk shake!

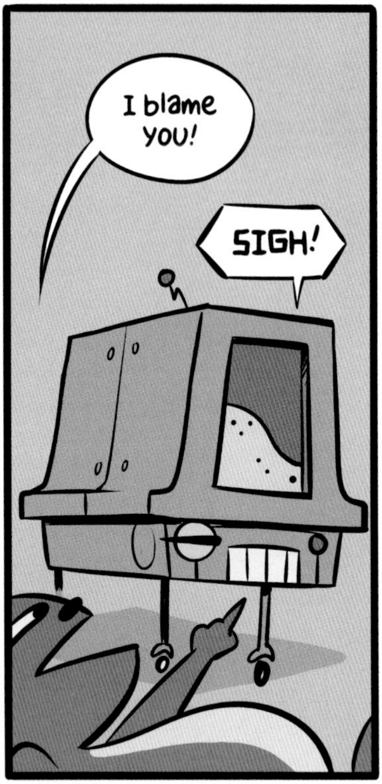
I blame YOU!
SIGH!

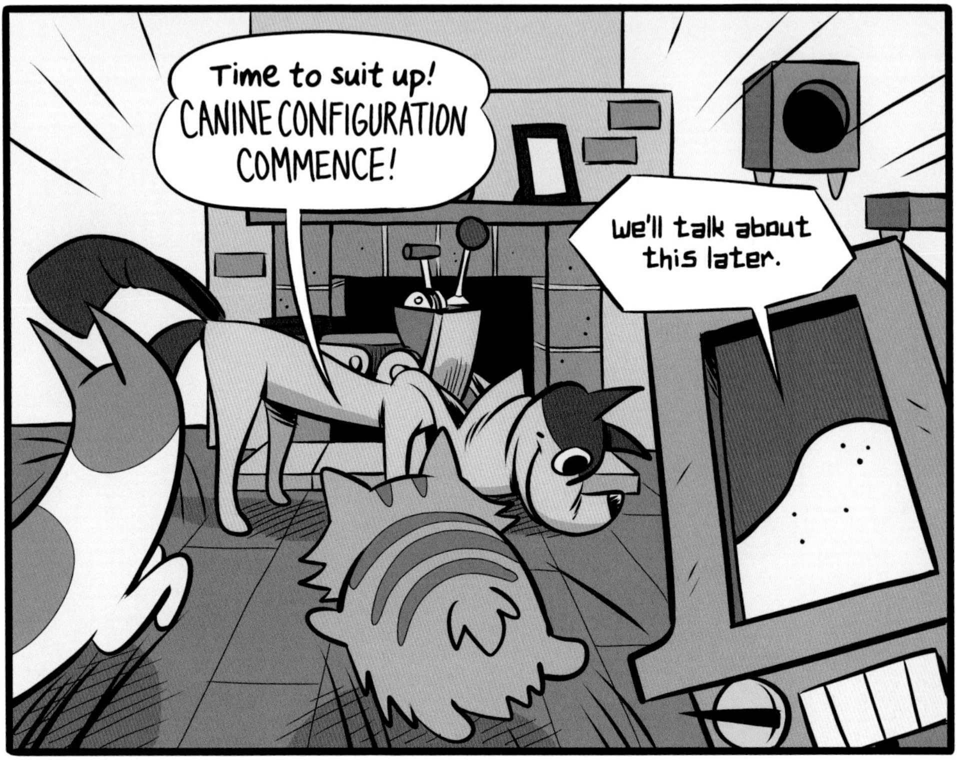
Time to suit up! CANINE CONFIGURATION COMMENCE!
We'll talk about this later.

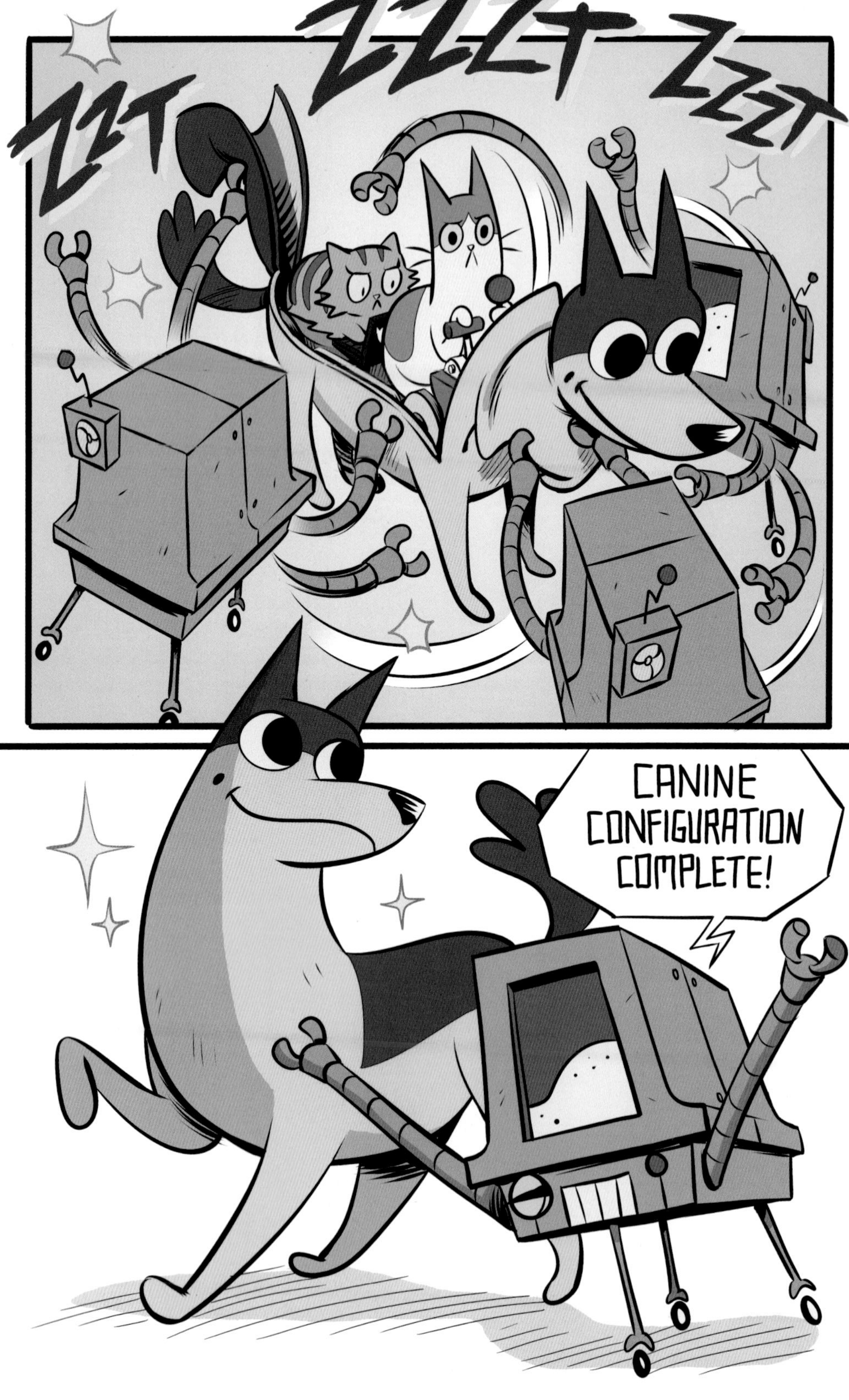
ZZT
ZZZT ZZZT
CANINE CONFIGURATION COMPLETE!

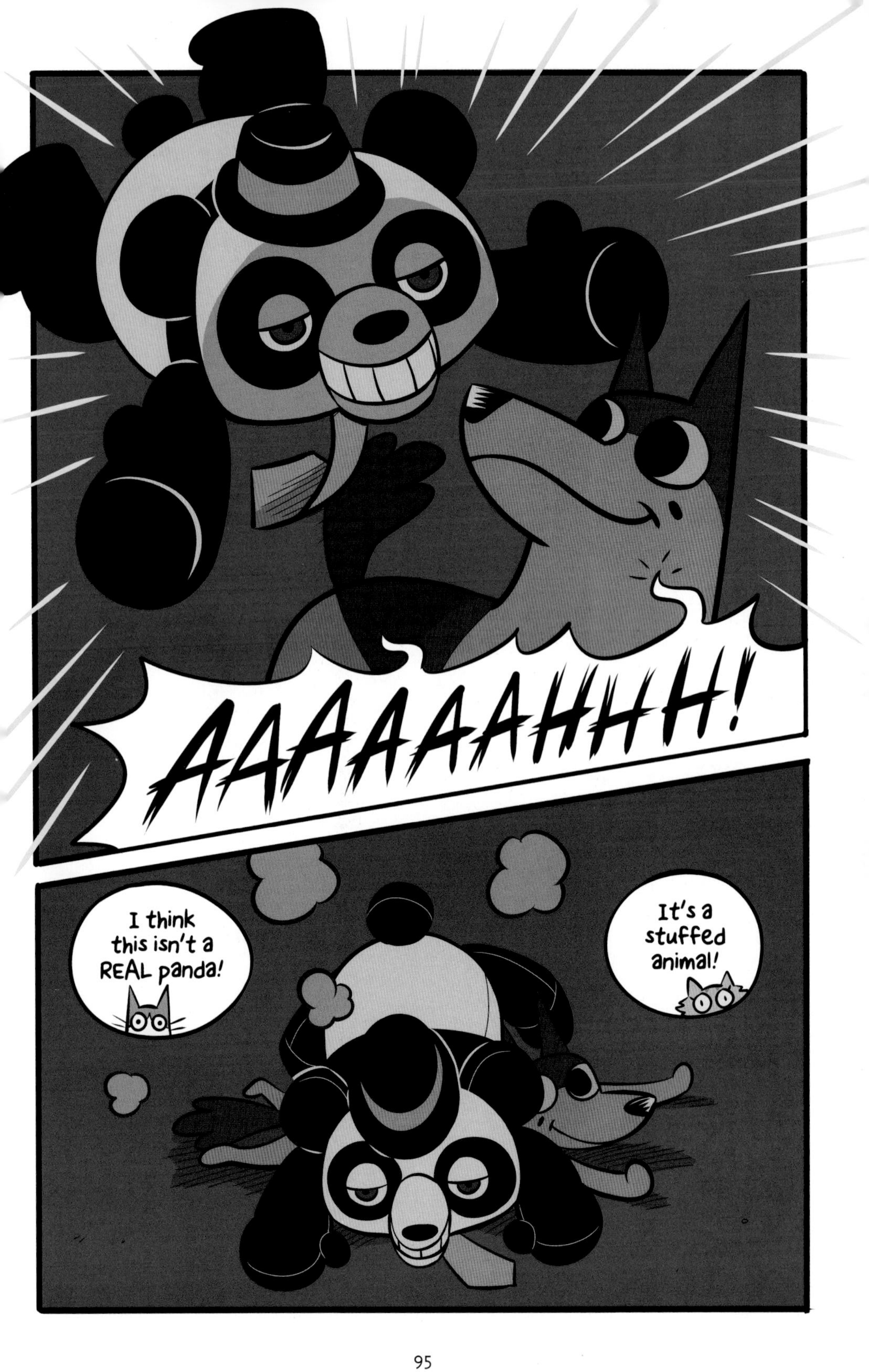
AAAAAAHHH!
I think this isn't a REAL panda!
It's a stuffed animal!

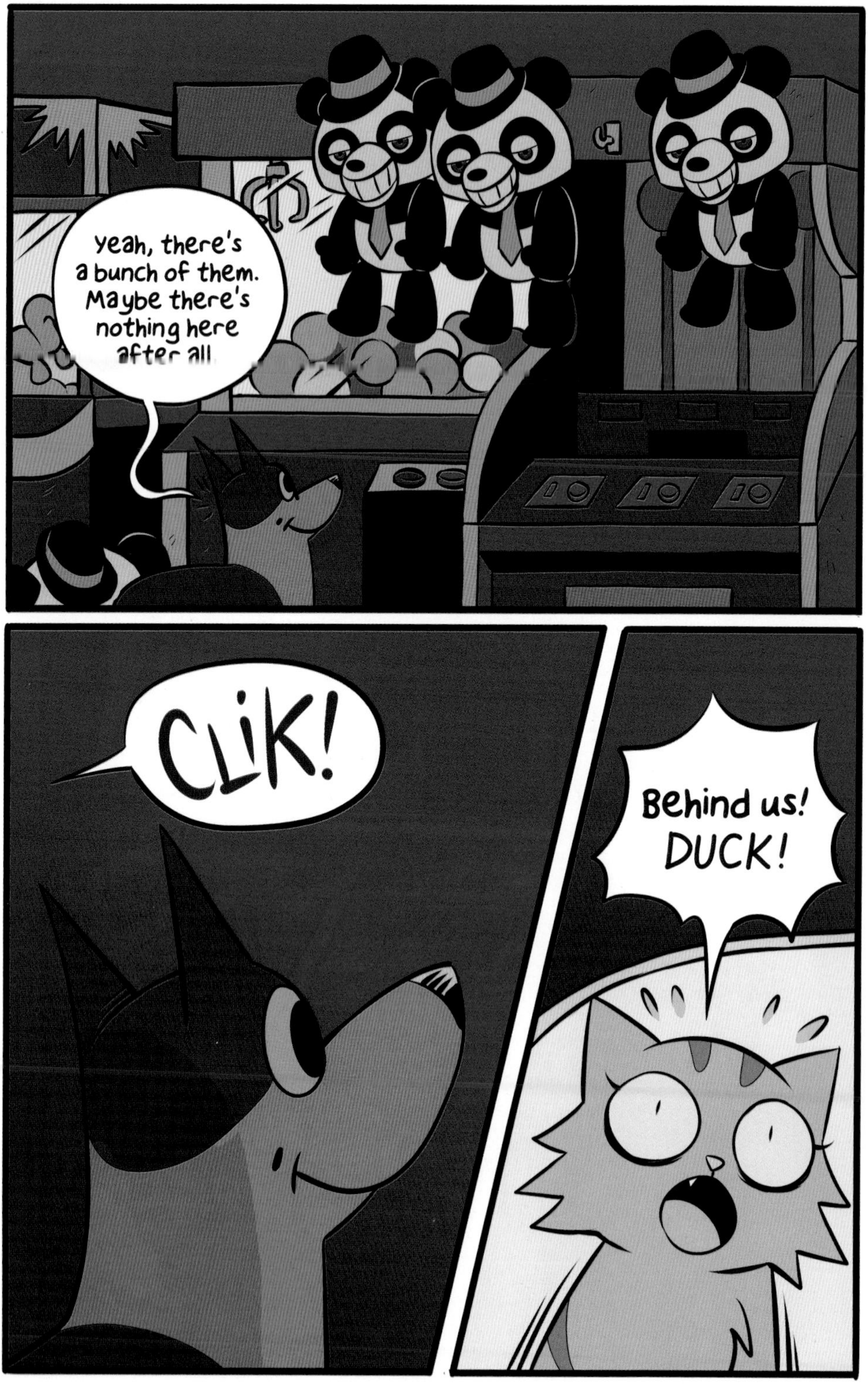

yeah, there's a bunch of them. Maybe there's nothing here after all.
CLIK!
Behind us! DUCK!

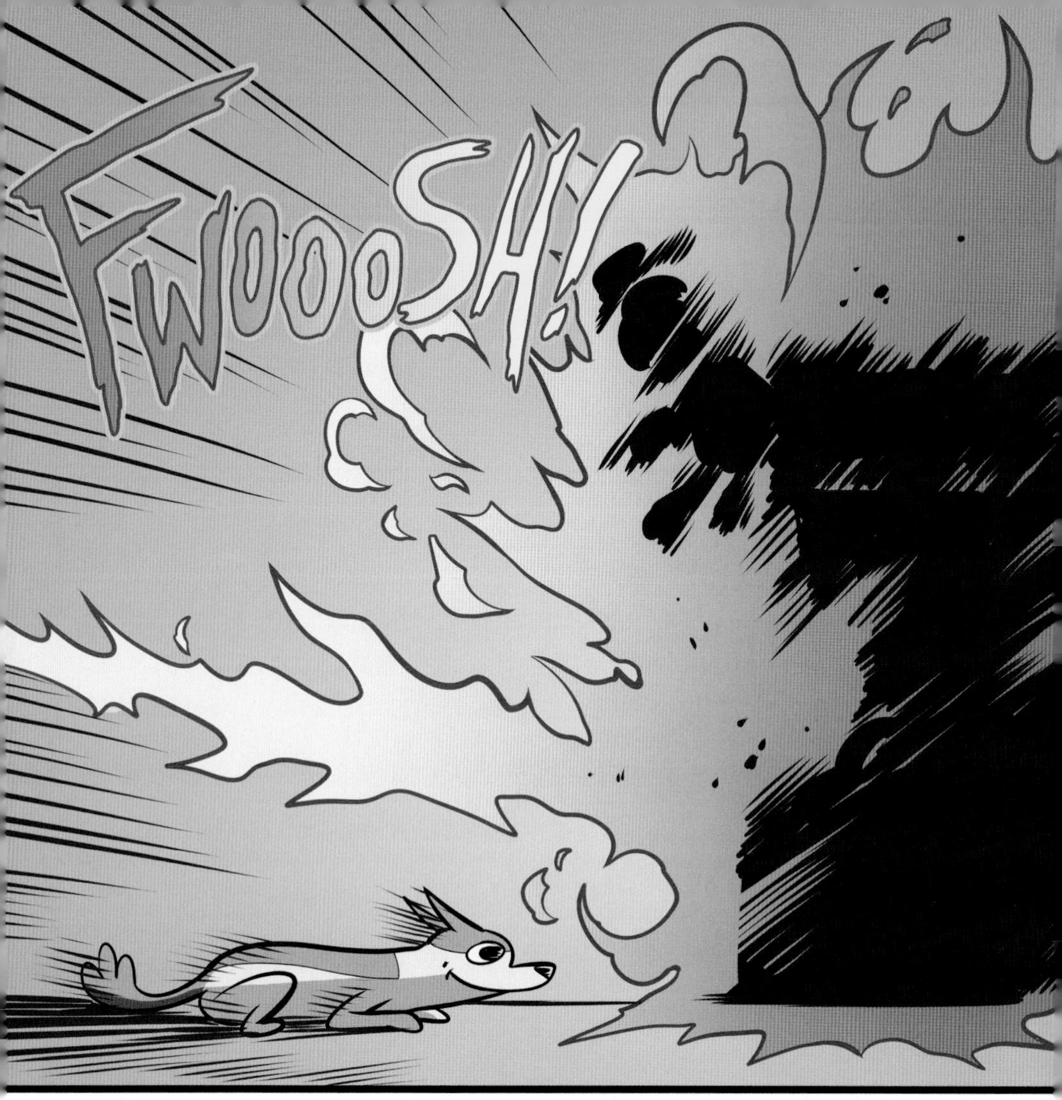
FWOOOSH!

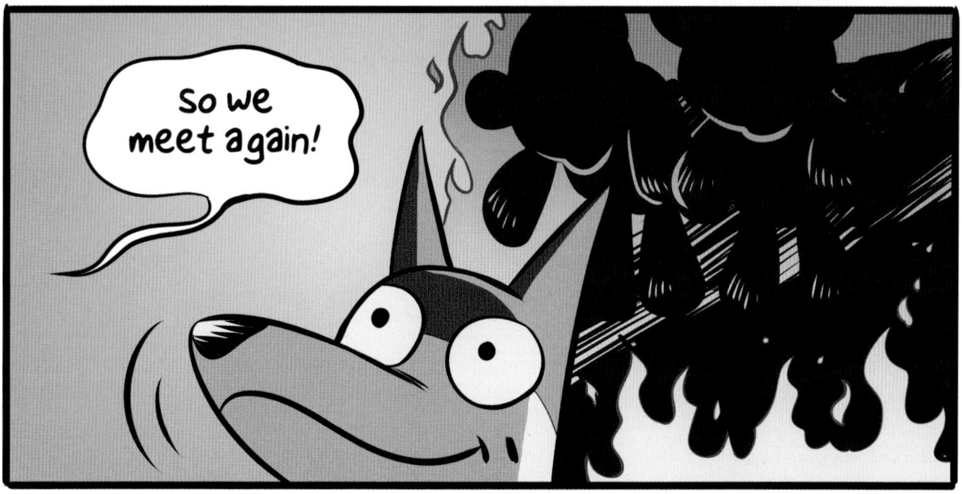
So we
meet again!

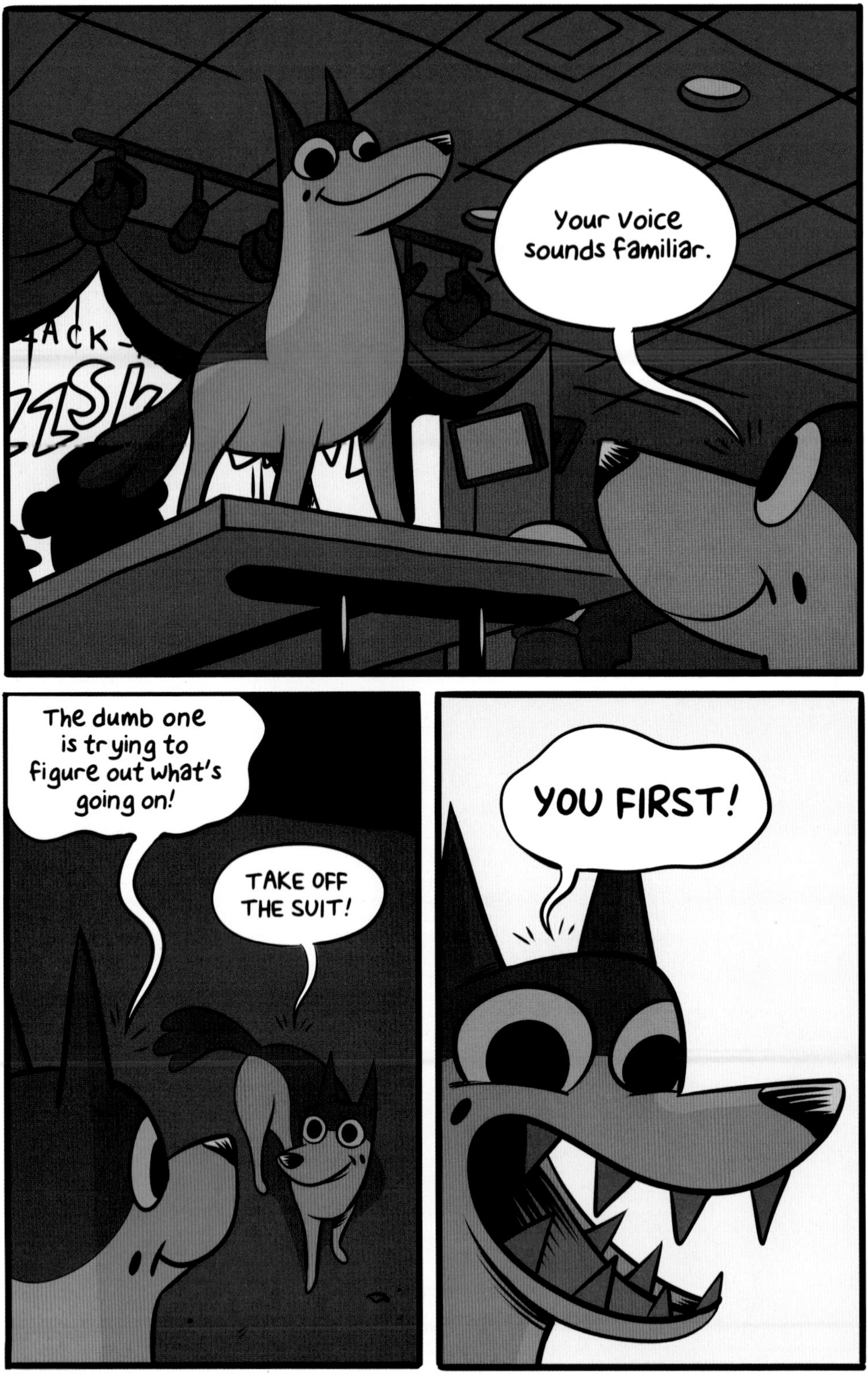
Your voice sounds familiar.
The dumb one is trying to figure out what's going on!
TAKE OFF THE SUIT!
YOU FIRST!

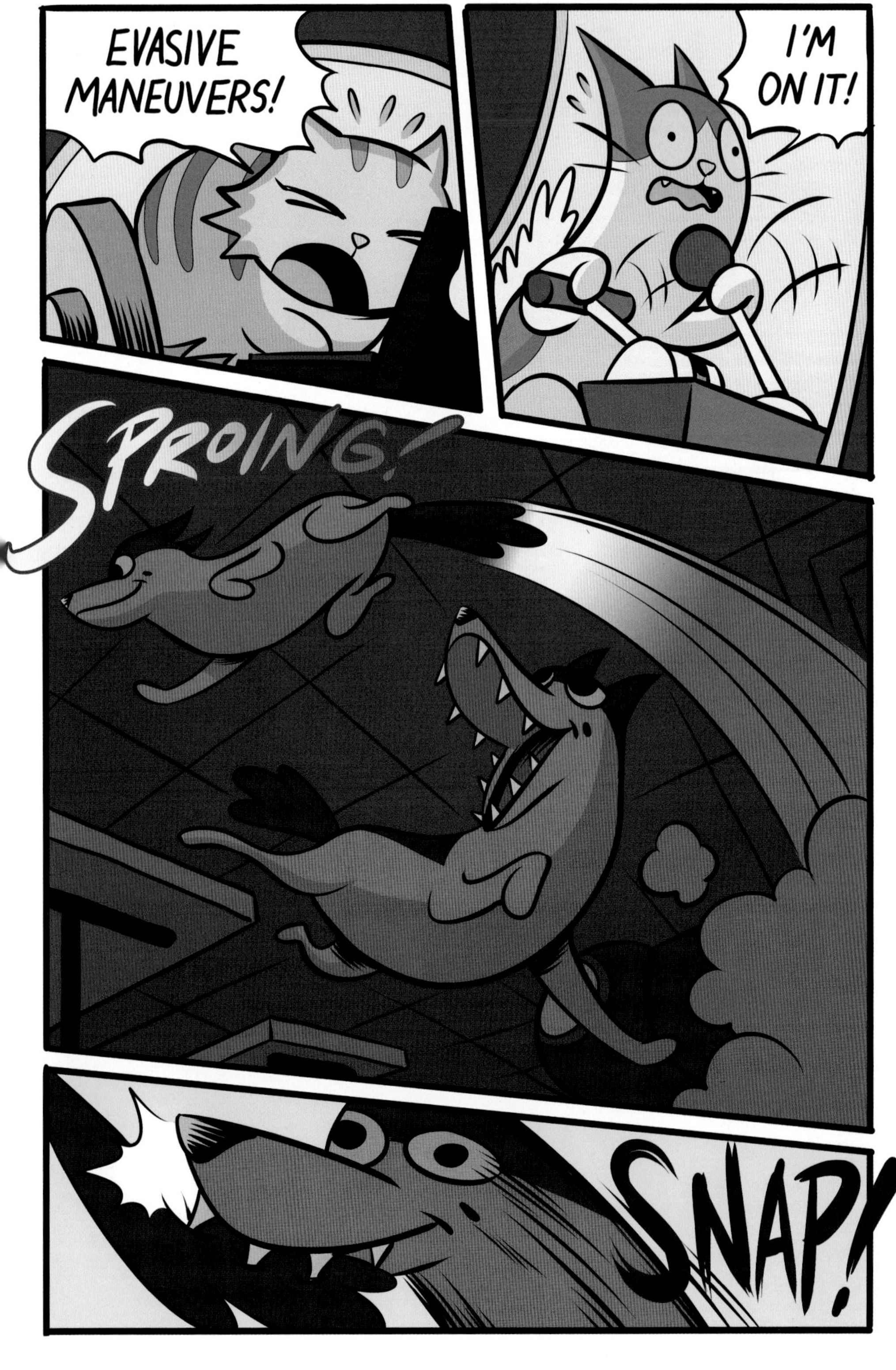
EVASIVE MANEUVERS!
I'M ON IT!
SPROING!
SNAP!

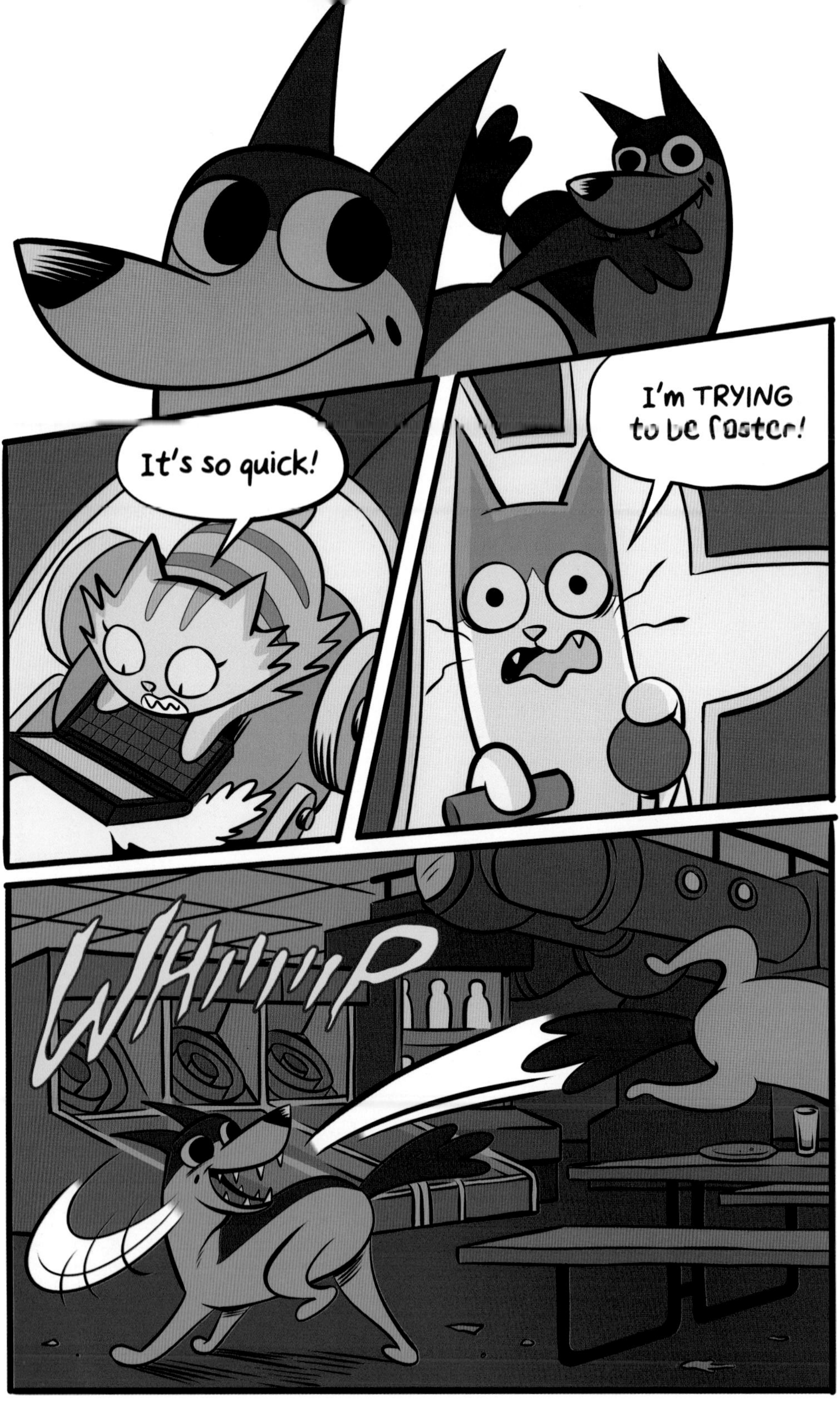
It's so quick!
I'm TRYING to be faster!
WHIIIP

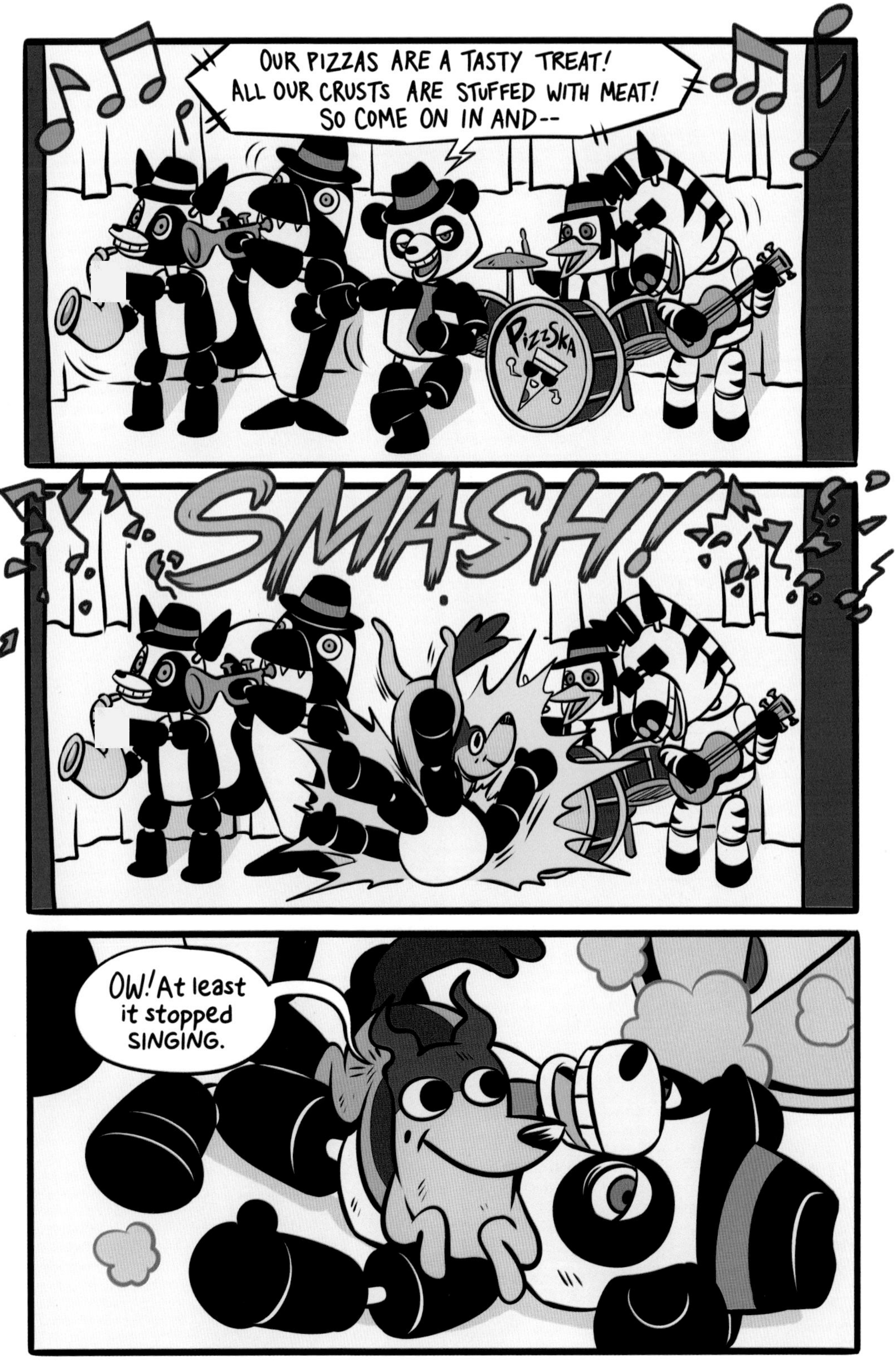
OUR PIZZAS ARE A TASTY TREAT! ALL OUR CRUSTS ARE STUFFED WITH MEAT! SO COME ON IN AND--
PizzSka
SMASH!
OW! At least it stopped SINGING.

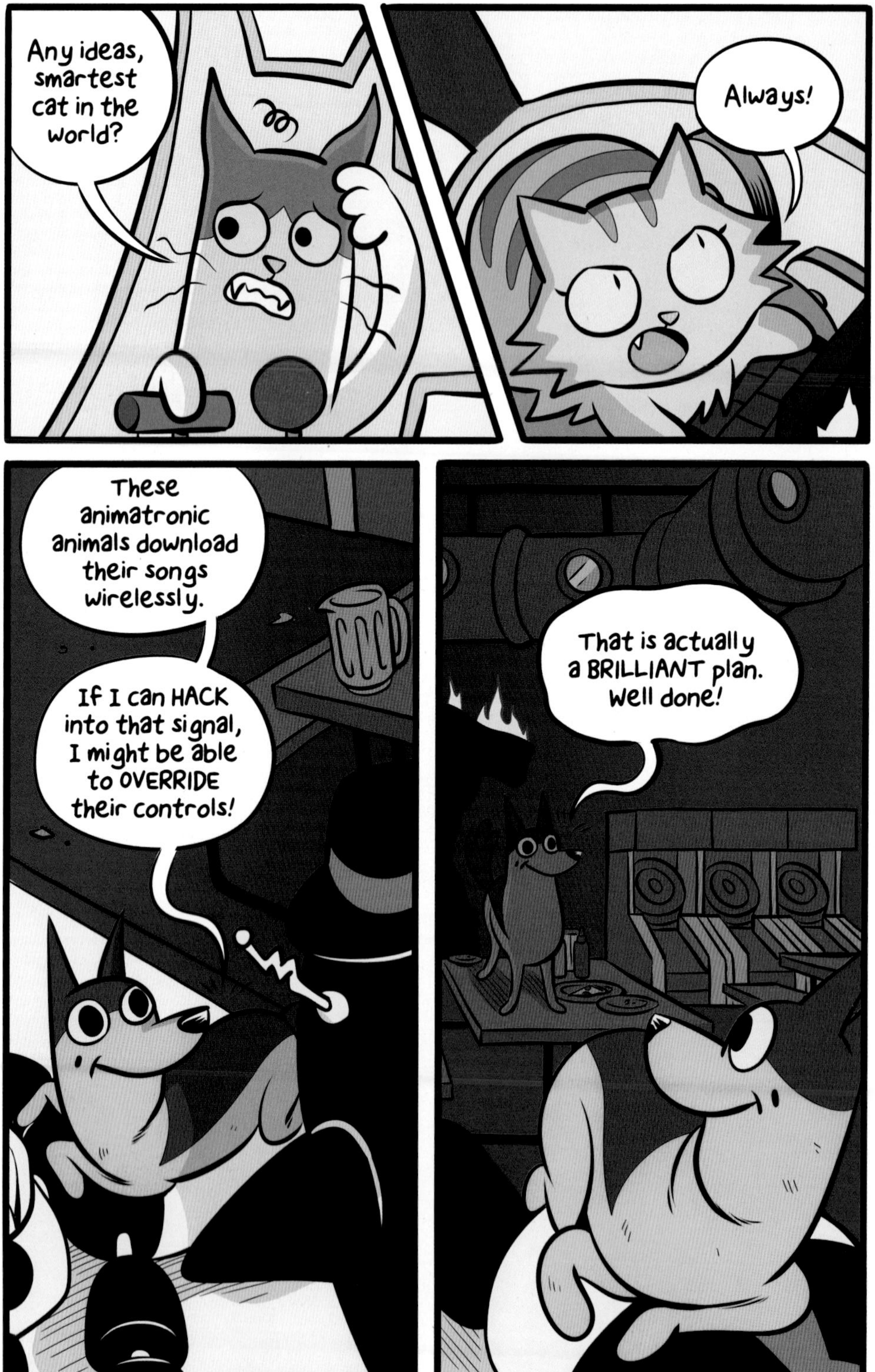
Any ideas, smartest cat in the world?
Always!
These animatronic animals download their songs wirelessly.
If I can HACK into that signal, I might be able to OVERRIDE their controls!
That is actually a BRILLIANT plan. Well done!

103

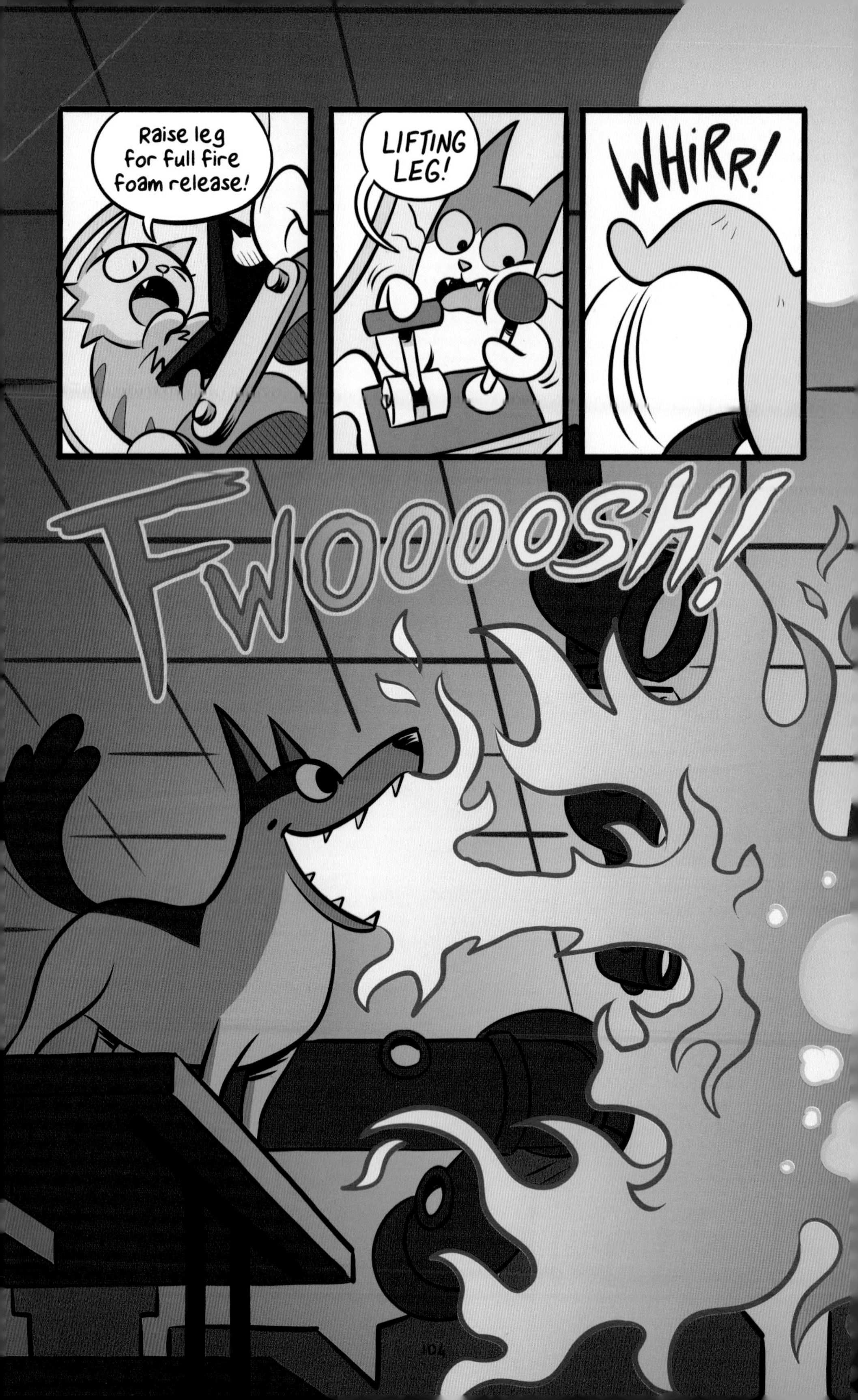
Raise leg for full fire foam release!
LIFTING LEG!
WHIRR!
FWOOOOSH!

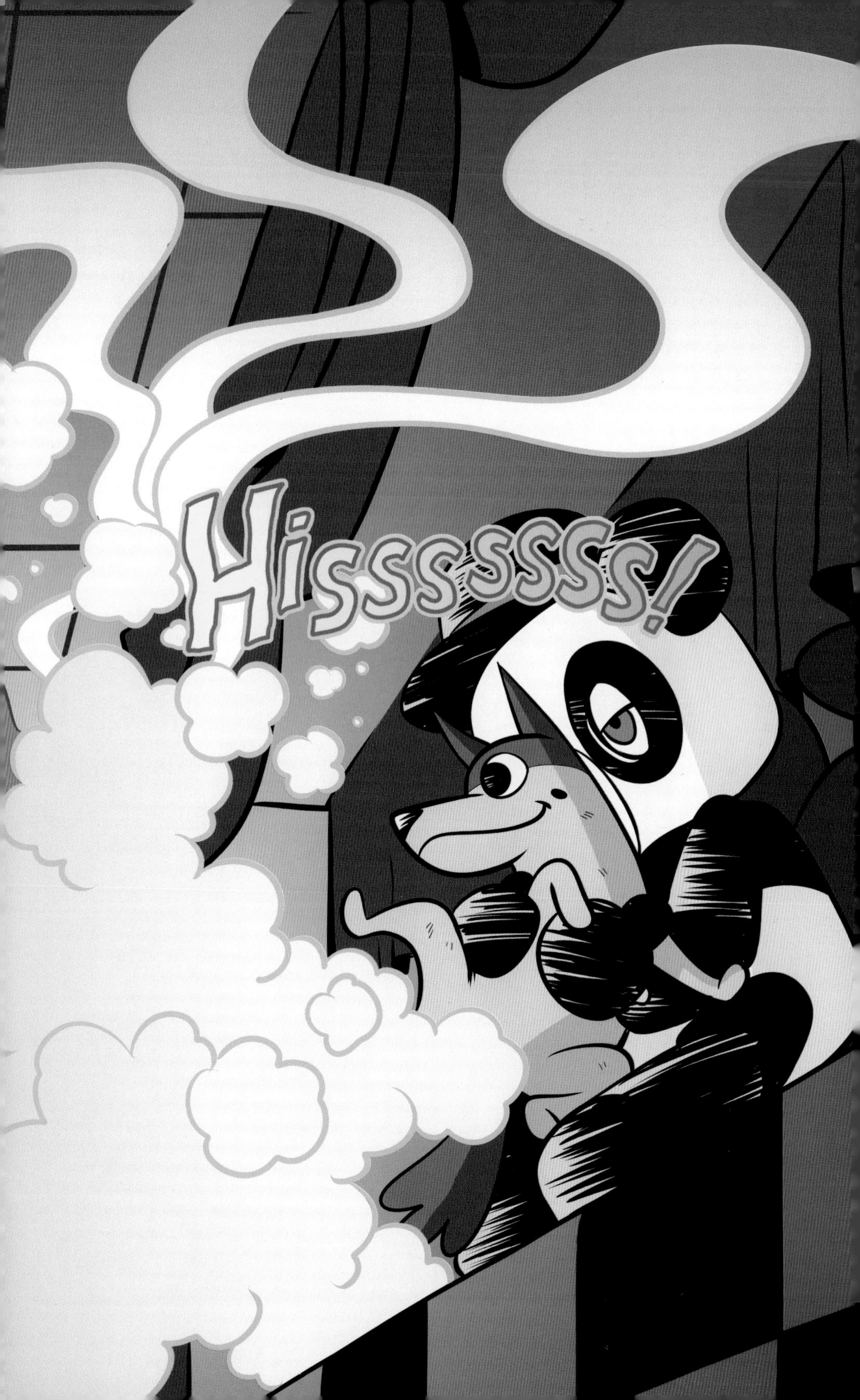
Hisssssss!

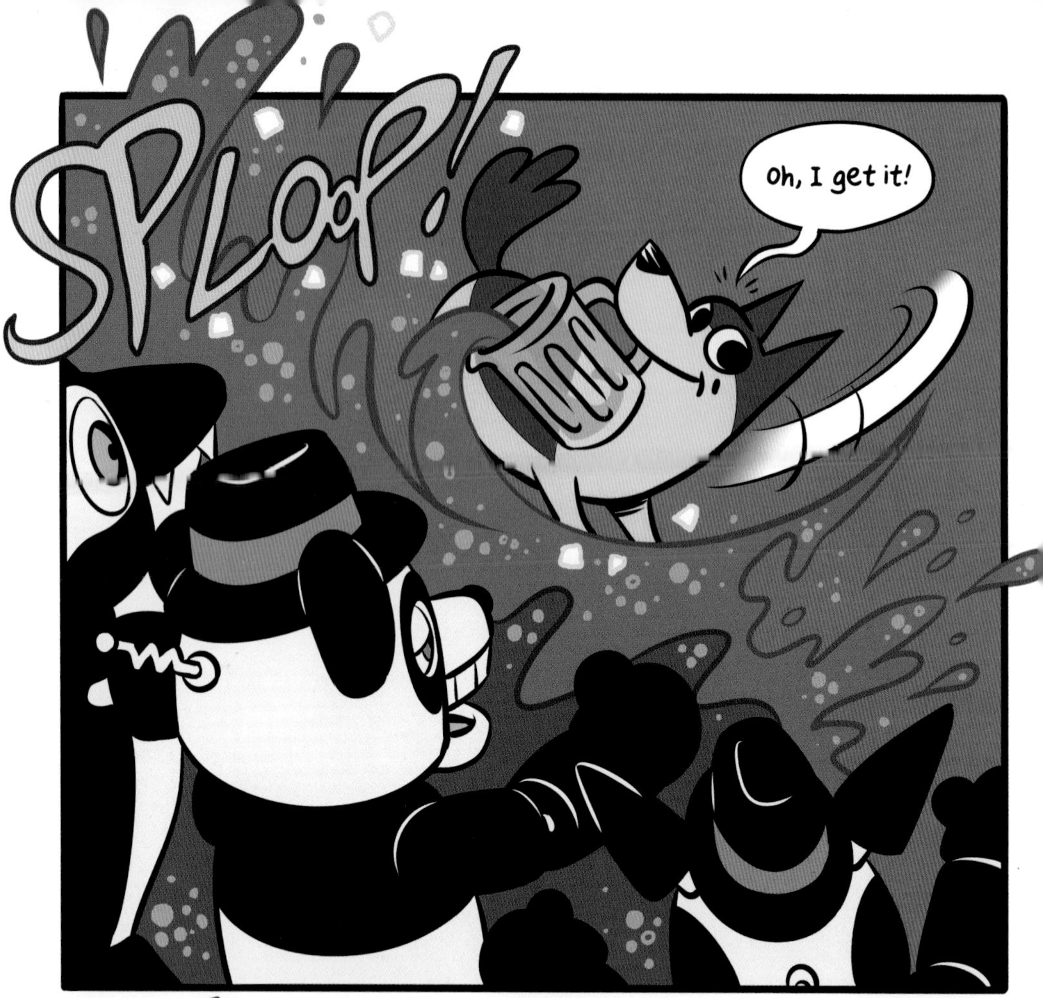
SPLOOP!
Oh, I get it!

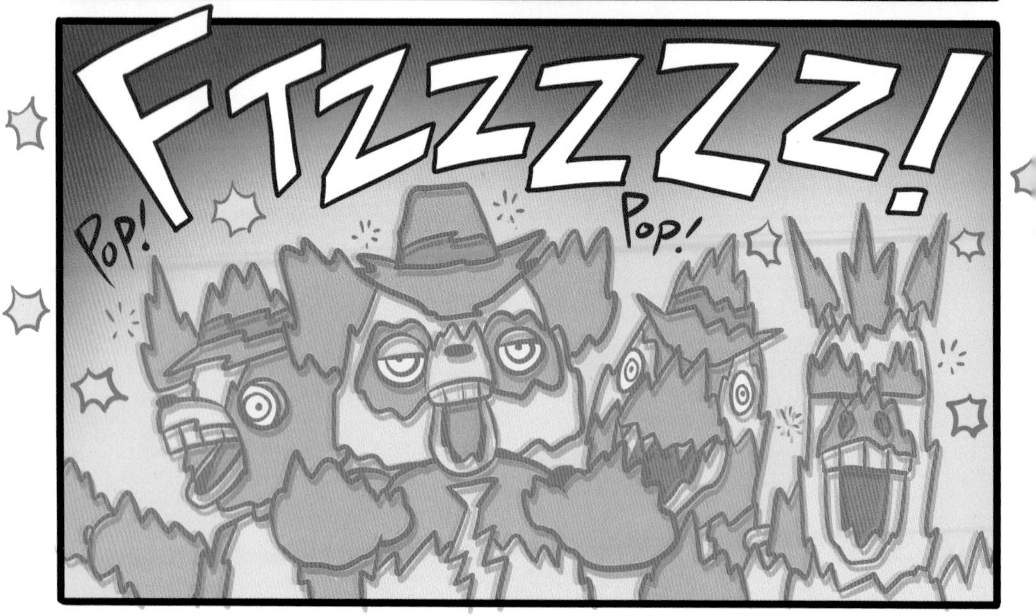
FTZZZZZ!
Pop!
Pop!

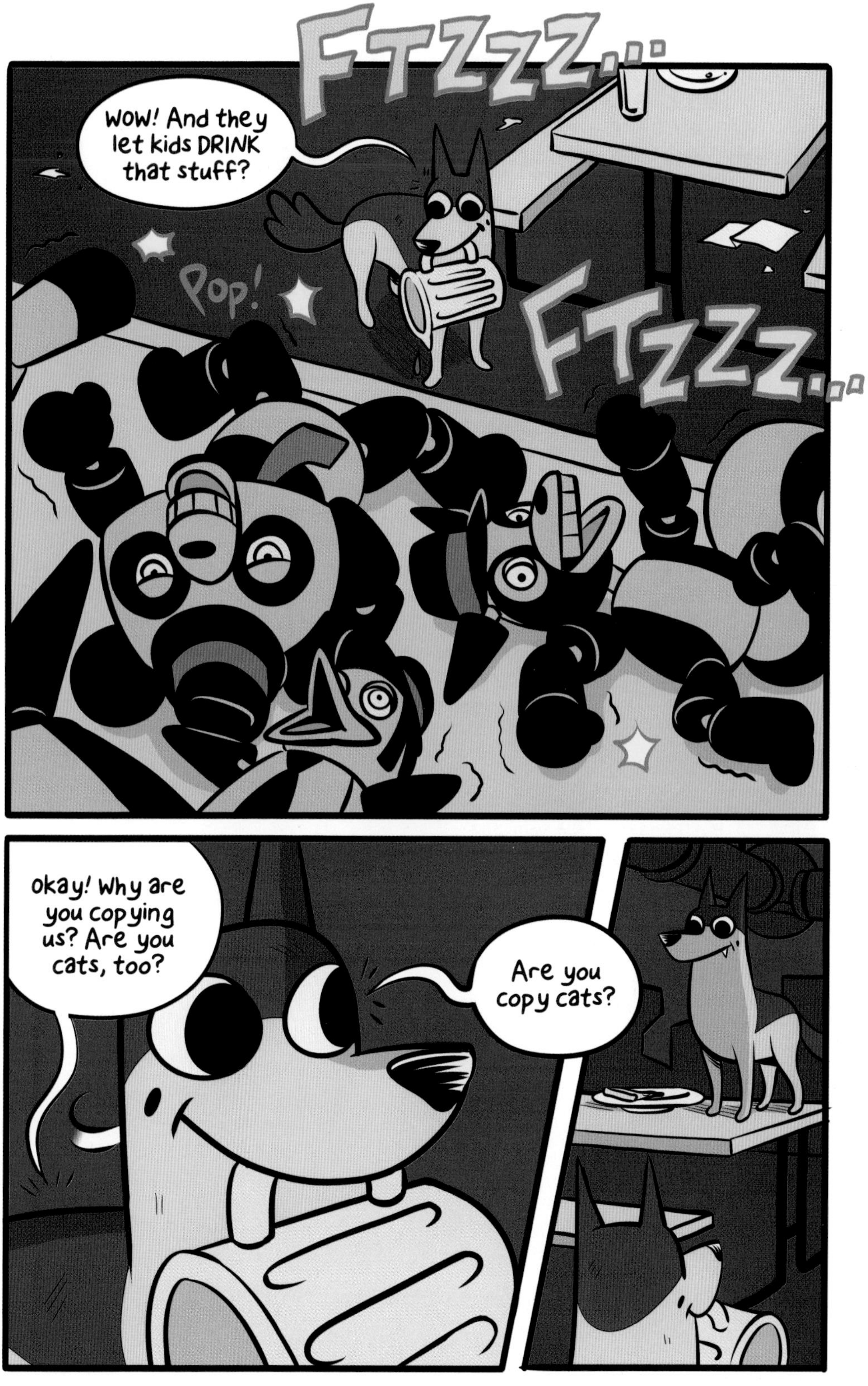
FTZZZ...
WOW! And they let kids DRINK that stuff?
POP!
FTZZZ...
okay! Why are you copying us? Are you cats, too?
Are you copy cats?

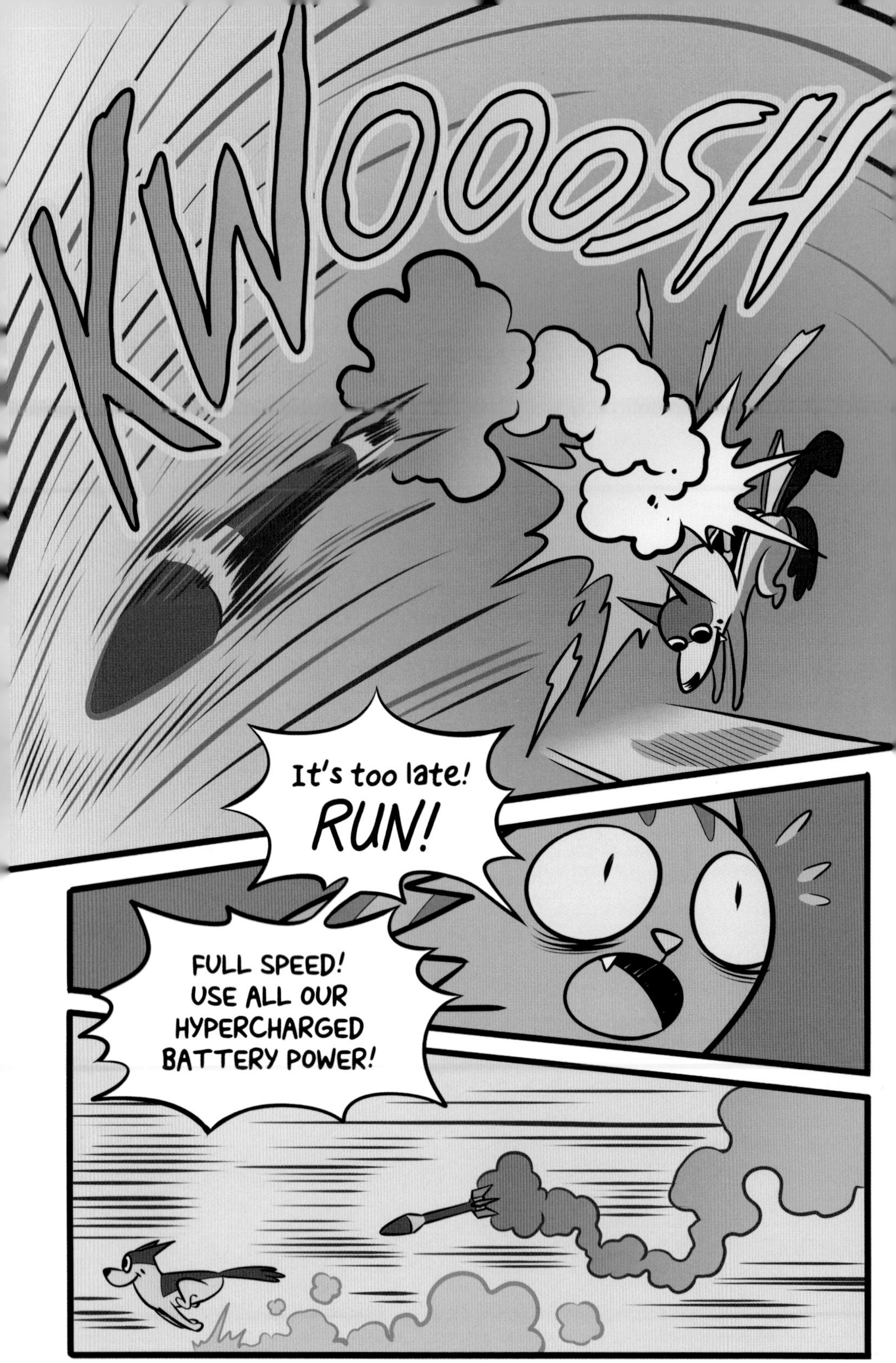
KWOOOSH
It's too late! RUN!
FULL SPEED! USE ALL OUR HYPERCHARGED BATTERY POWER!

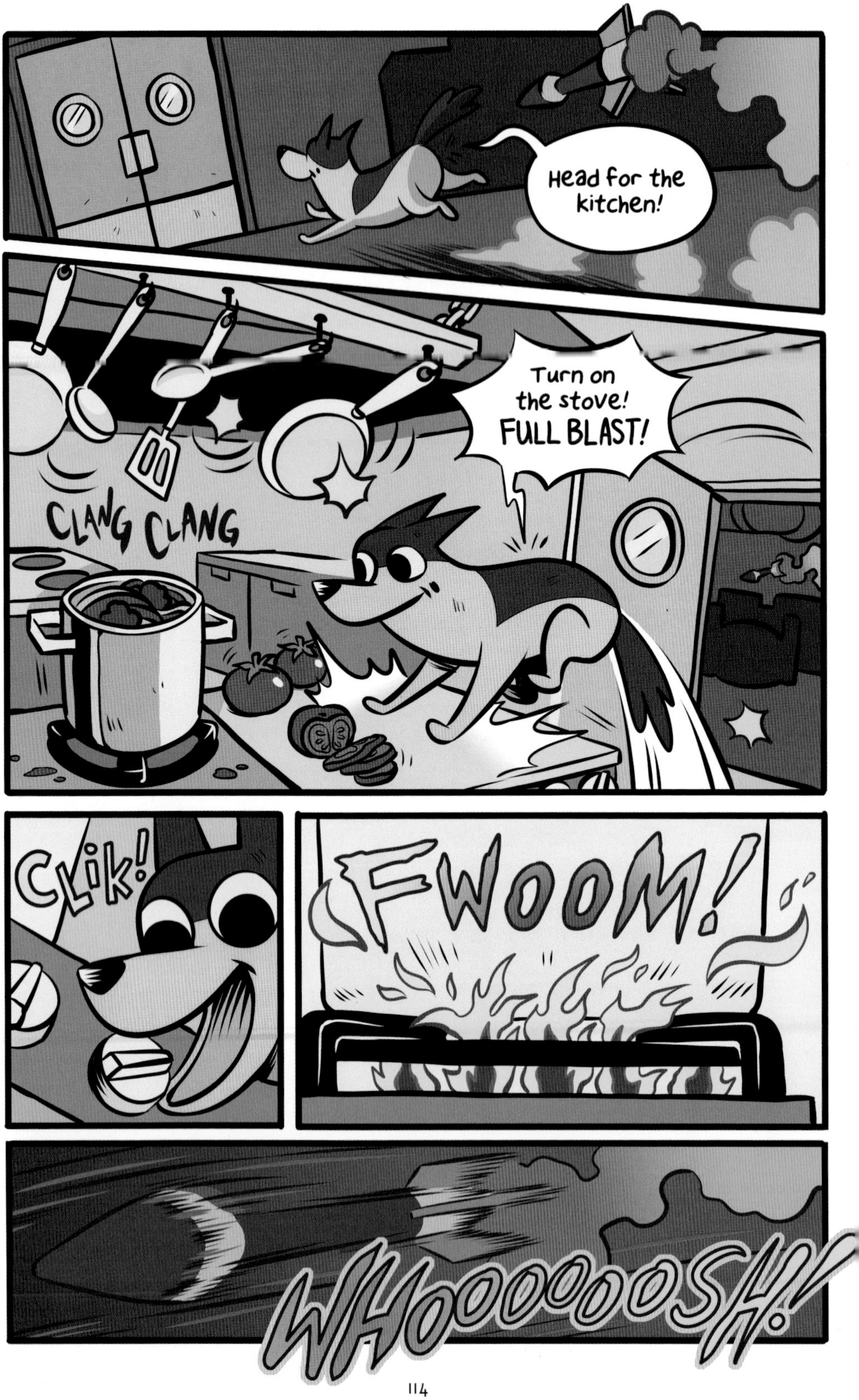
Head for the kitchen!
Turn on the stove! FULL BLAST!
CLANG CLANG
CLIK!
FWOOM!
WHOOOOOOSH!

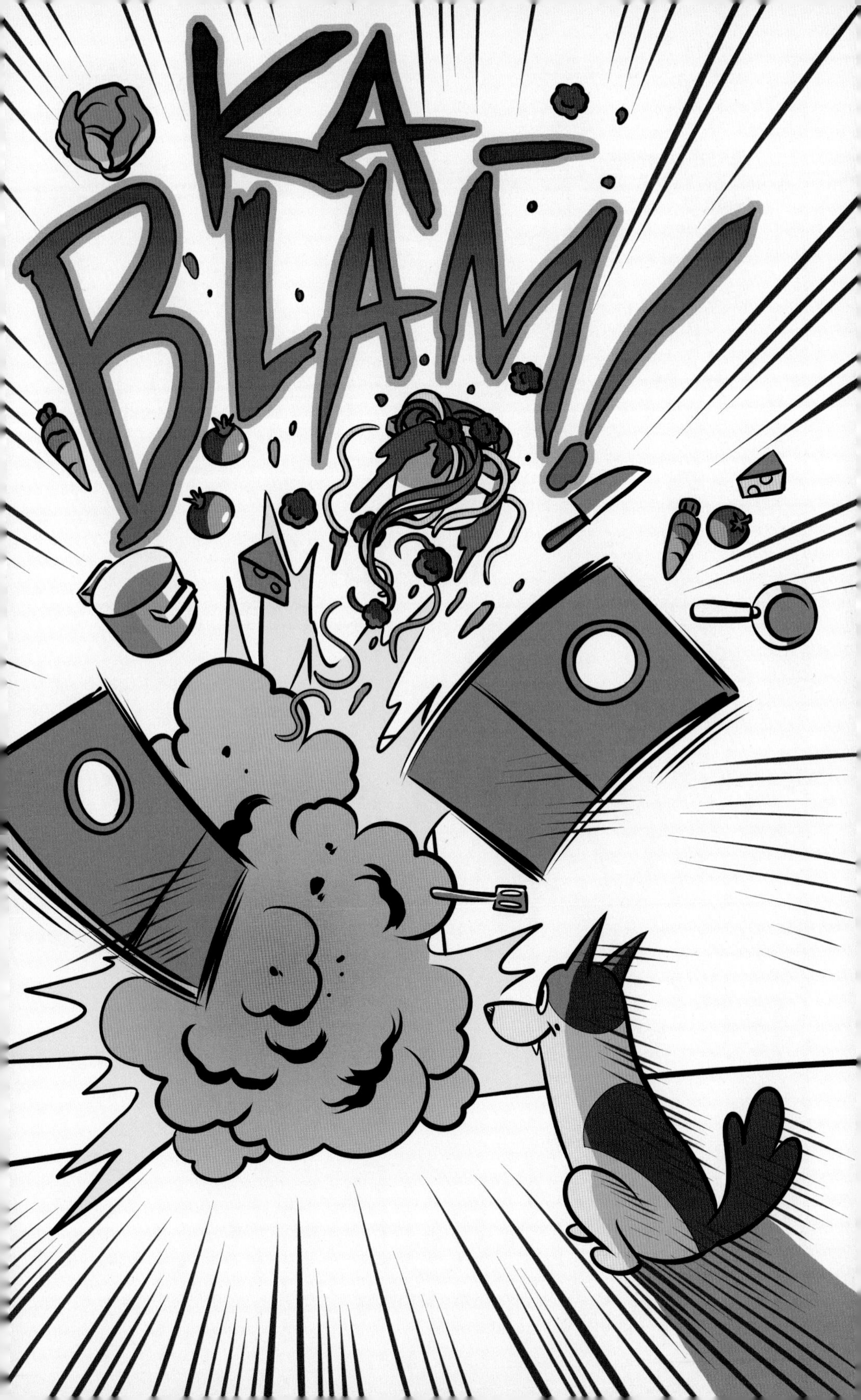
KA-BLAM!

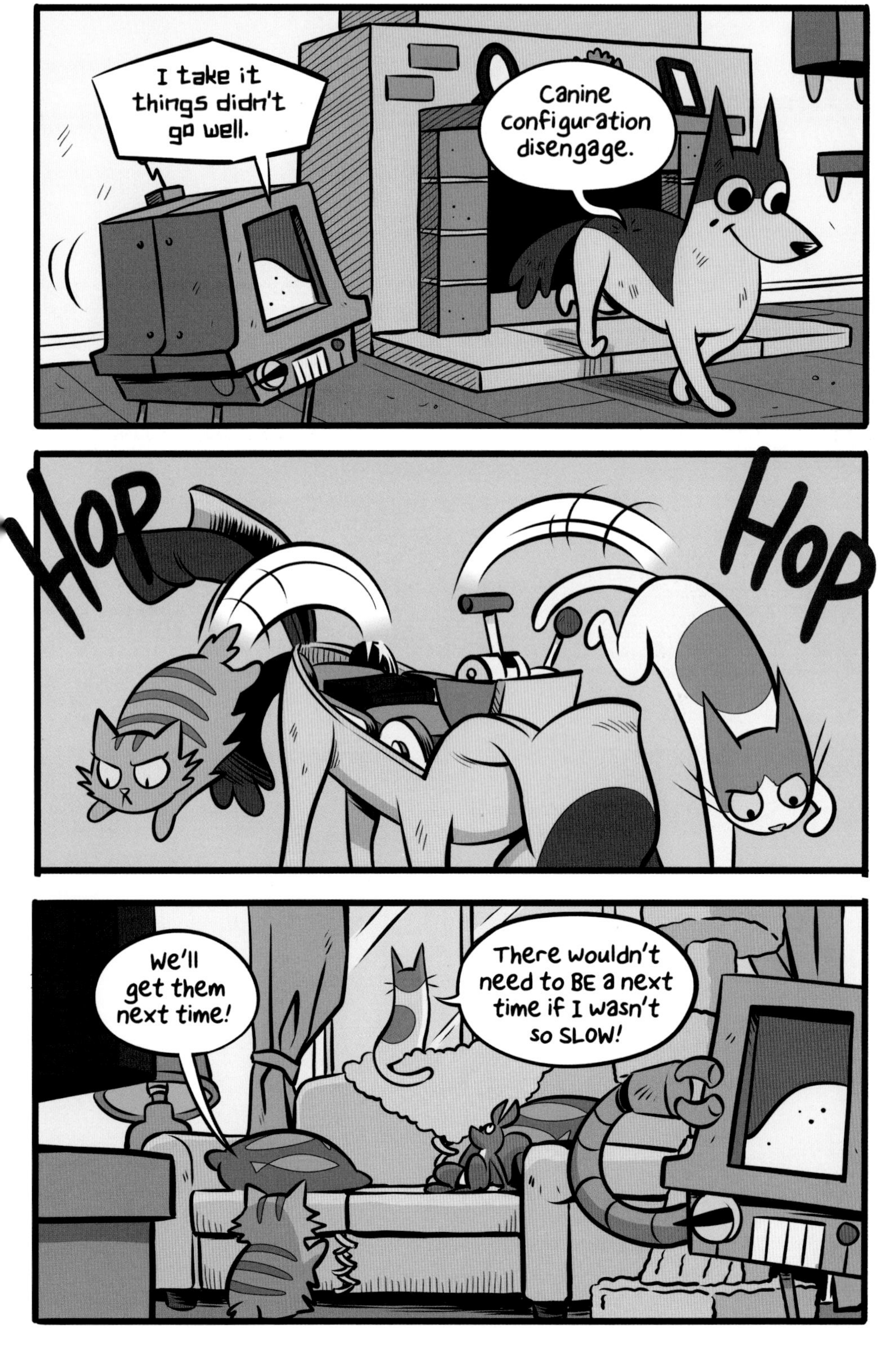
I take it things didn't go well.
Canine configuration disengage.
HOP
HOP
We'll get them next time!
There wouldn't need to BE a next time if I wasn't so SLOW!

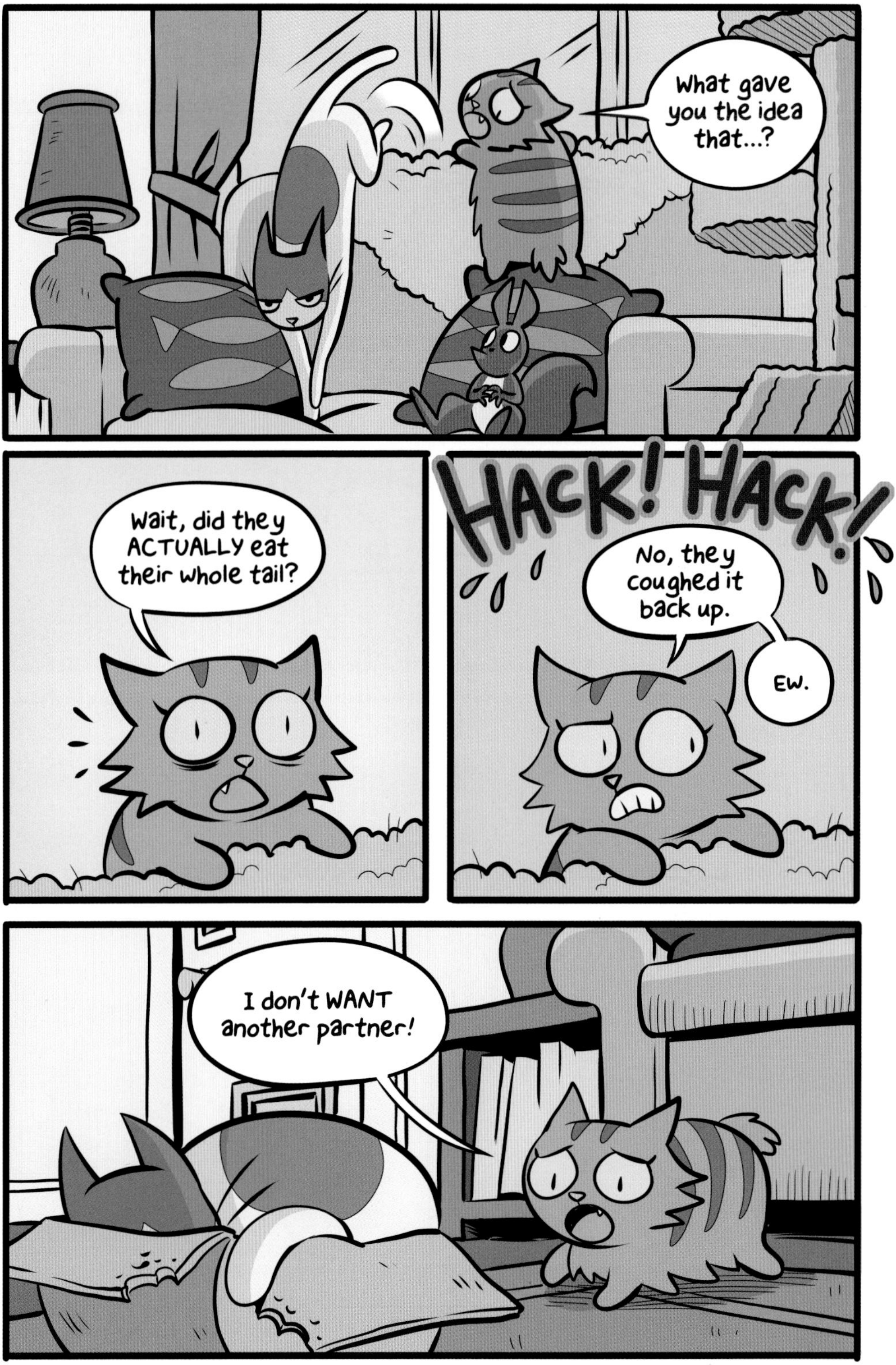

What gave you the idea that...?
Wait, did they ACTUALLY eat their whole tail?
HACK! HACK!
No, they coughed it back up.
EW.
I don't WANT another partner!

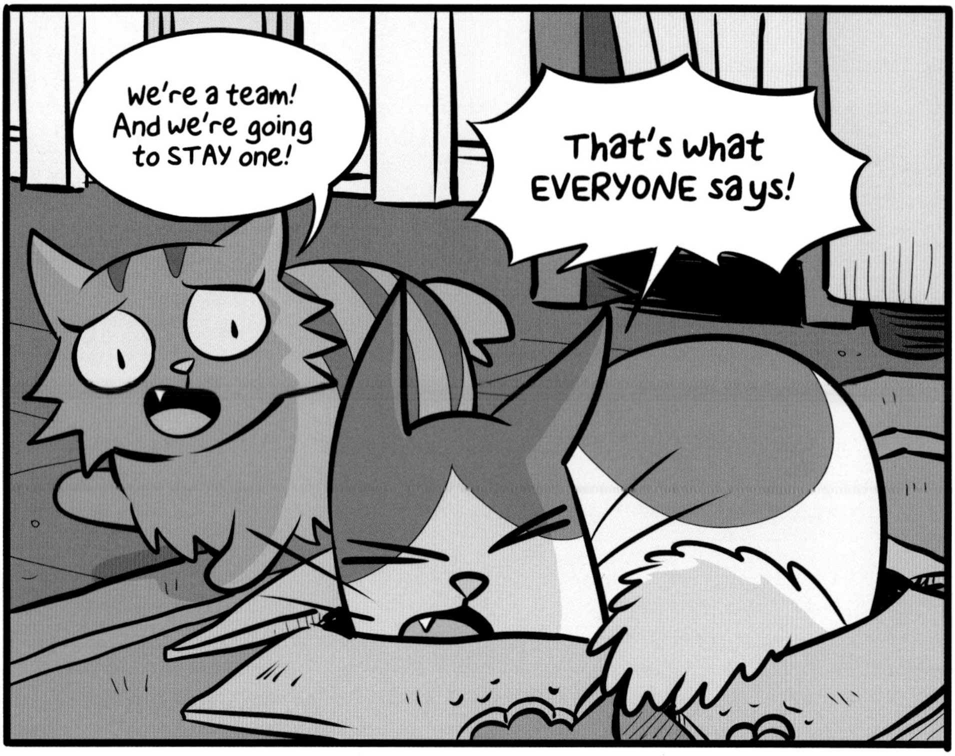
We're a team! And we're going to STAY one!
That's what EVERYONE says!

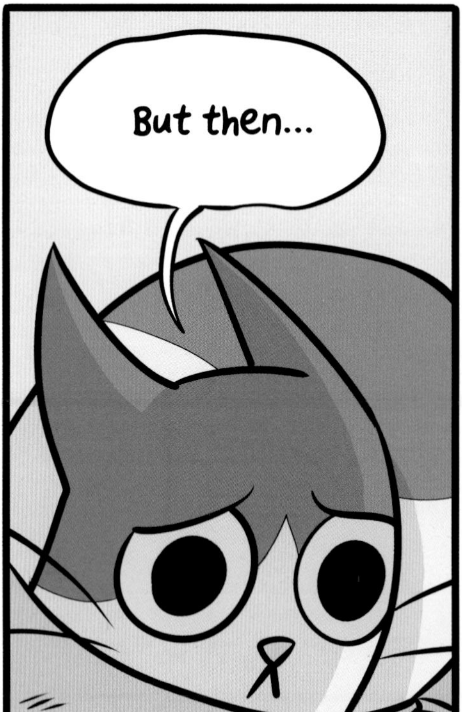
But then...

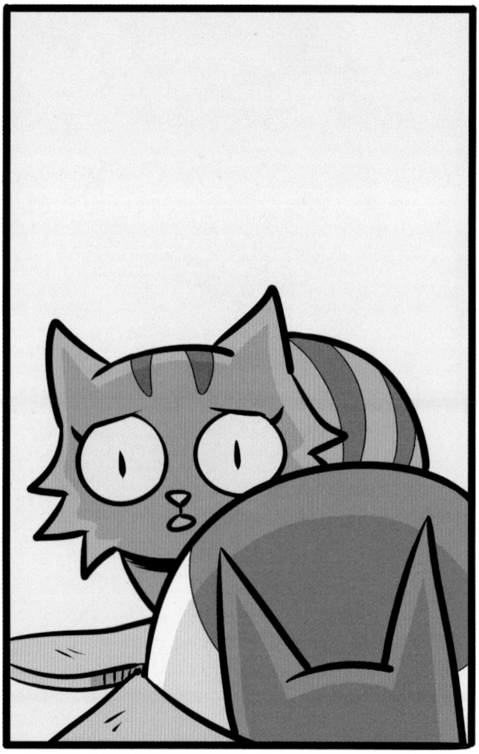

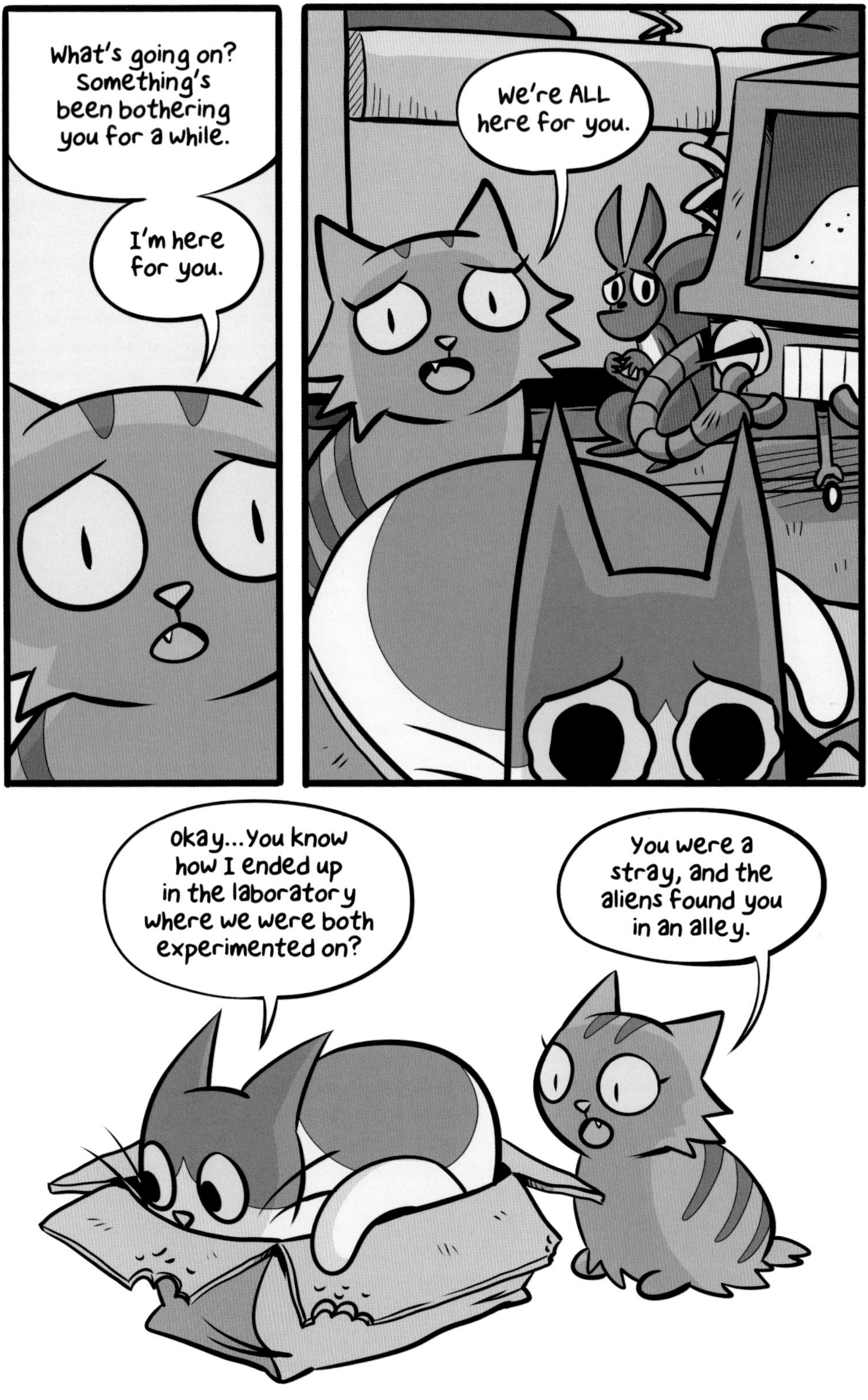
What's going on? Something's been bothering you for a while.
I'm here for you.
We're ALL here for you.
okay...You know how I ended up in the laboratory where we were both experimented on?
You were a stray, and the aliens found you in an alley.

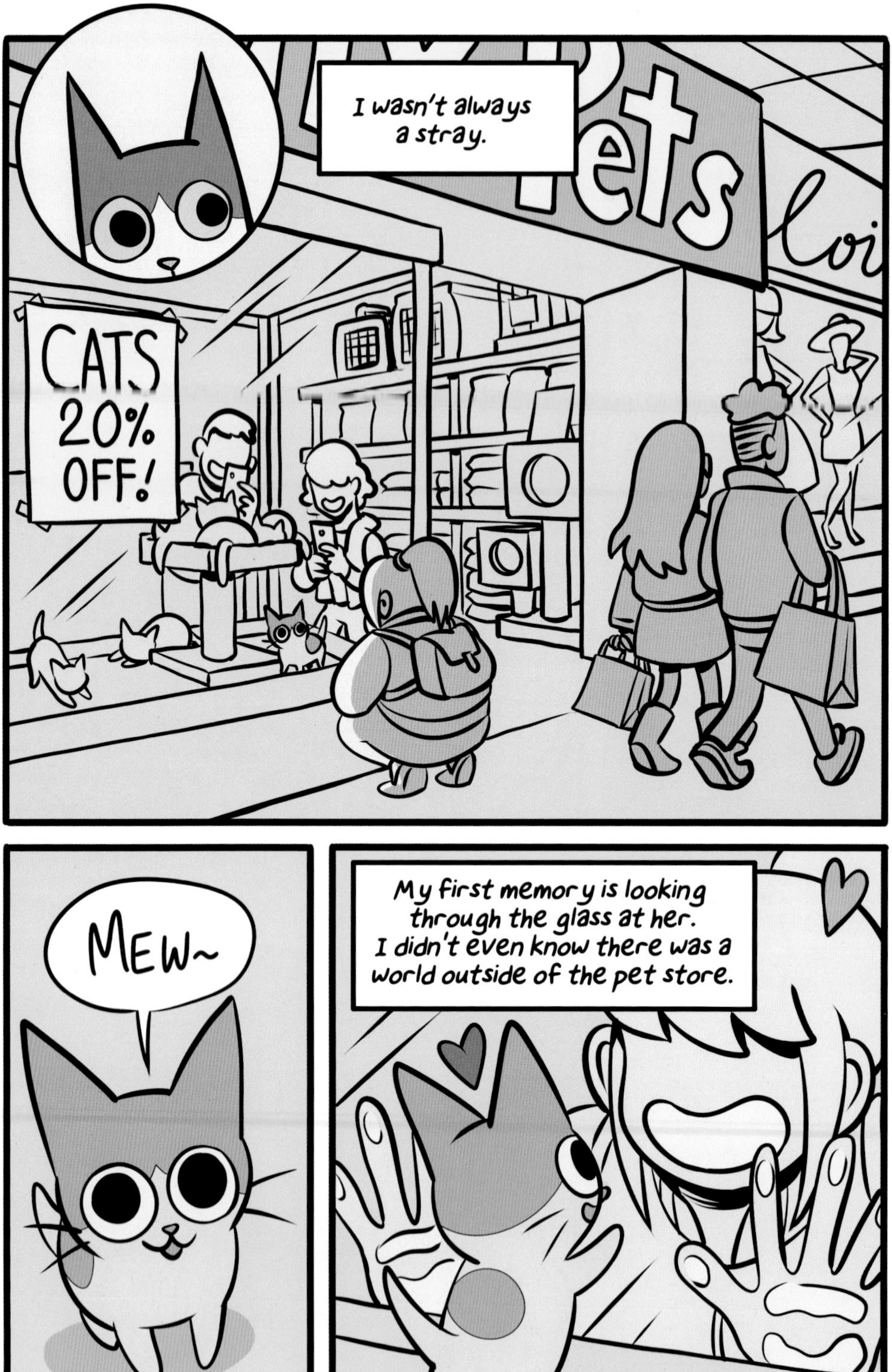
I wasn't always a stray.
Pets
CATS 20% OFF!
MEW~
My first memory is looking through the glass at her. I didn't even know there was a world outside of the pet store.

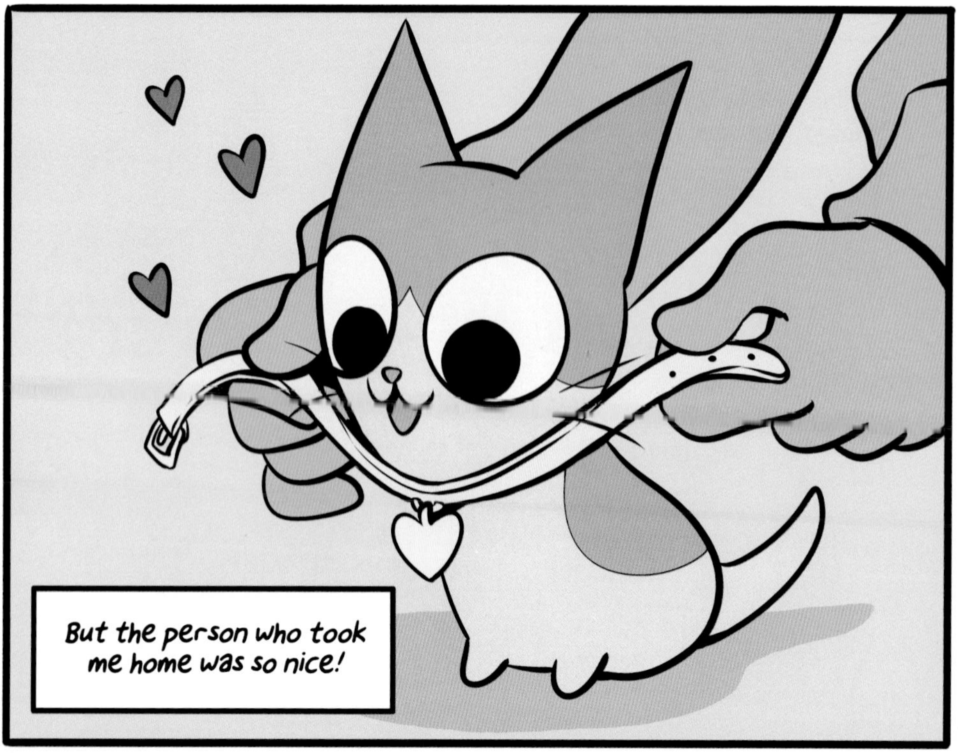
But the person who took me home was so nice!

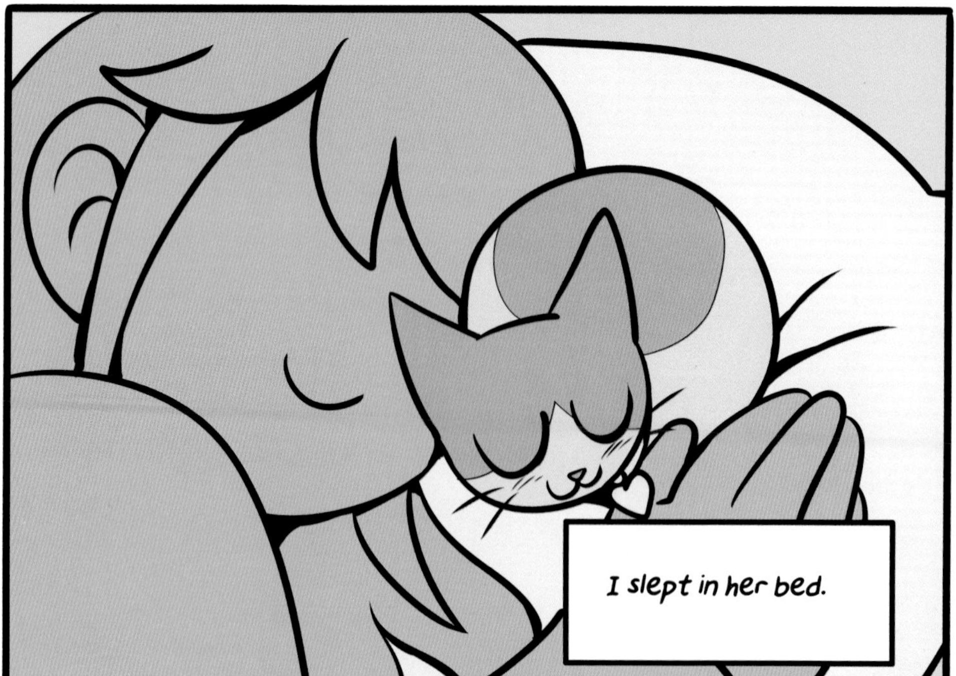
I slept in her bed.

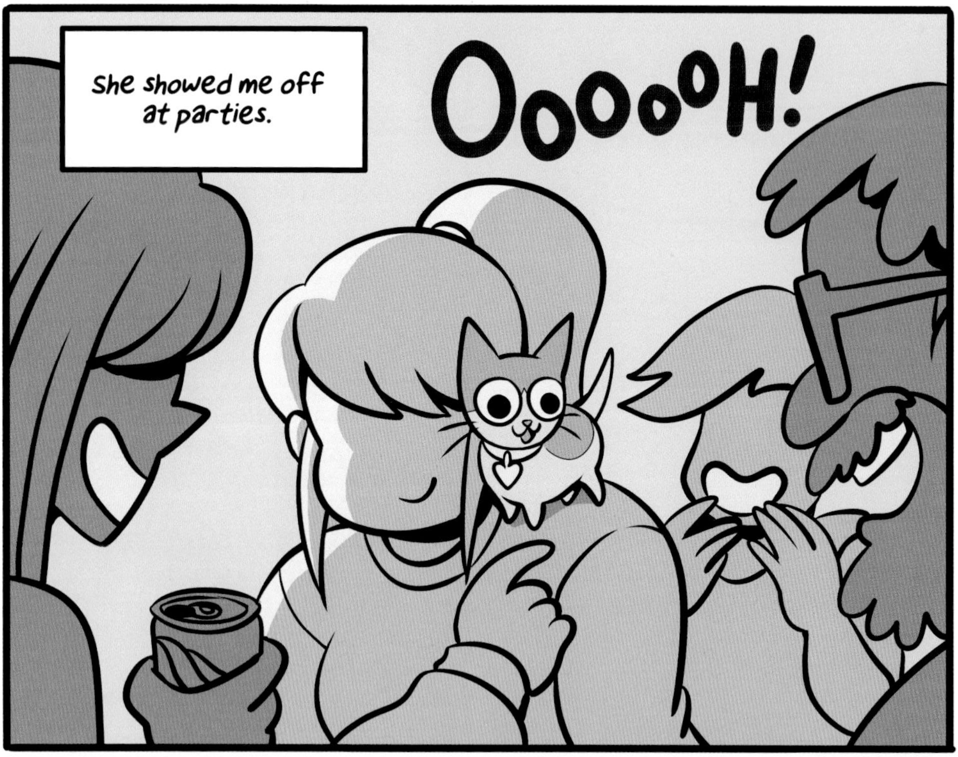
She showed me off at parties.
OooooH!

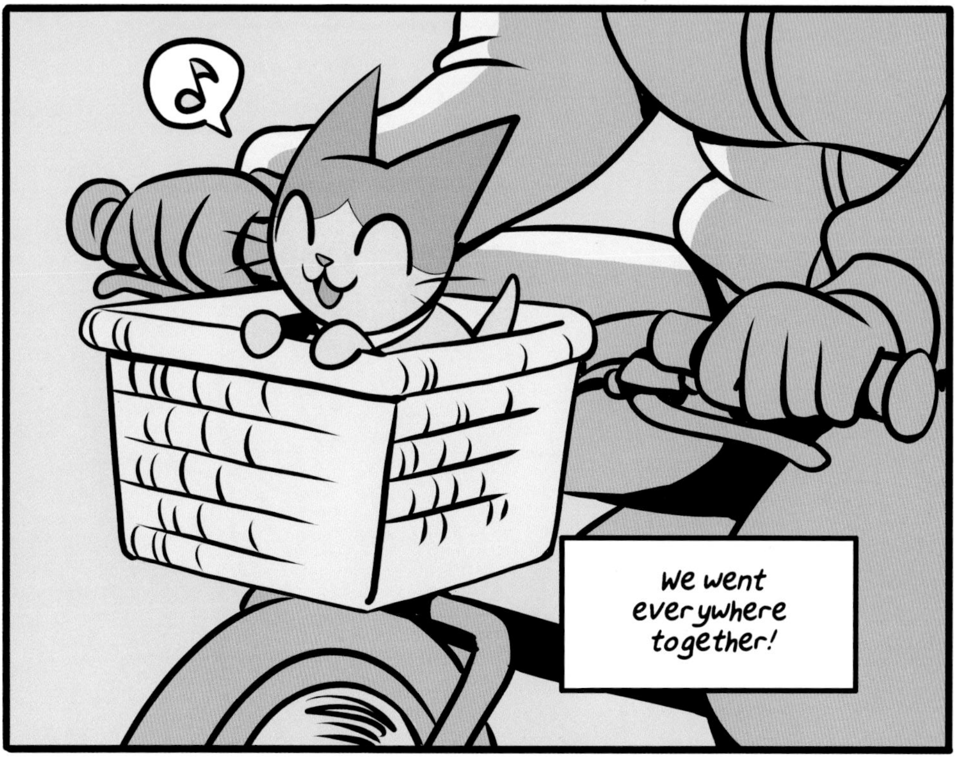
We went everywhere together!

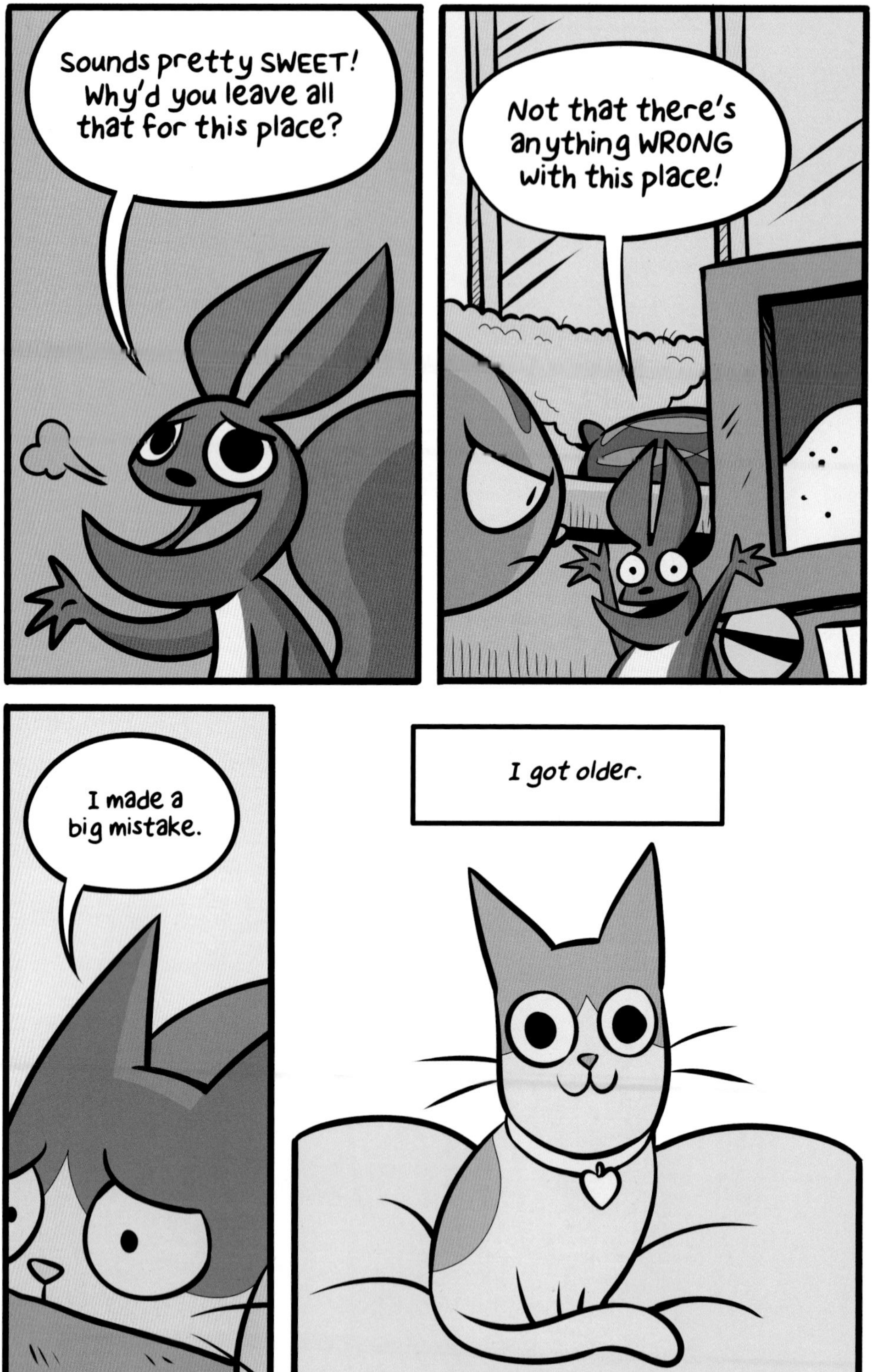
Sounds pretty SWEET! Why'd you leave all that for this place?
Not that there's anything WRONG with this place!
I made a big mistake.
I got older.

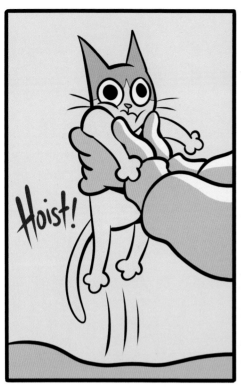

She said I was too big for the bed.

I think your cat got out again.

MEW~

SIGH!

SKRITCH SKRITCH SKRITCH

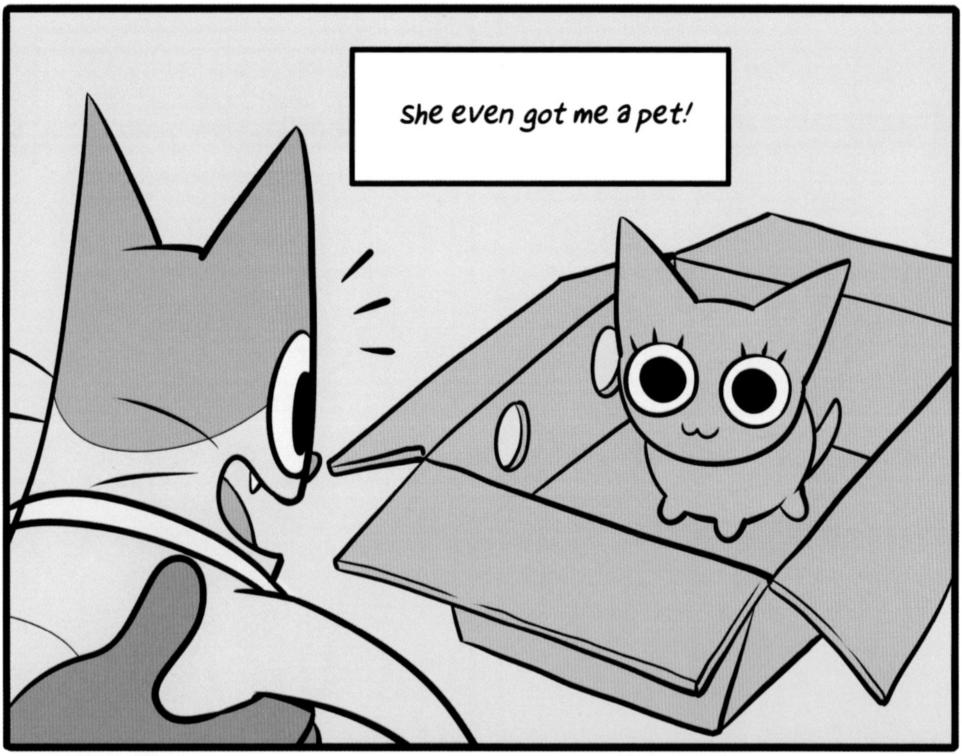
she even got me a pet!

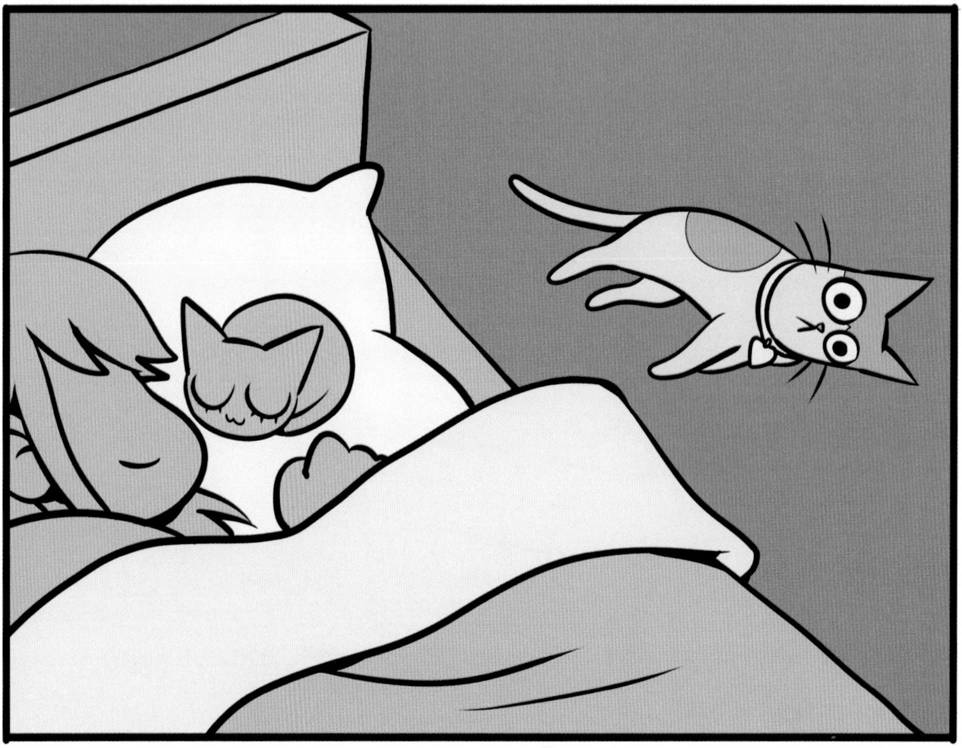

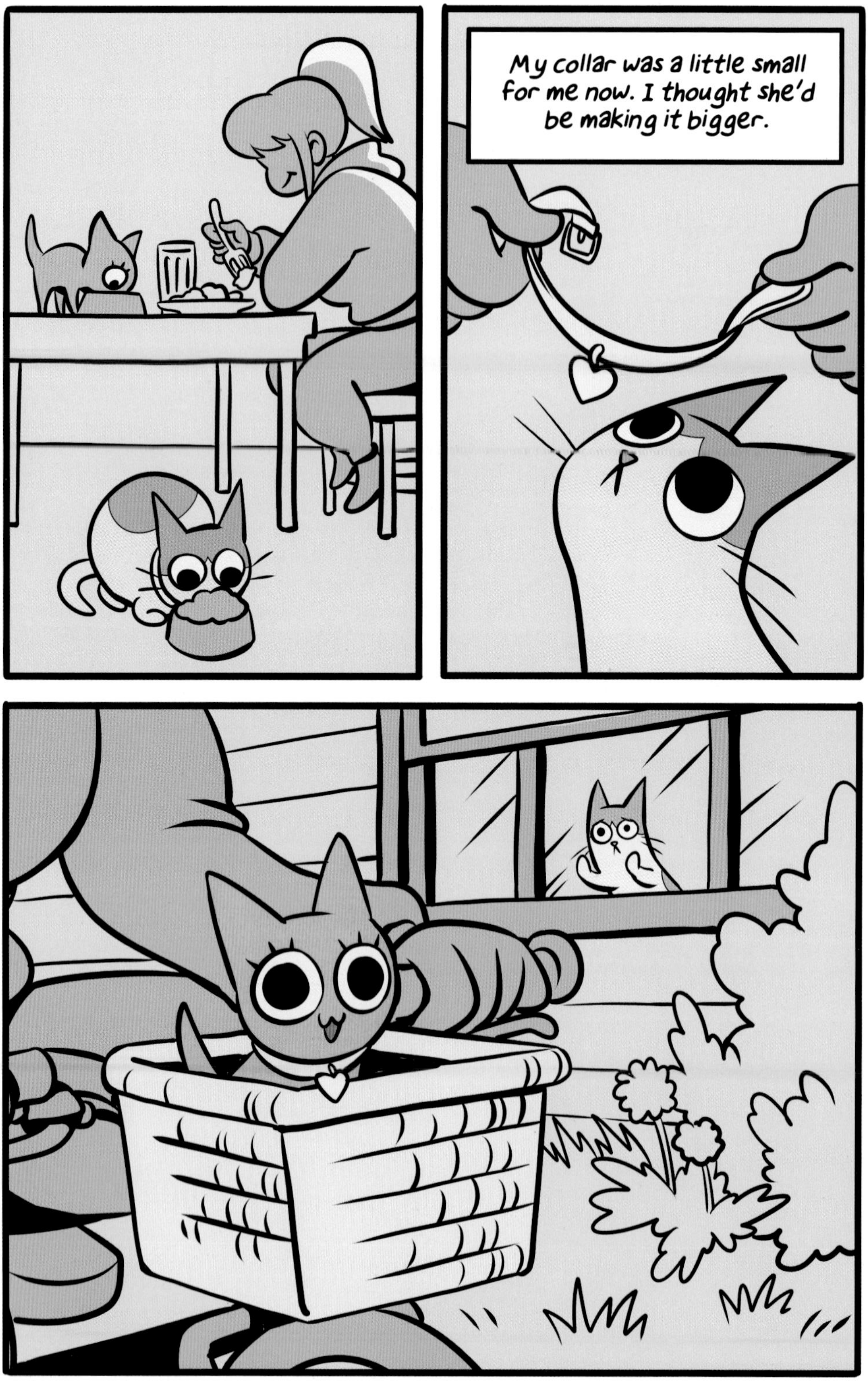
My collar was a little small for me now. I thought she'd be making it bigger.

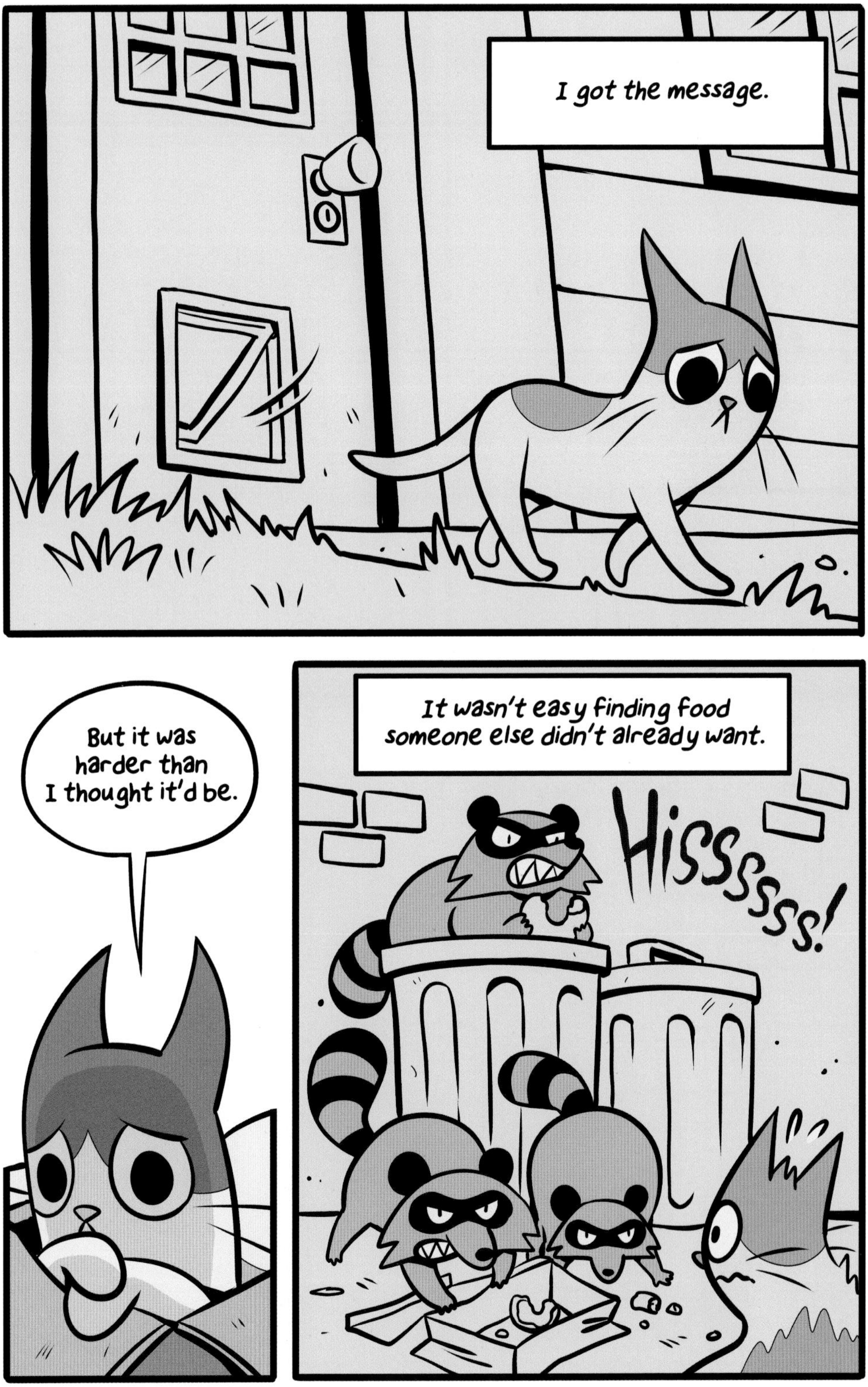
I got the message.
But it was harder than I thought it'd be.
It wasn't easy finding food someone else didn't already want.
HISSSSSS!

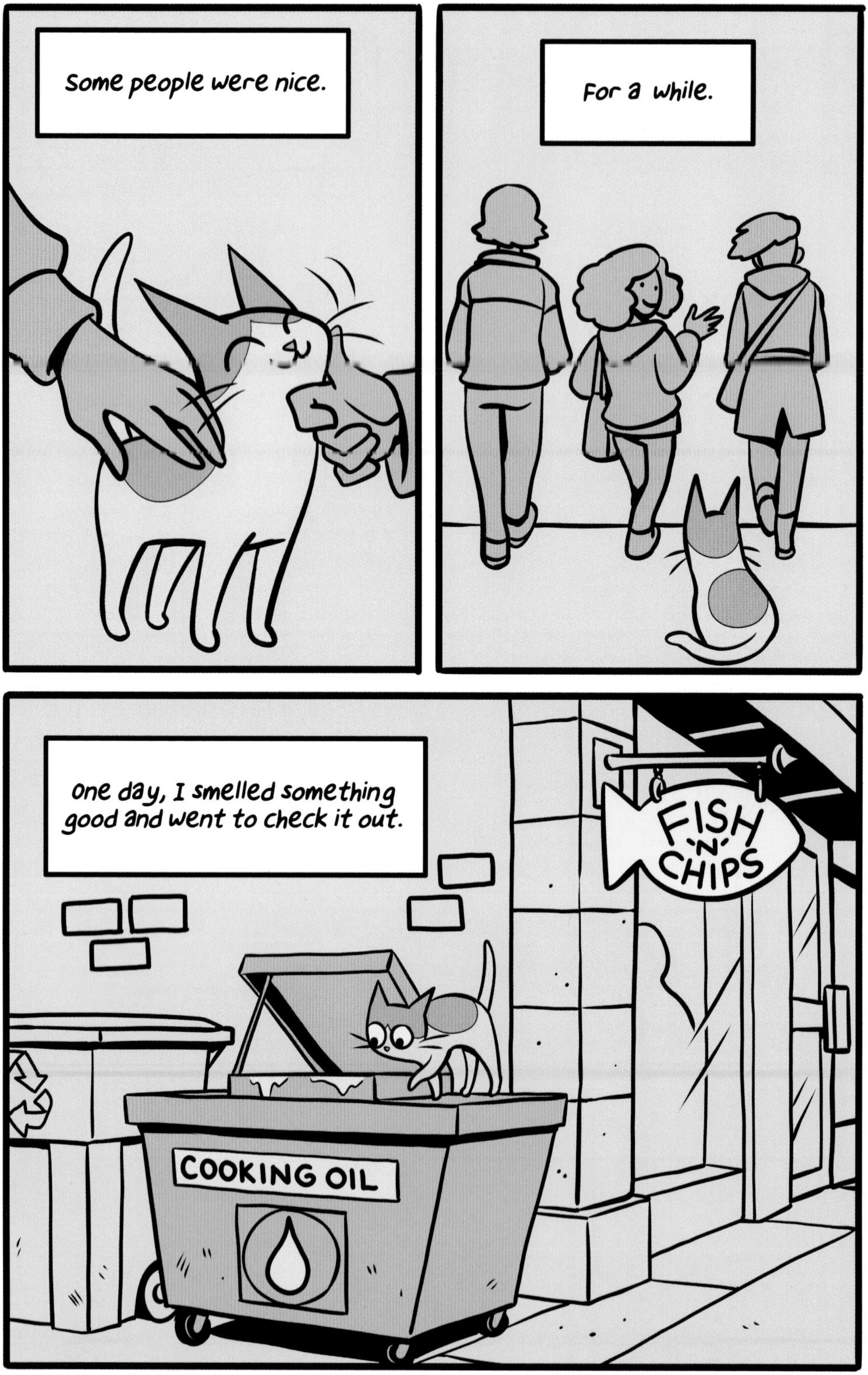
Some people were nice.
For a while.
One day, I smelled something good and went to check it out.
FISH -N- CHIPS
COOKING OIL

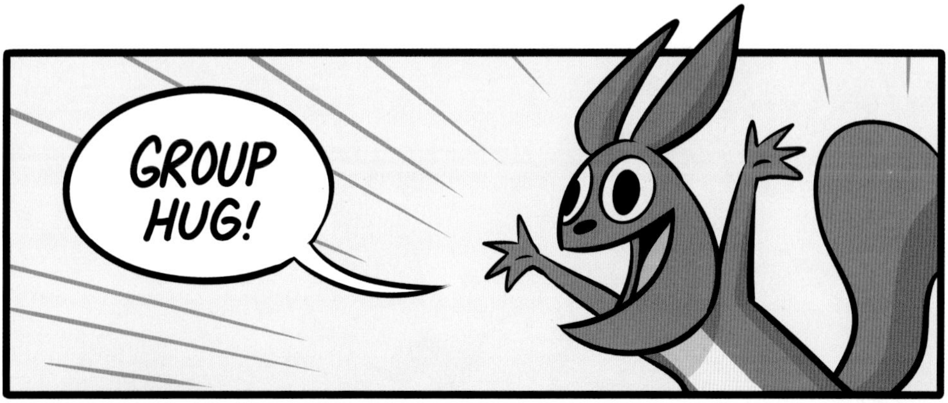
GROUP HUG!

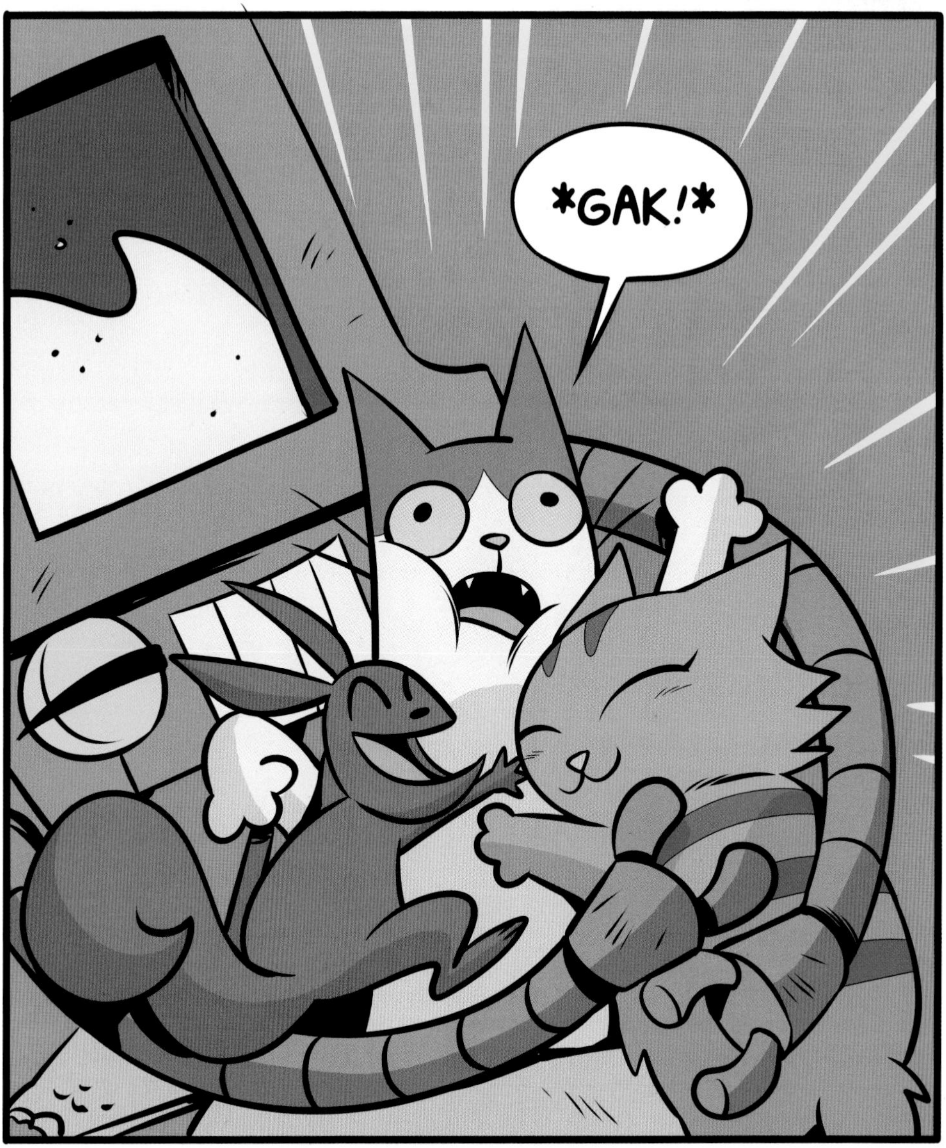
GAK!

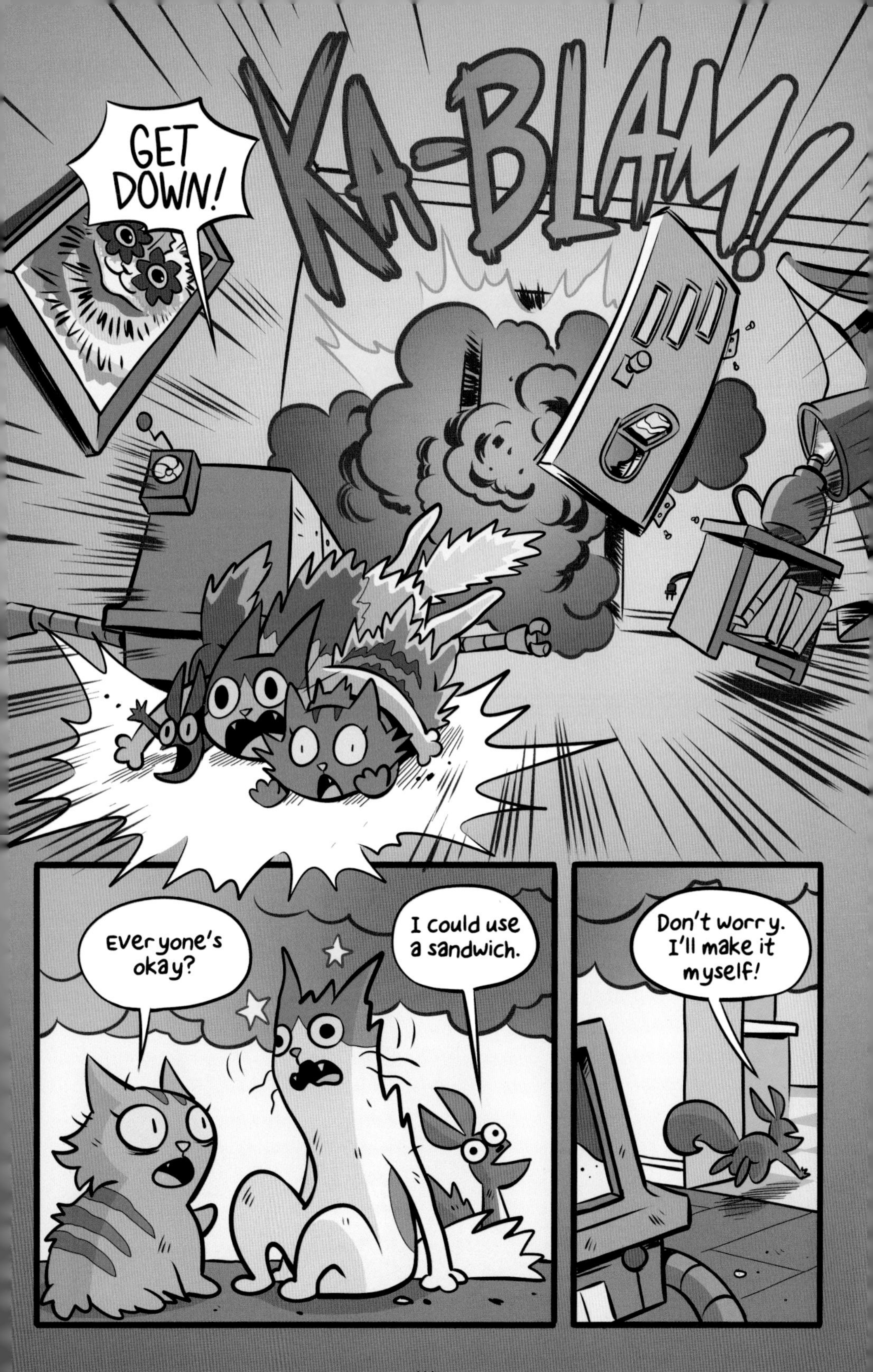

GET DOWN!
KA-BLAM!!
Everyone's okay?
I could use a sandwich.
Don't worry. I'll make it myself!

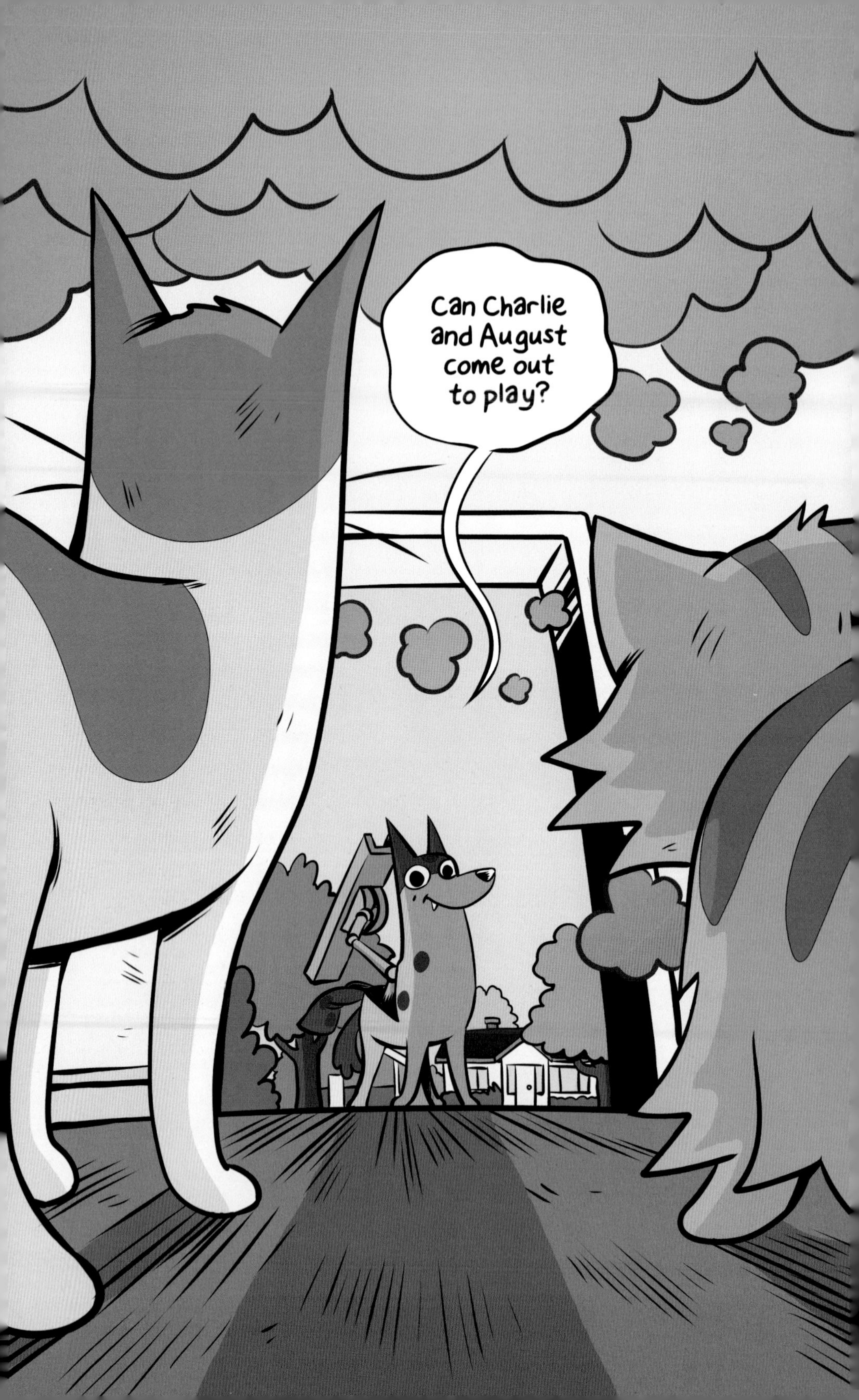
Can Charlie and August come out to play?

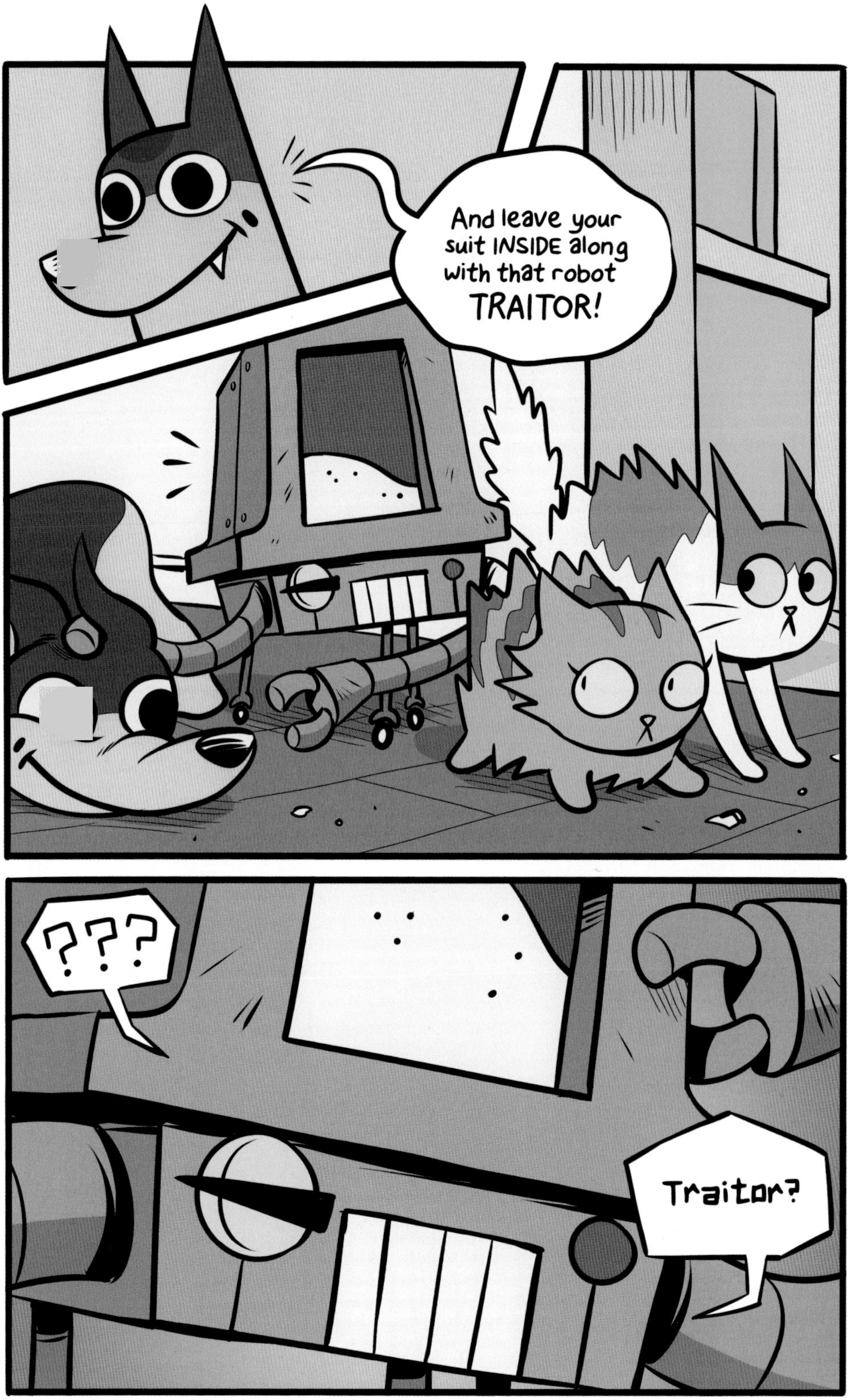
And leave your suit INSIDE along with that robot TRAITOR!
???
Traitor?

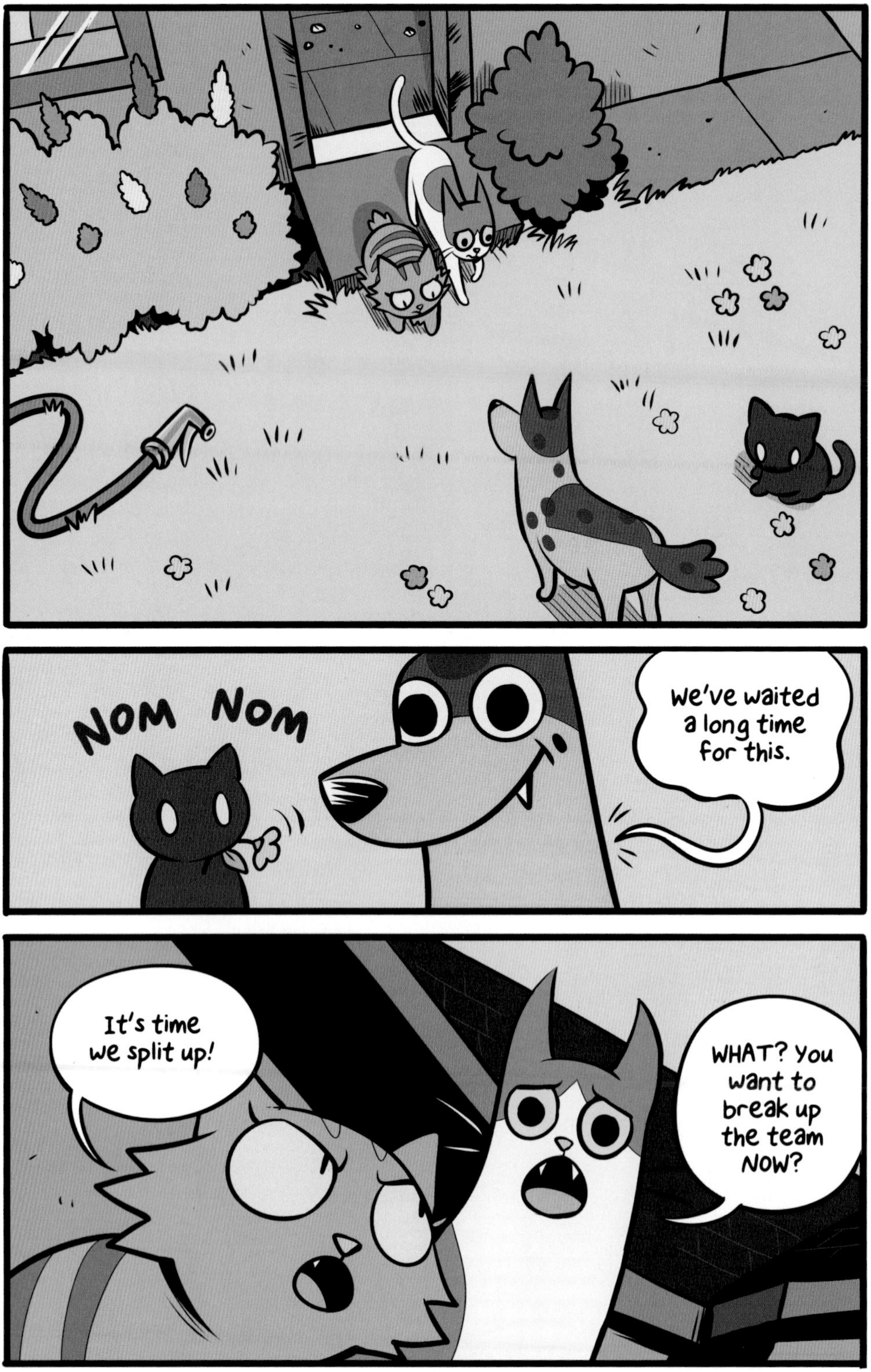
NOM NOM
We've waited a long time for this.
It's time we split up!
WHAT? You want to break up the team NOW?

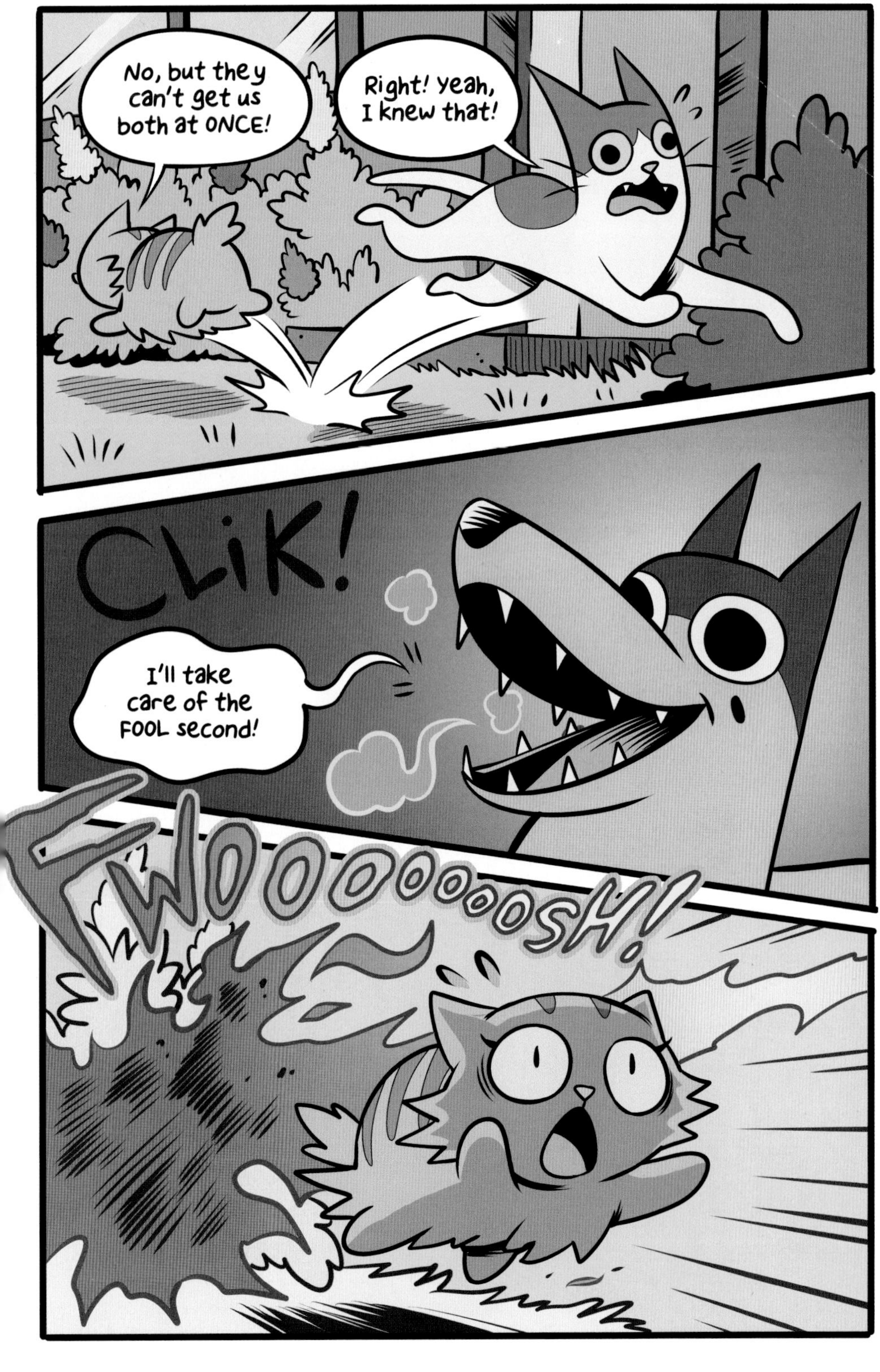
No, but they can't get us both at ONCE!
Right! yeah, I knew that!
CLIK!
I'll take care of the FOOL second!
FWOOOOOOOSH!

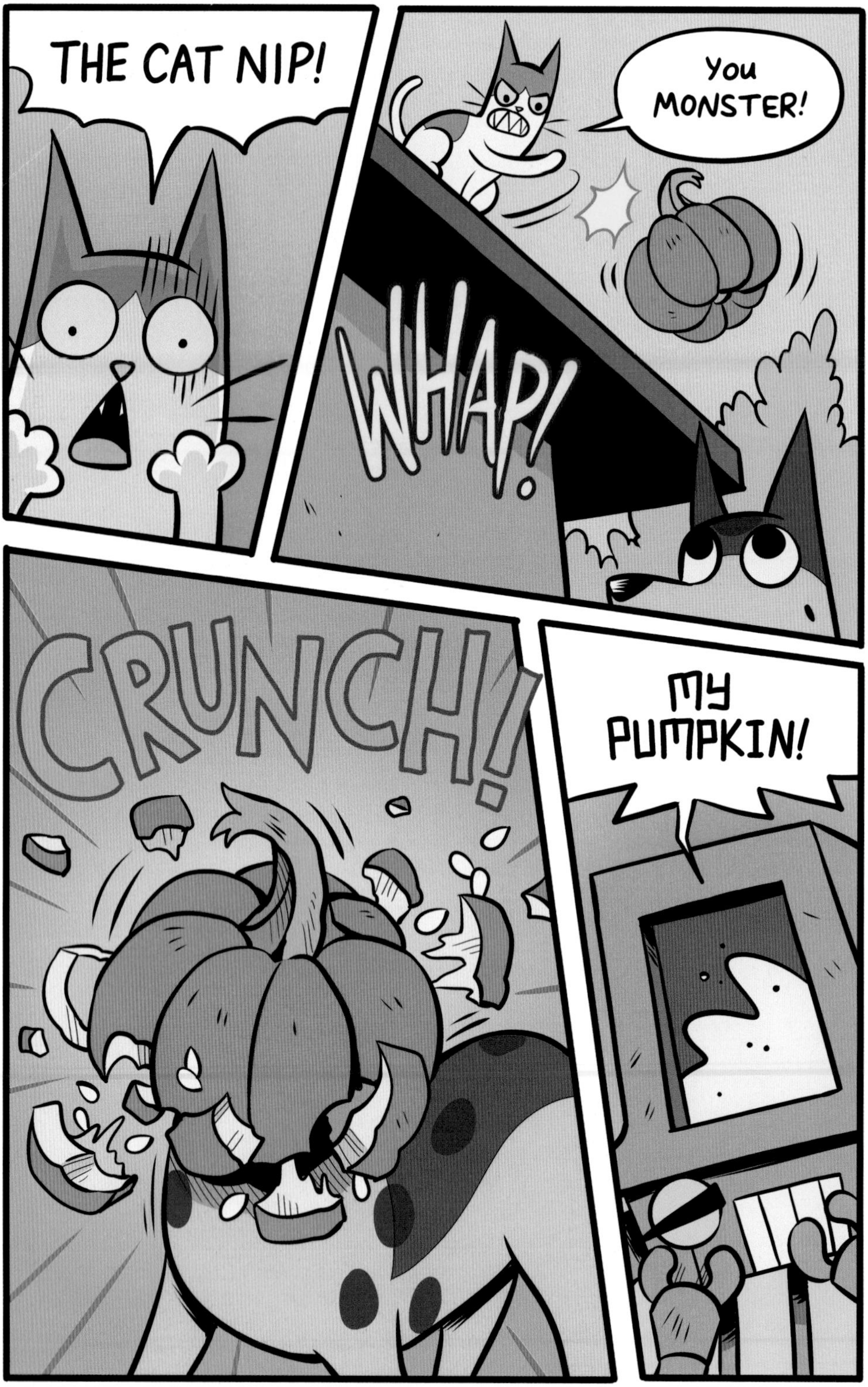
THE CAT NIP!
You MONSTER!
WHAP!
CRUNCH!
MY PUMPKIN!

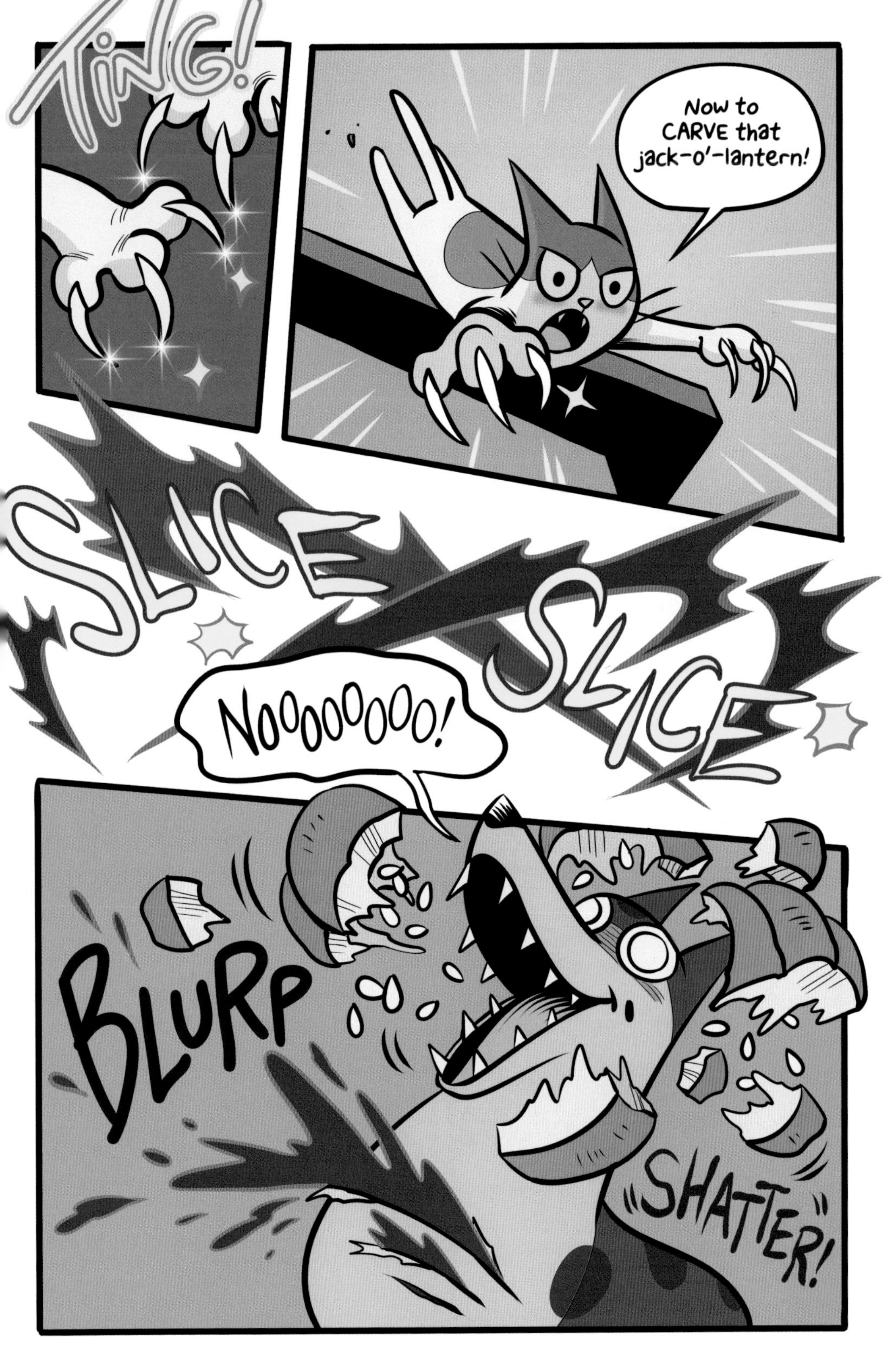
TING!
Now to CARVE that jack-o'-lantern!
SLICE
SLICE
NOOOOOOOO!
BLURP
SHATTER!

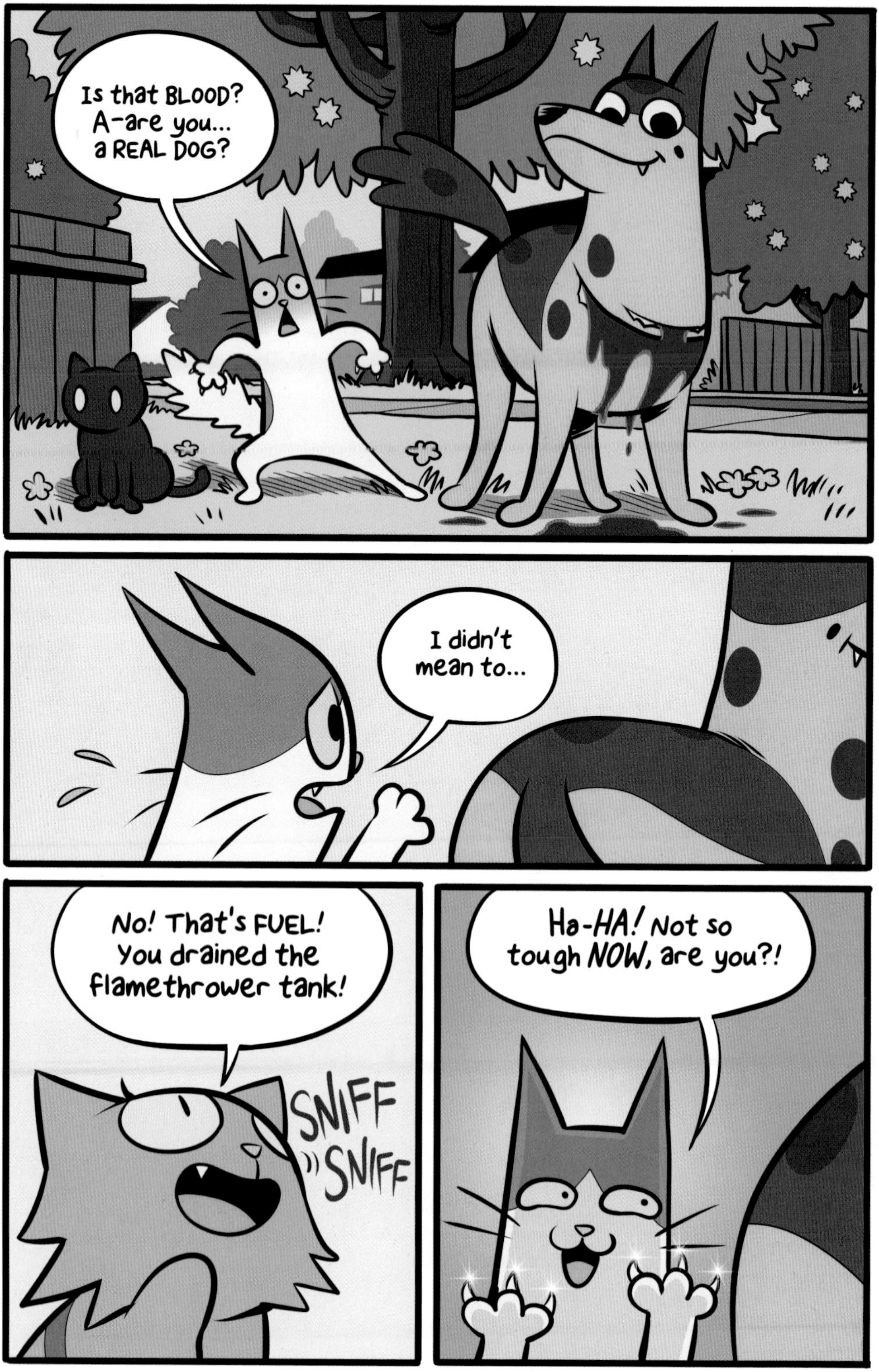
Is that BLOOD? A-are you... a REAL DOG?
I didn't mean to...
No! That's FUEL! You drained the flamethrower tank!
SNIFF
SNIFF
Ha-HA! Not so tough NOW, are you?!

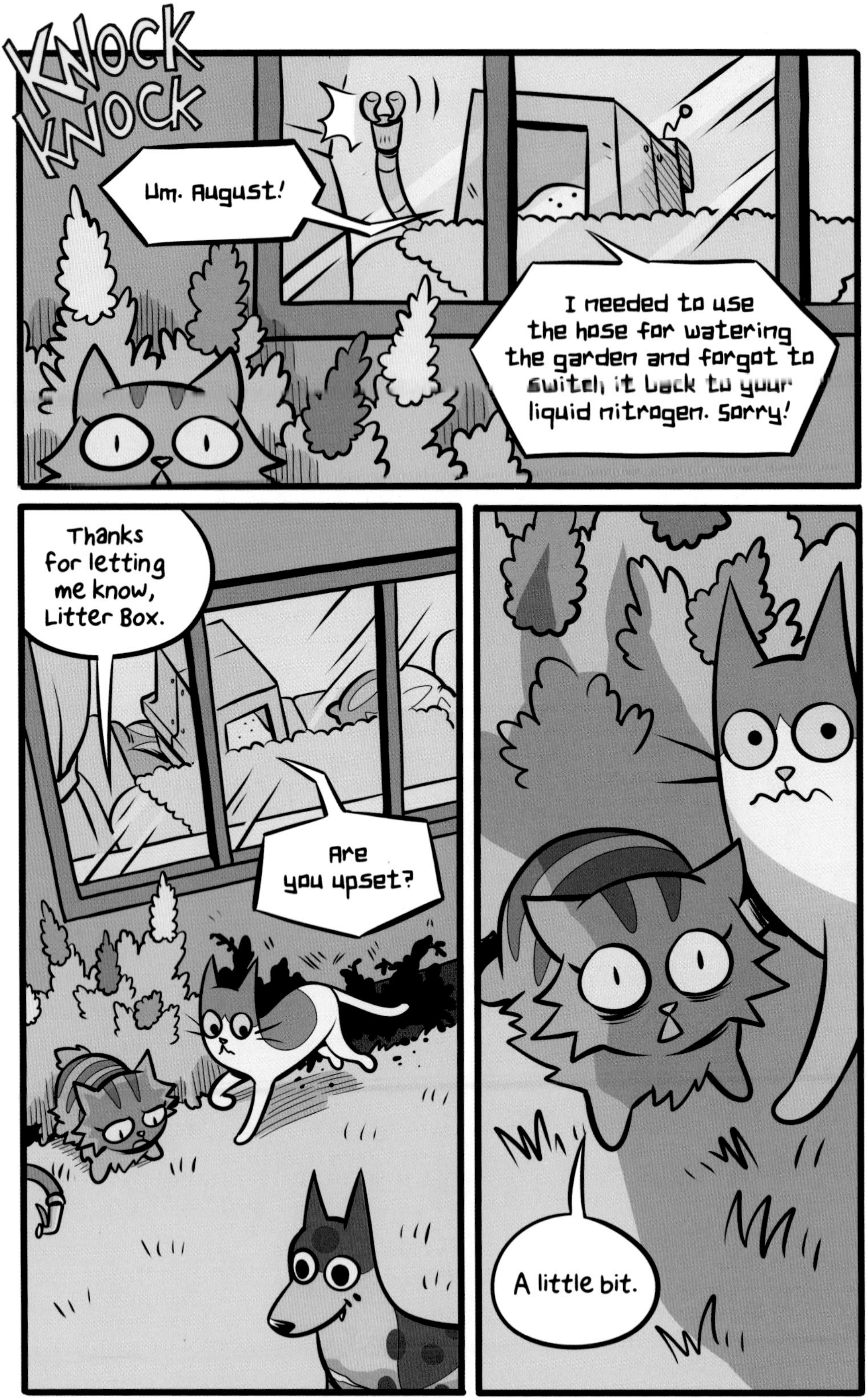
KNOCK KNOCK
Um. August!
I needed to use the hose for watering the garden and forgot to switch it back to your liquid nitrogen. Sorry!
Thanks for letting me know, Litter Box.
Are you upset?
A little bit.

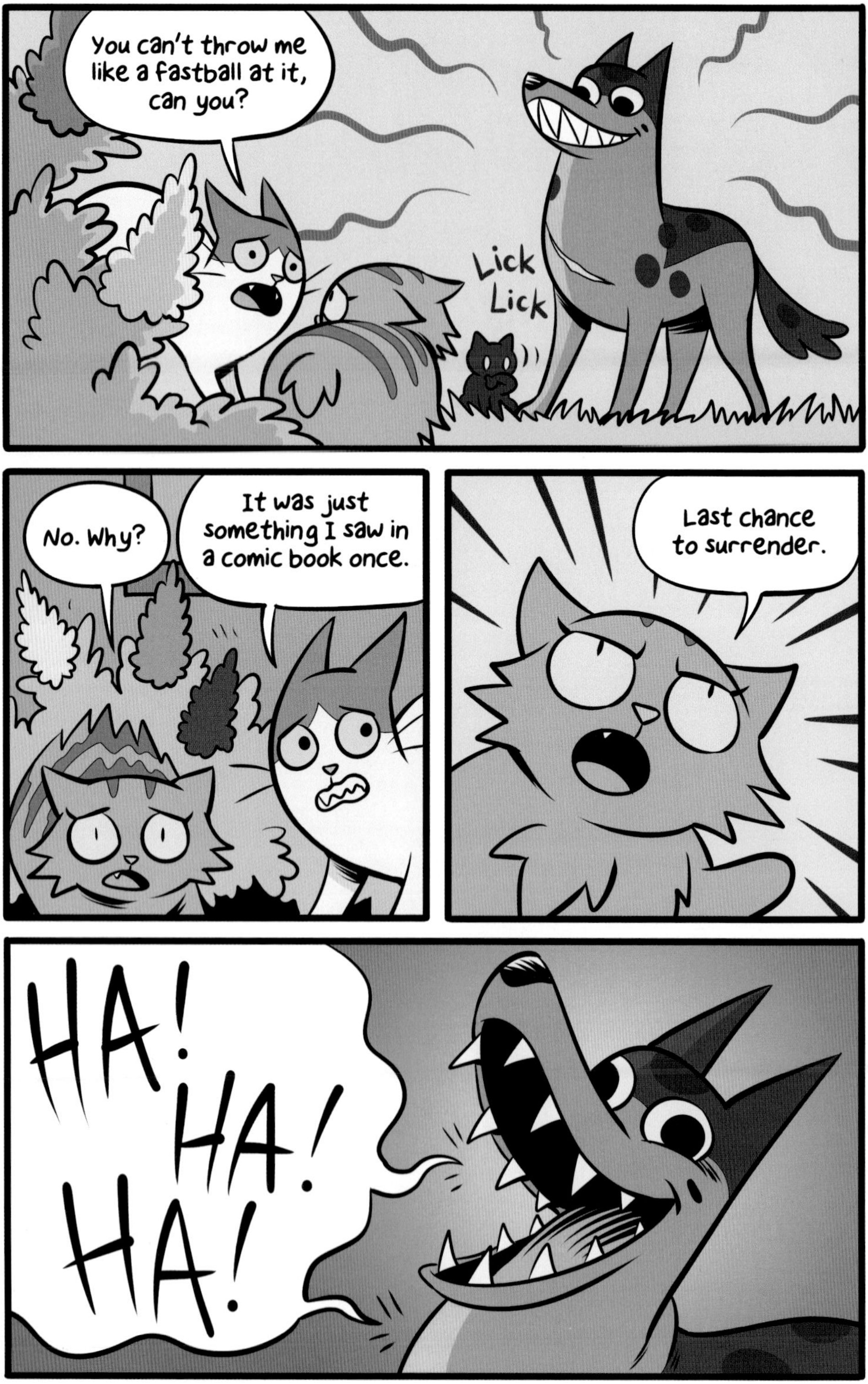
You can't throw me like a fastball at it, can you?
Lick Lick
No. Why?
It was just something I saw in a comic book once.
Last chance to surrender.
HA! HA! HA!

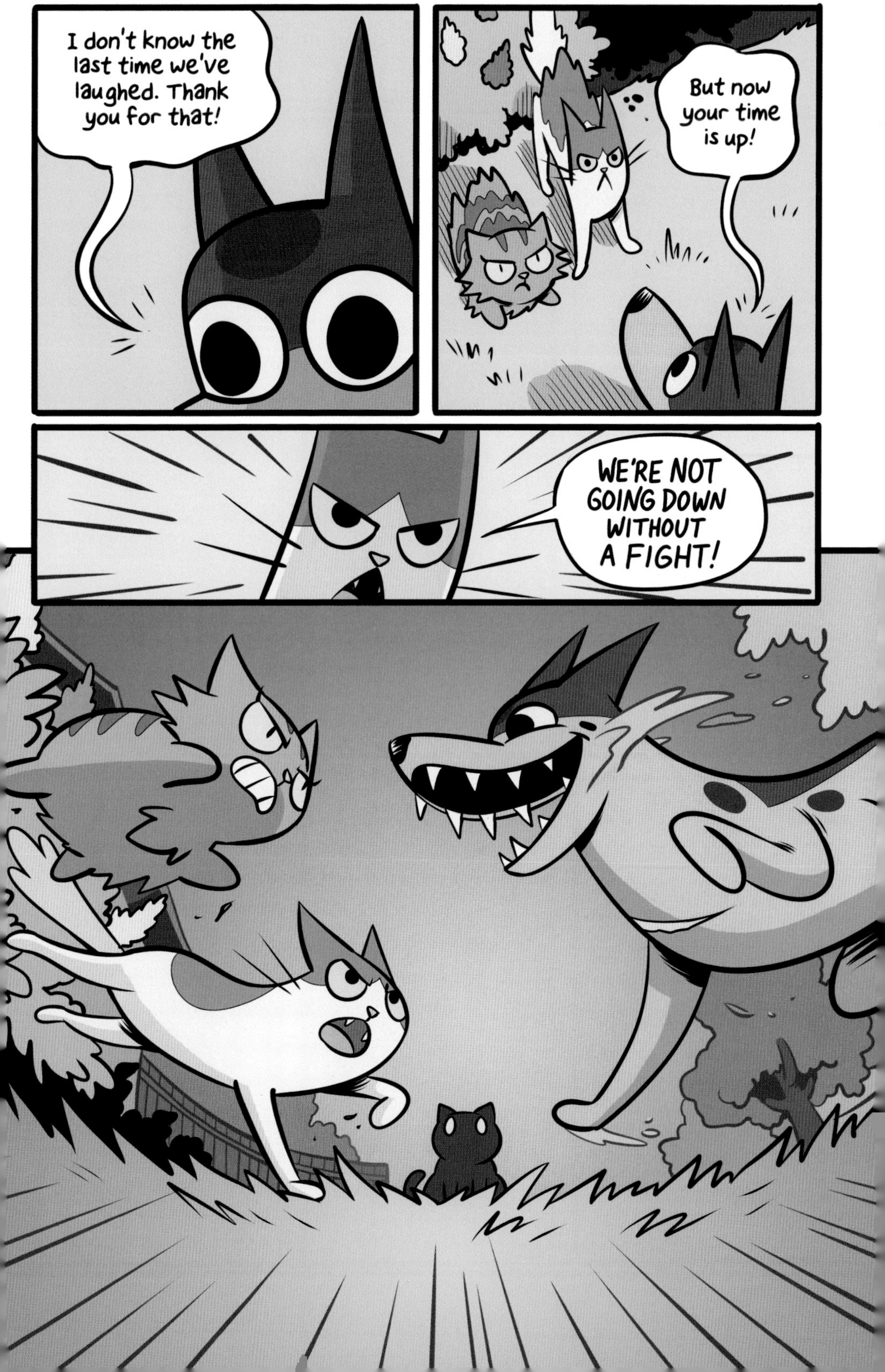

I don't know the last time we've laughed. Thank you for that!
But now your time is up!
WE'RE NOT GOING DOWN WITHOUT A FIGHT!

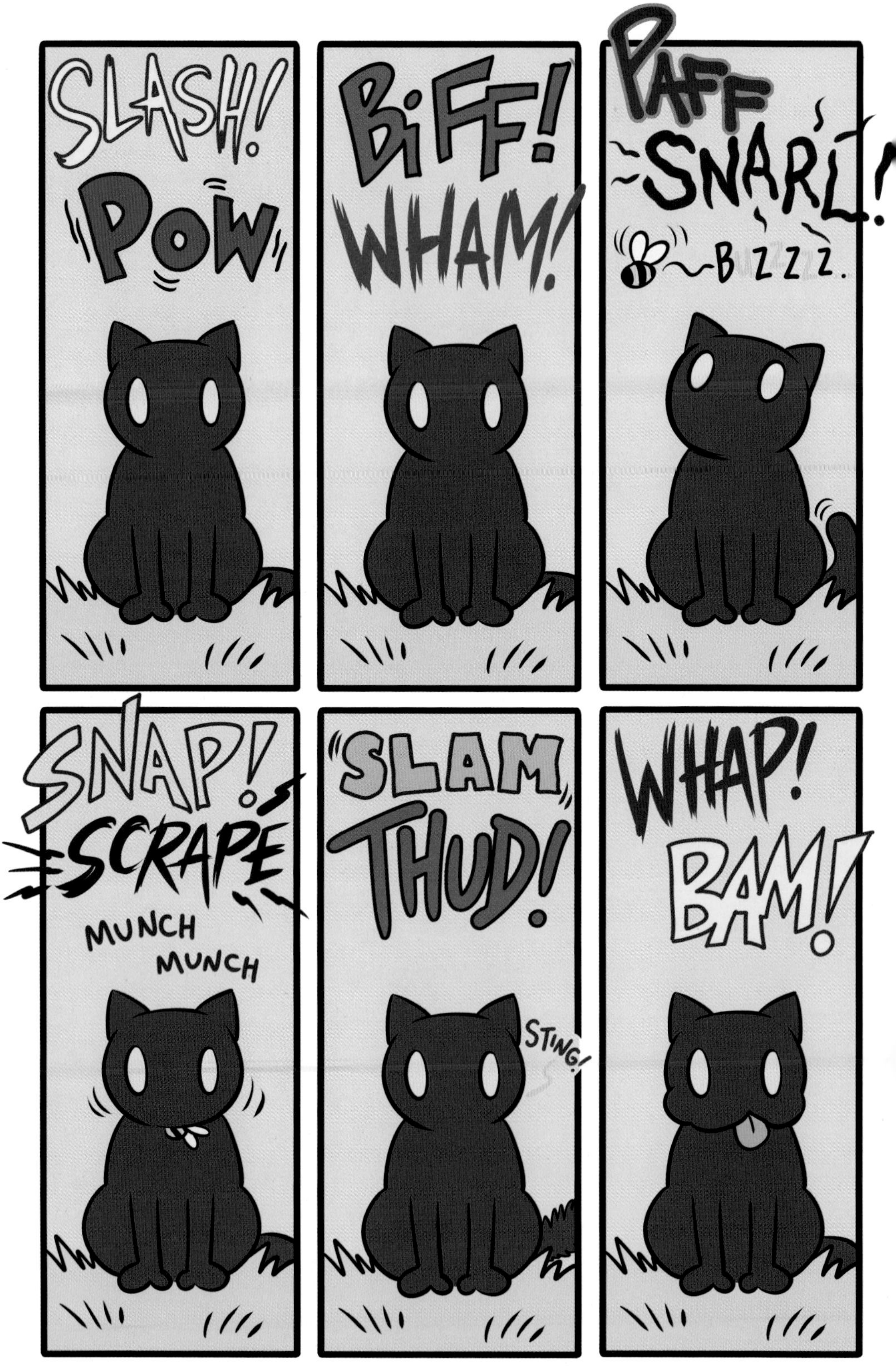
SLASH!
POW
BIFF!
WHAM!
PAFF
SNARL!
BZZZZ.
SNAP!
SCRAPE
MUNCH
MUNCH
SLAM
THUD!
STING!
WHAP!
BAM!

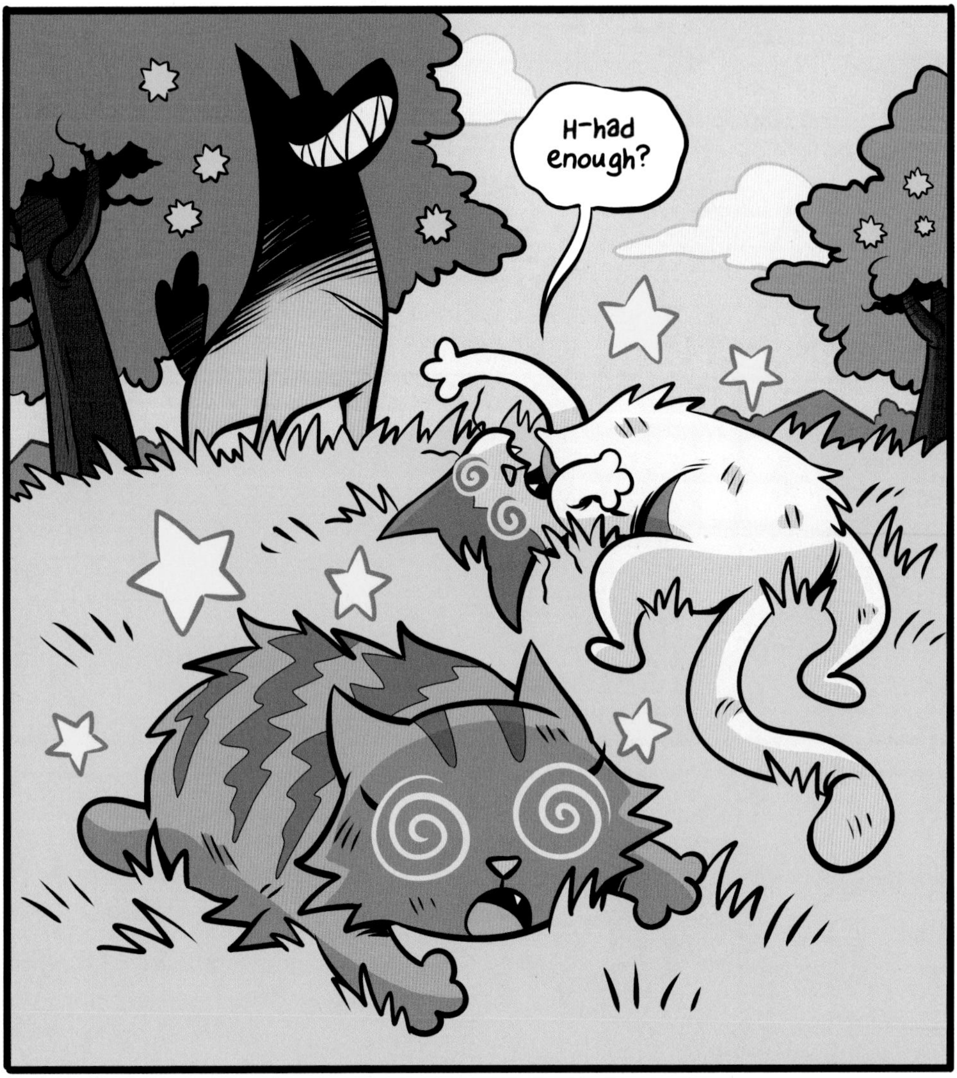
H-had enough?

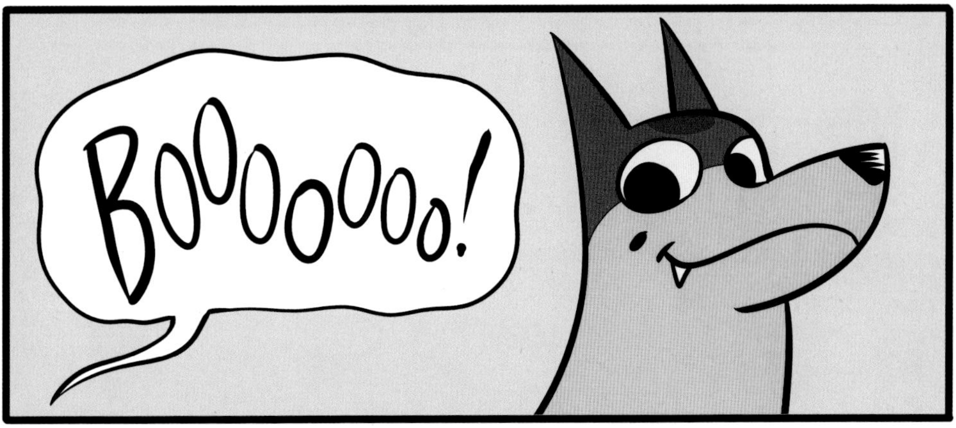
BOOOOOOO!

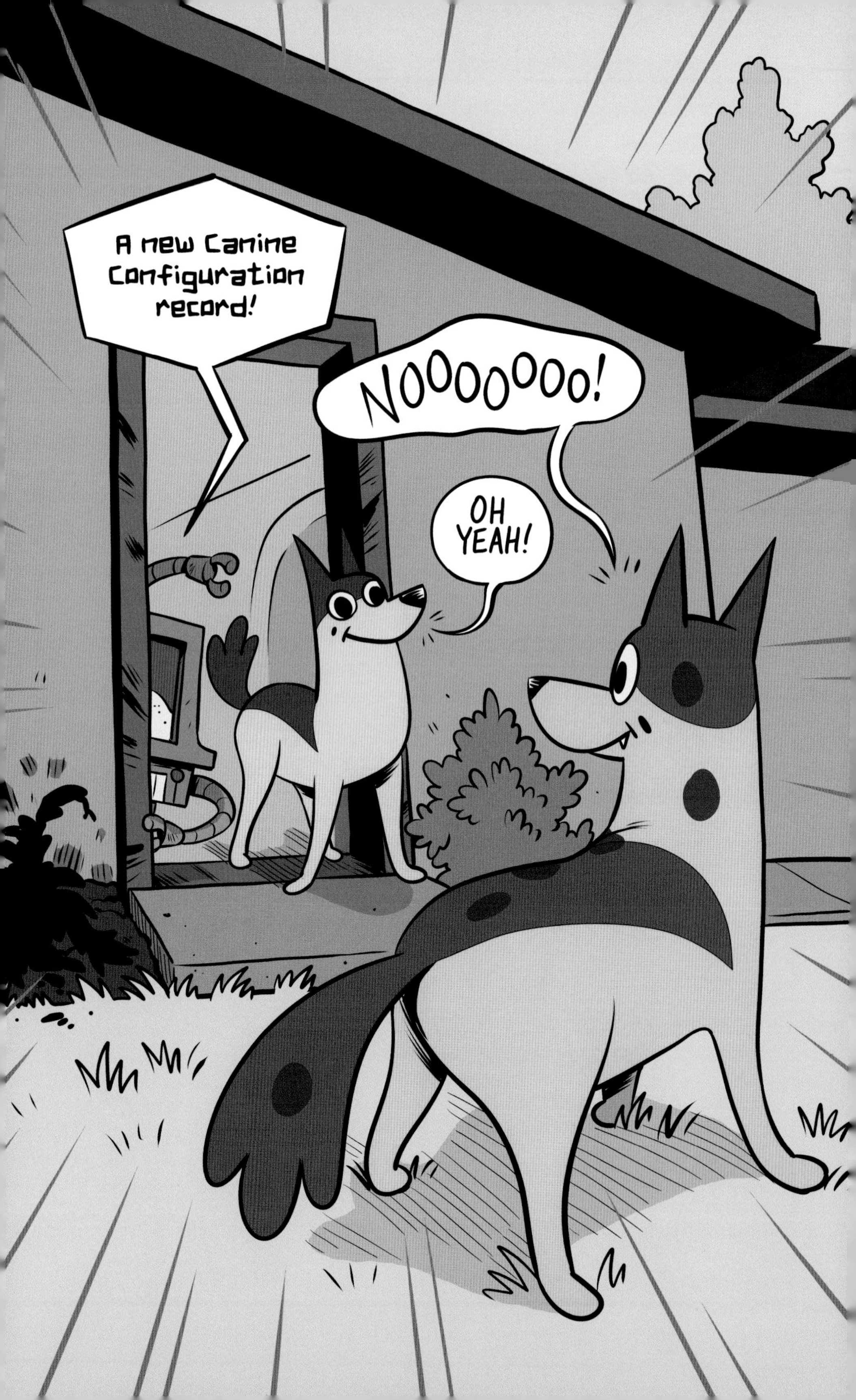
A new Canine Configuration record!
NOOOOOOO!
OH YEAH!

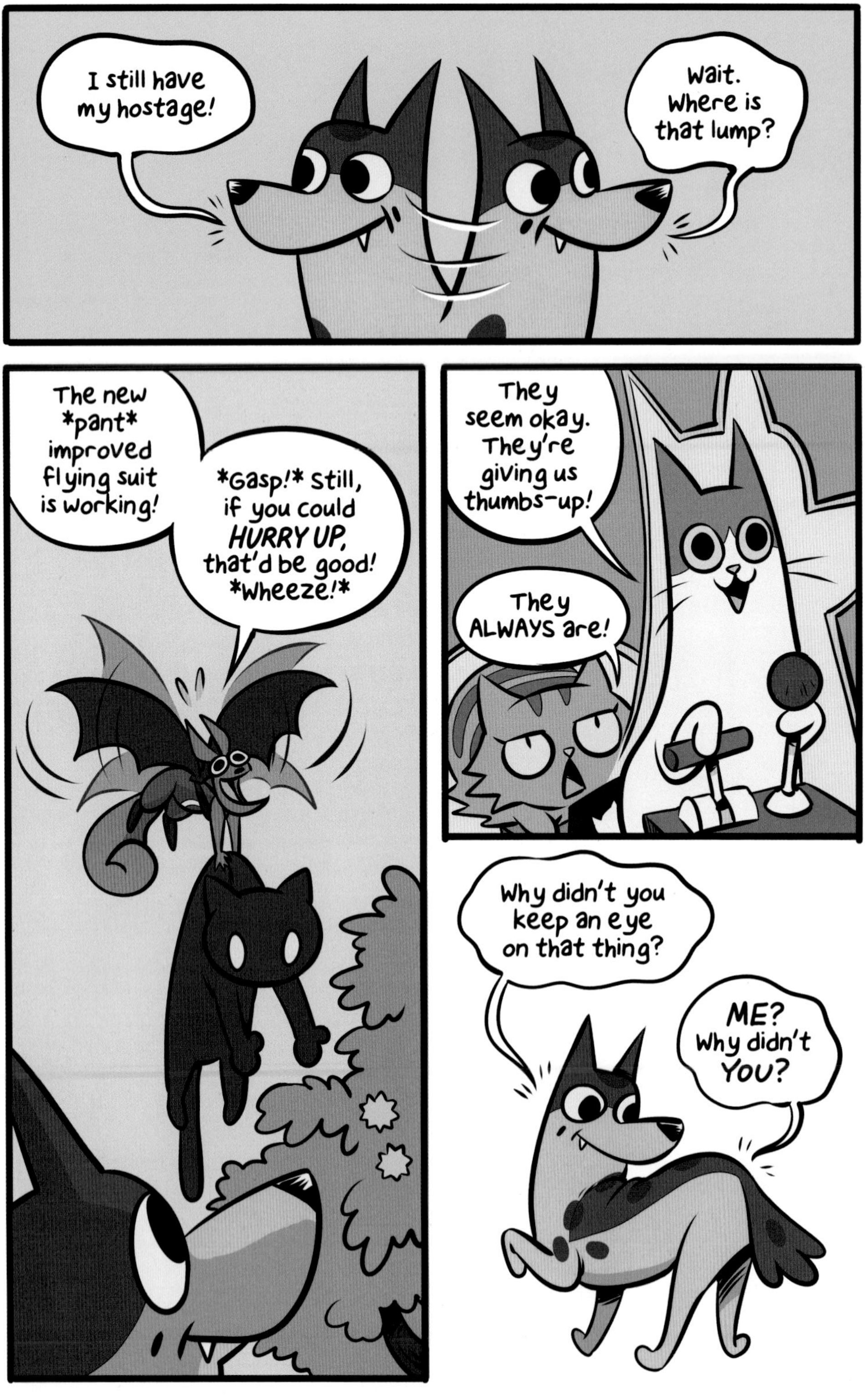
I still have my hostage!
Wait. Where is that lump?
The new *pant* improved flying suit is working!
Gasp! Still, if you could HURRY UP, that'd be good! *Wheeze!*
They seem okay. They're giving us thumbs-up!
They ALWAYS are!
Why didn't you keep an eye on that thing?
ME? Why didn't YOU?

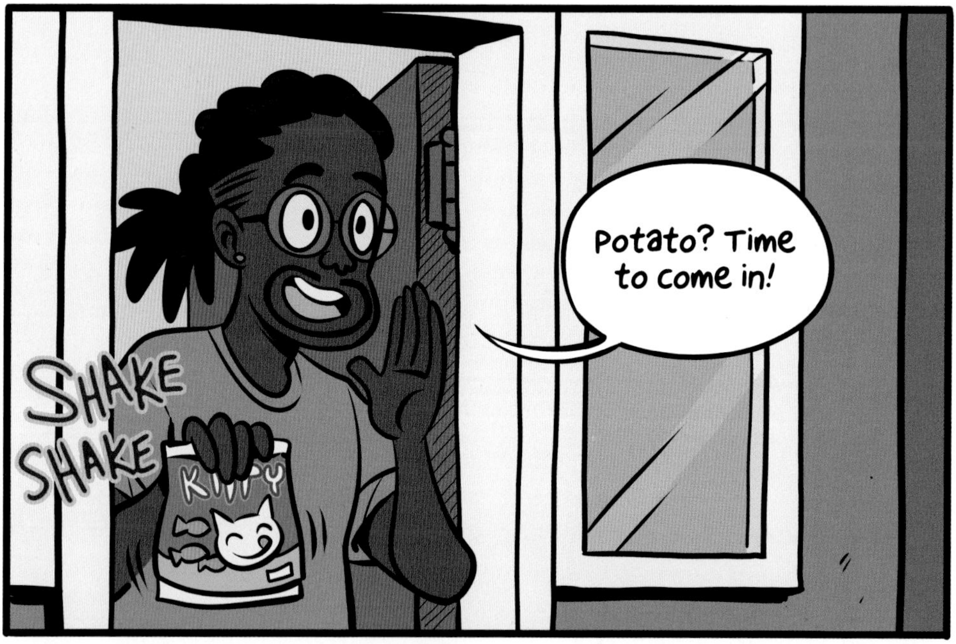
Potato? Time to come in!
SHAKE SHAKE

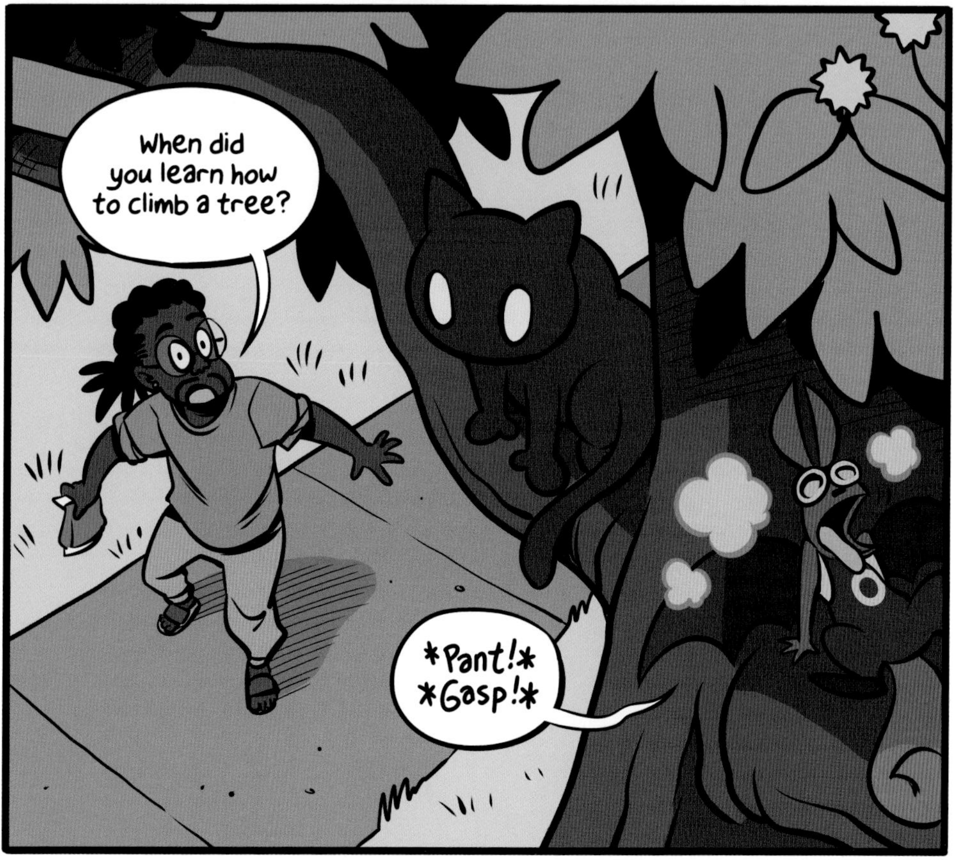
When did you learn how to climb a tree?
Pant!
Gasp!

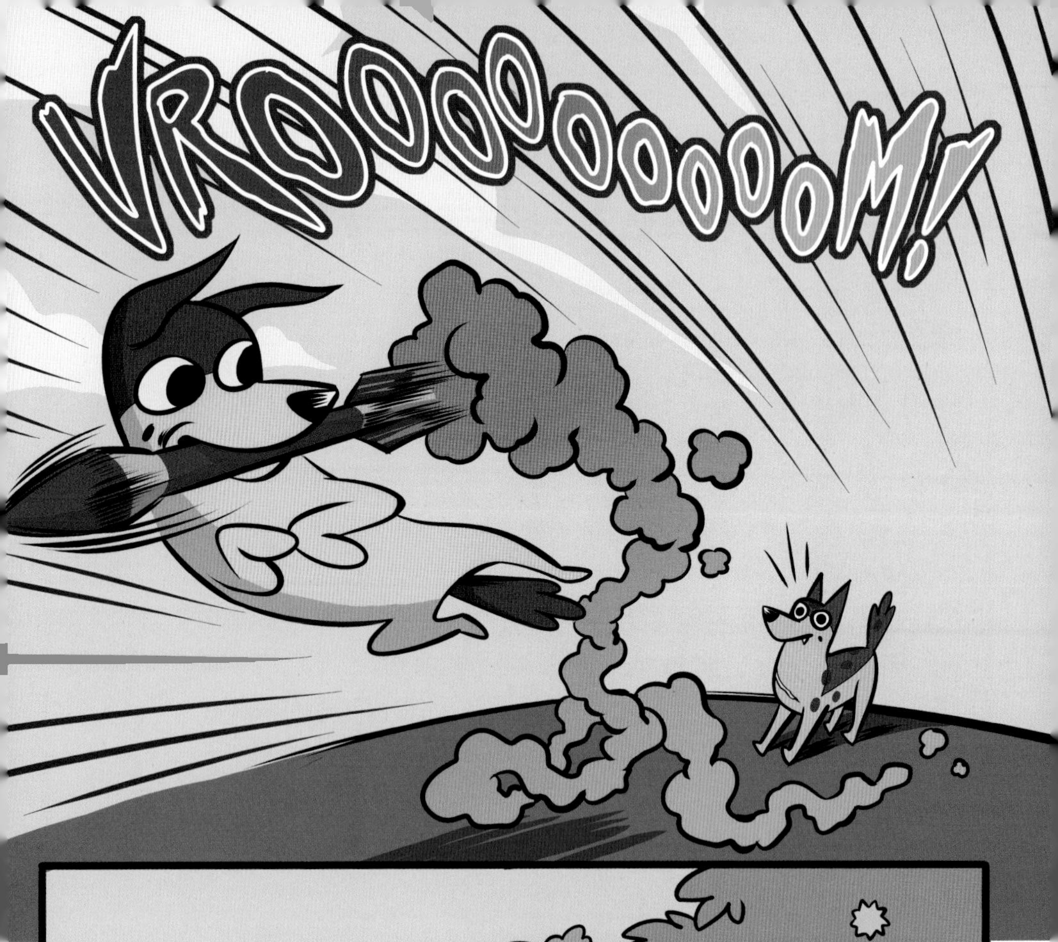
VROOOOOOOOOOM!

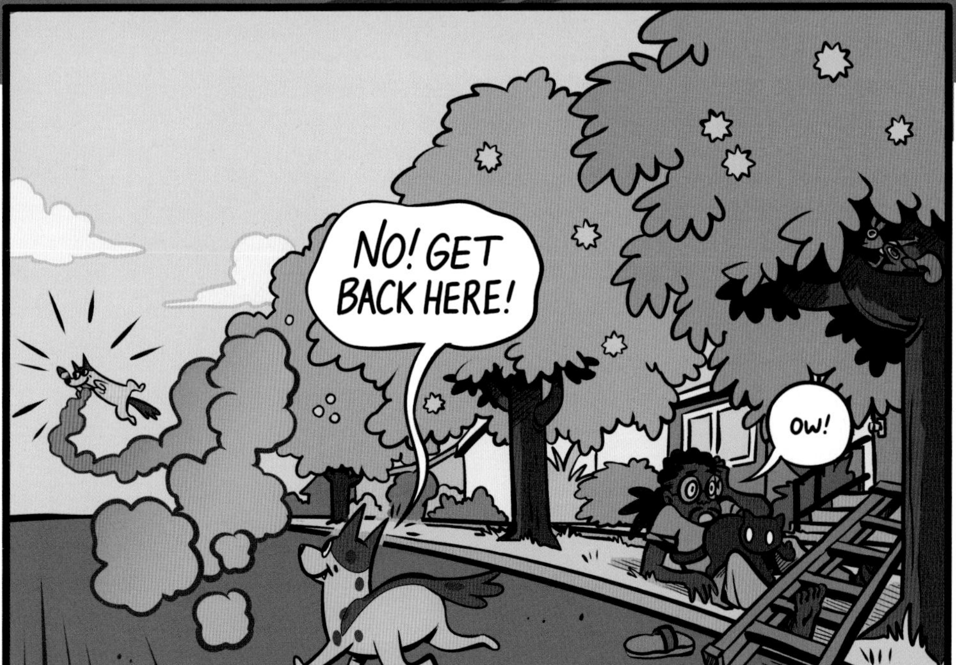
NO! GET BACK HERE!
OW!

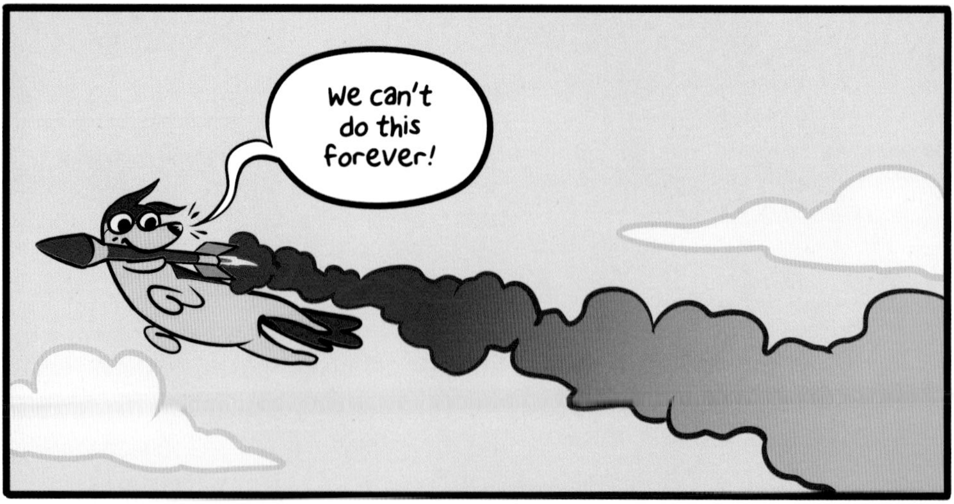
We can't do this forever!

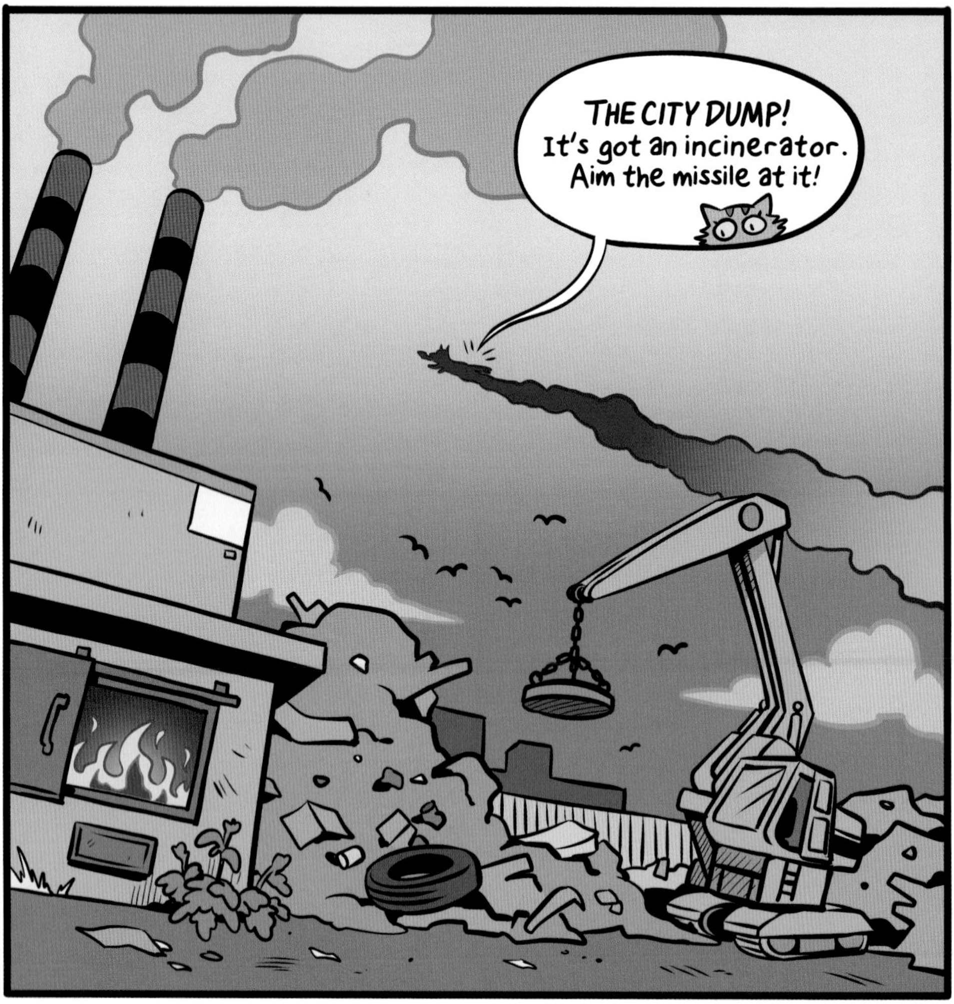
THE CITY DUMP! It's got an incinerator. Aim the missile at it!

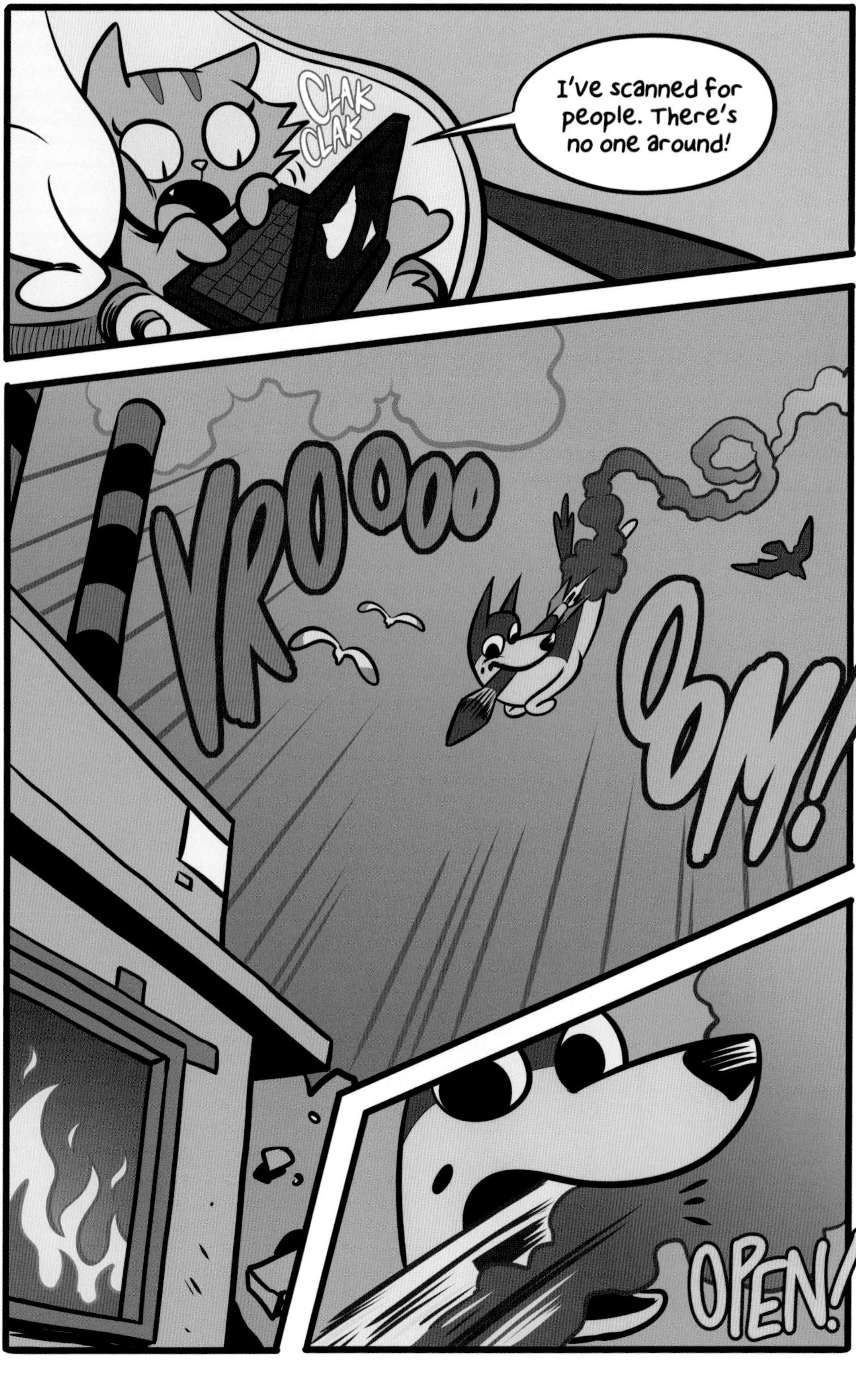
CLAK CLAK
I've scanned for people. There's no one around!
VROOOOO
OOM!
OPEN!

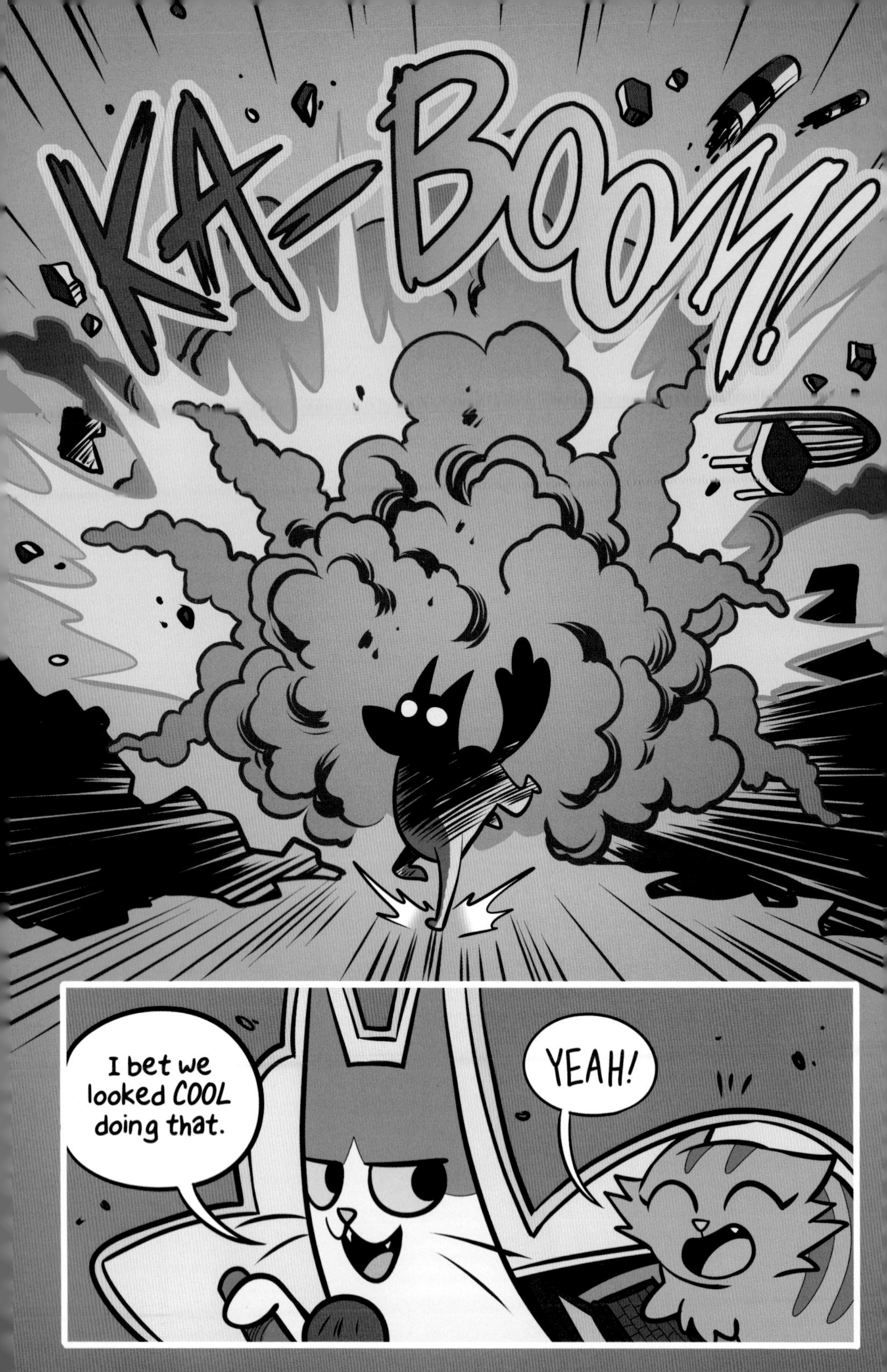
KA-BOOM!
I bet we looked COOL doing that.
YEAH!

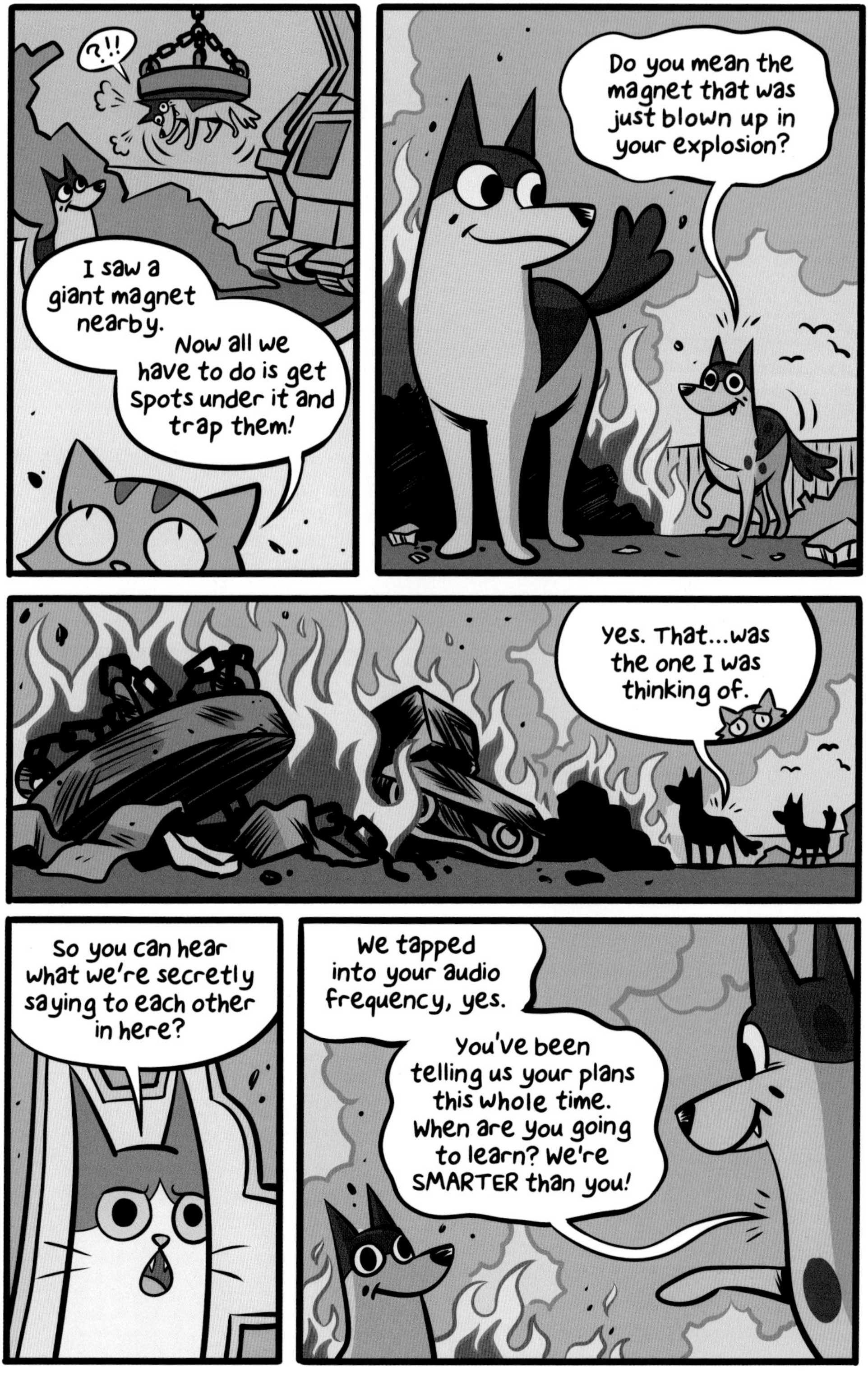
?!!
I saw a giant magnet nearby.
Now all we have to do is get Spots under it and trap them!
Do you mean the magnet that was just blown up in your explosion?
Yes. That...was the one I was thinking of.
So you can hear what we're secretly saying to each other in here?
We tapped into your audio frequency, yes.
You've been telling us your plans this whole time. When are you going to learn? We're SMARTER than you!

We'll see about that! FULL SPEED AIR JUMP!
KA-BOING
CRUUUUSH!
CRUUUUSH!

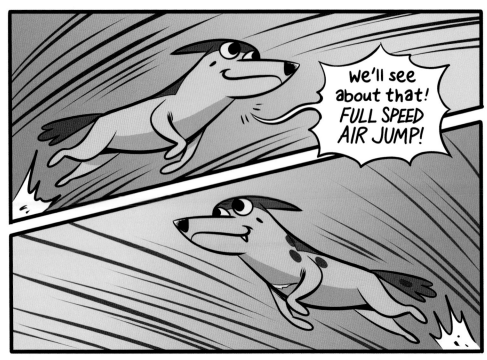

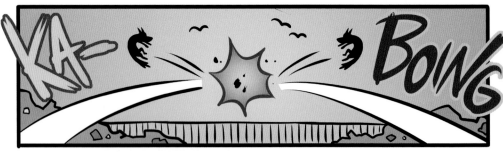

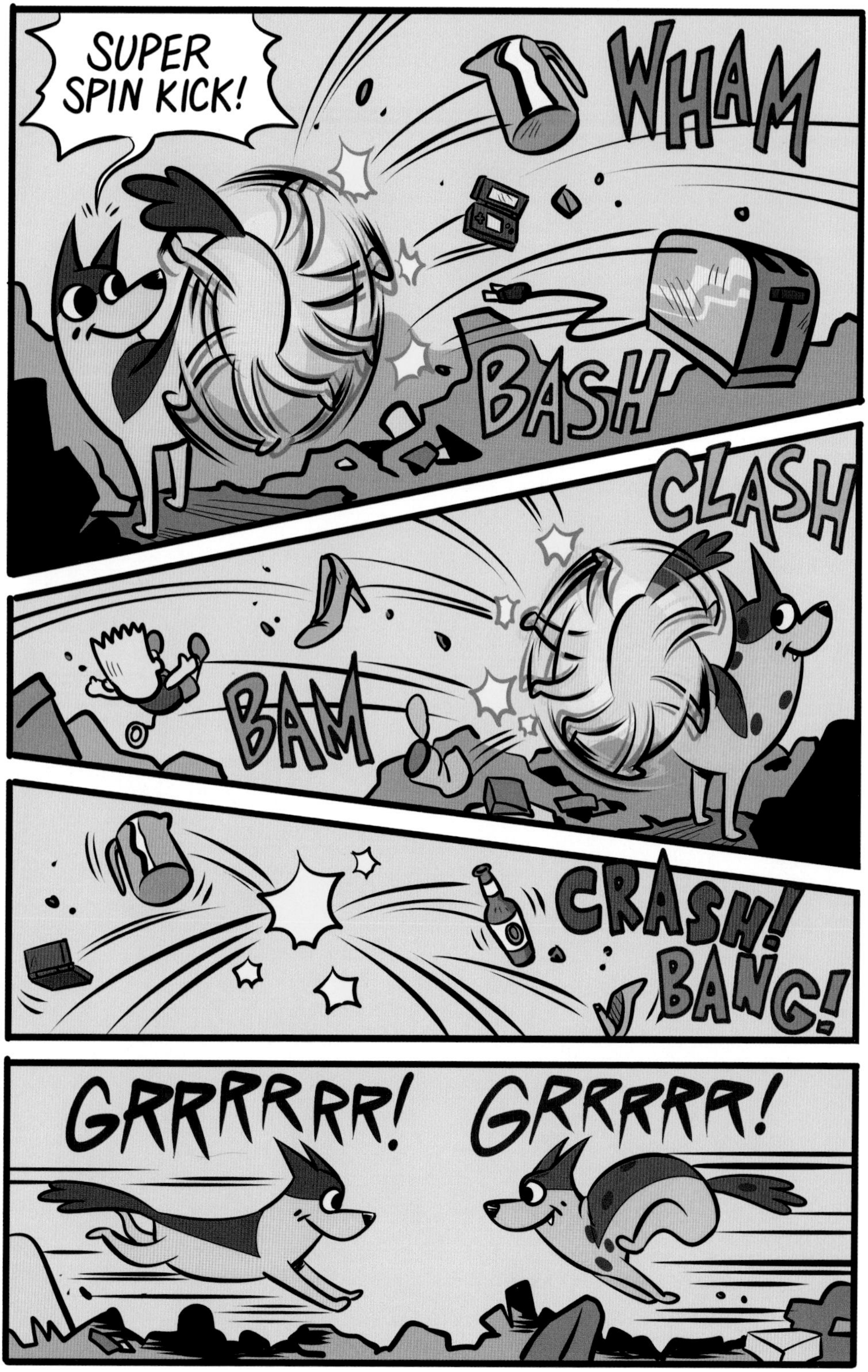
SUPER SPIN KICK!
WHAM
BASH
CLASH
BAM
CRASH!
BANG!
GRRRRRR!
GRRRRR!

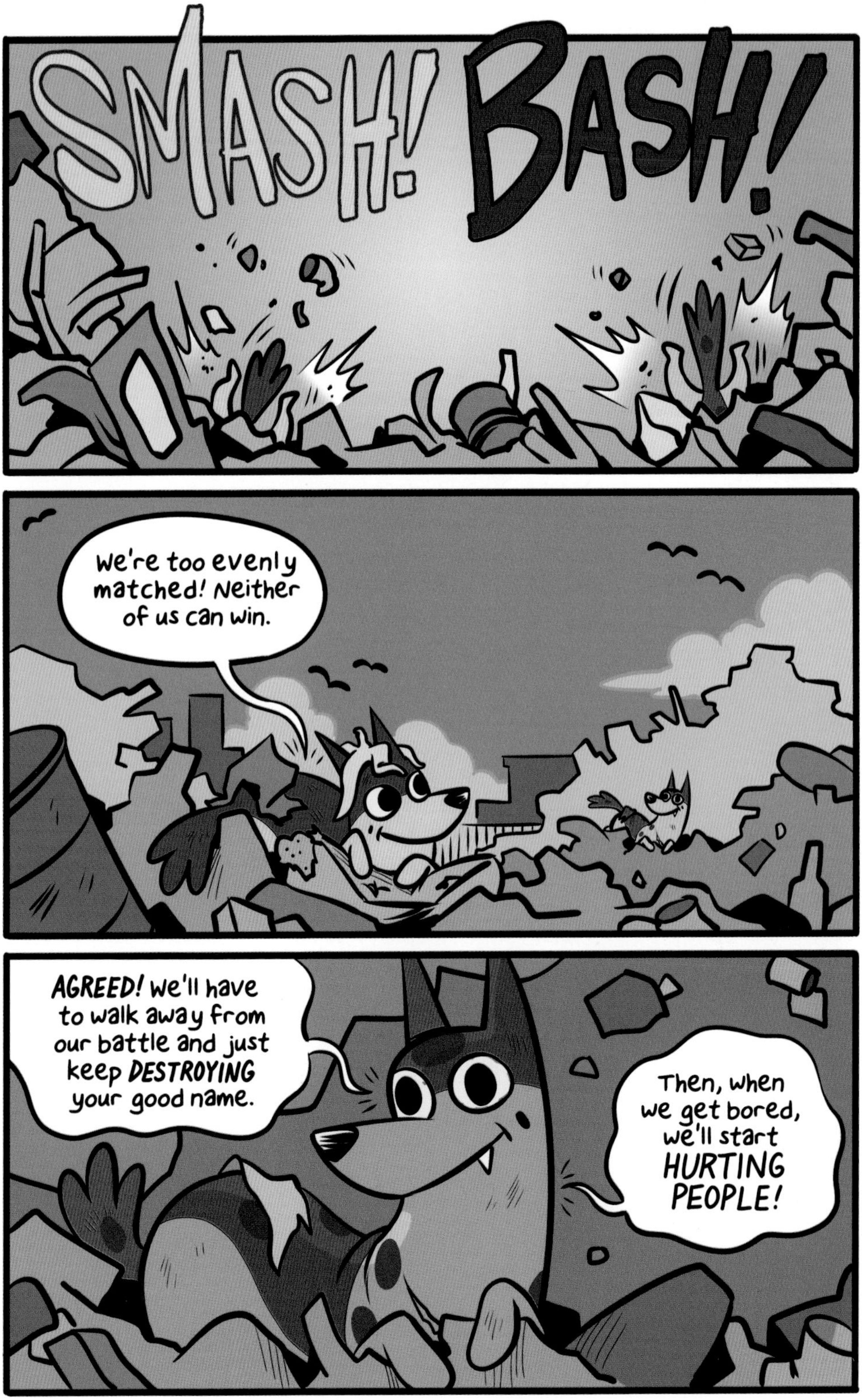
SMASH! BASH!
We're too evenly matched! Neither of us can win.
AGREED! We'll have to walk away from our battle and just keep DESTROYING your good name.
Then, when we get bored, we'll start HURTING PEOPLE!

176

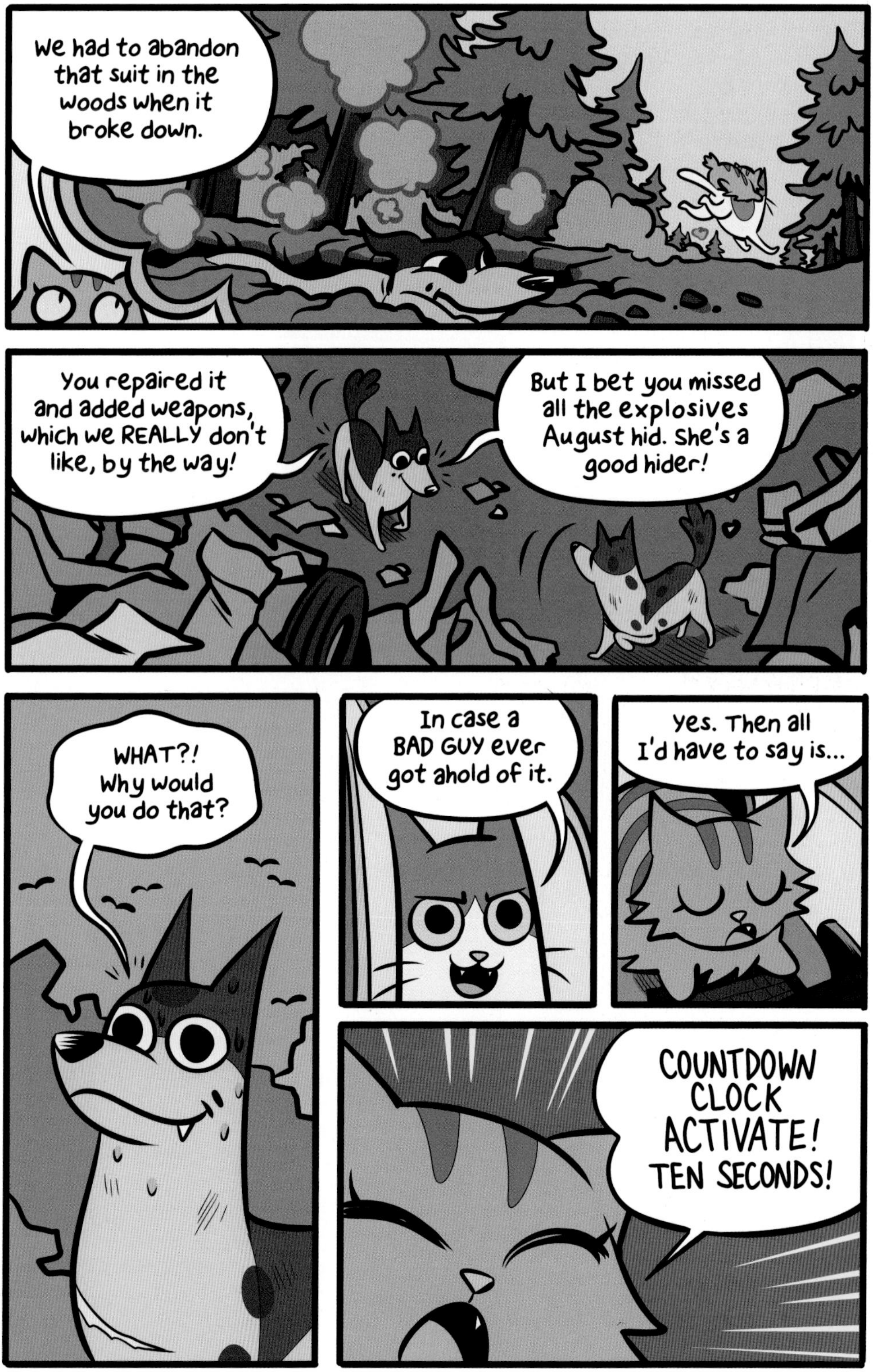
We had to abandon that suit in the woods when it broke down.
You repaired it and added weapons, which we REALLY don't like, by the way!
But I bet you missed all the explosives August hid. She's a good hider!
WHAT?! Why would you do that?
In case a BAD GUY ever got ahold of it.
Yes. Then all I'd have to say is...
COUNTDOWN CLOCK ACTIVATE! TEN SECONDS!

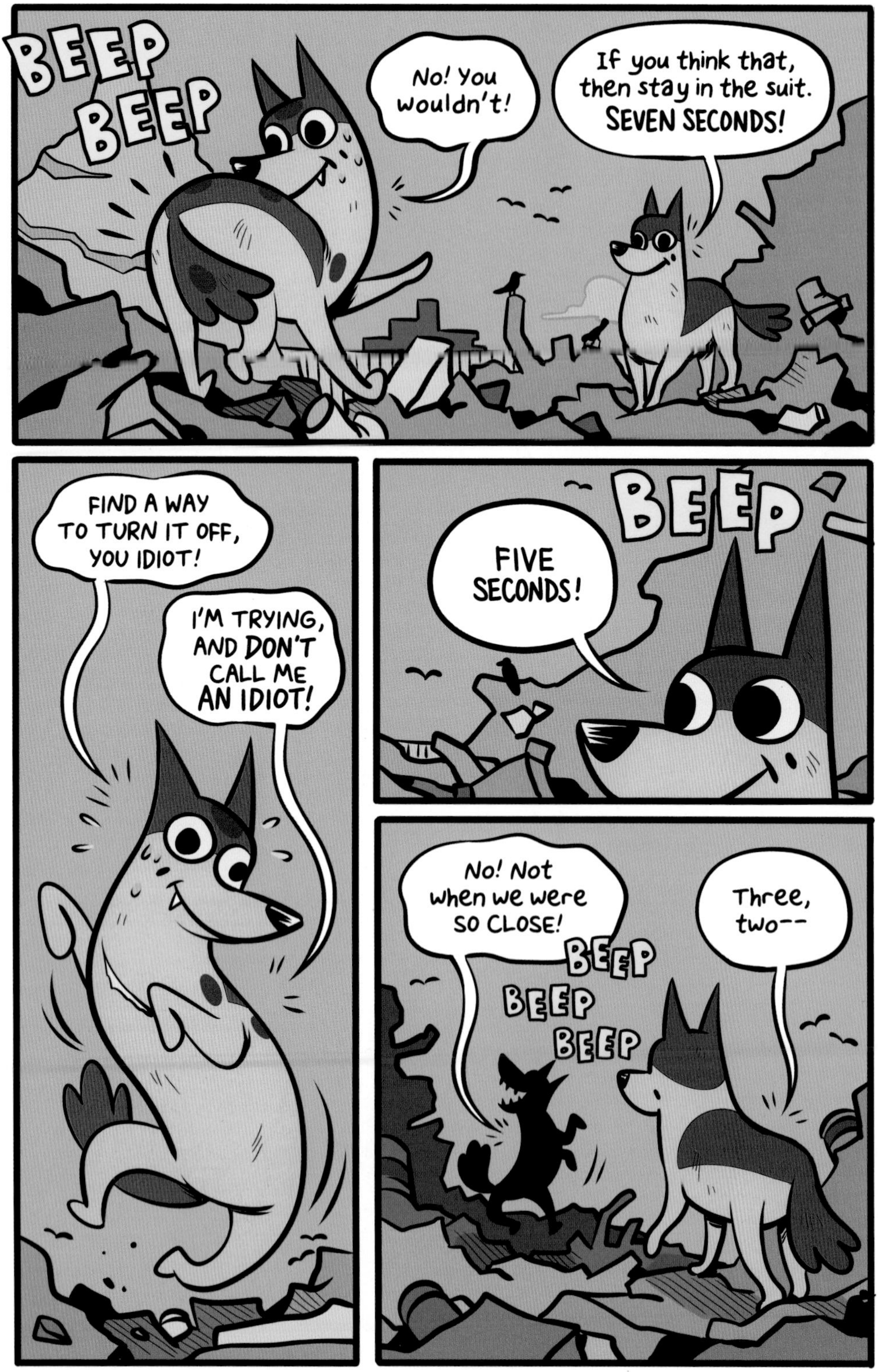
BEEP
BEEP
No! You wouldn't!
If you think that, then stay in the suit. SEVEN SECONDS!
FIND A WAY TO TURN IT OFF, YOU IDIOT!
I'M TRYING, AND DON'T CALL ME AN IDIOT!
BEEP
FIVE SECONDS!
No! Not when we were SO CLOSE!
Three, two--
BEEP
BEEP
BEEP

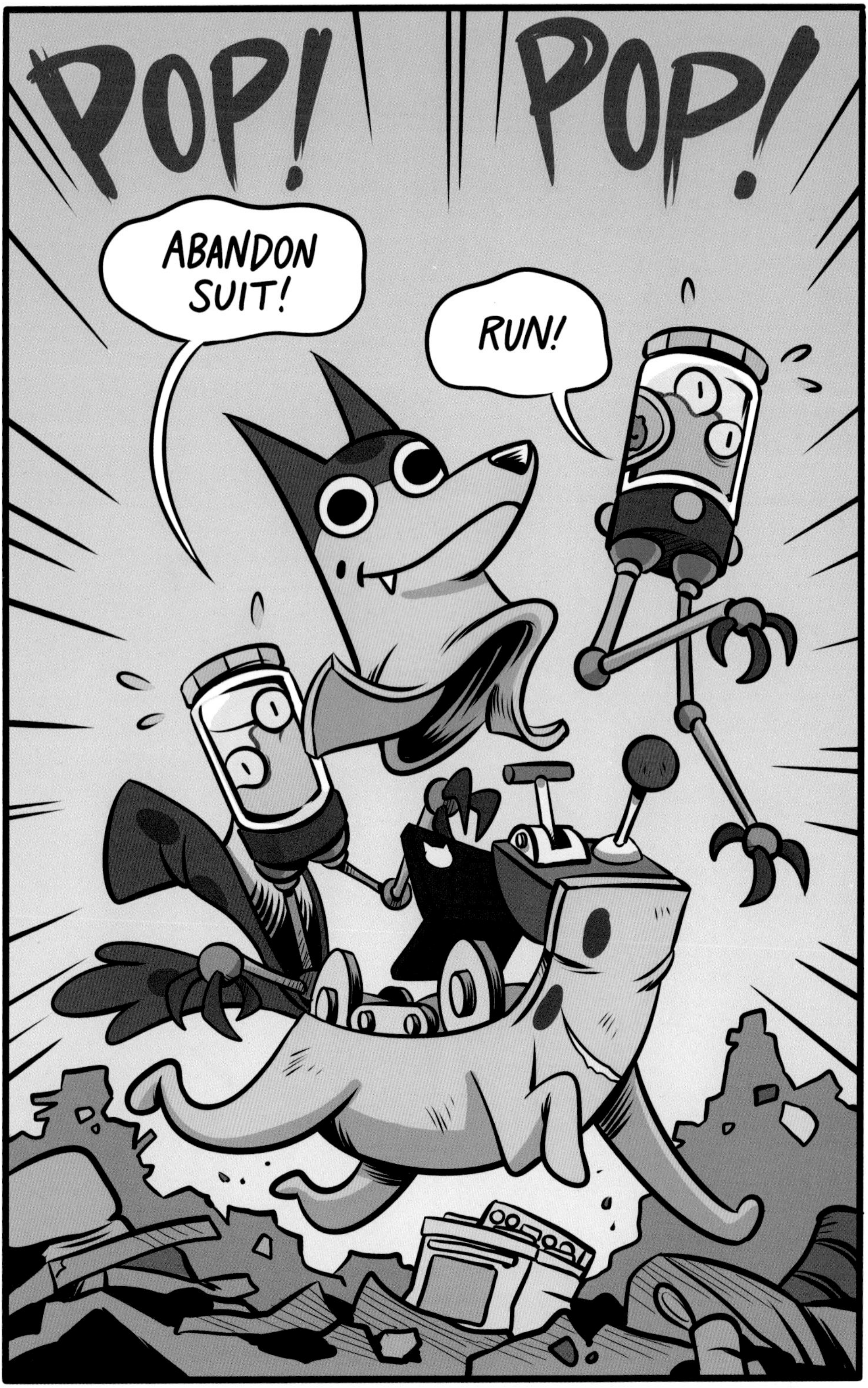
POP! POP!
ABANDON SUIT!
RUN!

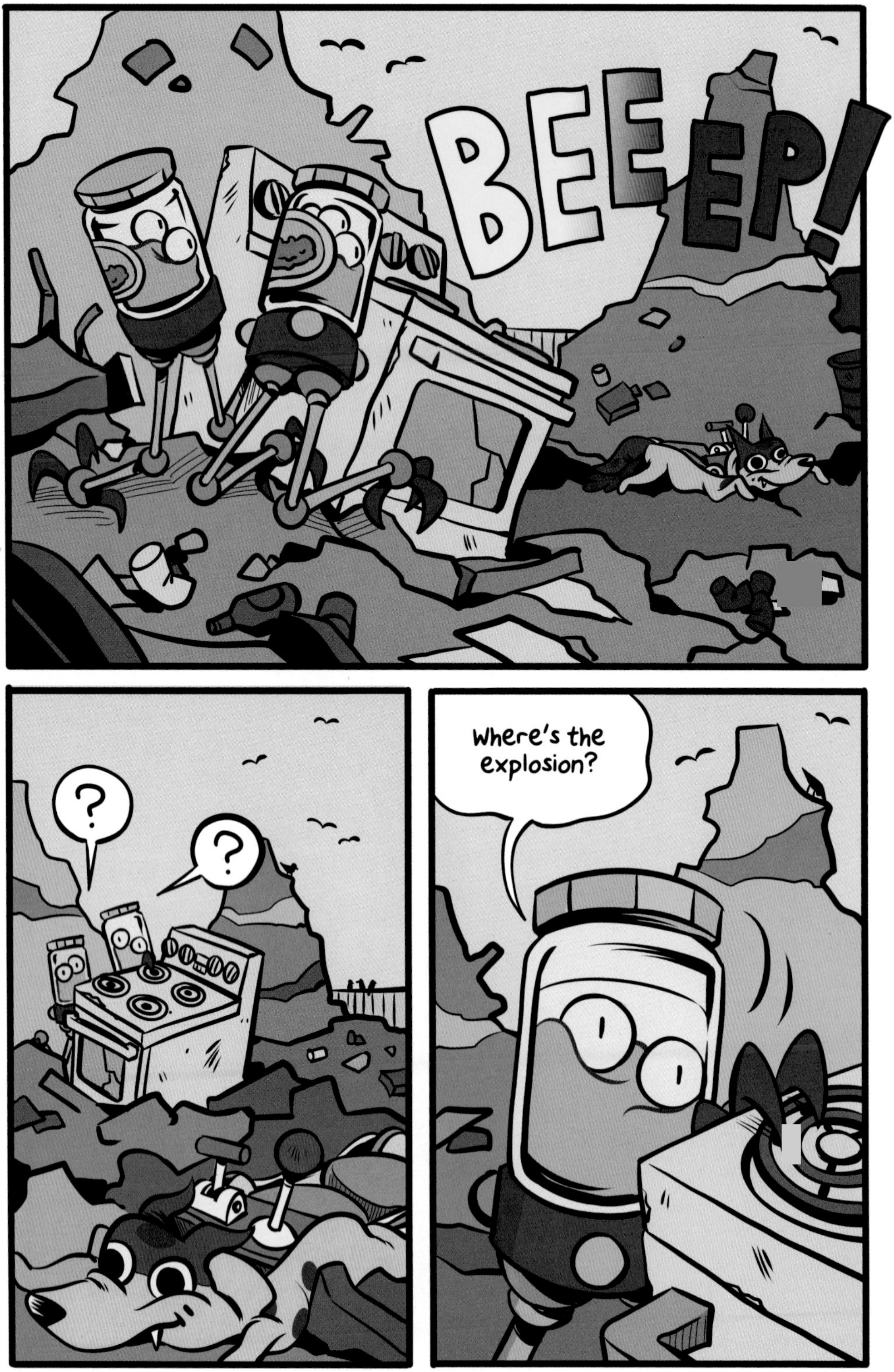
BEEEP!
?
?
Where's the explosion?

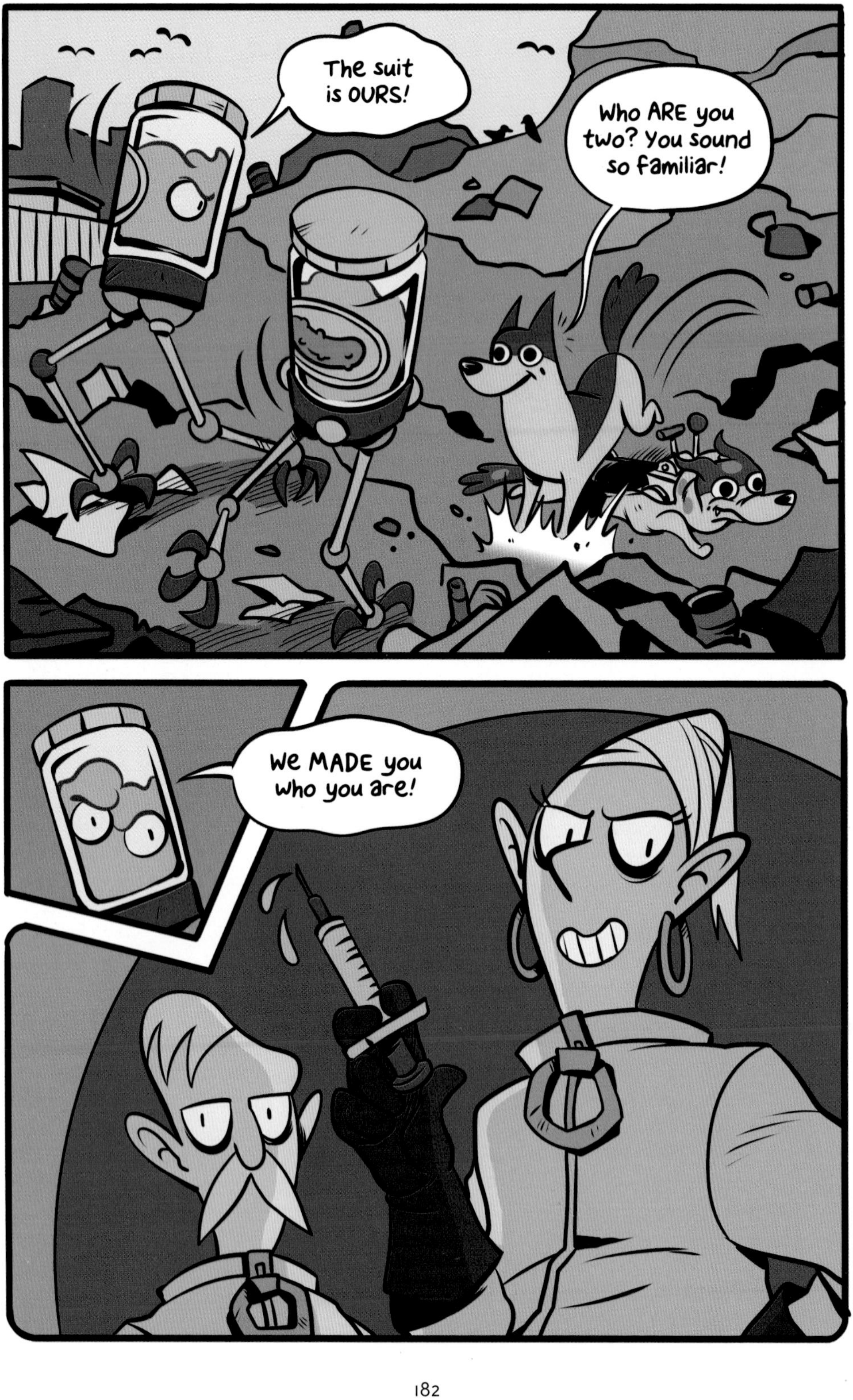
The suit is OURS!
Who ARE you two? You sound so familiar!
We MADE you who you are!

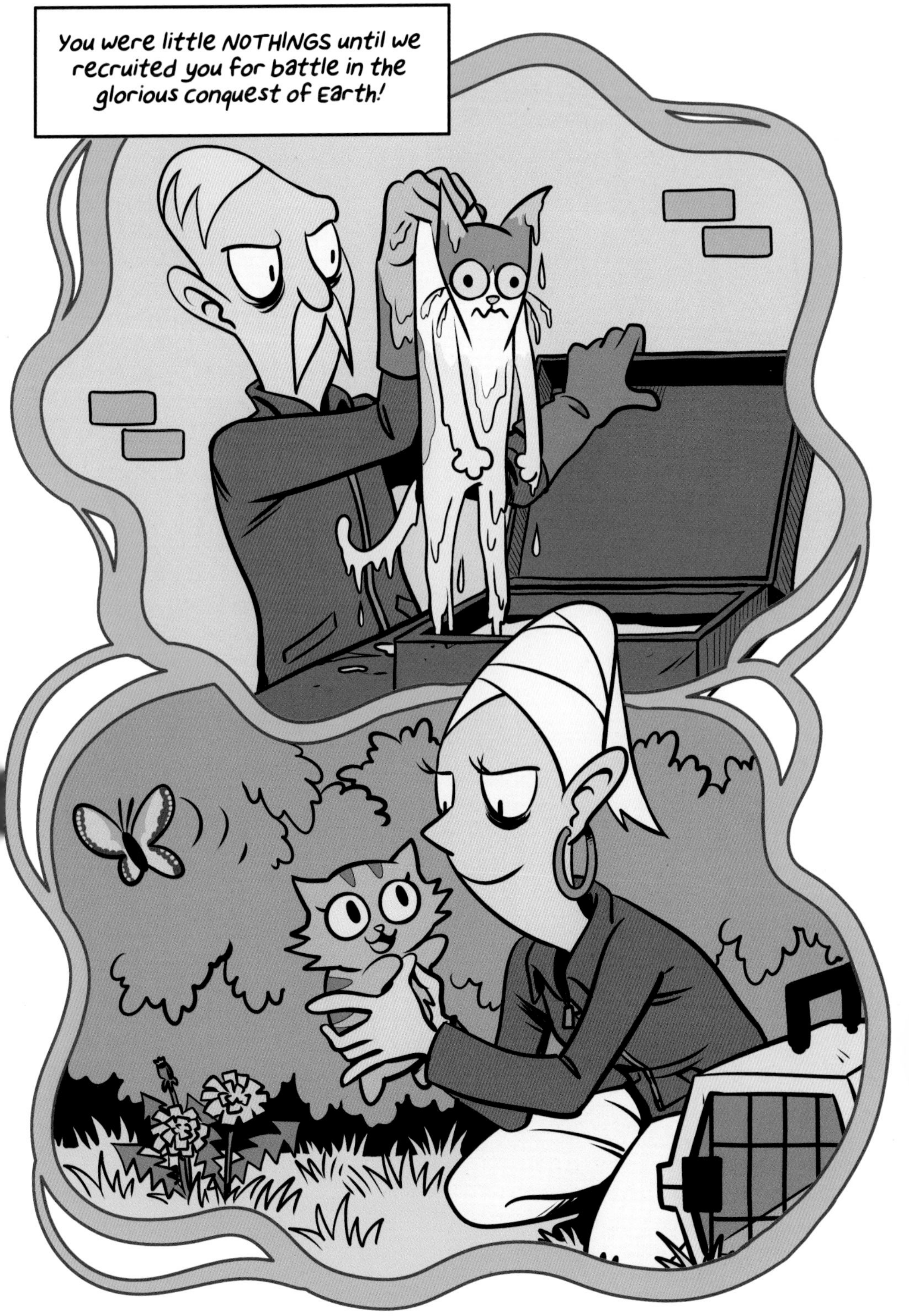
You were little NOTHINGS until we recruited you for battle in the glorious conquest of Earth!

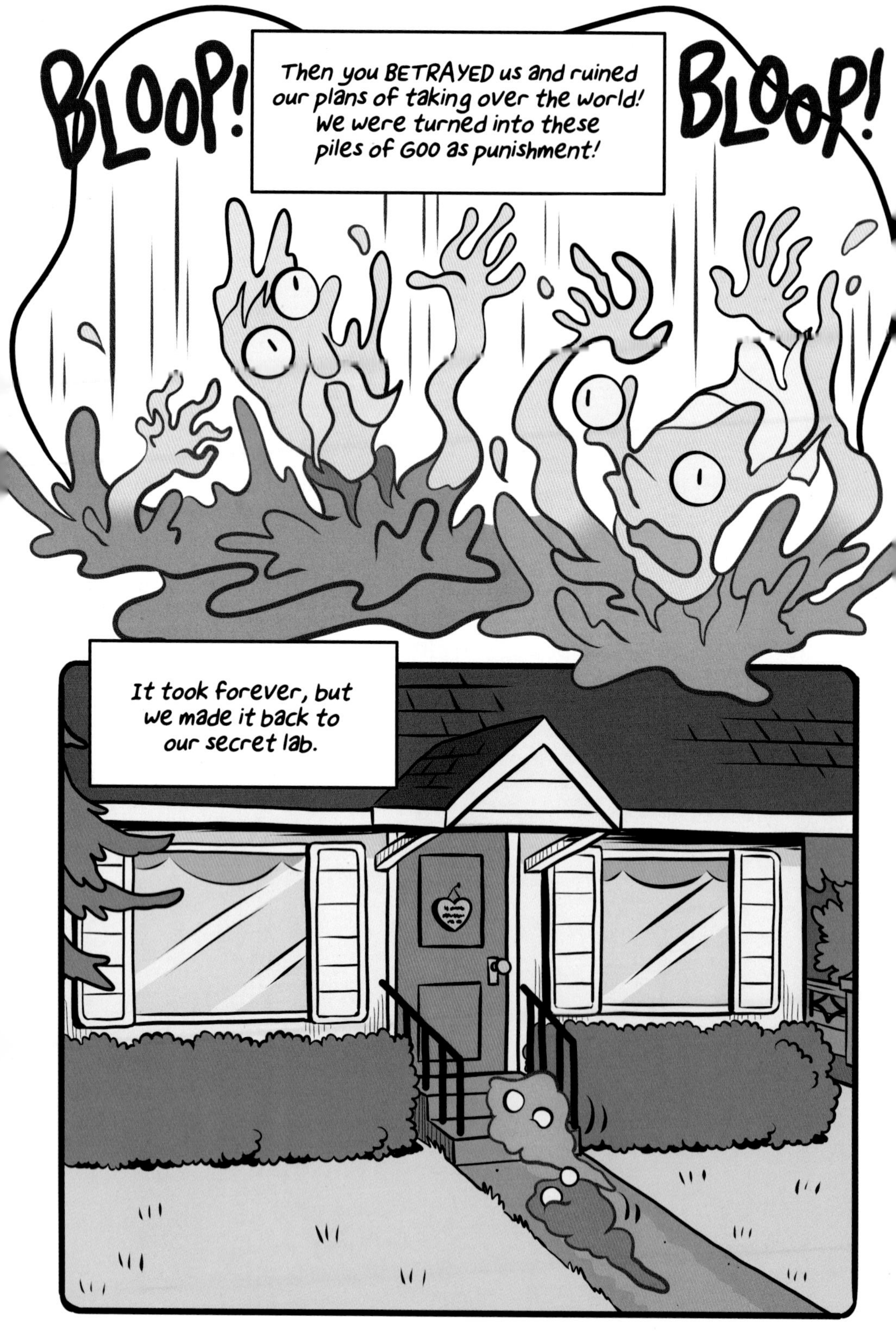
BLOOP!
Then you BETRAYED us and ruined our plans of taking over the world! We were turned into these piles of GOO as punishment!
BLOOP!
It took forever, but we made it back to our secret lab.

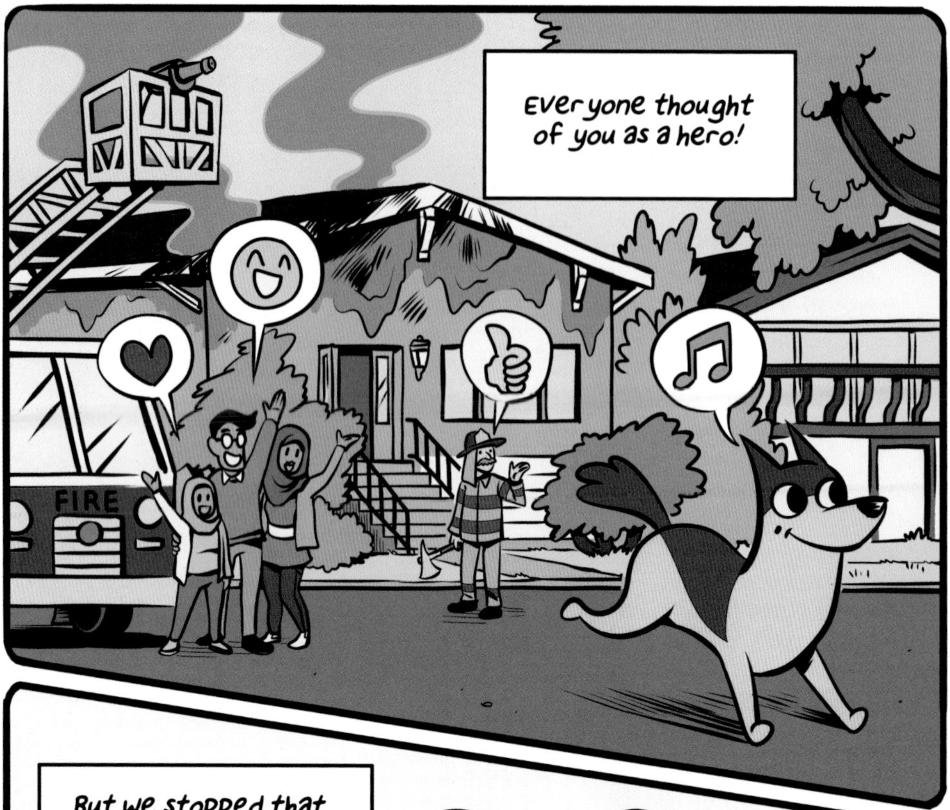
Everyone thought of you as a hero!
FIRE

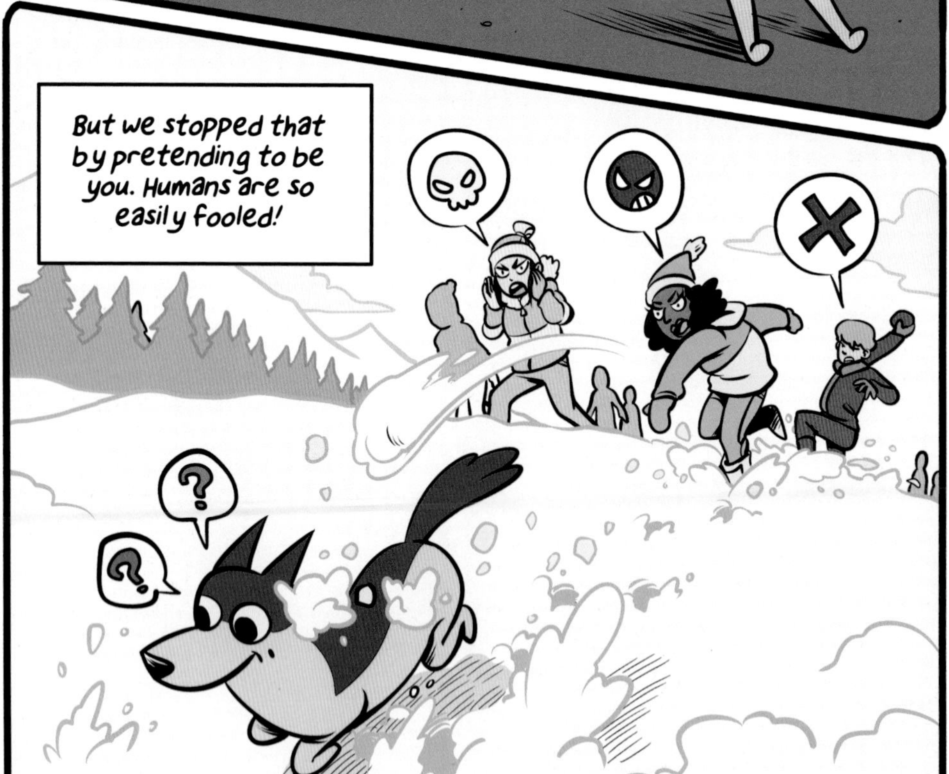
But we stopped that by pretending to be you. Humans are so easily fooled!

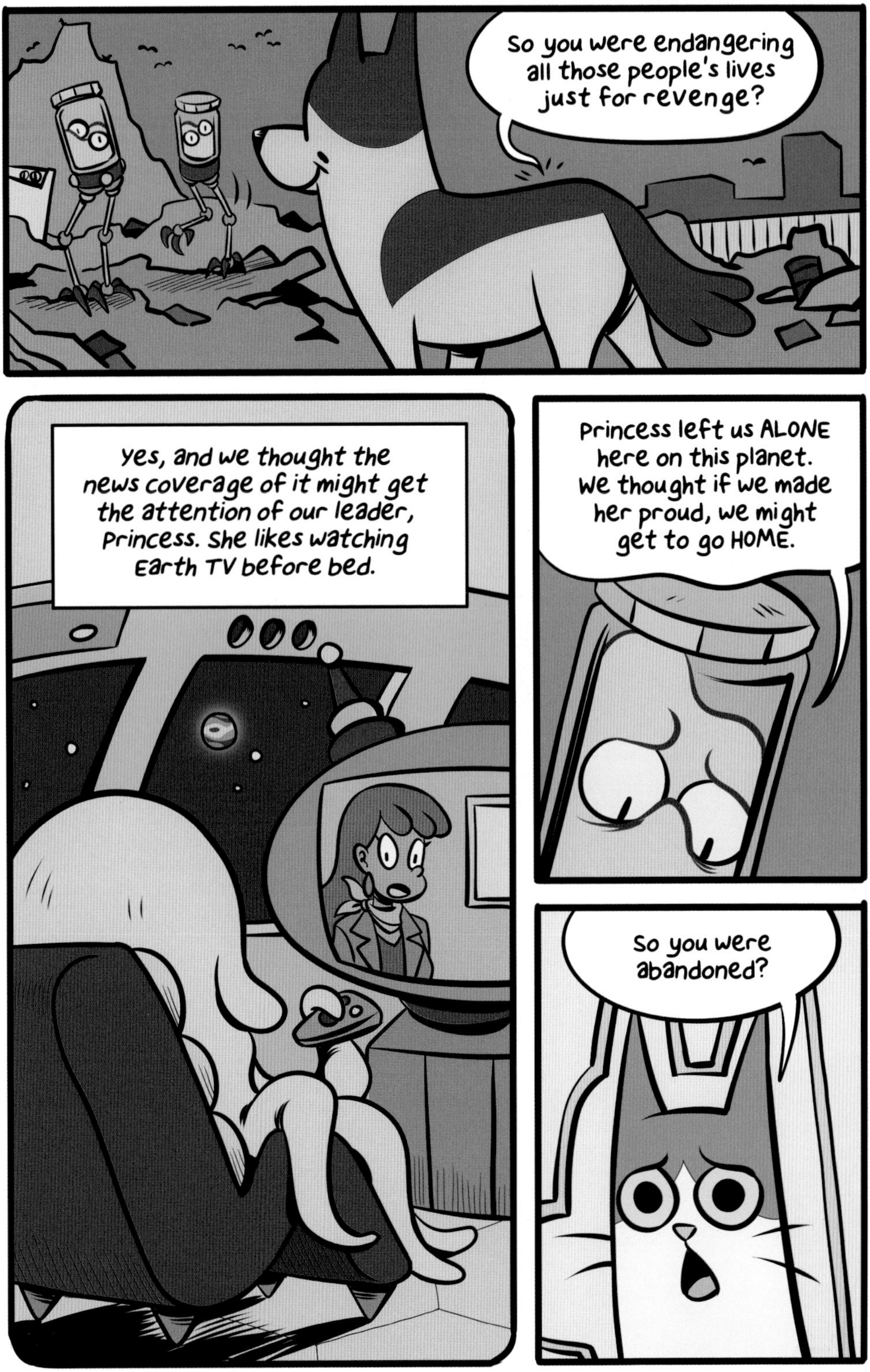
So you were endangering all those people's lives just for revenge?
Yes, and we thought the news coverage of it might get the attention of our leader, Princess. She likes watching Earth TV before bed.
Princess left us ALONE here on this planet. We thought if we made her proud, we might get to go HOME.
So you were abandoned?

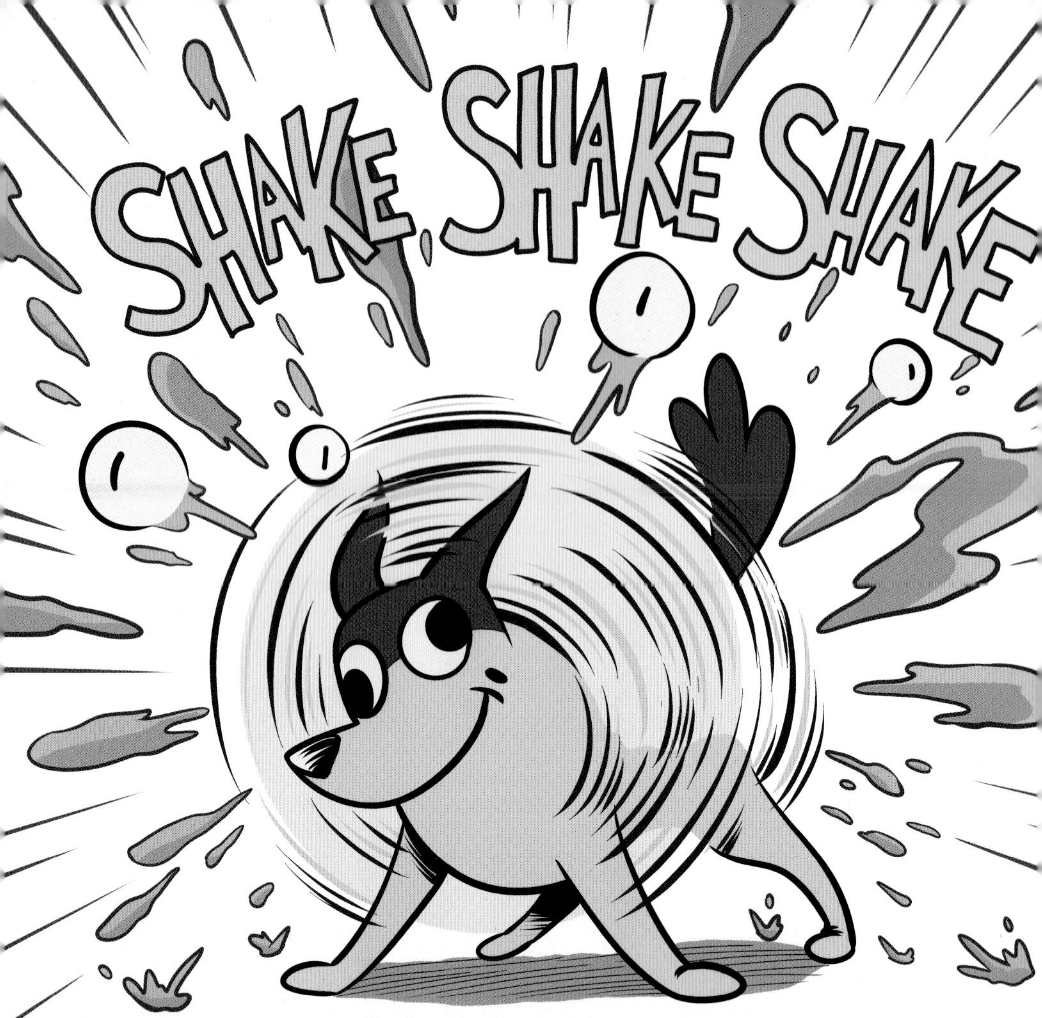
SHAKE SHAKE SHAKE

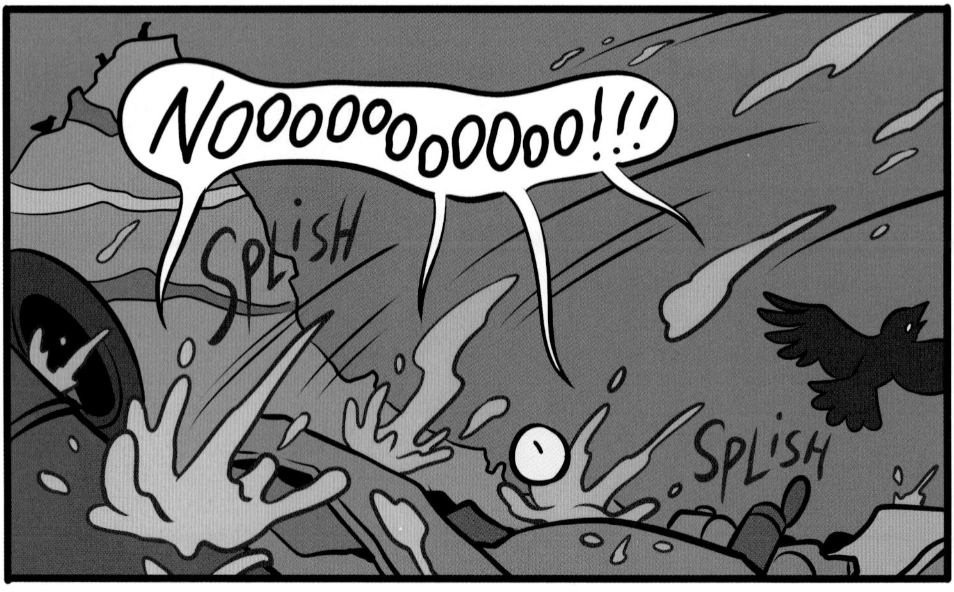
NOOOOOOOOOOOO!!!
SPLISH
SPLISH

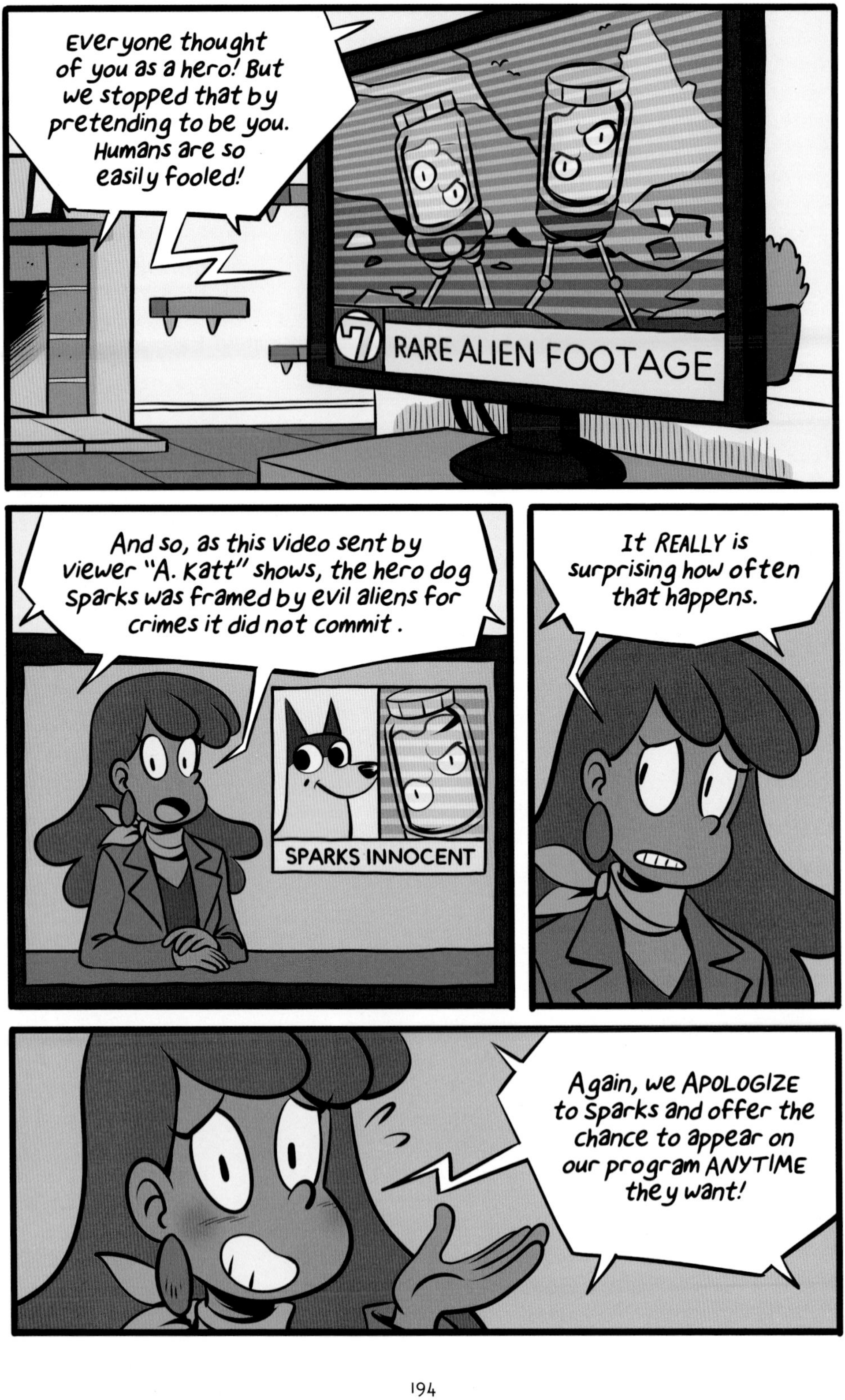

Everyone thought of you as a hero! But we stopped that by pretending to be you. Humans are so easily fooled!
RARE ALIEN FOOTAGE
And so, as this video sent by viewer "A. Katt" shows, the hero dog Sparks was framed by evil aliens for crimes it did not commit.
SPARKS INNOCENT
It REALLY is surprising how often that happens.
Again, we APOLOGIZE to Sparks and offer the chance to appear on our program ANYTIME they want!

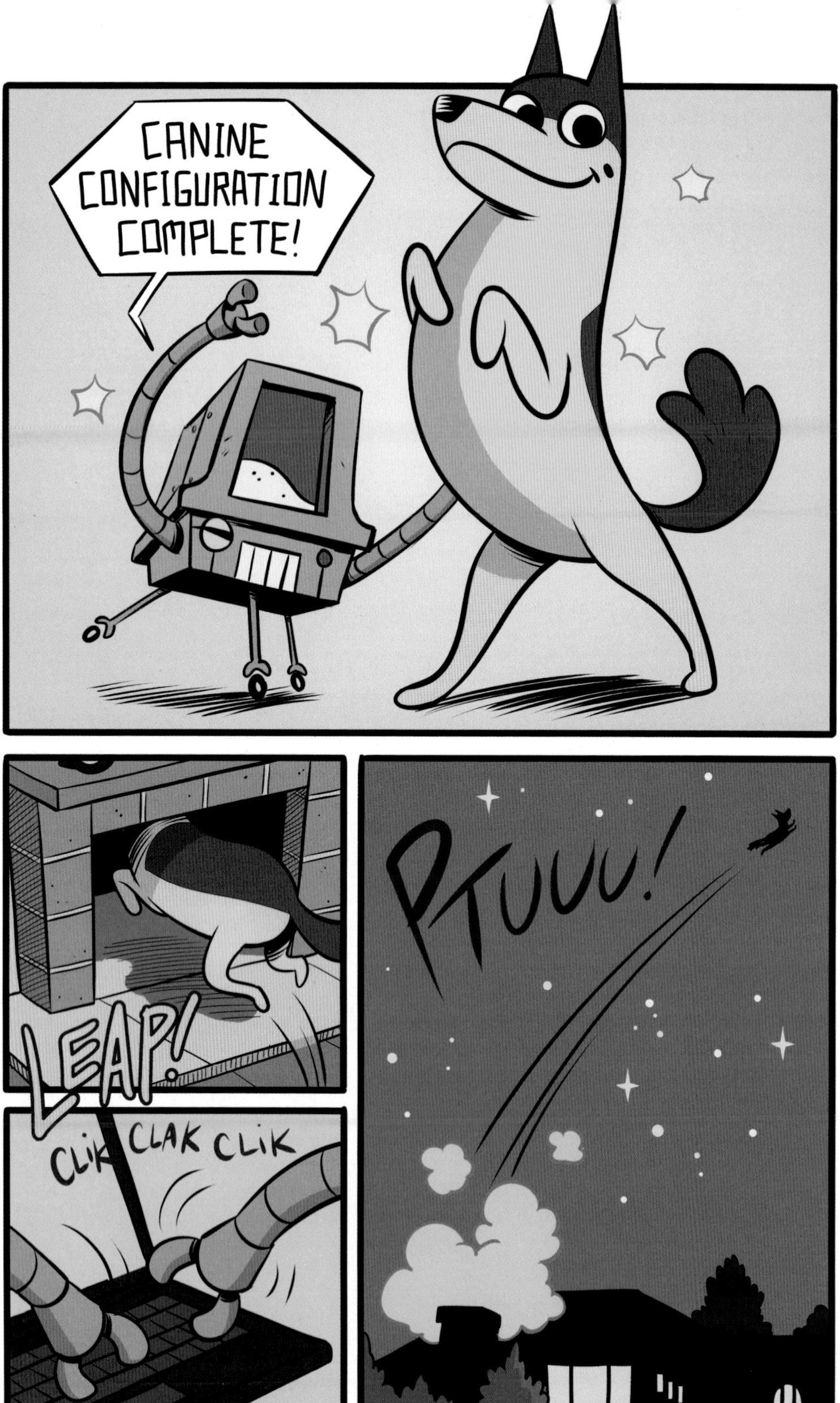
CANINE CONFIGURATION COMPLETE!
LEAP!
PTUUU!
CLIK CLAK CLIK

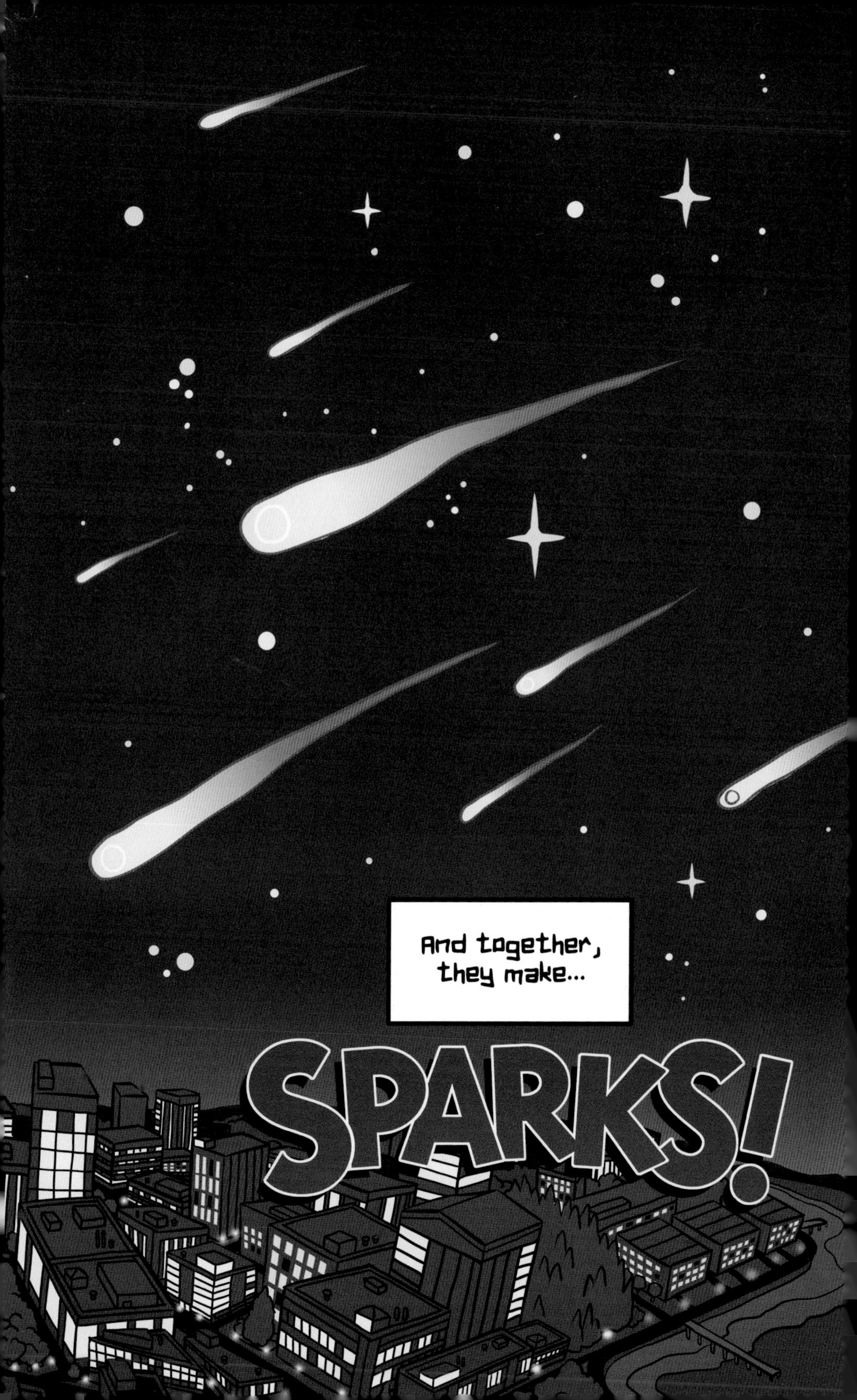
And together, they make...
SPARKS!

IAN BOOTHBY has been writing comedy for TV, radio, and comics since he was thirteen. Ian has written for *The Simpsons* and *Futurama* comics as well as being a regular cartoon contributor to *MAD* magazine and the *New Yorker* with his wife, Pia Guerra. Ian has also won the Eisner Award for Best Short Story with his friend and *Sparks!* cocreator Nina Matsumoto. Ian loves cats but has a hard time drawing them.

NINA MATSUMOTO is a Japanese Canadian who designs video game T-shirts and merchandise for Fangamer. She has been drawing comics for over ten years — most notably for *Simpsons Comics*, which won her an Eisner Award for a story she drew written by Ian. She loves every type of pizza and believes all toppings are valid.

DAVID DEDRICK has been writing and drawing funny pictures his whole life. This is his second time coloring a book. He lives with his wife, two daughters, two dogs, one cat, one horse, one pony, and two chickens — but only some of them actually live in the house!